COMEBACK

and

FLASHFIRE

Also by Richard Stark

COMEBACK

and

FLASHFIRE

Richard Stark

This omnibus edition published in 2009 by Quercus
Comeback first published in Great Britain in 1997
Flashfire first published in Great Britain in 2000

Quercus
21 Bloomsbury Square
London
WC1A 2NS

A CIP catalogue record for this book is available
from the British Library

ISBN 978 1 84916 097 1

Printed and bound in Great Britain by CPI Bookmarque, Croydon

10 9 8 7 6 5 4 3 2 1

COMEBACK

This is for Abby,
who said do it

The outcome you have waited for is assured.
Continue to persevere.
—Chinese Fortune Cookie

PART ONE

ONE

When the angel opened the door, Parker stepped first past the threshold into the darkness of the cinder block corridor beneath the stage. A hymn filtered discordantly through the rough walls; thousands of voices, raggedly together. The angel said, 'I'm not sure about this . . .'

'We are,' Parker told him. Holding the door open with one splayed hand, he nodded back at Mackey and Liss, who slipped in quickly past him, carrying the duffel bags. Parker shut the metal fire door and pulled up on the bar to lock it again, while Liss stood his duffel on the floor with a muffled clank and loosened the loop of rope that closed the top. Mackey's duffel was full of other duffel bags, and for now stayed on his shoulder. Liss slid the rough canvas cloth of the bag down past the blunt metal barrels, then took out the three shotguns, giving one each to Parker and Mackey, then flipping the empty bag over his shoulder.

The angel blinked, watching. His heavy white robe and strapped-on feathery wings must have been hot, even in the air-conditioned arena; the white makeup on his face ran with perspiration, giving him the look of somebody who'd been dead a long time. Inside the costume and the makeup and the sweat, he was scared, with frightened pinpoint eyes. 'There's too many guards,' he said. His voice squeaked with the requirement that he keep it guarded and quiet. 'Too much going on. We'll do it another time. A better time.'

'We're set up now, Tom,' Liss said. 'You got nerves, that's all.' He and Parker and Mackey had taken shells from their shirt pockets, broke open the shotguns, and were thumbing the shells into place.

'I don't want to do it now!' The angel's voice was more and more shrill, echoing around the echoes of the distant hymn. 'We'll get caught!'

This amateur, this inside man, was Liss's pigeon; let Liss smooth his feathers. Parker saw Liss's jaw muscles set on the left side, where they worked. Liss didn't like his pigeon acting up in front of the string. He said, 'Don't worry about it, okay? Lead the way.'

But the angel wouldn't move. Blinking sweat out of his eyes, fidgeting his hands together as the limp wings moved on his back, he said, 'We can't do it. I told somebody.'

They all became very still. They looked at the angel, whose name was Tom Carmody. Liss said, 'A woman?'

The angel looked ashamed. 'Yes. I thought it was all right, but . . .'

'But what?'

'She's gone. She isn't at home. She isn't at work. Nobody knows where she is.'

Parker said, 'She's with this bunch? Your bunch?'

'No, she teaches at a special school for disturbed kids. They don't know where she is.'

Mackey leaned his duffel bag against the wall. He said, 'You live with her?'

'No. Not really. She has her own place.' The angel was miserable, he was scared and embarrassed and unhappy.

4

He was also an asshole. He said, 'I don't know what she'll do.'

Liss said, 'Tom? You two have a fight? She mad at you? Maybe go to the cops?'

'No, no, nothing like that, she just disappeared. I don't *know* why.'

Liss looked around at his partners. He'd brought them into this, and now a decision had to be made. 'What do you think?'

Parker said, 'How much did he tell her? Everything—'

'Just a little!' the angel cried.

Parker looked at him. 'Shut up.' To the others he said, 'Everything she wanted to know, that's how much. So she has the route in, she has a little idea what's going down inside, but not the route out. We're here, so if it's trouble, it's already trouble.'

'That's right,' Mackey said. 'No point stopping.'

Liss turned back to Carmody and gestured with the shotgun. 'Lead the way.'

'Please.' Carmody spread his hands like a holy statue. 'Please let's just call it off, it's just a mistake, it would be better to *burn* the rotten money than—'

Parker reached out and closed his left hand around Carmody's right thumb, bending the thumb in on itself, applying only the slightest pressure. Carmody's face turned almost as white as the makeup smeared on it, his knees bent, his mouth opened in a wide O. Parker said, 'Shut up, now. You said your say. Now we walk to the money room.'

Carmody tried to say something else, but Parker squeezed just a little bit harder, and no sound but a faint whimper came out of the angel's mouth. Obedient, wide-eyed, he turned, his sandals shuffling on the concrete, and they all walked together along the gently curving corridor, lit by widely spaced fluorescent tubes mounted on the ceiling. Parker and the angel looked like they were holding hands, flanked by the other two as they walked from light to light, the three big hard-boned men in dark clothing, carrying shotguns, all round the bedraggled angel, shoulders slumped beneath the useless wings.

The hymn-singing got louder as they progressed, more aggressive, ridding the world of evil by shouting at it. A side corridor went up to the left, and they paused there to look.

That corridor, tunnel-like, was dark and low-ceilinged, with a closed mesh gate at the end. Beyond the mesh were the bright field lights, washing the arena in a glare of white, so that from where Parker and the others stood it was impossible to make out exactly what was taking place on the artificial turf out there. A mass of people, their backs turned, all swaying so that the light glinted and shifted, harsh white bleaching out the colors, making the shadows blacker than black. Except for the rolling roar of the hymn, almost anything could have been going on out there; a political rally, a demolition derby, a football game. At one time or another, the arena had been used for all of those, but tonight the attraction that had brought twenty thousand souls to this domed arena in the American heartland was William Archibald and his Christian Crusade.

The hymn ended. The people shuffled and stirred, and the amplified fruity voice of Archibald himself sounded above and around and among them all as though speaking from a cloud: 'Brothers! Sisters! Fellow mortals!'

6

'Come on,' Parker said, and tugged gently on the thumb.

Tom Carmody's resistance was all used up. As the other two followed, he plodded along at Parker's side, shaking his head slowly. 'I hate that bastard,' he muttered, but in an exhausted way, without passion. 'I hate his lying voice. I hate everything he does. I ought to *burn* the money, and him in it. Burn him in his own rotten piles of cash.'

Parker tightened his grip on Carmody's bent thumb, just a little, just enough to bring him back to earth. 'Where's the money room?'

'Ahead!' Pain and surprise were in Carmody's voice; he hadn't known he deserved punishment. 'Just up ahead.'

'Keep your mind on what we're doing.'

They walked a little farther, the corridor constantly curving, appearing ahead of them, disappearing behind their backs, and then they came to a brown metal door on the interior side of the curve, with white block letters reading NO ADMITTANCE. Parker released the angel's thumb, and Carmody immediately closed his other hand around it, like one small animal comforting another. 'Do it,' Parker said, and prodded him in the side with the shotgun barrel, the blued metal poking into the white folds of the robe.

As the three armed men stood against the shadowed wall, Carmody stumbled forward and stood in front of the door. His left hand reluctantly released the aching thumb and pressed the button beside the door. He stood there blinking, the sharp fluorescent light above his head making him look more like a clown than an angel, and then a harsh voice sounded from the grid below the button: 'Yes?'

'Hi, Harry. It's Tom Carmody.' The angel's voice sounded almost normal; it hardly quavered at all.

'Hi, Tom,' said the voice from the grid. 'Come on in.' A raspy buzzing sound came from the door.

Carmody pressed his non-painful hand to the door and it clicked open. Holding it that way, opening inward toward the corridor to the money room beneath the stands, he looked at Parker and said, 'All right?'

Mackey moved forward to take the door. 'You did fine,' Parker said, and hammered the angel with the shotgun butt.

TWO

It began with a phone call. Parker didn't hear it ring, because he was out on the lake, in the rowboat, oars shipped, doing nothing, feeling the pulse of the water through the wood hull. Early May, this lake in northern New Jersey was still too cold to swim in, most of the vacation houses around its fringe still closed down, waiting for their owners to come back from the city when weather and water got a little warmer. Parker and Claire were among the few year-round residents, Claire establishing her presence in the community, Parker more aloof, being someone whose work let him stay at home for periods of time and then took him away sometimes. Claire was the one who made the home here, being Claire Willis because Parker had been Charles Willis a long time ago, before they'd met. She liked the idea of reaching back into the world when they hadn't known one another, to make a link, throw a line back into the past.

Movement. He always reacted to movement, no matter how small, anywhere in his vision. This was three-quarters behind him, and when he turned his head it was Claire, at the dock, waving. The lawn stretched behind her up to the dark house. He lifted a hand, then rowed back, and as he stepped up onto the dock she said, 'Man called. Pay phone. Says he'll call back in ten minutes.' She looked at the slender watch on her slender wrist and corrected herself: 'Six minutes.'

'Did he give a name?'

'George Liss.'

Parker frowned at that, and tied the boat to the stanchion, and they walked up to the house, she holding his wrist in her cool fingers. She said, 'He seemed like he knew you.'

'To a point,' Parker said.

Parker and George Liss had never worked together, though they'd come close. Twice, they'd met on other guys' deals that hadn't panned out. He had no real opinion about George Liss, except he thought he probably wouldn't want to count on him if things turned sour.

The money situation at the moment was all right, but not perfect. There was cash here and there, stowed away. He could wait for something that smelled good. Even in a world of electronic cash transfers and credit cards and money floating in cyberspace, there were still heists out there, waiting to be collected.

When the phone rang the second time, Parker was in the enclosed porch that faced the lawn and the lake and the boathouse, standing there, looking out. The day was overcast, and looked colder than it was. He picked up the phone on the third ring and said, 'George?'

'I've got something.' The voice slurred a little, making a furry sound in the phone lines.

Parker waited. George Liss could have a lot of things, including a need to turn someone else over to the law to take his place.

Liss said, 'It's a little different, but it's profitable.'

They were all different, and they were all supposed to be profitable, or you wouldn't do it. Parker waited.

Liss said, 'You still there?'

'Yes.'

'We could get together someplace, talk it over.'

'Maybe.'

'You want to know who else is aboard.' And again Liss waited for Parker to say something, but again Parker had nothing to say, so finally Liss said, 'Ed Mackey.'

That was different. Ed Mackey was somebody Parker did know and had worked with. Ed Mackey was solid. Parker said, 'Who else?'

'It only takes three.'

Even better. The fewer the people, the fewer the complications, and the more the profit. Parker said, 'Where and when?'

They came together first in the parking lot of a lobster restaurant on Route 1 just south of Auburn, Maine, a place where a couple of rental cars from Boston's Logan Airport wouldn't look out of place. Parker left his Impala and crisscrossed through the parked cars to the Century Regal where Ed Mackey, blunt and taciturn, sat at the wheel with his girlfriend Brenda beside him and George Liss in the back seat. Parker joined Liss, a tall, narrow, black-haired man with a long chin, who nodded at him and smiled with the side of his mouth where the nerves and muscles still worked, and said, 'Have a good flight?'

This wasn't a sensible question. Parker said, 'Tell me about it.'

'It's a stadium,' Ed Mackey said, half-turning in the front seat, knees pointed at Brenda as he looked back at

11

Parker. 'Usual stadium security. Twenty thousand civilians inside.'

Parker shook his head. 'All you walk out with,' he said, 'is credit card receipts.'

'Not this one,' Liss said, and the left side of his face smiled more broadly. A sharpened spoon handle had laid open the right side, in a prison in Wyoming, eleven years ago. A plastic surgeon had made the scars disappear, but nothing could make that side of his face move again, ever. Around civilians, Liss usually tried to keep himself turned partially away, showing only the profile that worked, but among fellow mechanics he didn't worry about it. With the slight slurring that made his words always sound just a little odd, he said, 'This one is all cash. Paid at the door.'

'They call it love offerings,' Mackey said, deadpan.

Parker tried to read Mackey's face. 'Love offerings? What kind of stadium is this?'

Liss explained, 'The stadium's the usual. The *attraction's* a guy named William Archibald. A TV preacher, you know those guys? Evangelists.'

'I thought they were all in jail,' Parker said.

'The woods are full of them,' Liss said, and Mackey added, 'Mostly the back woods.'

Parker said, 'He's preaching at this stadium, is that it?'

'To make a movie,' Mackey said, 'and show it on the TV later.'

'The people walking in,' Liss said, moving his hands around in the space between himself and Parker, 'they put down a twenty-dollar love offering, every one of them. No exceptions. Twenty thousand people.'

Brenda spoke for the first time: 'Four hundred thousand

12

dollars,' she said in her husky voice, rolling her full lips around the words.

'Brenda does my math for me,' Mackey said.

'Plus,' Liss said, 'they got these barrels up front by the stage, you get inspired along the way, you want to help the preacher spread the word on the TV, you can go up and toss whatever money you want in the barrel.'

'On TV,' Mackey said. 'On the big screen up behind the preacher. I seen it work, Parker, it's like hypnotizing. These people *love* to see themselves on that big screen, walkin right up there, tossin their cash in the old barrel. Then a month later, they're at home, TV on, there they are again. Live the moment twice. The day you gave the rent money to God.'

'We figure,' Liss said, 'that doubles the take.'

Brenda opened her mouth, but before she could say anything Mackey pointed at her and said, 'Brenda. He can work it out.'

Parker said, 'There's going to be more than the usual security, if it's all cash.'

'Archibald has his own people,' Liss agreed. 'But we got a guy on the inside. That's what made it start to happen.'

'Not one of us,' Parker said.

'Not for a minute,' Mackey said.

'He works for the preacher,' Liss said. 'And now he's mad at him.'

'Greedy? Wants a bigger slice?'

'Just the reverse,' Liss said, and half his face laughed. 'Ol' Tom got religion.'

'Just tell it to me,' Parker said.

Mackey patted the top of the seatback, as though

calming a horse. 'It's a good story, Parker,' he said. 'Wait for it.'

People had to tell their stories their own way, with all the pointless extras. 'Go ahead,' Parker said, and sat back to wait it out.

Liss said, 'I had twenty-nine months' parole last time I got out. It was easier, just hang around and do it, then have a paper out on me the rest of my life. This guy Archibald, one of his scams is, his people volunteer to give this *counseling* to ex-cons. It's all crap and everybody knows it, it's just to find new suckers, and to get some kinda tax break.'

'A cash business,' Parker said. 'He's doin okay with taxes anyway.'

'Oh, you know he is. But William Archibald, he's one of those guys, the more you give him to drink, the thirstier he gets. So I drew this guy Tom Carmody to be my counselor, once a week he'd come around the place I was living, and then when he'd fill out the sheet, that meant I didn't have to go in to the parole office. A good deal for everybody. And after the first few weeks, we pretty much come clean with each other, and after that we'd just watch basketball on the tube or something, or have a beer around the corner. I mean, he knew what I was and no problem, and I knew what scam *he* was on, so we just got on with life. Except sometimes he'd go on crusades, and—'

Parker said, 'Crusades?'

'When Archibald takes his show on the road,' Liss explained. 'Rents a hall, a movie house, a stadium, someplace big, does his act three, four times, brings in a couple mil, takes it all home again. Tom was one of the staff guys he brought along on these things, so then I'd get

14

some gung ho trainee from the office instead, and I'd have to be real serious and rehabilitated and grateful as hell to Jesus and all this shit, and then when Tom came back we'd laugh about it. Only, then, about the last six months – yeah, two years we're dealing bullshit and we both knew it, and then the last six months he began to change it all around. Not trying to reform *me* or nothing. It was Archibald he got agitated about.'

Brenda spoke again, this time drily: 'He noticed Mister Archibald was insincere.'

'He got hung up on the money,' Liss said. 'How Archibald takes all the suckers for all this money, and it doesn't go anywhere good. I dunno, Parker, it wasn't the *scam* that got ol' Tom riled up, it still isn't. It's what happens with the money *after* Archibald trims the rubes. He'd talk about all the good that money could do, you know, feed the homeless and house the hungry and all this, and then he wanted to know was there any way I knew that he could *get* a bunch of that cash. Not for himself, you see, but to do good works with it.'

Parker said, 'It was his idea?'

'Absolutely. The guy's a civilian, I only know him two years, and he's tied to the parole board. Am I gonna say, "Hey, Tom, let's pull a number"? No way.'

'But you went along.'

Liss shook his head. 'Not at first. One of the few big words I know is *entrapment*. So at first I'd just nod and say well, that's a real bitch, Tom, and all this. And when he finally came out with it – 'Hey, George, let's do it together, you with your expert background and me with my inside information' – I told him no, I told him I'm retired, it isn't

15

I'm reformed I just don't want to go back inside. Which was almost the truth, by the way.'

Parker nodded. For a lot of people, that was almost the truth almost all the time.

'Also,' Liss said, 'I told him I didn't much care where money went that didn't come to me, whether this money fed Archibald or fed some other people made no difference to me, and he said he understood. He understood for me it would be more of a business proposition. So he suggested we split fifty-fifty, and I'd put my share in my pocket and he'd give his to the poor.'

'Us poor,' Mackey said.

Parker knew what Mackey meant. Glancing at him, 'If,' he said.

'Naturally.'

Liss went on, saying, 'Finally I said I'd pass him on to somebody who was still active in the game, but he said no, he wouldn't trust anybody but me, so then I figured I could take the chance. If he was out to trap somebody for the law, he wouldn't care who he brought in, right? He'd let me pass him on to somebody else, work his number just as good. Since he didn't do that, then he probably wasn't pulling anything. So then we started to get kind of serious, talking it over, him giving me the details about the money, and I saw how maybe it could be done. And here we are.'

Parker said, 'And the theory is, the inside guy takes half, and we split the other half. However many of us it is doing the thing.'

'That's the theory.'

'Does he buy it?' Parker shook his head, rejecting his own question, rephrasing it: 'What I mean, does he believe it?'

'That he'll get his half?' Liss did his lopsided smile. 'That's the big question, isn't it? He's kind of hard to read since he changed, you know. Used to be, he was an easygoing guy, now he's all tensed up. Relaxed guys are harder to fool, but tensed-up guys are harder to read.'

'Anyway, Parker,' Mackey said, 'what's he gonna do if he *doesn't* believe it? We're the takers, not him. Is he gonna take it from the takers? No way.'

Parker ignored that. He said to Liss, 'How many parole guys does this fella have beer with?'

Liss half-frowned; that face of his took some getting used to. He said, 'You mean, he puts together a backup crew to take it away after we get it? But what's the point, Parker? If he's afraid *we're* gonna cut him out, what's he gonna do about the second crew? Come up with a third?'

'What I think it is,' Mackey said, 'I think the guy bought his own story. He's not buying from us, he's buying from himself.'

Parker said to Mackey, 'You meet this wonder?'

'Not yet.'

'That can be arranged,' Liss said. 'Easiest thing there is. I'll call him tonight, say we're—'

'No,' Parker said. 'You say he goes out with this preacher on his crusades. When's the next one?'

'Couple weeks. I figured that's when we could pull it.'

'No. Where they gonna be? The whole tour.'

Liss's face went out of whack again. He said, 'Beats me. I guess I could find out.'

'Good,' Parker said. 'Then somewhere along the way, without any invitations or planning or setting things up,

17

we're there, and we say hello. Mackey and me.'

'And Brenda,' Mackey said.

Parker looked at Brenda. 'Naturally,' he said.

THREE

In a not-very-good restaurant in St. Louis, with old bored waiters and old-fashioned dark red-and-brown decor, Parker and Mackey and Brenda ate dinner, taking their time over it. Liss had said he'd get the pigeon here between eight and ten, and it was already nine-thirty. 'I gotta go to the john again,' Brenda said, fooling with her coffee cup, 'but I know, the minute I leave the table, they're gonna walk in.'

'Then do it,' Mackey told her. 'I'd like to see *something* make them walk in.'

'Only for you,' she said, and left the table, and a minute later Liss walked in with a sandy-haired nervous-looking guy in his late twenties, wearing tan slacks and a plaid shirt.

'There, you see,' Mackey said. 'That's why I keep Brenda around. She's magic.'

Parker said nothing. He already knew why Mackey kept Brenda around – she was his brains – and his interest was in the guy over there with Liss. And also with whoever might come into the restaurant next.

Which was nobody. If Carmody was being watched, it was a very long leash. Watchers couldn't have been planted in the place ahead of time, because Liss wouldn't have told Tom where they were going until they got here.

'This looks like a good place, Tom. I'm ready for dinner, how about you?'

And why would a watcher wait outside, when the whole point of keeping an eye on your bait was to see who came around and what happened? So Tom was not under observation. Which didn't mean he wasn't a Judas goat, only that, if he was, they were letting him float on his own. Not important to them, in other words, or not yet. Not until he starts to come home with somebody.

Liss had seated himself at the table in a chair where he could give the doddering waiter his good side, about which the waiter cared nothing. Tom Carmody, across from Liss, was quiet, low-key, ordering as though he didn't care if he ate or not, then sitting there in a funk. Liss gave him a minute or two of cheery conversation and then ate rolls instead.

Brenda came back to the table and Mackey said, 'Your magic worked.'

'So I see.'

While Mackey signaled to the waiter for the check, Brenda studied the guy sitting over there with Liss. Mackey repeated his hand gesture at the waiter – signing his name in the air – then turned back to Brenda to say, 'What do you think?'

'He's too gloomy.'

'I don't want you to date him, honey.'

'I don't want you to date him, either,' she said. 'That's what I mean, he's too gloomy.'

Parker listened, while across the way Liss and Carmody got their salads. Liss tucked in, while Carmody pushed the lettuce and tomato slice around in the shallow bowl.

Meantime, Mackey said, 'Explain yourself,' and Brenda

said, 'He already gave up. Look at him, Ed. He doesn't care if anything good happens or not. You know what a guy like that does when there's trouble? He lies down.'

'Good,' Mackey said. 'He'll give us traction.'

The waiter brought the check then, and stood around as Mackey brought out his wallet and, despite the hand signal, paid in cash. While he did that, Brenda said to Parker, 'How's Claire?'

Unlike Mackey, Parker didn't bring his woman to work. 'She's fine,' he said.

'Will I be seeing her?'

'I don't think so.'

Mackey left a little tip, and said, 'Let's go look at our boy up close.'

Parker let Mackey and Brenda go first; they were better at the social niceties, like pretending to be happily surprised at the sight of Liss sitting there: 'George! How you doing, old son?'

'Hello, Ed! How are you? And Brenda!' Liss rose, shaking Mackey's hand, kissing Brenda's cheek, giving Parker a bright-eyed look of non-recognition.

Mackey said, 'George Liss, here's a pal of ours, Jack Grant.'

'How you doing, Jack?' Liss said, grinning, extending his hand.

'Fine,' Parker said, shaking the hand briefly. Play-acting wasn't what he did best.

On the other hand, Liss was having a good time. 'And this is a pal of *mine*,' he announced, with a big wave at the pigeon. 'Tom Carmody. Tom, this is Ed and Brenda Fawcett, and a pal of theirs.'

Tom Carmody had been raised as a mannerly boy; he

got to his feet and managed a smile at Brenda, with his how-do-you-dos. Mackey squeezed Carmody's hand, grinning hard at him, saying, 'I'm a salesman, Tom, but I guess you can see that. Most people pipe me right away. You I don't get, though. You teach?'

'Not exactly.' Carmody was clearly uncomfortable at having to explain himself. 'I'm in rehabilitation,' he said.

Mackey did a good job of misunderstanding. Looking concerned, he said, 'Hey, I'm sorry. Whatcha rehabilitating from?'

'No, I'm – I—' Carmody's confusion made him blush. He finally managed to get it out: 'I work for a preacher. We do rehabilitation work for, uh, people.'

'Well, that's fine,' Mackey told him. 'There's a lotta people *need* that stuff.' With a big jokey grin he said, 'What about old George here? You gonna rehabilitate him?'

Carmody began to stumble and stutter all over himself again, but this time Liss came to his rescue, saying, 'Not me. I'm a hopeless case.'

'Us honest citizens shouldn't be seen with the likes of you,' Mackey said, and whacked Liss playfully on the arm. 'See you around, George.'

Everybody said good-bye, Carmody sat down with obvious relief, and Parker and Mackey and Brenda went out to the parking lot, where Mackey had a laughing fit, leaning over the hood of their car. When he got himself under control he said, 'That was touching, Parker. Do you know that? He didn't wanna blow the gaff on George being on parole. I call that touching.'

'He's a very straight citizen,' Parker agreed.

Mackey leaned against the car, wiping his eyes, and said to Brenda, 'Well? What do you think? Still too gloomy?'

'I think you can take a chance,' she said. 'If everything else is okay. If Parker's going in.'

'Yeah?' Mackey was interested. 'How come the change of heart?'

'He isn't a liar,' Brenda said. 'He isn't trapping anybody, or double-crossing anybody, or anything like that, because that fella couldn't lie about what *time* it is without the whole thing showing on his face.'

'Well, that's true.' Mackey nodded, thinking it over, then grinned again and looked at Parker. 'Ever work with a guy on *that* recommendation before? He can't tell a lie. Parker, we're signing on with George Washington.'

FOUR

They waited in the parking lot, and when Carmody came out with Liss half an hour later he stopped dead at the sight of them. Eyes round, he stared off toward the street for rescue, but before he could do anything foolish Liss took his elbow and said, reassuringly, 'It's okay, Tom. This means they like you.'

'What? What?'

Gently, Liss explained: 'These are the people gonna help us, Tom. They wanted to see you first, see what they thought. If they figured you were okay, they'd wait here until we came out. And here they are.'

'You mean, the, the—'

Mackey said, 'That's right, Tom. The reverend's millions.'

Startled, Carmody said, 'Not millions!'

'I know, I know.' Mackey grinned at himself. 'I was just exaggerating, Tom, it's a bad habit I got. The number's four hundred grand, am I right? Two for us, two for you.'

'Approximately,' Carmody said.

Mackey spread his hands, looking at Liss. 'How can we not love this guy, George?' he asked. 'He doesn't want to mislead us or anything.'

Parker said, 'Carmody, you'll give George a list of the

places where your preacher's going to be doing his thing the next four or five months.'

Carmody said, 'That long? I was hoping—'

'Maybe we'll do it next week,' Parker told him, although he knew they wouldn't. 'Maybe not till later. We'll do it when we got the right place, the right circumstances. You don't want any risk, right?'

'That's right,' Carmody said. He stared at Parker like an antelope looking at a lion. 'Mr. uh, Grant, is it?'

'Yeah.'

'I never did anything like—'

'We know,' Parker said. 'George told us what your idea is. You want to do good.'

'Whereas,' Mackey said, '*we* want to do well.'

Ignoring that, Parker said to Carmody, 'If something goes wrong, the cops won't ask you what your motive was. You see what I mean?'

'Absolutely,' Carmody said.

'So we'll pick the right time, the right place, the right circumstances,' Parker told him. 'We'll decide when it's safe to make our move. And then we'll say to you, *now*.'

FIVE

The money room was long, low-ceilinged and windowless. There were bright fluorescent lights in the ceiling, the walls were off-white plasterboard, and a pale gray industrial carpet was on the floor, but even with all that lightness and brightness the place had the feeling of being a cave or a tunnel, far underground. Air conditioning produced a flat dry atmosphere, in which sounds became muffled and small. The hymn-singing could not be heard in here.

Parker and Liss and Mackey came into the room fast, ski masks on their faces, the shotguns pointing outward, slightly over the occupants' heads, the blued-steel barrels moving back and forth as though looking for a target. Liss cried out, 'Everybody stop! Stop now! Hands on desks! *You!* You'll die!'

The fat man with the black necktie stopped reaching for the phone. He and the other five people in the room all became very still. Three of them – the fat man and two middle-aged women, all seated at desks with open ledgers and calculators and video terminals – were employees of the arena, and would calm down when they stopped to remember it wasn't their money in any case. The other three, all slender short-haired young men in dark slacks and white shirts and narrow ties, were Reverend Archibald's people, and might take a robbery more personally.

These three had all been on their feet, standing around the long tables piled with money, still only partially counted. Now they all stood bent slightly forward, palms flat against the counting table as their eyes darted around, glancing quickly at one another, at the money, at the shotguns, at the lights and the floor and everything in the room. All three were thinking about trying something, even against the guns.

Mackey stepped forward toward the money table, keeping to the side so he didn't block Parker's and Liss's aim. He was jittery on his feet and bunching his shoulders up and down, giving them all kinds of body language about how wrought-up he was. His voice loud and ragged, full of tension, he yelled, 'You three! Get away from the money!'

They stared at him, not moving. Mackey shook the shotgun in both hands. He bobbed on his feet. He yelled, 'I gotta blow one of you bastards away! I gotta! So *move!*'

Liss angrily yelled, 'Don't get blood on the money!'

'Move away!' Mackey screamed at the three. 'Move away!'

Now finally one of them found voice. Frightened, gasping through the words, he said, 'What do you want to shoot us for?'

Parker stepped forward. 'Ed, don't do it,' he said. 'Not unless they give you a reason.'

Mackey jittered forward close enough to touch the shotgun barrel against the white shirtsleeve of the one who'd spoken. 'Give me a reason,' he begged. 'Give me a reason.'

Parker, as though he wanted to calm Mackey down as much as anybody, said to the trio, 'Down on the floor.

Right where you are. On your backs. Ed won't shoot unless you're stupid.'

The three went down fast, and lay blinking up at the ceiling. Like upended turtles, they felt more exposed and helpless on their backs than if Parker had let them lie face down, where they could have felt hidden and coiled. Between their position on the floor there and Mackey's apparent blood-hunger, they wouldn't be causing any trouble after all.

Parker had taken the bag of duffel bags from Mackey on the way in, to leave Mackey's arms free for when he went into his act. Now Parker turned to the two women seated at their desks, trying to be invisible, and tossed the duffel at them. 'Take the bags out and fill them. The faster you do it, the sooner we're out of here.'

The women hurried across to the money table, stepping over the supine men. Awkward with haste, they stuffed money into the gray canvas bags, while Mackey kept pacing around, muttering to himself and rubbing the top of his head. Liss stood near the door, the shotgun in his hands moving in arcs, like a surveillance camera. Parker went past him and back out to the small anteroom, where they'd left Carmody, who was still out, lying on the floor where they'd dragged him. He went back inside and Mackey was fidgeting back and forth, pointing his gun at the men on the floor and mumbling incomprehensible things, while the two women kept sneaking terrified looks at him and filling the duffel bags as rapidly as they possibly could.

Parker went around the room, unsnapping the phone cords connecting all the phones to their jacks, then bringing the phone cords over to the money table and stuffing them into a bag that was already half full.

Liss said to the fat man, 'You can make that important call now.'

The fat man was doing dignity; he sat, unmoving, head bent forward, gazing at a spot on the desk midway between his splayed-out hands. He pretended Liss hadn't spoken.

They'd brought six bags, but it only took five for all the money. 'Give me the empty one,' Parker told the women as they loaded the last of the cash, and they did. While he moved the duffels two at a time out to the anteroom, Liss told the people, 'You'll stay in here a while. Ed's gonna hang around outside the door, hoping to shoot somebody. I don't know how long it's gonna take Jack and me to get him to leave, so don't be in any hurry to go anywhere.'

Liss then joined Parker and the money in the anteroom, while Mackey raved at the people a while on his own. Looking down at Carmody, some dried blood on the side of the fellow's head looking fake against the angel makeup, Liss said, 'Is he gonna hold?'

Parker had already put his shotgun in the empty duffel bag. Holding it open for Liss's weapon, he said, 'He'll hold.'

'I'm the one he could identify,' Liss said. He didn't put the shotgun in the duffel. He said, 'I'm the one exposed if he breaks.'

'If you kill him,' Parker said, 'they'll know he was the inside man. They'll look at who he knew, through that parole scam. They'll get to you for sure.'

Liss thought about that. Mackey came out, shutting the door, and looked at them. 'Something?'

29

'No,' Liss said, and put his shotgun in the bag.

Mackey put his weapon with the others and said, 'They'll stay in there a while. They'll stay in there until their pants dry.' Then they tossed their ski masks into the bag with the guns, and left, each carrying two bags, Mackey carrying the heavier one with the guns.

Back where they'd come into the building, Parker cautiously opened the door and looked out. The parking lot was full of cars and empty of people. This was why they'd given up the idea of going for the money outside in the barrels. They would have had to wait until the crusade finished and everybody was out and moving. This way was cleaner and simpler.

The three moved quickly across the asphalt lot through the cars. It was a bright sunny fall day, temperature in the fifties, air very crisp and clear. They seemed to shimmy and disappear as they moved through the varicolored parked cars.

At the far end of the parking lot, five days ago, a construction company trailer had been set up here, wheeled in behind a semi cab, then chocked up and the perimeter beneath closed with concrete blocks. A sign on the side of the trailer read, in large blue letters on a white ground, MORAN CONSTRUCTION, SITE MANAGER'S OFFICE.

This was a legitimate trailer from a legitimate construction company, now bankrupt and shut down, but its assets not yet sold. The trailer had been stolen from the company's yard, using a cab that also belonged to the company. Once it was in position here, Mackey had hooked up the electric lines to a nearby power pole, and then they'd just left the thing alone. Archibald's crusade hadn't even been in this state when they'd moved the trailer into position. Such trailers are so often to be found in distant corners of large public parking areas that nobody looks twice at them. This one had been left undisturbed for five days.

Now, Parker did the combination on the padlock on the door and climbed up and in, followed by Liss and then by Mackey. They entered a cramped office, with desk and chair on one side and narrow hard sofa on the other, on and around which they dumped the duffel bags. To the right of the office was the john, complete with a very narrow shower – the trailer contained its own water supply and waste storage – and to the left was a compact living room, with built-in sofas, a bookcase full of magazines and paperbacks, and a small black-and-white television set. Beyond the living room was a galley-type kitchen; five days ago, they'd stocked that with beer and soda and canned food.

There was a small sliding window in the entry door, covered on the inside by a stretched-tight translucent plastic curtain. Once they were inside, Parker removed that curtain, unlatched the window, slid the openable half out of the way, reached out, and reattached the padlock to the hasp on the door, locking them in. Then he slid the window shut, latched it, and put the curtain back in place.

Mackey came in from the kitchen with three cans of beer. Distributing them, he said, 'Parker, I like this. It's very good. This is the most comfortable escape from a heist I ever made.'

'Bad news to be running around out there now,' Parker said.

'You know it.' Mackey popped open his beer. 'To a life of ease,' he said.

Liss knocked back about half his beer, but still looked troubled. 'Now,' he said, 'all Tom has to do is not make me sorry he's still alive.'

SIX

It was a mess in the parking lot for a couple hours. Police cars and police lab vans blocked the aisles. An ambulance came and went, yowling, most likely dealing with Tom Carmody. Long tables were set up near the main arena entrance, where clerical cops processed the crusade's attendees, taking their IDs and giving them a few quick questions each, as the former crusade audience stood in long nervous patient lines. More cops searched every car before permitting it to be driven away. Twenty thousand people; every one of them given personal attention. It took a while.

Twice in the course of the afternoon, cops came over to the construction trailer to fiddle with the padlock and test the door to be sure it was locked and then knock on it, just in case. The second one did even more, walking all around the trailer to see if there was any other way in, then trying to look in through the three windows; the one in the door leading to the office, the large one in the living room through which Parker and Mackey and Liss occasionally watched the action outside, and the small high one in the john. But they were all covered by the translucent plastic curtains, so he gave up, and contented himself with copying down the Moran Construction Company phone number from the sign on the trailer's side. He wouldn't get much satisfaction if he actually dialed that number. *Out of service*, most likely.

The cops were nowhere near finished when it started to get dark, so three floodlight trucks were brought in and parked strategically to drench the area in light. Even at the fringe of the action, where Parker and the other two waited, there was plenty of illumination. It spilled into the trailer, giving them all the light they needed, softening into a pale coral color as it filtered through the curtains.

In that soft illumination, Parker and Mackey and Liss sat around the desk in the office and counted the money, which came to three hundred ninety-eight thousand, five hundred eighty dollars, all in fives and tens and twenties, and even some wrinkled singles. About as traceable as a drop of water.

After that, they mostly watched television, with the sound very low. Which meant they mostly watched other angles of what was going on outside. The half-million-dollar robbery at the arena – whether the exaggeration was Archibald's, the cops', or the television people's, was hard to guess – was the biggest event in this town since the last Rolling Stones farewell tour.

Around nine o'clock, Mackey moved the curtain slightly at the corner of the living room window, looked out, and said, 'Parker, they're gonna still be here tomorrow morning.'

The idea was, Brenda was expected at six in the morning. She'd drive by in a station wagon they'd promoted earlier, and if things seemed all right she'd come on into the parking area, they'd switch the goods, set the fuse on the bomb, and take off. (The only way to be sure they wouldn't leave incriminating evidence in the trailer was to blow it up.) But now Mackey, shaking his head as he looked out the window, said, 'When Brenda gets here, she's gonna have to check in with the cops.'

'They'll be gone,' Parker said. 'You're just getting antsy.'

'And that's the truth,' Mackey agreed, moving away from the window, sitting down again. 'I never lived inside a tin can before,' he explained. 'Now I know how minestrone feels.'

'How does Tom Carmody feel,' Liss said tensely, 'that's all I want to know.'

Parker said, 'He's got a concussion. He'll come out of it tomorrow groggy. They won't lean on him very hard, not right away. By the time they're really looking him over, he won't be nervous any more.'

'Tom,' Liss said, 'will *always* be nervous.'

Parker shrugged. 'So will you, I guess.'

Mackey leaned back, fingers laced behind his head, aggressive grin on his face. 'Snowbound with my pals,' he said. 'Everybody getting along. No problems. From here on in, everything's gravy.'

SEVEN

A flat metallic *click* woke Parker. He opened his eyes and in the darkness saw the dull glint of the shotgun barrels a foot from his face. Beyond them, Liss's eyes stood out, the whites luminous, as though lit from within.

Making a hoarse scared rale in his throat, Liss pulled the second trigger, and that *click* sounded again as Parker kicked him in the chest. Liss bounced backward into the wall, and Parker's left hand went up and closed around the barrels, yanking the shotgun away. Grasping the barrels with both hands, he surged up from the sofa and lunged the shotgun forward, the butt smashing into Liss's face.

'Hey! What the hell?' Mackey came boiling up from the other sofa, getting in Parker's way, the two of them stumbling around in the cramped space as Liss fell to the floor, then crawled quickly through the doorway into the other room.

'It's *Liss*,' Parker said, pushing Mackey away. 'Wanting it all.'

'Son of a bitch.'

Parker went to one knee, felt under the sofa cushion, came out with just one of the shells. Getting to his feet, he broke the shotgun as he went through the doorway. The exit door stood open. Thumbing in the shell, slapping the shotgun shut, Parker crossed to see Liss out there, hesitating over the three duffel bags.

They'd each crammed their third of the take into one of the bags, and Liss had moved all three outside before turning to rid himself of his partners: one barrel into Parker, then quickly one into Mackey, all of them together in the narrow room. If Parker hadn't quietly emptied the three shotguns earlier tonight, one time when he had gone to the john and the other two were watching television, he and Mackey would be dead.

Liss had thought he might grab one or more of the bags anyway, on his way out, but when he saw Parker in the doorway he gave that up and just ran. Parker jumped down to the asphalt and watched Liss dash across the parking area, bent low and weaving as he went. Parker stood where he was, shotgun in both hands, not pointing anywhere in particular.

Mackey leaped down beside him, empty hands closed into fists. 'Shoot the cocksucker! What's the matter with you?'

'No need,' Parker said. 'And a noise could draw a crowd.'

Furious, Mackey said, 'Don't leave him *alive*, God damn it.' He acted as though he wanted to pull the shotgun out of Parker's hands, and was restraining himself with difficulty.

Liss was out of sight now. The police had finished clearing out of here a little after ten, and the three in the trailer had gone to sleep around midnight, three hours ago, Liss on the sofa in the office, with the money and the guns. He could have just taken the money and left, but he hadn't wanted Parker and Mackey behind him the rest of his life.

Apparently, Mackey returned the feeling. 'Parker,' he said, 'that was a mistake. We could have afforded a little noise, not to have him around any more.'

Parker never saw any point in arguing over past events. He said, 'Can you call Brenda?'

'Yeah, you're right,' Mackey said. 'We can't stay here any more.' Peering away into the night where Liss had disappeared, he said, 'He'll need time to get guns and friends, but I'll bet you, Parker, he still thinks this money is his.'

EIGHT

Parker sat on the weedy ground, the chain link fence against his back, the reloaded shotgun on his lap. Out ahead of him, in the darkness, beyond the narrow strip of scrubland, the empty asphalt parking area stretched across to the big round bulk of the arena. Off to the right, its metal side picking up the glints of distant streetlights, waited the construction trailer. The three sacks of money were back inside it, and the padlock was once more in place on the door.

Parker had been seated here for twenty minutes, and so far nothing had happened. The only weapons they had were the shotguns, so Mackey had gone off unarmed to find a phone booth and call Brenda. She'd come to where he was, pick him up, and then drive on to the arena. This town wasn't George Liss's home base, so he shouldn't immediately be able to lay his hands on guns and colleagues. There was time enough.

The car that nosed into the parking area entrance, way over by the arena building, wasn't a station wagon. It paused just inside the parking area, then switched off its headlights. In darkness, it drove slowly around on the asphalt, stopping two or three times, pausing, then driving on, moving in apparently random ways.

Liss? With friends? Parker lay flat against the fence,

shotgun tucked in against his side, and watched the car move around the parking area like a hunting dog that's lost the scent.

Eventually the people in the car saw the construction trailer and drove over to it, still with no lights. They stopped beside the trailer and two men got out, one from the front seat and one from the back. When they opened the two right-hand doors, the interior light went on, and Parker could see that neither of them was Liss. Nor was the third man, the driver. The strangers shut the car doors, killing the light, and went over to look at the trailer, poking at its padlock.

Parker sat up, holding the shotgun in both hands. If they tried to break into the trailer he'd have to move against them. He had extra shells in his shirt pocket, but could only fire twice before having to reload. He should be closer, to put one charge into the two at the trailer door and the other into the driver. To give them something as a distraction while he reloaded.

Slowly, silently, he got to his feet and moved to his right, to put the bulk of the trailer between himself and the three newcomers. But as he edged up closer they moved away from the trailer, losing interest in it. Parker hunkered down, and the two guys got back into their car. In the brief moment when the interior light was on, he could see they were arguing among themselves, all three. He could hear the driver grind gears, and the car jerked away.

It made one more stop, over by the arena, and Parker saw the light come on briefly as the two guys got out again and went over to look at the accordion gates closed and locked over the broad arena entrance. They didn't seem to have anything particular in mind. They *were* dogs who'd lost a scent.

Finally they got back into their car, and this time it drove away entirely, out the exit from the parking area and out of sight. Two minutes later, another pair of headlights appeared way over there, and when Parker hunkered down next to the trailer to silhouette the car it was the station wagon.

This vehicle switched down to parking lights as it turned this way, then came straight across the empty lot to the trailer and stopped. Brenda was driving, Mackey beside her.

Mackey, more sensible than the strangers in the other car, had removed the bulb from the interior light, so nothing flashed when he climbed out and came across to Parker and said, 'Did you make those guys?'

'Don't know them,' Parker told him. He still held the shotgun and kept glancing toward the parking area entrance.

'Our delay is,' Mackey said, 'they were watching the motel. They followed Brenda when she left to pick me up. She took some time and shook them before she got to me, and told me about it, and damn if they weren't right ahead of us three blocks from here. We hung back and watched them come in and fuck around and then come back out. What did they do in here?'

'Looked lost,' Parker said. Now he leaned the shotgun against the trailer and did the combination on the padlock as he said, 'They know something, or they think something, but not enough. They came over here and sniffed around the trailer, but not as if they knew for sure this was it. It's like they think we didn't leave, but they don't know what happened instead. They were trying to figure out how to get into the arena, like maybe we're still in there.'

'Friends of Liss?'

'Or Carmody's girl friend,' Parker suggested. He pulled open the trailer door. 'Too many people hanging around.'

'Time to go someplace else,' Mackey agreed. He opened the station wagon's cargo door, and he and Parker carried the three duffel bags from the trailer to lay them side by side on the station wagon's floor, like mail sacks. Then Parker put the shotgun in the office with the other two and plugged the bomb into the electric outlet beside the desk. He and Mackey got into the front seat with Brenda. They drove away from there, and three minutes later the trailer exploded itself into a million guitar picks.

NINE

Brenda drove, Mackey sat in the middle, and Parker was on the right. He bent his head sometimes to look at the outside mirror on his door, but nothing showed behind them. Four in the morning, this was a quiet town.

Except, of course, when a construction trailer blows up with a force that rattles windows a block away. The trio in the car heard it go, and Brenda immediately pulled into the curb among a line of parked cars, cutting the lights and engine. They kept their heads down and waited, and a couple minutes later the parade of official vehicles started: fire engines, police cars, emergency service trucks, all thundering along at top speed, sirens wailing and red-and-white gumdrops and tootsie rolls flashing.

The flow of excited public servants lasted five minutes or so, and finally ebbed with the appearance of a bright red fire chief's station wagon, making a slower and more dignified approach to the scene.

They let that last one go by, and then Brenda started up their own station wagon and took them farther away from the center of excitement. 'Where next?' she said.

Mackey said, 'Well, we can't go back to the motel, I know that much. Those extra guys, whoever they are, that's where they'll go, back where they were watching Brenda, stake it out, wait for us.'

'I know,' Parker said.

Brenda said, 'I want to tell you, Ed, I'll be leaving a whole lot of cosmetics back in that room.'

'We'll buy you a suitcase of the stuff,' Mackey promised her, 'out of Liss's share.'

'Good.'

'But the other problem is,' Mackey went on, 'we can't go to that empty house where we were gonna stash the goods, because naturally Liss knows about that place, and he just might show up there.'

'Well, we can't drive around all night,' Brenda said, taking a random right turn. 'Some cop'll stop us just on general principles, and then he'll want to look at our laundry back there.'

Mackey said, 'The same thing would happen if we try to drive *out* of town. This is a very tense location right now. And if we go check into some other hotel somewhere at this hour in the night, we're still drawing too much of the wrong kind of attention.'

'What we want now,' Parker said, 'is an all-night gas station.'

Mackey frowned, leaning against Brenda to look at the gas gauge on the dashboard. 'Why?'

Brenda, quicker than that, said, 'I saw one out by the interstate.'

Looking past Mackey's confused frown at Brenda, Parker said, 'We'll get out a block before you reach the place. You go on in, you tell the guy you just got off the interstate because there's something knocking under the hood and you don't know what it is.'

'The dumb broad in the car,' Brenda said.

'That's right.'

Mackey's frown turned to a smile. 'He puts it on the rack,' he said. 'Inside.'

Brenda said, 'So I better tell him it's something with the brakes. Otherwise, we'll just stay outside by the pumps and he'll look under the hood.'

Mackey beamed at Brenda's profile. 'You see, Parker?' he said. 'You see what I mean?'

'Yes,' Parker said, and bent his head to look in the outside mirror once more. Something? He squinted at the distorting mirror – *objects in mirror are closer than they appear* was etched into the glass – but there was nothing back there but parked cars, dark houses, streetlights, traffic lights playing solitaire. *Had* there been something? Hard to tell. Nothing now. Maybe it had been a car crossing an intersection back there.

It was another ten minute drive to the gas station, during which one police patrol car passed, going the other way. It slowed as they came together, the two cops giving the people in the station wagon a *very* long stare, but Brenda smiled and waved at them, and they nodded with dignity and drove on.

'One thing I don't want to have to do,' Brenda said, sounding a little nervous as she watched the police car recede in her mirror, 'is outrun a lot of cops in *their* town.'

'At that point,' Parker told her, 'we give the whole thing up. Lose the car *and* the goods, and go to ground.'

'Don't even think it,' Mackey said.

They saw no more traffic, and then there was the gas station with all its gleaming lights, out ahead of them, an oasis of glitter in the surrounding dark. Beyond the station's lights, occasional smaller lights could be seen

45

going by, fifteen or twenty feet up in the air; the big trucks on the interstate overpass.

'We'll get out here,' Parker said to Brenda, 'and we'll give you five minutes.'

'Fine.'

Brenda pulled the station wagon to the curb, and the men got out. Looking back the way they'd come, Parker frowned. Had something moved back there? As Brenda drove away, Parker stepped into the street, peering down the long empty stretch of it. No movement. Just the darkness.

'What is it?'

'Nothing,' Parker said.

The gas station was on this side, a block and a half away. They crossed the street and walked down the opposite sidewalk. Facing the gas station was a closed tire store, with *sale* signs in the windows. They paused there to look across the way, through the large open doorway into the service area. Over there, Brenda was just backing the station wagon into the service area, on the side with the lift, being directed by a skinny kid in white company coveralls and his own baseball cap. He seemed to be the only one on duty tonight.

'We have time,' Parker said. 'I want a look at the ramp.'

They walked on another long block to the two on-ramps for the interstate, and saw a state highway patrol car parked on each one, tucked up partway along the ramp, so you'd already have made the turn before you saw it. 'Just like we thought,' Mackey said.

'Just like we *knew*,' Parker said.

The one advantage was, where the highway patrolmen were, they wouldn't be aware of anything going on at the gas station. Leaving them there, keeping to the shadows, Parker and Mackey walked back and went beyond the gas station again before crossing to its side of the street and making their approach.

The kid had the station wagon up on the lift now and was checking the brake fluid, which should have kept him occupied, except that there was a bell over the office door that sounded when Parker entered, Mackey coming in behind him. Parker went to the doorway connecting the office with the service area, while Mackey went straight to the messy metal desk and riffled through the drawers, shoving credit card slips and other junk out of the way.

The kid came in fast, polite and ready to serve, but holding the wrench he'd used to open the brake drum cap. 'Sorry, gentlemen, I didn't hear your car come—' He took in the absence of a car out by the pumps at the same time he saw Mackey at the desk. 'Hey!'

Mackey straightened, shaking his head at the kid, disappointed in him. 'You don't have a gun in here,' he complained.

Bewildered, the kid stared at Mackey and said, 'No! What do we want with a—? What are you *doing* there!'

Mackey came around the desk toward the kid, spreading his empty hands, saying, 'That's a hell of a thing. What if we were robbers?'

It had crossed the kid's mind that that's just what they were. Blinking from Parker to Mackey, both of them now too close to him, he said, 'You're not?'

'Not at the moment,' Mackey said, and grinned.

Parker held out his hand. 'If you give me the wrench,' he said, 'the lady behind you won't have to crack your head open.'

47

Everything was happening too fast; the kid could never get set, never get a response ready before the encounter took another turn. Looking over his shoulder, he saw Brenda there behind him, holding up a shiny large socket wrench for him to see. She wasn't smiling. She looked businesslike. The kid said, 'You're *with* these guys?'

Mackey laughed. 'She's the boss!' he announced. 'That's Ma Barker!'

'The wrench,' Parker said.

The kid shrugged, and handed it over. 'If you're not gonna hold the place up,' he said, 'then I don't get it.'

'We're all going to stay here a while,' Parker told him. 'Where do you turn off the lights?'

This astonished the kid more than anything so far: 'You want to *close*?'

'You're getting a vacation,' Mackey explained. 'An unexpected brief vacation.'

Parker tapped the kid's chest with the wrench, leaving a grease smear on the white coveralls. 'The lights.'

The kid blinked, then pointed at the circuit breaker box on the back wall behind the desk. 'We do it there,' he said. 'You can't turn them *all* off, though. There's some stuff we've got to leave on.'

'For now,' Parker said, 'just turn off the outside lights.'

Reluctant but obedient, the kid did as he was told, wide-eyed, as though it were some kind of sacrilege to close a 24-hour gas station.

Next, they had him lower the hydraulic lift, to bring the station wagon back down, and shut and lock the service area door, a double-width overhead garage door full of rectangular windows. Then they looked around at their new environment and found, at the right rear of the service area, a door to a storage room that was tucked in behind the office. Long and narrow, the storage room was full of fan belts and cans of oil and high wooden racks of tires. The door was open, but there was a padlock on the hasp on the outside.

Mackey said, 'Write down the combination, will you?'

'I'm not sure I know it,' the kid said, deciding to be crafty.

Mackey shrugged. 'That's up to you,' he said. 'We're gonna lock you in there now, so you won't be in our hair. I figured to let you out when we go, but you want to take your chances on somebody coming along, that's up to you.'

The kid remembered the combination then, and wrote it on a service order pad. He also asked if he could bring into the room with him the two magazines from the desk that he'd been reading, and they said okay. He went in without trouble, dragging along a wooden chair and carrying his magazines. He even grinned at them tentatively as they closed the door.

Fixing the padlock, Mackey said, 'Not a bad kid. A bright future, I think.'

'A smart kid,' Parker said. 'He knows he wants a future.'

They turned off the rest of the lights, shutting the station entirely. A little illumination seeped out from under the storage room door, where the kid was reading his magazines, but not enough to be seen out in the street.

Mackey and Brenda caught up on some of their missed sleep in the station wagon. Parker made himself as comfortable as he could on the vinyl stuffed chair in the office, feet up on the desk. He dozed off a few times, never

49

for very long, and then one time he opened his eyes and it was daylight; six or six-thirty in the morning.

And what had awakened him was a city police car out there, just pulling to a stop, this side of the pumps. There was only one cop in it. He got out on this side, and turned his back to look out over the top of his car at the street, looking left and right. His uniform was the wrong size, legs too short, jacket too loose.

Parker put his feet on the floor and leaned forward. The cop turned and started toward the office, right hand unhooking the flap on his holster, closing around the service revolver in there. Under the police cap, it was George Liss.

PART TWO

ONE

Seven hours before some atheistic sons of bitches robbed the Reverend William Archibald of four hundred thousand dollars, he woke up alone in bed. '*Now* where the hell is she?' he said.

Tina, having heard the familiar rich baritone voice, immediately popped out of the bathroom, saying, 'Here I am, Will.' Her heavy ash-blonde hair framed that willing face in a mad tangle, still mussed from sleep. She was naked, and remained the only woman in Archibald's experience to overflow her birthday suit. 'Is there something you want, honey?' she asked.

He looked at her standing there, open, amiable, those round cheeks bracketing a full-lipped mouth succulent with sleep. 'Come to think of it,' he said, 'there is.'

Fifteen minutes later, Archibald was whistling in the shower while Tina ordered breakfast from room service. By the time he was dressed in his pinstripe blue suit, white shirt and figured blue tie, his sleek jowls gleaming with aftershave and his pewter hair brushed into corniche waves, breakfast was waiting in the living room of the suite, set up at the table by the big window overlooking the view, which Archibald ignored. Every town was the same, finally, if you didn't live in it; just a collection of tall and short buildings containing people who might be helped by

Reverend Archibald's ministry, and might help the reverend in return. Now, seating himself before his bacon and eggs, home fries, orange juice, toast and coffee, he said a heartfelt, 'Thank *you*, Lord,' and tucked in.

Tina appeared ten minutes later, having completed her daily transformation. In her pale gray suit, white blouse with neck ruffle and low-heel black shoes, with her hair tamed into a bun, her pale and subtle makeup, and her horn-rim spectacles – she was blind as a bat, and wore those glasses everywhere except in bed, where she got along quite well by feel – she was no longer the compliant and indulgent Tina of their nighttime hours, but Christine Mackenzie, conductor of the Reverend Archibald's Angel Choir. The mouth was still loose and carnal now, when she smiled hello, but when singing 'Just a Closer Walk with Jesus' those lips could appear to be swollen with nothing more than heavenly love. Heavenly.

At Tina's place, across the table from Archibald, the breakfast consisted of half a grapefruit, two slices of dry toast and tea without milk. Tina was a lush girl inside that gray suit, but it was a lushness that could spill into over-ripeness, as they both well knew. Limiting herself to a diet that the monks of the Middle Ages would have chosen for penitent reasons, to the castigation of the body and the greater glory of God, but doing so for rather different reasons of her own, Tina managed to hold her abundance in check, to keep herself at a level that was no more than what the kikes call *zaftig*. (The bastards even have their own language.)

From the very beginning of his ministry, William Archibald had understood that *the appearance of propriety* was the name of the game. It wasn't merely that the appearance of propriety was as good as propriety itself, but that it was much better. If the appearance of propriety were steadfastly maintained – religiously maintained, you might say – a reasonably careful man could have it all; the rich rewards of religion *and* the rich rewards of life. And that's what he wanted: it all.

Archibald wasn't a hypocrite. He believed that man was a sinful creature and he said so, publicly and often, never excepting himself. He believed that his ministry had held back many a fellow human being from committing crimes and sins untold. He believed that his contributions to the social order, his civilizing influence on men and women who were in many ways still one small step from the apes, were practical and immense, and he *firmly* believed he was worth every penny he made out of it. His ministry had rescued drunkards, saved marriages, reformed petty thieves, struggled successfully at times against the scourge of drugs, cured workplace absenteeism and given a center and a weight and a sense of belonging to unnumbered empty, drifting, useless chowderheads. If, in his leisure moments, he liked to ball a big-titted woman, so what?

They were finishing breakfast when Dwayne Thorsen came in, looking brisk and competent in a gray suit that managed to be as respectable as Archibald's without competing with it. Dwayne's twenty years in the Marine Corps had left him lean and mean, and his seven years as Archibald's executive assistant had done nothing to change him. He still preferred his old cropped-short Marine haircut (the stubby hair pepper-and-salt gray now), his comfortable but ugly black oxford shoes, and his government-issue wire frame round-lens glasses, through which his pale eyes skeptically gleamed like the coldest sunny day in Norway, from which his thinlipped hard-working farmer forebears had emigrated a century ago.

'Morning, Dwayne,' Archibald said. 'Order yourself some coffee.'

'Ate.'

There was a third chair at the table, facing the view. Like the other two, it was armless, with a cushioned seat and delicately scrolled wooden back. When Dwayne's big-knuckled hand reached for it, the chair seemed to flinch, as though sure it would be kindling in a minute, but Dwayne merely pulled it out from the table, sat in it, ignored the view as much as the others had, ignored Tina as well – he usually did, facing her when he absolutely had to with a fastidious sneer – and said, 'All set.'

'Well, naturally.' Archibald smiled at his assistant. 'If you're in charge, Dwayne, it's all set.'

Dwayne shrugged that off. 'Morning news says six hundred of them camped at the arena last night.'

Not unexpected. Since Archibald's crusades offered no advance sales and had no reserved seating or credit card sales or anything else except cash on the barrelhead as the customer walked in the gate, and since his draw had only increased with the television ministry, it was usual these last few years for a number of people to bring sleeping bags or deck chairs and camp out the night before at the gate of the stadium or arena where he was to appear, to be certain of getting in. Still, six hundred was a pretty impressive number, and Archibald couldn't help a little smile of satisfaction as he said, 'Radio news or television news?'

'Both. Local insert on *Today*, and just about every local radio news spot.'

Good. Archibald would have no trouble selling out this twenty-thousand-seat arena, but it was nice anyway to let *other* people, people who so far were insufficiently aware of the Reverend William Archibald, know that this attraction was such a grabber it drew six hundred overnight campers. Better than the World Series.

Dwayne went on, 'Security's shitty at this place, though I don't suppose it matters.'

'Dwayne,' Archibald said comfortably, sopping up the last of his egg yolk with the last of Tina's second piece of toast, 'you say that every place we go.'

'It's true every place we go,' Dwayne said. 'These outfits today, they're not used to cash.'

'Dwayne, Dwayne,' Archibald said, 'who's going to steal from the ministry?'

'Well, we've had some, now and then.'

'Pilfering. Employees, misguided smalltime people. You find them out, Dawyne, you always do, and I give them a good talking-to.'

'And then I,' Dwayne said, 'kick their butts into the street.'

'But we haven't had anybody like that for a long time,' Archibald said. 'You pick those people with a great deal of care, Dwayne.'

'Which brings me,' Dwayne said, 'to this boy Carmody.'

Archibald sighed. 'A knottier problem than most,' he admitted.

'I think we ought to get rid of him.'

'For zealousness? Dwayne, we've never had to do anything like that before, and I just worry it could backfire on us.'

'He's making trouble,' Dwayne insisted. 'He's an infection that could spread. I like my troops motivated.'

'Yes, of course. But the press, Dwayne. The press is a constant affliction. If Tom Carmody's disaffection led him to the wrong reporter, if he found a sympathetic ear in the media to listen when he says we threw him out because he *got religion*, it could be very bad. Very bad.'

'Three days' wonder.'

'Maybe. And maybe it's open season on servants of the Lord right now, Dwayne, and we ought to, as our corporate friends say, protect our asses.'

'I don't like what he says to the troops,' Dwayne insisted.

Archibald understood what Dwayne's problem was. The Marine Corps method of dealing with rotten apples was to seek them out, identify them, and throw them away before they could infect the rest of the bushel. But the Marine Corps didn't have to worry about the combination of a naturally hostile press and a business dependent on voluntary contributions. What Tom Carmody could do to sow doubt in the minds of Dwayne's troops was *nothing* to what he could conceivably do, with the right reporter's help, to sow doubt in the minds of people like the six hundred drinking their thermos coffee at the moment out at the arena. Employees come and go, but the six hundred are needed forever.

Which it would not be politic to explain to Dwayne, an essentially simple soul whose range of comprehension was unlikely ever to extend beyond the perimeter of the brigade. If someone was troublesome to Dwayne's troops, that's all he would see or care to see; the larger picture was beyond him.

Archibald said, 'I tell you what. After the crusade today, I'll have a chat with Tom, see if I can bring him round a bit.'

'Fine,' Dwayne said. 'But, Will, *look* at him when you talk to him. Look him over. Keep an open mind. If he isn't gonna come around, tell me. I won't just fire him, I'll ease him out, so he don't get mad.'

The idea of Dwayne being tactful brought a faint smile to Archibald's lips. He said, 'I'll study him like the lesson of the day. How's that?'

Tina said, 'Maybe you could talk him into joining some monks or something. Go into a monastery. Then he'd be away from us, but he'd be happy.'

Dwayne always squinted a bit and looked away when Tina spoke, as though a bright light were being shined on him. He did that again now, and left it to Archibald to say, 'Tina, that's a very good idea. I'll sound him out. A monastery is an *excellent* place for a religious young man.'

'He's got a girl friend,' Dwayne said, with no inflection.

Archibald raised an eyebrow. '*Has* he? So much for the monastery. Is she part of the problem, do you think?'

'Probably. Don't know for sure.'

'Perhaps I should talk to them both together.'

'She isn't here,' Dwayne said. 'She isn't one of us. She lives back in Memphis,' he explained, Memphis being Archibald's home base, where he had his Eternal Jesus Chapel and where his television ministry was taped.

'Well, I don't think we should postpone the issue until we get back to Memphis,' Archibald said. 'I'll talk to Tom this afternoon, after the crusade, and if necessary, talk to the girl later, when we get home. What kind of girl is she?'

'Don't know,' Dwayne said, and shrugged. 'Mary something. Don't know a thing about her.'

TWO

Just around the time William Archibald was whistling in the shower, Mary Quindero was beginning to die. She knew it, or suspected it, or feared it, but couldn't warn her murderers because they refused to hear anything except the answers to their questions, and she had no more answers. They, Woody Kellman and Zack Flynn, didn't know she was dying because they had no idea of the cumulative effect of the strangle-and-reprieve, drown-and-reprieve methods they were using to get the answers they felt she was still holding back. And her brother, Ralph Quindero, couldn't know what was happening because he was over at Zack's place, watching an old horror movie on the VCR, unable to be present while his friends pressured his sister, and not realizing just how stupid they were.

'Don't hurt her, or— You know, don't do— She's my sister, you know, I gotta . . .'

'Don't worry, Ralph, when she sees we're serious, what's she gonna do? What's her choice? We gotta pressure her a little, that's all, so she knows we're serious. That's all.'

That it hadn't worked that way was simply a miscalculation on everybody's part, starting with Ralph, who hadn't believed his pals would actually harm his own sister, and continuing with Woody and Zack, whose knowledge of the world came from movies and TV, which hadn't told them that, in real life, you could kill a person by repeatedly holding her head underwater in a bathtub, and finishing with Mary herself, who was motivated by a foolish desire to protect her dumb younger brother and who couldn't believe until too late that he wouldn't at some point come in and make them stop. But he didn't.

No. Ralph watched the horror movie until the finish, then brooded at the telephone while the tape rewound, wondering if he should call Mary's place, just see what was going on. This was taking longer than they'd expected, wasn't it? An hour and a half. What could take an hour and a half? How much information could Mary have, after all, and how long before Woody and Zack got it out of her?

Without the movie to distract his thoughts, he found himself worrying a little more about his sister in the hands of those two guys. They wouldn't . . . fuck her or anything, would they? No, they wouldn't do that, because they knew she'd tell him about it afterward, and they knew he'd *kill* them if they went too far, if they even – if they did anything except what they'd already agreed on: Lean on her a little, get whatever else it was Tom Carmody had told her about the guys who were out to grab the preacher's money, then phone him here to go downstairs and wait at the curb.

When Woody realized her eyes were open underwater, and that some new kind of sullen limpness had come over her body, different from the times when she'd passed out, he had an instant of panic, quickly buried. Ignoring the knowledge he already possessed, he pulled her back up out of the tub and stretched her out once again on the white-tile bathroom floor. Her eyes stayed open, water drops standing on them, not at all like tears.

'Passed out again,' Zack said, disgusted, looking over Woody's looming back, his view obstructed.

Woody felt a sensation he hadn't known for years, had completely forgotten: Being a little kid on a swing, going too high, until his balls felt like they were being sucked downward right out of him, drawn into the frozen middle of the earth. It had been a scary, exciting, unpleasant but fascinating feeling then; now it only made him sick. 'Aw, shit, Zack,' he said, and moved to the side, a strong and heavyset but clumsy guy, to let the skinnier tenser Zack have a clear view.

When the tape rewound, Ralph popped it out of the machine and into its box, and considered the rest of Zack's tape library. The three of them, punks in their mid-twenties, inseparable schmucks since high school, were occasional burglars, and Zack loved to break into video rental stores, copping armful after armful of tapes while Ralph and Woody searched the cash register and drawers for chickenfeed.

'How can we *call* him? Jesus Christ, Zack, his sister's *dead!*'

'*He* doesn't know that. He doesn't know that till long after we got the money, till we're gone and *history*, man.'

'*Jesus*, Zack.'

'Call him, goddamit. You wanna run *with* money, or without?'

Ralph touched the rows of tapes. Was it too early in the day for porn? Nah; he selected a tape, and turned toward the VCR as the phone rang. And now he was almost reluctant to answer.

In the living room of Mary's apartment, the bedroom and bathroom doors both closed, Woody stood holding the phone, while Zack glared at him. They were both sopping wet, and hiding their fear from one another. 'Remember!' Zack hissed. 'She's locked in the closet! She's okay!'

Woody nodded impatiently and said into the phone, 'Ralph? Okay, everything's done here. She's fine, we locked her in the closet, you can let her out when we get back.'

Zack stared, wild-eyed, a ventriloquist no longer sure he controls his dummy. Woody said, 'Well, she didn't want to tell us for a while.'

Zack looked alert, worried, imperiled. Woody said, 'You know, she always wanted to keep you out of – wants to keep you out of trouble. You know how she is.'

Zack silently pounded the sofa back in frustration, and Woody said, 'Well, she seen we weren't gonna take no for an answer, that's all, so then she opened up. She didn't know much more than she already told you, by the way. Not as much as we figured.'

Zack nodded in exasperated agreement – so much effort, such a rotten accident, for so little return – and Woody said, 'Except the name of the motel where Carmody's supposed to get in touch with them, if anything changes. Yeah, where they're gonna be today. So that was worth it, huh?'

'I don't know,' Ralph said, hefting the porn tape in his other hand, thinking about how mad Mary was going to be, even when he came back successful, even when he had more money than *God* in his hands and all her irritating little doubts and sermons and putdowns were proved for once and all to be wrong, wrong, wrong. 'I guess so,' Ralph said. 'Okay, I'll see you downstairs.'

It was a five-hour drive from Memphis to where William Archibald's crusade had latterly taken him; they should get going, if they wanted to be there in time for the robbery. 'Ten minutes,' Ralph said into the phone. 'Right.'

He watched five minutes of the porn movie, rewound it, and went downstairs.

THREE

Lunch for the staff on crusade days was simple and short; bowls of salad, slices of bread, plastic cups of tea or apple juice, all laid out on long folding tables in whatever arena they found themselves. It's true this was an inexpensive way to feed a crowd, but Archibald's motives went beyond the squeezing of a dollar. He wanted his angels, his choir, his assistants, all his boys and girls to be cheerful and energetic and sparkling during the crusade to come, not bogged down by great sandwiches of cheese and meat, dulled by rich desserts, logy with milk shakes. And the staff enjoyed it, too, enjoyed the camaraderie of paper bowls and plastic forks, the rough fellowship of bleacher seats while eating and big open barrels for their trash afterward, the sense of coming together in peak condition to face the long and arduous campaign ahead: the saving of souls.

Dwayne Thorsen always ate like that anyway. He didn't see how people could stuff their faces with all that bad crap available to the idiots of this world. He'd eaten sparingly as a child back in Kentucky, out of necessity – they were *poor* – had turned necessity into virtue, and now virtue had become mere habit. But a good habit.

Among the first to start lunch, and the absolute first to finish, Dwayne discarded his implements in the empty trash barrel and began a roving tour of the facility, a kind of stubborn prowl, movement mostly for its own sake, to relieve the pressure he felt, the weight of responsibility on his shoulders. The rest of them could laugh and joke together down there in the bleachers, take it easy, pay no attention to their surroundings, and if something screwed up they'd just shrug and go on about their business. Because avoiding the screw-ups *was not their business*. Not even Archibald's business, not really. The smooth functioning, the seamless progress, the glitch-free continuation of the William Archibald Crusade; that was Dwayne's business.

This is what he'd learned in the Marines: Do not ask why, only ask how. That's the philosophy he'd carried out of the Marines and into his work with Archibald, and it's what made him so valuable. Irreplaceable. Whether Archibald were sincere or a phony, or some mingling of the two, wasn't Dwayne's concern. His only concern was that the crusade go forward with no bad publicity, no awkward snags, no loss of money, no distractions from the task at hand. None.

His roving of the stadium showed the security weak spots, showed the crowd-control difficulties, but showed also the advantages of the terrain, the narrow-funneled egresses, the vast clear space at the center of the stadium that meant no troublemaker could get very close to Archibald during the crusade without being seen and intercepted.

Dwayne visited the money room – fairly well concealed, fairly well protected – he visited the temporarily erected cubicles where counseling would be available at the end of the crusade, he visited the sexually segregated changing

67

areas where the choir and angels would soon be getting into uniform (he didn't think in terms of 'costumes' but 'uniforms'), he visited the public restrooms and the refreshment area, he personally tried every door that was supposed to be locked and opened every door that was supposed to be unlocked.

Half an hour before the gates were to be flung wide to the paying public, Dwayne noticed from high in the stands Tom Carmody making his way across the Astroturfed field toward the dressing rooms, and even from way up here something about the man's posture snagged his attention. When something within Dwayne's area of responsibility was *wrong*, out of alignment, not exactly where or how it should be, he'd always spot it right away, and in this moment he could see that something about Tom Carmody was well and truly bent out of shape. The discouraged slope of those shoulders, the defensive clench of that ass, the fatalistic half-grip of those dangling hands as he made his way across the great open space; if they'd been back in the Marines together, Dwayne would know those signals could only mean one thing. A fellow bent on desertion.

But desertion? Here? If that were it, if Tom Carmody were merely planning to quit this livelihood and take his miserable long face somewhere else, Dwayne Thorsen would do nothing but cheer him on his way. Help him pack. But Tom wasn't leaving, not willingly, Dwayne was sure of that much. And here, in William Archibald's crusade, what would be the equivalent of desertion?

Dwayne followed Carmody into the dressing rooms, and came upon him hanging up his angel robe on a hook on the wall of the small and simple doorless cubicle he'd been assigned. His makeup tubes were already laid out on the narrow white Formica shelf in front of the mirror. His jacket was tossed on the floor in the corner; another bad sign. Dwayne said, 'How you doing, Tom?'

Carmody jumped, guilt all over his face and in his every move. Guilt about what? Had the son of a bitch *already* found his reporter? Was he in here wired? Was he walking around with camera and tape recorder to expose the villainy of the William Archibald crusade? Dwayne considered, for just an instant, having Carmody searched, right here, right now, but realized at once and reluctantly what a mistake that would be if it turned out he'd jumped the gun, if Carmody were still merely gearing up for his betrayal, whatever form that betrayal would take.

The son of a bitch can't even look me in the eye, Dwayne thought, as Carmody said, 'Oh, hi, Dwayne,' and busied himself with an unnecessarily long search in his canvas tote bag for his clothesbrush.

Dwayne stood in the cubicle doorway and watched Carmody brush the robe, too hard and too long. Unconsciously echoing the counselors who would be at work in nearby cubicles in just a few hours, he said, 'Anything you want to talk about, Tom?'

'What? *No*, Dwayne, everything's fine!'

Scared eyes, weak mouth, defensive hunch of shoulders. Oh, you'll bear watching, my lad, Dwayne thought. 'Well, if you get troubled about anything, Tom,' he said, doing his damnedest to put some warmth into his voice and failing even more than he knew, 'I want you to think of me as somebody you can count on, somebody you can trust. A friend.' He choked on the word, but got it out pretty smoothly, all in all.

A panicky smile played like summer lightning over

Carmody's ashen sweating face. 'I apprcciate that, Dwayne,' he said. 'Thank you for – Thank you for worrying about me.'

'Oh, I worry about everybody,' Dwayne told him, with his own ghastly smile. 'You know me.'

'I sure do, Dwayne,' Carmody said.

Dwayne nodded, and turned away. I wish I could send the son of a bitch on night patrol, he thought, and shoot him.

FOUR

Zack sat behind the wheel of the maroon Honda Accord, Woody beside him, Ralph in back. In the parking lot at the Seven Oaks Professional Building – three law firms, three dentists, one interior decorator, one office for rent – diagonally across from the Midway Motel, they remained in the positions they'd held since they'd driven away from Memphis. There was nothing to do now but wait.

Ralph leaned his forearms on top of the front seat, so he could be part of the conversation. If you could call it a conversation; Zack said almost nothing, and Woody kept babbling on and on about nothing at all, as though silence were something to be feared, like a fatal disease. As he babbled, they all kept looking at the station wagon parked across the way at the motel, in front of room 16. The woman and one of the men were in that room, George Liss and the other man next door. They were tough-looking, all of them, even the woman.

Mary had pointed out George Liss to Ralph a couple of weeks ago, as the crook her friend Tom Carmody was mixed up with, that she was so worried about. (So worried, in fact, that she'd made the mistake of talking it over with her stupid kid brother.) The hardness of Liss's face had been daunting, but nevertheless, the instant he'd heard Mary's story Ralph had known what he had to do.

And while he and Woody weren't real tough guys, Zack was, wasn't he? Zack could front for them in the toughness department. And Ralph, the way he saw it, was the brains.

Nothing happened for a long time, except that Woody just kept on talking, never saying anything at all interesting but never letting up. After a while, Ralph took his forearms off the seat and sat back to relax, not needing to follow every word. And when he looked out the left rear window, he could still see that station wagon over there, just as well.

The chatter was getting to Zack, too. He started saying things like, 'You already told us that, Woody. Shut up.' Or, 'Who gives a fuck, Woody?' Finally, he turned around in exasperation and said to Ralph, 'Remember that pizza place? Back a couple blocks.'

'Yeah?'

'Go get us something. Maybe if we put a lotta food in this asshole's mouth he'll shut up a while.'

Woody said, 'I'm just filling the time, Zack. Jeez, what's wrong with just—'

'Shut your *face*.'

Ralph said, 'What if they go before I come back?' Gesturing at the station wagon across the street.

'They won't,' Zack said, and looked at his watch. 'It's an hour before the fucking crusade even starts. They won't go before the money's in.'

'Boy, am I gonna spend *that* money,' Woody said, grinning like Bozo the clown at the two of them. 'I dunno, do I get a Jap bike, or a Harley?'

Woody had already thrown this question out to general

consideration twice before. Zack leveled a furious glare at Ralph: '*Go.*'

'Okay, okay,' Ralph said, and got out of the car.

Zack watched in the rearview mirror as Ralph went sloping away in the sunlight, goofing along like some stumblebum on his way to the soup line. Woody continued to yak away. When Ralph passed out of sight, Zack took the spring knife out of his pants pocket, opened the four-inch blade, turned sideways, and slipped the knife point past Woody's arm and into his side, maybe a quarter-inch deep, just above the lowest rib.

Stunned, scared, Woody recoiled against the door to his right, and Zack pursued him, pressing the blade against his flesh, maintaining that slight and dangerous penetration, his expression grim and intent.

'Jesus, Zack! Jesus! What are you doing?'

Quiet, but very serious, Zack said, 'If Ralph tumbles what happened to his sister, I'm putting this in there to the hilt.'

'What'd I say? Jeez, all I—'

'You been too jumpy,' Zack told him, holding the knife in place. 'Too jumpy just for what we're doing here. You're running off like an idiot. When Ralph comes back, you shut up.'

'Come *on*, Zack—'

Zack pressed the knifepoint into Woody's side just a little deeper. 'Wake *up*, you fucking asshole.'

'*Don't*, man! That hurts!'

In the rearview mirror, Ralph was coming, a six-pack of soda on top of a pizza box. So soon. Zack frowned at the mirror, then at Woody. 'You will shut up now, asshole, or

73

I start cutting. You got me?' He gave the knife a quarter turn.

'*Aaaaa!* That hurts!'

'*And*, he figures out what happened back home, you're dead meat. You got it, Woody?'

'Yes!'

Walking back toward the parking lot in the sunlight, carrying the pizza box in front of himself in both hands like a page boy carrying the queen mother's crown, Ralph saw Zack leaning way over to talk at Woody, and from the menacing shape of Zack's posture Ralph knew Woody was being told to *shut up*. Scaring the shit out of him, Ralph thought, and grinned at the idea. Yeah, Zack would be their tough guy, against those other people.

As Ralph opened the right rear door of the Honda, Zack moved leftward, wiping both sides of the knife blade against Woody's thigh, leaving a small faint streak of bloodstain. Woody, grimacing in pain, put his right hand over the wound like a compress and pressed it there with his left elbow. Zack, in better humor, said, 'So what'd you get? Pepperoni?'

'They could do halfies,' Ralph told him, sliding into the car, pushing the box ahead of himself across the seat. 'Half plain, half pepperoni.'

Zack held up the knife, showing it. 'I got my knife out, to slice.'

'The guy did it at the place. Eight slices.'

'I'll just leave it here,' Zack said, putting the open knife on top of the dashboard, 'in case we need it.'

Woody looked at the knife open on the dashboard, and blinked, and didn't say a word.

They ate the pizza, and drank three cans of the soda,

and then across the way the doors of 16 and 17 opened, and the four people came out. The woman got behind the wheel of the station wagon. Two of the men were carrying duffel bags that they put in back, then all got into the car.

'She's the driver,' Ralph said, surprised. 'I didn't think she'd be part of it.'

'Some women are,' Zack said. 'Why not.'

'I'll have to tell Mary when I get back,' Ralph said. 'How good things could go, if you had a woman along you could trust to be on your side, and not be nagging you and putting you down all the time.'

Woody put his right fist up to his mouth and gnawed gently on the knuckles. His left arm was pressed to his side. He wasn't talking, he was just staring at the glove compartment door. His left side ached, as though he'd been hit there by a baseball bat or something, not the sharper pain he would have expected from being stabbed. I've been stabbed, he thought, with dulled surprise. How did I get to be here, in this place, stabbed? Jesus, what did I do that I'm here in this place?

Zack started the Honda engine, and they followed the station wagon, keeping well back, and it did what they'd expected it to do, it went straight to the stadium. There, the wagon stopped, and the three men got out. They collected their duffel bags and strode away across the full parking lot, and the station wagon moved on, and Zack followed.

Back to the motel. The woman went indoors, and Zack found their old parking spot beside the Seven Oaks Professional Building still waiting for them. 'This is nice,' he said, as he pulled to a stop in the same old space. 'They pull the job, and if it works out she goes and picks them up, and gets them out safe, away from the law. And then we go in and take it away.'

Nobody said anything. Zack gave Woody a hard smile. 'Pretty good, huh, Woody?'

I don't want to be here, Woody thought. I don't want to know these people any more, or be in this place, or anything. I don't even want that pizza, it feels like shit in my stomach, I don't know if I'm gonna throw up or cry.

He didn't do either. Zack reached out with his middle finger and tapped the bloodstain on Woody's thigh and repeated his question: 'Pretty good, huh?'

'Yes,' Woody said.

FIVE

During football games, this was the replay booth, where guys with video equipment could second-guess the referees. It wasn't an ideal command post for Dwayne, being so far from the center of activity, but its overview of the stadium couldn't be beat, and the communications between here and the rest of the complex were perfect. Dwayne, not a sitting-down type, paced back and forth behind the long plywood table containing all the electronic equipment, and looked out past it through the line of big windows at the crusade making its measured practiced way far below.

The main part of the crusade, exclusive of counseling and other activities scheduled for afterward, was planned to take just two and a half hours, and the second hour was not quite over when the phone call came. There were four telephones spaced along the plywood table, and the low-pitched ring was supplemented by a white light that blinked on the appropriate one. Dwayne picked it up, said, 'Thorsen,' and heard a frightened young male voice say a scrambled nervous sentence in which one word stood out.

'Robbed.'

Dwayne made it to the money room before the police, but not by much. The normally locked door was propped open, and inside Tom Carmody lay unconscious on a sofa, his gray-white angel makeup blotched with dark dried blood. Dwayne looked at that unconscious discontented face and knew: 'So this is what you did, you stupid fuck,' he said, and turned as the first cops came in.

In every organization, there's the one guy who manages things. Not the boss but someone at the middle level, the equivalent of a master sergeant in the army. Dwayne was that one in William Archibald's Christian Crusade, and whenever he had to deal with another organization of whatever kind he always sought out his opposite number, and would settle for nothing less. This time, it was a fellow named Calavecci, a Detective Second Grade.

Tom Carmody had been ambulanced away still unconscious, the six people in the money room had been questioned and turned over to the medics for tranquilizing, and now the money room had filled up with technicians. Dwayne stood to one side, observing, waiting, and when he heard a voice say, 'Who's in charge of security here?' he smiled and turned around, knowing the manager-type on the other side would be just as anxious to make contact with *him*.

'Me,' he said, and felt an instant coolness toward the man filling the doorway. Large but not beefy, with an irritable yet patiently amused expression, he was the kind of guy, in the Marines, who liked war too much. Well, you worked with who you had. 'Dwayne Thorsen,' and he approached with hand stuck out.

The man considered him briefly, considered his hand, then took it. 'Calavecci, Detective Second Grade. What happened here?'

'Three men with shotguns.'

'Inside help?'

'Yes.'

Calavecci looked surprised: 'Usually we get denials,' he said, 'this early on.'

'This isn't early,' Dwayne said. 'They're already gone with the money. I don't have time for denials.'

'Good. Got a candidate for the inside guy?'

'Tom Carmody. The one went to the hospital with a concussion.'

Calavecci considered that. 'Trouble before?'

'He's been building,' Dwayne said. 'I had my eye on him. I expected something different, though.'

Calavecci looked around the room. 'They whomped him to give him cover,' he said. 'Whomped him pretty good, but that was it.'

'That's right.'

'Be nice,' Calavecci said, 'if he knows where they went, because *we* sure as hell don't.'

Dwayne didn't like that. 'You mean they're long gone?'

'I mean they're pros,' Calavecci said. 'Like you and me. So they're on the next page already. Maybe the loot's in the trunk of a car outside and they're back in here with the audience. Congregation? What do you call this crowd?'

'The crowd.'

'Well, maybe they're with them. Or maybe they're burning rubber on the interstate, but if they are we've got them, and I assume they know that, so I assume they're not. So maybe they come to town last month and rented a little apartment two three blocks from here. We're checking that. We'll check everything. But it would be nice if your fella, whatsisname—'

'Tom Carmody.'

'Be nice if he knew what was supposed to happen next,' Calavecci concluded. 'Take all the guesswork out of it, that's what *I* like.'

Carmody was conscious when Dwayne and Calavecci got to the hospital, but the doctors wouldn't let him be questioned. 'Bullshit,' Calavecci said, which was the wrong thing to say to the doctors.

'Hold on,' Dwayne said. 'Let me try something.'

'Try anything,' Calavecci offered, 'just so your friend can tell us where *his* friends got off to.'

So, while Calavecci went to ask the Memphis police to question Mary Quindero, just in case Tom had told the woman anything useful, Dwayne called the hotel, and Archibald was there in the suite all right, raging in the background when Tina answered the phone in that breathless lisp that made Dwayne's skin crawl. Listen to the man back there, yelling his way around the hotel suite; how he hates to lose money. 'Let me talk to Will,' Dwayne said.

'Oh, *Dwayne*, he's *so* upset, I know he wants to talk to you.'

He did. Dwayne stood there at the pay phone in the hospital corridor and listened to a certain amount of unnecessary oratory and then at last cut in with, 'Will, you can help down here.'

That caused a stumble in the oration. Archibald said, 'Help? Down where?'

'I'm at the hospital with Tom Carmody. They won't let the law question him, so it's up to you and me. They can't very well keep the man's religious advisers away from him, so *we* do the questions.'

80

'Questions? Tom?' Dwayne could almost hear the penny drop. 'Dwayne! Do you really think that filthy little pervert— You think it's *him?*'

'He's part of it. Come on down, Will.'

In a small bare conference room borrowed from the hospital administration, Dwayne gave Archibald a little orientation talk before they went in to see Tom: 'Now, listen, Will. If we get mad, or we make him scared, we won't get a thing out of him.'

'I'd like to get his liver and lights out of him, that wretched little . . .' Archibald sputtered, at a loss for words he could permit himself to use.

'Will, that's the wrong attitude,' Dwayne said patiently. 'What we want is whatever information Tom Carmody has inside his head, and the *only* way we're gonna get it is if we go in there and preach sweet forgiveness.'

'Sweet for—!' Archibald choked on the word, his beefy neck flushing all the way around his collar.

'Shit, Will, you play it to millions all the time. This once, play it to one. We want the money back, dammit.'

'Yes, we do,' Archibald agreed, and sat back, and nodded. 'All right, let me just get myself settled.'

'Sure.'

Archibald sat there a minute longer, eyes half closed, and when he made a steeple of his hands Dwayne thought in astonishment that the man was going to pray, but he didn't. He took a deep breath instead, managed a smile, got to his feet, and said, 'All right, Dwayne. Let us go pour oil on the little prick.'

SIX

Miserable, hurt, alone, knowing at last what an utter fool he was, Tom Carmody lay on his back in the high hard bed in this small bare-walled one-patient hospital room and tried to decide what to do. Suicide; confession; silence followed by a life of atonement; silence followed by revenge on—

On whom? Revenge on whom? Which brought him full circle to suicide once more. Who else should he be avenged on, except himself?

Mary. Would they think Mary had anything to do with the robbery? Just because they were friends? Because he'd told her about— That he would *never* let them know! Never bring her name into it at all, never, never.

His head was heavily bandaged, all across the top and around the back, the thick white layers covering his ears and even pressing his eyebrows down lower over his eyes. He lay cocooned, sounds muffling as they made their way through the swaths of cotton. Why had Grant hit him so hard? Why hit him at all?

Of course, this way at least the police would never suspect, would have no reason to believe the person brutally attacked by the robbers was himself a part of the scheme. So, if he *didn't* confess—

He kept remembering Grant, on that first meeting, look

at him with his cold eyes and say, 'If the police catch you, they won't ask your motive.' No, they won't.

But he could ask his own motive. Had he ever expected to get away with it, or had he unconsciously been trying to get himself caught all along? Had he ever realistically expected to collect his half of the take? When he didn't even know where they were going with the money from here, where to find them afterward? He knew George Liss's name; the others had probably used aliases. If George wanted to go on pretending to be an honest citizen, if he actually showed up next month at the parole office, Tom could make contact that way. What were the chances?

And what did it matter? An IV tube fed something or other into a vein in his left forearm; surely, if he wanted to kill himself, he could use that needle somehow. He might even be able to get to his feet and go out that window over there.

Wait, he told himself, trying to keep control of his mind, fighting the panic, the guilt, the fear. Wait. Wait to see what happens.

And then Archibald himself came in, followed by Dwayne Thorsen. Tom looked at that smug fat face – he barely registered Thorsen's colder harder face behind the preacher – and his resolve hardened. I'll admit nothing, he promised himself. Nothing.

There was one chair in the room, armless with tubular chrome legs and green vinyl seat and back, and of course Archibald immediately took that for himself, pulling it over to the right side of the bed and sitting where he could comfortably peer into Tom's face, his own face a mask of false sympathy. Naturally it was false, Tom knew better than to trust any emotional display from William Archibald. His skepticism, however, did not yet lead him to believe that Archibald's falseness was anything beyond the normal insincerity that defined the man's life. He did not at all guess that this time the fakery covered an absolute certainty in Tom's guilt.

'How *are* you, Tom?' Unctuous, oily, the moist eyes melting with sympathy. Meanwhile, his hatchet man, Dwayne, leaned his forearms on the footrail of the bed, watched Tom like a specimen in the zoo, and made no attempt at all to show anything other than his normal cold indifference.

'Not feeling so good,' Tom said, and was surprised to hear the quaver in his voice. He didn't have to pretend weakness, did he? Weakness and confusion. No pretense at all.

'Guess that fella hit you pretty hard,' Archibald said, and nodded in faux sympathy, agreeing with himself.

'Yes, sir.'

'Shows you what can happen with those bad companions,' Archibald said, face and voice as smoothly caring as ever.

Tom didn't absorb the meaning of the words for the first few seconds, and then a sudden jolt of icy cold ran along his spine, as though a great icicle had all at once formed there. His lips trembled. Tears filled his eyes, but didn't fall. 'S-s-s-sir?'

'What I think happened, Tom,' Archibald said, gazing into Tom's eyes as though Tom were the greatest TV camera ever made, 'I think we all just got caught up in the money too much. You, and me, and Dwayne here, and all of us.'

'I don't know what you mean,' Tom said. He tried to keep his own face expressionless, but couldn't help staring at Archibald like a bird in front of a snake.

Archibald ignored Tom's feeble protest. With a theatrical sigh, he said, 'I don't excuse any of us, Tom, no, I don't. We've all been culpable in this matter. I should have spent more of my time talking about what the money *does*, not just how we have to go out and get more of it.'

He's a liar, Tom reminded himself, he's a liar and a charlatan, and he's just trying his usual crap on me, that's all it is. Tom *knew* that's all it was, and he was right, and he knew he was right, and yet he found himself being tugged in nonetheless, drawn by that syrupy voice and those smooth words. Grasping at inessentials because he didn't dare think about the essentials, he said, 'The money doesn't do any *good*.'

'Oh, but it does, Tom,' Archibald said, 'and that's where I've been remiss. Remiss, Tom. I've failed you, and I've failed the Crusade, and I've failed every good soul who has ever put his or her trust in me. Because all I've been saying is, "Give me money," and I have *slighted*, I have *ignored*, I have failed to make clear, what the money is for.'

'It's for you,' Tom said, feeling amazingly brave to confront the man like this, to throw the truth in his face for once, with no softening of the blow at all.

'It's for the Crusade,' Archibald corrected him, but gently, the milk of human kindness still sheening on his face. 'The television costs us *so* much, Tom, but without the television how will we reach God's creatures? And the counseling, the crusades in the field, all our efforts . . . Now, I know some of the good we do is strictly speaking not in His service, is more social work than religious work,

85

but I believe God can and will forgive us for our lunch programs and our school crusades and—'

'The money's for *you*!' Tom cried, feeling himself sink under Archibald's platitudes, drown in his false pieties, lose his own hard certainties in the undifferentiated sludge of Archibald's philosophy. 'It's all for you! The rest of it, it's all just fake, it's all just to cover for you, for you, for you!'

Archibald sighed, more sinned against than sinning. He sat back in the small chair, gazing with sad forgiveness at Tom as he contemplated what had just been said, and finally he replied, 'I had suspected that was what you believed of our mission, Tom. I'm glad you've unburdened yourself of it, brought it out in the open where we can look at it.'

'It's true, and you know it.'

Another sigh. Archibald said, 'And I suppose that's why you helped those men.'

A hard wall. There, right there, in the path of Tom's life. A huge hard impenetrable wall, right there *now*. His throat pained him, his eyes pained him, with the emotional sense of his loss. He looked at the stolid Dwayne Thorsen, then back at Archibald. They were waiting for an answer. And he too was waiting to hear his answer. He and they all wanted to know: Would Tom lie? At this point in his life, at this nexus, at this nadir, would he lie? or would he tell the truth?

'Yes,' Tom said.

Archibald's long sigh this time seemed more honest, more human, and even Dwayne shifted position slightly, though his face didn't alter. Archibald, as though the question hardly mattered, said, 'And do you know where they are now, Tom?'

'No.'

'Oh, Tom,' Archibald said. 'Don't disappoint me at this stage, Tom. You have started to open your heart, don't close it again.'

'I don't know where they are,' Tom insisted. 'And that's the truth.'

Archibald and Dwayne shared a glance. Tom knew they were trying to decide whether or not it *was* the truth, and he knew Archibald didn't really and truly care whether Tom believed all that stuff about the money, all that face-saving garbage about lunch programs and counseling and of course his own work with former convicts. *There's* a laugh; the work with former convicts. How do you like your social programs now, Reverend Archibald?

Archibald turned his attention back to Tom. 'I hope to do what I can to help you,' he said, 'in your difficulties with the law. And I equally hope *you* will—'

A knock at the door interrupted him. Archibald frowned at Dwayne, the unctuous mask slipping slightly, and Dwayne silently crossed to the door, opened it, spoke briefly in a low voice with someone outside, accepted a sheet of paper, and shut the door again.

While Archibald and Tom watched, Dwayne came back to the bed, reading the sheet of paper, which was white but flimsy, curling at the edges. Archibald, tension at last apparent in his voice, said, 'Dwayne? What is it? Do they have the rascals?'

'No,' Dwayne said, and extended the sheet of paper for Archibald to take. The paper curled like parchment as it changed hands, so that for one instant there was something almost Biblical in the transaction.

Archibald unrolled the paper, read it, and the blood drained from his face. *That* expression of shock wasn't false. Tom stared at the soft clean hands holding the sheet of paper; he burned with both fear and curiosity, wondering if they would even tell him what the paper was all about. And then Archibald looked at him with something new and incomprehensible in his eyes. Sympathy? The genuine article?

Extending the rolled-up sheet of paper, Archibald said, 'You should see this, Tom. And I am truly sorry.'

What in God's name could it be? Fear clenched Tom's chest as he took the paper and fumblingly unrolled it. A fax, on the letterhead of the Memphis police. It was addressed to Detective Second Grade Lewis Calavecci, and the body of the message read:

'Mary Quindero discovered dead in her apartment. Preliminary medical exam suggests death by drowning. Body found in a closet. Under the circumstances, we'd appreciate more particulars regarding your interest in this person. Please forward your response to—'

'NO!'

'I'm sorry,' Archibald said, and this time he sounded as though he really meant it. 'Do you have any idea why they would do such a thing?'

'No.' Tom gestured vaguely with both hands, too distracted to think. 'No! They didn't have to— They didn't even *know* about her until . . . I didn't think they knew about . . . There's no *reason*.'

Softly, almost whispered, Archibald said, 'Who are they, Tom?'

Tom let the paper go, and it curled into a tube on the blanket covering his legs. 'The first one,' he said, in a dead dulled voice, 'is called George Liss. I met him in the parole program . . .'

Around midnight, one of the night nurses foiled Tom's suicide attempt. He'd been trying to slit his wrists with the IV needle torn from his forearm. The tool was inefficient, making a number of shallow gashes, painful and disfiguring but not in any way fatal.

A doctor from emergency was called, who oversaw the cleaning and bandaging of the wounds. Tom spent the rest of the night strapped into the bed, horribly awake, thinking unwillingly about Mary and the people who had killed her. Why? *Why?*

George Liss. Let them find him, please, God. Let them find George Liss.

SEVEN

When George Liss ran across the dark parking lot away from the construction trailer, he expected a bullet in his back at any second. He had no idea what had gone wrong, why Parker and Mackey weren't dead right now and he on his way with the four hundred thousand, but Liss was not a man to gnaw at the past. All he would do now was run, as fast as he could, bent low to make a smaller target but nevertheless expecting that bullet every step.

Which didn't come. He hadn't run directly toward the lights flanking the entrance, not wanting to silhouette himself, but had angled off toward the darkness along the perimeter fence, and when he reached that fence with neither a bullet in his body nor even the sound of shots having been fired behind him, he began to believe he might be still alive. And with work to do.

Hunched over, Liss trotted along the straight chain-link fence, and slowed when he got near the brighter illumination around the entrance. Looking all around as he moved, he decided there was no one there, no one watching, nothing to worry about, at least not in this particular spot at this particular moment, so he sprinted on through and out to the public road.

And now what? He still wanted the money, that was the whole purpose, but Parker and Mackey were alerted now, would be harder to deal with. And right this minute, this town was a dangerous place to be wandering around in, alone and unarmed and with no good explanation for his presence. There were going to be cops all over the neighborhood tonight. Somehow he had to go to ground, get out of sight.

What were the choices? He couldn't get to the motel and Brenda and the station wagon before Mackey called to warn her what had happened. And if he went to the empty house where they'd planned to stash the goods once they'd left the construction trailer, Parker and Mackey were sure to show up eventually, cautious and armed.

But if he just hid out in some alley or parked car for the night, Parker and Mackey could clear out entirely, find some other place to wait for the heat to grow less intense, and Liss would never get his hands on that money. There had to be a way to stay out of sight, and yet keep an eye on those golden duffel bags.

Across the road from the stadium parking lot was a row of old three-story houses, with small shops downstairs and apartments above. Shoe repair, deli, dry cleaners, all shut down solid for the night, with heavy gates closed over their windows and doors. The apartment windows were all dark, too. Was there something useful there?

A nearly full trash barrel stood by the curb. Out of it Liss plucked a newspaper. Folded in quarters, he put it under his left arm, and now he was a nightworker on the way home.

Headlights coming. Liss turned and strode purposefully the other way, not too fast, not trying to conceal himself. Two cars went by, civilians, and then one in the other direction. At the corner, Liss crossed the street away from the stadium, and when he walked past the side of the final row house he saw that it had a back yard, all those houses had back yards, separated here from the sidewalk by an eight-foot-high wooden fence, vertical boards tapering to points at the top.

With a door? Yes; a simple narrow door of the same vertical boards, probably nailed to horizontal support pieces on the inside, and with a little round metal Yale-type lock inset in the wood. No knob.

Liss looked left and right, and saw no one. Dropping the newspaper onto the sidewalk, he lifted his right knee high, and slammed his heel flat against that lock. The door popped open with one loud *crack*. Liss stepped through, pushed the door closed again behind himself, leaned against it, and looked around at where he was. Illumination from the streetlight on the corner showed him a messy untended yard, scattered with junk. A shorter wooden fence of the same style but only about five feet high defined the other border. An exterior flight of metal stairs against the rear of the building led up to a second-story door. The back door of the ground-floor shop was under the stairs.

Liss made his way through the junk across the yard to the other fence, and looked down the row of yards. Some were neater than this, some as messy. A few had been turned into cared-for gardens and some had outdoor furniture in little conversational groups. Almost all the yards were defined or separated by some kind of fence. Every house had the exterior metal staircase giving access to the second floor. Every window down the entire block was dark, and the outside darkness was deeper the farther you went toward the middle of the block.

Liss went over four fences, looking for the yard with the

least sign of activity; neither a garden nor an accumulation of junk. He wanted a yard that suggested either a vacant apartment or a stay-at-home tenant, and when he found the right one he went silently up the stairs to that second-floor door, and just as silently through the door with a credit card.

He was in a kitchen, small and old-fashioned, not remodeled for maybe thirty years. There was very little light, just enough to suggest the place was neat, cared for. He opened the small old refrigerator with its rounded corners and found it contained small amounts of just a few things; milk, orange juice, a few eggs, some tiny leftovers in plastic. A solitary; good.

The refrigerator's interior light, in the few seconds he'd had the door open, had spoiled his night vision. He stood patiently in the middle of the room, one hand touching the refrigerator door, until shapes took form in his sight again, and then he moved forward, through the deeper darkness of the doorway on the other side of the room.

Night vision no longer helped. Shuffling forward very slowly, as silent as possible, both hands moving to the sides and out ahead, Liss made his way down a short black hall with a pair of closed doors facing one another partway along. A little farther, his groping right foot touched the saddle of a doorway. He stopped. He felt the wood of the frame, then the closed door itself, and then the old faceted glass knob. He turned the knob as slowly and gently as though it were a safe in the back of a store still open for business, and when it gave a tiny *chick* sound he eased the door open, out away from himself.

Light, thin diffuse gray light defining the rectangles of two windows. This was the small living room, facing the street. Liss came on through, still holding the doorknob turned, and reached his other hand around to grasp the knob on the other side. He held that one in the same position as he eased the door shut again, then turned to look the place over.

A living room, underfurnished. Two sagging armchairs, one near each window. A small TV, on a low wooden crate. A couple of end tables and lamps. One side wall was absolutely empty; that's where the sofa would have been.

Liss crossed the room and looked out a front window, just in time to see a car turning in at the parking lot entrance across the way. Brenda? No, it wasn't the station wagon. Liss sat on the arm of the chair behind him, and watched through narrowed eyes. Who was in that car? What did they want?

The car made its hesitant moves around the parking lot, and Liss tensed up when it stopped over by the construction trailer. People out of the car, fucking around over there at the trailer. He didn't like that, he didn't want anybody else around his money. That's my money, he thought. Keep away.

'Who's there?'

Liss automatically rose to his feet, while his mind registered that voice. Old, male, querulous. Liss moved catlike away from the windows.

'Who's there? *I* hear you!'

Liss slid along the empty wall, coming the long way around to the door, so he'd wind up behind it when it opened.

'You better speak up! I've got a gun!'

Oh, have you, Liss thought. Good; I need a gun.

The doorknob rattled. 'I'm warning you! I'm coming in!'

Do it and get it over with, Liss thought.

The door opened. Liss leaned close to it, eyes fixed on the gray rectangle of window past the dark vertical line of the edge of the door. A figure moved into that space, and Liss clubbed down with his forearm, hitting the top of a shoulder, the side of a neck. The old voice cried out, and Liss swung around the door, punching hard into the indistinct figure, connecting three times before it could fall.

Light switch. Should be beside the doorway, same side as the knob. Yes; Liss flipped it, and a ceiling light came on, the bulb discreetly behind a round pink glass saucer.

The unmoving old man on the floor bled slightly from nose and mouth. He wore gray pajamas and a thick wool maroon robe and dark blue slippers. Liss rolled him over, frisked him, searched the floor all around him, and there was no gun. The old son of a bitch lied.

Liss switched off the light, hurried back to the window, and was just in time to see that unwelcome car come across the parking lot, moving as slowly and hesitantly as ever, and jounce out the exit onto the street. It drove away, out of sight.

Good, Liss thought. I don't know who you people are, but stay out of the way.

EIGHT

Zack was still driving. He steered them out of the stadium parking lot and down the empty street, as Ralph said. 'All for nothing, the whole thing for nothing.'

'We don't give up,' Zack said. He'd grown less cocky, but more sullen and just as determined, since he'd lost the woman in the station wagon.

When she'd come out of the motel, moving with purposeful speed, all three of them in the car had perked up, even Woody, who'd been sulking about something for hours. And at first they'd liked it that she was pushing hard, driving a little too fast for the city streets. It meant action at last, something happening.

They'd heard on the car radio about the half-million-dollar robbery – a half a million dollars! – and they knew the robbers had gotten away with it clean and clear. They were still at large. And this woman in the station wagon would lead them right to it.

Except she didn't. 'Shit,' Zack said at one point, 'she's onto us.'

'Oh, goddamn it,' Woody said. 'I knew it'd be something.' His brief return of high spirits was over, already.

Ralph was leaning forward again, forearms atop the front seat. 'Maybe she isn't,' he said. 'What makes you think she is?'

'We went down this block before,' Zack said, angry and disgusted, 'and made that *fucking turn*!'

Half a block ahead, the woman took a right turn very hard and fast, the heavy body of the wagon sagging way leftward as she went around the corner and out of sight. Zack took the turn as fast as he could, not quite as quick as the woman, and when they came around— Goddamit, the station wagon's coming the other way!

How did she *do* that? A hard right, an impossibly tight U-turn to the left, and coming back the other way as Zack completed his own turn. All three of them gaped at her, and she pretended they weren't even there. A good-looking woman, dramatic in the rose-glow of her dashboard, jaw set, eyes facing front as she flashed on by.

Ralph twisted around to look out the back window, and saw her take a left so fast and so sharp she left rubber all over the street back there. Going back the way they'd come. And of course, by the time Zack got them turned around and back to the intersection she was long gone.

Still, he drove in her imagined wake for a while, as they argued about what it meant and what to do next. 'It doesn't come out right,' Woody kept saying. 'Everything screws up, it just gets worse and worse, we should never of got into this, we're fuckups, that's all, we're just fuckups.'

'Shut up.' Zack's knuckles were white, he held so hard to the steering wheel. His teeth were clenched, the veins stood out on the side of his neck, he looked like he'd explode. But he never shouted. 'Shut up shut up shut up.' Low, quiet, but with such intensity that Woody withdrew down into a sullen lump in his corner of the front seat.

Ralph said, 'Shit, Zack, we did lose her. I mean, we *lost* her.'

'So we'll *find* her.'

'How?'

'The stadium. That's where she was headed, before she saw us. So that's where we'll go.'

And that's where they went, and got nothing for it. Nobody at the stadium, all locked up and dark. Parking lot empty except for some construction trailer way at the far end, padlocked and empty. Nobody and nothing. No trail of breadcrumbs. With no alternative, they drove away from the stadium at last, the car moving along in its own gray cloud of depression.

'What we did,' Woody mumbled, feeling so sorry for himself he was almost in tears. 'What we did, and for nothing.'

'Shut *up*, Woody.'

'What we did, what we did.'

Ralph frowned at Woody's miserably unhappy profile. 'What are you talking about?'

'He's talking about,' Zack snarled, 'what an asshole he is. It isn't over, all right? We aren't done, all right?'

Ralph said, 'Zack, we don't know where they are. If the cops can't find them, how are *we* gonna find them?'

'Luggage,' Zack said.

Woody was still deep in his own misery, but Ralph bit: 'Luggage?'

'She didn't take any luggage when she left the motel,' Zack said. 'None of them did. Just those duffel bags, and that was for the job. Remember, the radio said. So they didn't take their luggage, so they're going back.'

Ralph felt a sudden surge of hope, and even Woody looked up. Ralph said, 'To the motel!'

'They're going back,' Zack said, absolutely sure of himself. 'And so are we.'

Same parking space. The nearby pizza place was closed, but they found another and settled down in their usual vantage point to eat and to wait. Across the way, the windows of rooms 16 and 17 were dark. No car parked in front. Not back yet.

After a while, Ralph said, 'Maybe they're hiding the loot. Maybe they're doing that first, so it won't be on them if they get stopped.'

'That's okay,' Zack said.

'But maybe it won't be with them,' Ralph said, because Zack didn't seem to be getting the point.

'That's all *right*,' Zack said. 'If it isn't with them, they'll tell us where it is. Okay?' Zack pulled that switchblade out of his pocket again, snapped it open, whapped it down onto the dashboard where he'd kept it before. 'With *that*, okay? We'll ask with that, and they'll tell us.'

Ralph looked at the knife, the blade glinting sharp, reflecting a nearby streetlight. Troubled by a sudden thought, he licked his lips and said, 'Zack? That isn't how you asked Mary, is it?'

Woody made a small sound deep in his throat. Loud, covering Woody, Zack said, 'Of course not! Jesus, Ralph, we didn't cut her, all right? I never even showed her the knife. Jesus Christ.'

'Okay,' Ralph said. 'Okay.'

Zack gave Woody a disgusted warning look, then reached out to switch on the radio. 'Let's hear something cheerful for once,' he said.

They listened to Top 40s, interspersed with news

reports. They kept hearing about the three robbers and the half million dollars and how the three robbers were still on the loose, and it never occurred to them. They sat there in the parking lot, visible to the street, three guys in a car with out-of-state plates, listening to the news reports about how every cop within five hundred miles was looking for the three robbers, and it never occurred to them for a second, not until about twelve million watts' worth of searchlights and floodlights were suddenly beamed at them from every direction in the universe, including a helicopter up above.

'Jesus!' Zack cried, blinded by all the light, and would have made the fatal mistake of switching on the car engine if Ralph hadn't been just smart enough to yell, 'No!' and grab his elbow.

They sat in the car in the empty parking lot, impaled by all that light, specimen bugs on a display board, and shadows moved out there. Cops, armed to the teeth, easing through the light as through heavy fog, moving cautiously in this direction.

'*You in the car!*' A hugely amplified voice, coming from everywhere. '*Don't move! Make no movements!*'

Woody started to cry. 'I don't fucking believe this,' Zack said, but it wasn't clear whether it was the cops' sudden presence or Woody crying that he didn't believe.

Ralph, amazed at his own capacity for quick thinking, leaned another inch forward over the seat back and said, 'We didn't break any laws. We're driving to the coast, we stopped here for a pizza and rest a while.'

'Right right right,' Zack said. He was blinking like mad, his fingers twitching on the steering wheel.

One cop, braver than the others, approached Zack's

door, opened it, and stepped back. He was carrying a shotgun – a freaking *shotgun*, for Christ's sake! – at port arms, and what he said was ridiculous: 'Sir, would you step out of the car, please?' *Sir!*

'Officer,' Zack said, his voice sounding much younger and more vulnerable than usual, 'officer, uh, something wrong, officer?'

'Just step out of the car, please, sir.'

So Zack, fumbling a bit in nervousness, stepped out of the car, and the cop asked to see ID, continuing with the horrible grotesque parody of politeness. In the car, Woody hunched down in his corner of the front seat, moaning, while Ralph kept unwillingly looking at that switchblade knife on the dashboard, as big as a bayonet in all that light.

Zack's driver's license was handed on back to some other cop, and then more cops approached the car, also loaded down with weapons, and called on Ralph and Woody to get out, which they did. Woody, no longer crying, just stood there and trembled, like a horse on the way to the dogfood factory, while Ralph looked all around, trying to see, interested despite himself in what was happening.

More *sirs*, more requests for ID, more licenses passed back into the darkness behind all that light. Then the frisk. *Sir*, would you face the car? *Sir*, would you place your hands on the car roof? *Sir*, would you move your feet back? Farther apart, *sir*. Thank you very much, *sir*.

Pat pat pat; nothing. They were permitted to stand normally again, feeling a little better. Damn good thing the two pistols were stashed with their bags in the trunk.

'Sir, would you mind opening the trunk?'

They stared at one another, stuck, screwed, completely fucked over, and another cop came out of the darkness into the light to say, 'Which one is Quindero?'

A distraction from the question of the trunk. But was this a good thing, or a bad thing? 'Me,' Ralph said, raising his hand like a kid in school. 'Ralph Quindero.'

The cop was a little older than the other cops, and not in uniform, and with no guns in his hands. It was hard to see people's faces in all this light, expressions and features got washed out to nothing, but still Ralph had the feeling there wasn't much he'd like in that face. The plainclothes cop, no inflection in his voice, said, 'You're from Memphis?'

'Yes, sir.'

'You know a Mary Quindero?'

Woody made the weirdest sound Ralph had ever heard, like a screen door being crushed or something. Ralph looked at him, just as Woody dropped to his knees, arms hanging at his sides. What the hell?

'Sir? You know a Mary Quindero?'

'She's my sister,' Ralph said. 'What's going on?'

The plainclothes cop turned away to the other cops. 'Bring them in,' he said, and walked away into the darkness, and Woody began to keen, like a dog when somebody's died.

NINE

Dwayne was in Archibald's suite, waiting. He didn't want to be there, but if he went to his own room down the hall Archibald would just keep telephoning every five minutes, so it was better to be here in the comfort of the man's suite, with Calavecci given this number to call if anything happened, even if that did mean he had to put up with Tina marching back and forth in a tight robe all the time, like a hooker on a runway, flashing those heavy legs.

Archibald marched, too, back and forth, back and forth, stopping every once in a while to glare at the phone, as though it had betrayed him in some fashion. 'Why don't they *call*?'

'Cause they don't have anything to say,' Dwayne suggested.

Tina, voice dripping sympathy, said, 'Will? You want a massage? Come on in the bedroom, I'll give you a nice massage.'

Well, Dwayne knew what *that* meant, but Archibald was too distracted by the loss of the money even to respond to his harlot. 'No, I can't think,' he said. 'You go to bed, Tina, I'll be along later.'

'I want to wait with you,' she said, and so she did.

What was this like? In some ways, it was like a wake, sitting around being polite in the presence of a death in the family. More than that, it was almost as though the money hadn't been stolen, it had been kidnapped, and they were waiting to hear from the kidnappers, hear what the terms were for getting the money back.

When the phone finally did ring, at almost three in the morning, it seemed at first as though nobody was going to answer it. Archibald and Tina, both pacing, stopped to stare at the instrument, on a round table at one end of the sofa. Dwayne, seated at the other end of the same sofa, also looked at the phone, but didn't reach for it because this, after all, wasn't his suite. Then he realized that while he was deferring to Archibald, Archibald was deferring to him, as the professional in this situation. Once that became clear, Dwayne lunged across the sofa, scooped up the receiver, and said, 'Thorsen.'

'Calavecci. You want to come down to Broad Street?' That was what they called police headquarters, a big old pile of limestone built during the Wobbly scares, back in the twenties.

'You got them?'

'No, I don't,' Calavecci said, 'I'm sorry to say. I got something else, though. Very interesting.'

'Be right there,' Dwayne said, but of course he had to give Archibald about ten minutes of explanation about that one-minute phone call before he could leave.

Calavecci met him in a small barren office that had the look of a place whose regular occupant had just been fired, but which was in fact nobody's regular space. It was a meeting/conference/interrogation room, with an extra chair in one corner for the stenographer, for when the confession was to be taken, and a phone on the desk for calling the stenographer.

Calavecci and Dwayne sat across the desk from one another, both comfortable in this room, and Calavecci said, 'We couldn't believe we were so lucky, so of course we weren't. What we had was three white males in a car with Tennessee plates, where you people are from, and it's parked for hours in a professional building parking lot, where the building's closed for the night.'

'Three's the right number,' Dwayne agreed.

'But the wrong guys.' Calavecci grinned and shrugged. 'But interesting nonetheless. Your boy Tom Carmody—'

'The inside man.'

'The clown,' Calavecci agreed. 'His girlfriend Mary Quindero turns up drowned in a closet. Not a usual way to go.'

Dwayne, trying to be patient, said, 'That's right.'

'One of the three guys in the Tennessee car is her brother Ralph.'

'Ah,' Dwayne said, getting it. 'Tom to George Liss to a couple of his pals, so that's our doers. Then Tom to Mary Quindero to her brother Ralph to *his* pals, they decide to do the doers.'

'The sheer quantity of assholes in this world,' Calavecci said, 'never ceases to amaze me. You want some know-nothing clown come in, louse things up? No problem.'

'But the sister's dead,' Dwayne said. 'How does that come into it?'

'The other two,' Calavecci said, 'Isaac Flynn and Robert Kellman—'

'Isaac Flynn?'

Calavecci shrugged. 'That's what it says on his driver's

license. Twenty, twenty-five years ago, people named their kids all kinds of stuff, like they were brands of cereal. Anyway, these two, Flynn and Kellman, they leaned on the sister because she clammed up when she realized what her brother had in mind. Of course, these are not guys who get the details right.'

Dwayne shook his head, having trouble here. 'They killed his sister, and the brother kept on with them?'

'He didn't know. He still doesn't know.' Calavecci smiled like a wolf. 'I thought you'd like to be here when we tell him, see what falls out of the tree.'

He's tougher than I am, Dwayne told himself, a thought that didn't come to him often and which left him slightly uneasy. But if this was a test, he'd have no trouble passing: 'Should be interesting,' he said.

Ralph Quindero was about what Dwayne had expected: Beetle Bailey without the comedy, a sad sack who would always be in the wrong place at the wrong time. Just smart enough to get into trouble.

What do you do with such people? Dwayne had dealt with a number of them in his Marine years, and they were a real problem. They weren't mean or vicious, they were just inevitable losers who screwed themselves up and made trouble for everybody near them along the way. Your only hope was a war; you'd put them on patrol till they didn't come back.

It was too late for a war to help Ralph Quindero, who came shuffling into the interrogation room with his guard and, at Calavecci's direction, sat in the chair Dwayne had vacated, Dwayne now being in the corner on the stenographer's chair, to observe. Quindero gave him one curious look on his way in, but Calavecci was clearly the authority figure here, and Quindero was doing what his brand of clown always did; once it's too late, be polite and cooperative with everybody. Ingratiating.

With Calavecci and Quindero seated facing one another, Dwayne in the corner, and the uniformed guard leaning against the door, Calavecci said, 'Well, Ralph, you're a lucky man.'

Quindero looked confused, as well he might: 'I am?'

'Oh, absolutely,' Calavecci said. 'After all, what've we got on you? Eating a pizza in a parking lot. No crime there.'

Quindero's slumped spine was beginning to straighten, hope was lifting him up. 'That's right,' he said, his voice tinged with awe.

'Of course,' Calavecci went on, 'there's the issue of those handguns in the trunk, but they weren't yours, right?'

'No, sir. They're not mine.'

'And the car isn't yours. The car's Zack's, so the guns are *his* problem.'

'Yes, sir!'

'Of course,' Calavecci said, 'if we wanted to get really technical . . .' He waited, and grinned at Quindero, a sly and nasty little grin.

Hope stumbled. Quindero began to fidget in the chair. 'Sir? Technical?'

'Well,' Calavecci said, 'there's the matter of the robbery out at the stadium.'

Quindero blinked, confused now. 'Sir? I didn't have anything to do with that, we didn't, we didn't rob anybody!'

'But you knew it was going to happen,' Calavecci pointed out. 'That's why you came to town, because you knew the robbery was going to happen, and the problem is, you didn't inform *us* about it. You knew a felony was going to be committed, and you didn't inform the authorities, and that's called accessory before the fact. If we want to get technical, you know, just to be a pain in the ass with you.'

Quindero didn't know exactly how to respond. He snuck another look in Dwayne's direction, then said to Calavecci, 'The reason we came here? Sir, we were just—'

'Now, take it easy, Ralph,' Calavecci said. 'Be careful you don't say anything to make me think you're trying to be a smart guy.'

'No, sir, no, sir, I'm cooperating.'

'That's right. So's your pal Woody, by the way. That boy's singing like a miner's canary, on videotape. He's the one told us why you're here.'

'Woody?' You could see Quindero trying to figure out where the bullet was coming from, so he could dodge it. Or try.

'Now, Tom Carmody,' Calavecci said, 'he was the inside man in the robbery, we know all that, Tom told us in the hospital. And Tom was good friends with your sister. Mary, is it?'

'My sister— Yeah, she's Mary. But she doesn't have anything to do with this!'

'Well, she did,' Calavecci said. 'Tom told Mary what was gonna go down here, and she told you, and so you and your pals thought you'd come on out, see what there might be in it for you. Isn't that right?'

'I, uh, I guess. But Mary isn't part of it!'

'Take it easy, Ralph,' Calavecci advised. 'The point is, you may have had something naughty in mind, but you didn't *do* anything yet. Unless, that is, like I said, we want to get technical with this accessory-before-the-fact business. But I don't think that's going to happen,' he finished, and grinned at Quindero.

Who grinned back, falteringly, and said, 'I'm glad. Thanks.'

Calavecci nodded. 'After all, we're gonna want you as a witness, because the *other* two, you know, Woody and Zack, we got them on all kinds of stuff. The handguns, the accessory count, murder one—'

'What?'

'Oh, that's right,' Calavecci said, snapping his fingers, 'you don't know about that part. Still, your testimony's gonna be very important there.'

'Nobody got killed!' Ralph's eyes were actually bulging, his breathing had become audible.

'You're wrong about that, Ralph,' Calavecci said. 'Somebody got killed, all right. Drowned in a bathtub. Took a long time at it, too, what I hear.'

Panicky, Quindero leaned forward, hands gesturing out in front of himself as he said, 'We didn't kill anybody! We just drove here, we parked, we didn't—'

'*Before* you drove here. Now, we could almost pull accessory on you there, too, but I accept it, you didn't know about the murder, so that's—'

'*What* murder? Nobody was murdered!'

'Oh, come on, Ralph,' Calavecci said, grinning in high good humor, 'figure it out. You can figure it out.'

Quindero could, too, though he didn't want to. Watching the young fool's profile, Dwayne saw him struggle with it, shaking his head, half-saying words, taking them back, finally saying, as though it were all just nothing but a joke in bad taste, 'No, come on.' And then again, asking for mercy, decency, humanity, something, 'No, come on, no.'

'You know who it is,' Calavecci told him, almost crooning now. 'Spit it out, Ralph. Tell me the name.'

Quindero's mouth hung open. His big eyes filled with tears. He couldn't seem to move or breathe or blink; certainly he couldn't talk. Calavecci studied him with mock sympathy, and then said, 'Ralph? You really don't get it? Come on, boy, you're smarter than that.'

Dwayne got to his feet, surprising everybody, breaking the moment. Ignoring the punk, he went over to the desk and nodded at Calavecci. 'You're having too good a time,' he said. 'I'll be going off on my own now. That was the Seven Oaks Professional Building? Where you picked these people up?'

Calavecci didn't like being interrupted. Irritated, he said, 'What do you mean, off on your own?'

Dwayne turned away, finished with Calavecci, and looked at Quindero's tear-stained face. 'Shut up, kid,' he said, 'until you see a lawyer.' And he left.

Sending them out on patrol was a lot cleaner.

TEN

When Bill Trowbridge woke up, he had to pee real bad. Also, he'd finished the magazines those crooks had let him bring into the locked storage room with him, when they'd taken over the service station. He'd slept for a while, curled up on the hard floor, but now he was awake, and he had to do something, soon.

He'd figured out who those people had to be. The news of the robbery at the stadium had been all over TV and radio yesterday afternoon, before he'd come to work. They'd said it was three men that had done the job, but they must have gotten that part wrong; it was two men and one woman. And they were hiding from the cops *here*.

What to do? They were tough and mean, no question about that. They'd beat up one guy at the stadium so bad he was in the hospital. They were, like the radio and TV said, armed and dangerous. He was lucky all they'd done was lock him in here with the batteries and fan belts.

On the other hand, he did have to pee. And he didn't have any more magazines to distract his mind. And who knew how long they meant to keep him in here, or even if they'd remember to let him out before they left. Or if they even intended to let him out. So, for all those reasons, Bill Trowbridge was climbing the walls.

Literally. The room was deep and narrow, crowded with

deep high wooden bins and shelves on both sides, all the way to the top, full of auto parts of various kinds. Fourteen feet up was the ceiling, obscured in darkness, far above the hanging light. Bill climbed up the shelves and bins, finding it easy, using the construction on both sides, and when he got to the top the ceiling was Sheetrock. He punched a hole in it with a length of tailpipe from one of the bins, yanked Sheetrock down and out of the way, dumping the pieces as quietly as possible into nearby empty bins – all the bins above the ten-foot level were empty, dusty, dry – and found two-by-six beams up there, sixteen inches apart. The roof, resting on those beams, was made of planks.

The storage room had plenty of tools. All Bill had to do was be careful about noise. Using screwdrivers, pliers, a flat-sided tire iron and a wrench, he gouged away sections of plank, exposing the tar paper and then the gravelly tar of the surface of the roof itself.

The more he worked, the easier it got, because the more room he had to work in. When he first broke through a section of tar paper and tar to the outer air, the sky was still black, but as he worked it began to lighten out there, and when he finally squeezed himself up between two of the support beams and out onto the rough-surfaced roof it was morning. Real early morning, but morning.

The first thing Bill did was go to the edge of the roof at the back of the building, where it overlooked a narrow stretch of scrubland with bushes and skinny little plane trees on it, and pee over the side, trying to hit branches that wouldn't make too much noise. Then he looked around, wondering how best to get himself down off this roof, and saw the police car!

Oh, boy; talk about luck. The police car was even coming *here*. Bill moved as quickly and silently as he could across the roof, seeing the cop get out of his car over there by the pumps and then walk this way, toward the building.

Standing at the front edge of the roof, just above the office door, Bill waved his arms over his head to attract the cop's attention. 'Hey!' he called.

The cop looked up.

ELEVEN

The police were stretched thin, having so many places to
search, so many routes to guard, so many barricades to
man, so many possibilities to think about. That was why
they were doing one-man patrols in what they considered
the safest places, and how it was that Liss found a cop all
alone in his patrol car, half asleep, parked next to a ramp
for a narrow rusty iron bridge over old freight yards. There
were a few bars and diners in this neighborhood, a few
junkyards and machine shops and auto-repair places, but
no homes, and no commercial places open at this hour.
Liss circled around into the grassy steep slope above the
freight yards, where an old chain-link fence was half
broken-down, bent out of the way, rusted and useless.
Along there, he found a two-foot length of the metal pipe
that had originally been part of the frame of the fence, and
held it close along his right leg as he came loping down the
empty street toward the patrol car, clutching his upper
right arm with his left hand as though he'd been wounded
and yelling, 'Help! Help!'

The cop, startled out of a moony doze, saw this
wounded man running forward, scrambled rapidly and
awkwardly out to the pavement, and took the metal pipe
directly across the face. He fell backward, half in and half
against his car, dazed but trying to reach his holstered

pistol, and Liss slammed the open door into him, pinning him there while he swung the pipe three more times at that head.

When Liss pulled the door open, the cop slid to the ground. Liss quickly stripped the uniform off him, not wanting blood on it, and stuffed the body into the trunk, noting the shotguns on racks in there, the first-aid equipment, even a small red-handled ax. Couldn't be better.

The uniform fit fairly well; good enough. Sitting behind the wheel, engine and heater on, uniform cap on his head, police radio giving him the ebb and flow of movement through the night, Liss waited. No rush any more.

He'd had to rush earlier, hurrying out of the old man's house across from the stadium when Brenda showed up in the station wagon. As they'd loaded the duffel bags over there, Liss had looked around frantically for a car to steal, but there wasn't time, and in any case, with so little traffic at this hour, how could he follow them in a car without being spotted?

So he'd had to do it a different way. It was hard, there were times he thought he was going to fail, but he kept going. Out of necessity, he trailed them on foot.

What made it a little easier, they were driving slowly, carefully, obeying the law, calling no attention to themselves, stopping at every stop sign, waiting at every traffic light. They parked at the curb for quite a while when the construction trailer blew up and the streets filled with fire trucks and police cars and ambulances and all the rest of it, and he could take a breather then, hidden beside an exterior staircase to an old tenement building.

After that, when they moved he ran; when they stopped he walked. Sometimes their lights were just faint red dots far away, and once when they made a turn he thought he'd lost them completely. But he managed to keep up, and to see what their idea was at the gas station, and he admired the move. Indoors, safe, warm. They wouldn't leave till morning, and by then he'd be ready.

In the meantime, he dozed in the warm comfort of the police car, the crackly snarl of the radio's infrequent reports keeping him from the mistake of a deeper sleep, and at first light he got out of the car, stretched, went down the slope to relieve himself, got back into the police car, and drove over to the gas station to get rid of Parker and Mackey and Brenda and get, at last, the goddam money.

Would they be awake or asleep? It was still very early. They wouldn't expect trouble after so many peaceful hours hidden away. They didn't know anyone had any idea they were here. And what would they see when he first showed himself to them? A cop.

He parked at the gas pumps, like a regular customer, and walked toward the station building, getting the cop's handgun out of its holster. Advertising posters and grease-pencil announcements obscured much of the office windows, but as he came nearer he saw there was somebody in there, seated at the desk. Parker? Staring at him?

Did they still have the shotguns?

Liss was deciding to shoot through the plate glass, get it over with, when movement suddenly made him look up. There was something on the roof! Nothing but a silhouette against the gray morning sky, looming over him, a black figure like something out of horror stories, waving its arms and yelling. Without any thought at all, in quick panic, Liss raised the pistol and squeezed off a wild shot.

And then all hell broke loose.

PART THREE

ONE

Parker looked past the notices taped to the gas station window and watched Liss come this way across the blacktop, that handgun sliding out of the holster. Parker's hands splayed on the metal tabletop in front of him, and he looked down, remembering the shotguns, seeing only the wrench they'd taken away from the kid. He reached for it, even though it was useless, even though he knew Liss was smart enough to shoot him through the window, not bother to come inside. Why should he?

Parker picked up the wrench, and heard a shot. He stared out at Liss, almost a silhouette against the flat gray morning light out there, and the silhouette was arched backward, the arm with the pistol aimed upward. Liss had fired at what? Something on the roof?

Parker heaved the wrench through the plate glass and launched himself out of the chair toward the open doorway to the service area. Would the racket wake Brenda? Would she know to get that station wagon moving?

The answer was yes, but she was even faster than Parker hoped. As he dove through the doorway, meaning to roll, to come up beside the wagon and yank open its rear door, the engine was already kicking over. Before he was on his feet, it was moving, and he came up to see the garage door splinter as the station wagon roared through it. Brenda hunched and grim over the wheel, Mackey just opening his eyes, his mouth a big astonished O, the car screamed through the wreckage it made of the door, spinning and sliding rightward over smashed plywood, bent metal, crushed glass.

Parker dropped to the concrete floor as the station wagon's rear wheels rifled broken pieces back into the garage, peppering the walls and tools with chunks of wood, metal and glass. He lay there, listening, hands and feet poised under him, trying to figure what was the best route now. What's the way out of this now?

A burglar alarm high on the front of the building began to scream, and Parker wriggled hurriedly backward, toward the office. If Liss came in here . . .

The doorway. He climbed it, trying to be invisible on both sides, and when he leaned leftward for a quick look out the office's smashed window he saw Liss running for the police car, the pistol waving in his hand.

Sure. Whether or not he knew Parker was still in here, and still alive, it was the money Liss wanted, the money he couldn't lose sight of.

Parker watched, because whichever way Liss went, that's where the money had gone. Liss jumped into the police car, kicked the engine on, spun the wheel, made a sharp U-turn around the pumps, and headed away to the left. Away from that interstate over there. Toward town.

Some ricocheted something had sliced Parker's left arm, not deep, but enough to sting. Rubbing it, he went out of the building through the opening where the garage door used to be, and above the insistent wail of the burglar alarm he heard a voice, some voice yelling. He looked around and saw nothing, but then remembered that Liss had fired upward, so he stepped farther from the building to look up, and the kid was up there, sitting on the roof. The kid they'd locked away in the storeroom was up on the roof, sitting there, both hands pressed to his left leg because that's where Liss had shot him.

He saw Parker down below, and yelled some more: 'Help! Help!'

'Everybody needs help,' Parker said, and turned away, and went loping toward town.

TWO

Parker walked two blocks. In the second, two police cars raced by him, shrieking, on their way to the burglar alarm at the gas station. At the far end of that block was a diner, just open for the morning's business. Parker went in there, where a dozen delivery men and salesmen yawned over coffee in their separate spaces. He found a stool at the counter with empty stools on both sides of it, ordered breakfast, and in the mirror on the back wall he watched the street behind him, where an ambulance screamed past, toward the gas station. The waitress brought his ham and eggs and toast and coffee and the ambulance screamed back the other way. Carrying the kid.

Parker ate, and looked at his own reflection in the mirror, and except for the stained cut on his left sleeve where he'd been nicked he looked all right. Like this is where he would eat breakfast.

Time to think. He knew the people. Did he know them well enough to find them?

Liss was the newcomer, but he was the easiest to peg. It was the dead side of his face that told the truth. A competitor, he'd never team up with anybody, not for long. If he had to go in with others to get what he wanted – like the money in those duffel bags – he'd take the absolute first chance that came along to get rid of his partners, and to get rid of them in a way that wouldn't leave anybody spreading complaints. Single-minded, he'd only look forward; never back. He wouldn't care if Parker was coming, because in his mind it would simply be somebody else trying for the same thing, the money. It wouldn't occur to him that for Parker that wasn't enough, that he wanted more than the money. That he needed Liss dead.

As for Mackey, he was a mechanic, like Parker. If Parker knew himself, he knew Mackey. He knew he wouldn't ever bother to cheat Mackey, because they were useful to each other and there'd always be enough for both of them. And he also knew he'd never go out of his way to give Mackey an assist, because Mackey was supposed to be a grown-up who could take care of himself. So that's the way Mackey would feel.

Which meant, at this point, Mackey would just keep moving, straight ahead. He wouldn't even consider the idea he could circle back and find Parker. Why should he? He couldn't even be sure Parker was still alive, back at the gas station. So Mackey would keep on, and Liss would keep on, right behind him, and if that's all there was to it, Parker would be the lame third, already out of sight and out of mind.

But that wasn't all. Brenda was also in the mix, and Brenda was the only one of them who thought about the future. She would want everything settled, now, today, before they all left this town. She would never want anything out of the past to come catch up with her, farther down the road. She was fast, and she was smart, and she was decisive – look how she tore that station wagon out of there – and Mackey deferred to her, because he'd learned long ago that when he followed Brenda's advice things worked out okay. So Brenda was the key.

Liss was following Mackey. Mackey would follow Brenda. Where would Brenda lead?

The station wagon was marked up now, it had to be. They couldn't keep it for long. Brenda would lose Liss, she was that good, but then she couldn't just drive around all day because very soon the cops would be on the lookout for the station wagon that had ripped through that garage door. And the kid would have already told them about the duffel bags in the station wagon, so the law would know it was the heisters from the stadium inside that car.

Brenda would lose Liss. They change cars, somewhere, somehow. Now there are three possibilities. They make a run for it, try to get out of town without being stopped by the law or Liss or anybody else. Or, the second choice, they hole up at the empty house where they'd all originally meant to wait out the police search. Or, third, they go back to the motel they'd been in before the heist.

If it was just Mackey, he'd choose to run. But Brenda's too smart and too careful. Does she go to the house? She knows Liss will be waiting for her someplace. And Liss will figure her to go to the house, right? Because that was the original plan for after the heist, and because, as far as Liss is concerned, the motel is used up. And Brenda will know that's what Liss is thinking.

What did Brenda say in the car, about the motel? 'I'll be leaving a whole lot of cosmetics back in that room.'

They'll have a different car. They already have a civilian cover in that motel. Brenda will believe that Liss will look for them in the house.

Parker paid for his breakfast, and left.

126

THREE

The Midway Motel occupied a wide shallow parcel of land on Western Avenue, across the street from the Seven Oaks Professional Building. The motel, red aluminum siding over concrete block, with metal room doors painted to look like wood, presented its long face to the street, with blacktop across the front for guests' cars to park, nose in. At seven-thirty that morning, cars and pickups stood in front of eleven of the twenty units, but not in front of either 16 or 17.

Parker walked down the other side of Western Avenue and climbed the concrete steps to the squat brick professional building. He stood in the little lobby, looking at the directory, aware of what was happening in the street. A few cars went by; nothing else.

'Can I help you?'

It was a caretaker, looking nosy. Parker said, 'No.'

'Well . . .' The guy was miffed. 'I'll be over here,' he said, and went away.

Parker stepped outside and paused, like anybody, to study the weather and the day. Going to be sunny, not hot. Nobody moving around the motel. No cars yet this morning in the Professional Building's parking lot, no cars with occupants inside stopped up or down the street.

Parker still had the key to room 17 in his pocket. When

no traffic was in sight, he crossed the street, moving directly to 17, watching for movement from inside any of those windows along the front, and there was nothing. Now the key and its rectangular plastic tab were in his palm.

He went in fast, slapping the door shut behind him as he crouched down and ran across the room, looking left and right. Nothing, nobody. In the bathroom, dark. Nothing, nobody.

The drape was already closed across the front window beside the door. Parker switched on lights and looked around, and nobody had been in here since they'd left except the maid. They all traveled light, all except Brenda and her cosmetics, and their goods, Parker's and Liss's, were still here where they'd been left, nothing but some clothing and toothbrushes and other things that didn't matter, weren't traceable, could always be bought new.

The original plan, now nothing but a memory, was that they'd wait in the construction trailer until the excitement was over. Then, at six in the morning, Brenda would pick them up, and they'd drive the three miles to the empty house, in town but isolated, and stash the money there. Then they'd come back here and stay in the motel until it seemed safe to leave town, when they'd go by the house once more, pick up the money, and be off.

Now everything was random. Mackey and Brenda and the money were somewhere in this city. Liss was somewhere else, looking for them. And Parker was counting on Brenda, sooner or later, wanting to come here.

There was a connecting door to the room where Brenda and Mackey had stayed. They hadn't bothered to unlock it before but Parker did now, and this room was also empty.

And in this bathroom were Brenda's famous cosmetics, spread over every surface.

Parker switched off the lights in Brenda and Mackey's room, went back to his own, and closed the connecting door almost completely, leaving just a crack to see and hear through. Then he went into the bathroom in here, stripped off his shirt, and washed out the angry red line along his upper left arm. He found one last fresh shirt, put it on, moved a chair over near the connecting door, switched off the lights in this room, and sat down in the dark to wait.

Click.

Parker sat up straighter, and a vertical line of gray light appeared in front of him, brightened, darkened, went out.

Somebody'd come into Brenda and Mackey's room; that was daylight when the door had opened. It was no more than two hours, Parker thought, that he'd been waiting in here.

The lights didn't go on, in the next room. Parker leaned close to the door and heard very small movements.

Brenda and Mackey would switch the light on, right away. Was this Liss? Parker listened.

Now the lights did come on. And the sounds of movement stopped. Then there was brisk walking, past this door and beyond, and Parker heard the bathroom light click on. He eased the door open a bit more, but his angle of view was toward the front of the room. He could see most of the bed, on the opposite wall, and the bedside table, and the round table and two chairs and swag lamp in front of the window, and part of the window with its drape pulled across. He couldn't see the door.

More footsteps. The closet door was slid open. Ruffling sounds as somebody went through whatever clothes were in there. Then a drawer was opened, and shut.

Somebody searching. Somebody neat searching; he shuts the drawer. Knowing this wasn't Brenda, coming to believe it wasn't Liss, wondering if it was one of the three guys from that car that had nosed around the stadium parking lot, Parker waited, and then a guy he'd never seen in his life before came around the end of the bed and crossed over to look in the drawer of the bedside table.

Parker looked at this guy, trying to fit him in. A friend of Liss's? Was Liss waiting at the empty house, and he sent this other guy just in case the money showed up at the motel?

No. Liss wouldn't trust anybody else that far, and nobody else would trust him that far. Also, this guy didn't look the type. He was a very trim fifty, with short-cropped gray hair, wire frame eyeglasses, and a look of competence and self-assurance. He was dressed in a neat gray suit that made him look more like a cop than a banker, but this wasn't a cop.

Something like a cop? Somebody who doesn't mind breaking and entering, and who feels there might be something here he's looking for. Somebody who's dealt himself in.

Parker's eyes were now once again used to the light. As the guy turned away from the empty drawer in the bedside table, Parker stood, pushed open the door, and stepped into the room.

The guy saw him. His eyes focused, his body became still, and his right hand snaked inside his suit jacket, coming out with a small flat automatic. 'Stop right there.'

130

Not law, but close to law. 'Don't be stupid,' Parker told him, and spread his own empty hands. 'Put that thing away, or I'll take it off you.'

The guy ignored that. He waggled the gun toward the table and two chairs by the front door. 'Sit down over there,' he said.

'So you are stupid,' Parker said, and walked toward him.

'Hey! Hey!' the guy said, startled, and backed up two steps to the wall. Then, before Parker could reach him, he holstered the automatic, just as rapidly as he'd taken it out. Showing his palms, he said, 'All right.'

Parker backed away, and now he was the one who pointed at the table and chairs, saying, 'Why don't we both sit down?'

The guy frowned at him. 'Jesus Christ,' he said thoughtfully. 'What if I was the excitable type?'

'I'd calm you down,' Parker told him. He went over and sat in the chair that didn't have its back to the door. Watching the guy, still standing there, indecisive, he said, 'You're looking for the money.'

The guy nodded, still frowning; not so much in agreement that he was looking for the money but accepting the force of the statement. 'I know who I am,' he said. 'Who the hell are you?'

'John Orr,' Parker told him. 'Midwest Insurance.'

'You're an *insurance man*?'

'Investigator.'

'You got ID?'

'Never,' Parker said. 'Not on the job. How about you?'

Now at last the guy came over and sat in the other chair.

He put one forearm on the table and said, 'Dwayne Thorsen. Head of Security for the Christian Crusade.'

'Archibald's guy.'

'He's who I work for,' Thorsen said. 'You've got no ID on you at all?'

Parker pulled his wallet out of his hip pocket and dropped it on the table. 'I've got papers on three different names in there,' he said. 'None of them true. It makes you feel better, look em over.'

Thorsen looked at the beat-up wallet, then at Parker, and laughed. 'You'll tell me when you're telling the truth,' he said, 'and you'll tell me when you're lying, and I can believe you or I can go fuck myself.'

This was true, and there was no need for Parker to confirm it. There was a persona he wanted Thorsen to believe, and the more that persona was Thorsen's own invention, instead of a razzle-dazzle fed him by Parker, the better.

Thorsen said, 'Midwest Insurance. Who's your client? The stadium?'

Parker put his wallet away. 'Nobody,' he said. 'Not on this one.'

Thorsen nodded, considering that. 'What you mean is, you were already on their trail, for something else.'

'One of them,' Parker said. 'A fellow named George Liss.'

'That's a name I know,' Thorsen agreed.

So Carmody had broken; not a surprise.

Thorsen went on, 'Seems to be his real handle, Liss. What do you have on the others?'

'Nothing,' Parker said. 'They're not part of my job. Or

132

they weren't. I guess they are now. Do you have names on them?'

'Not names I like,' Thorsen said. 'Jack Grant. Ed and Brenda Fawcett.' He waggled a hand, to show doubt. 'That's what they told Carmody, for what it's worth.'

Parker decided an insurance investigator following George Liss would have some knowledge of Carmody. He said, 'Carmody. He's something in Liss's parole, isn't he?'

'He's also the inside man on the robbery,' Thorsen said.

'It looked like there had to be somebody inside,' Parker agreed. 'And they holed up in that trailer that blew apart, I suppose.'

'From there,' Thorsen said, 'God knows where they went.'

'Who's running the investigation?'

Thorsen shook his head. 'I don't like him,' he said, 'and you won't either. Detective Second Grade Calavecci.'

'Is that why you're looking around here yourself? He's incompetent?'

'No, he's good at the job,' Thorsen said. 'I think the whole department's good. He just enjoys himself a little too much.'

'Maybe I'll stay out of his way,' Parker said.

'That's what I'm doing,' Thorsen said. 'Came over here to see what's what, when I couldn't stand him any more.'

'You knew about this place from Carmody?'

'And also from another bunch, trying to cut themselves a piece. Calavecci didn't want to come here, said they wouldn't be back, but you never know. Their stuff is here.'

Parker said, 'Another bunch?' That must be the trio in the car in the stadium parking lot. Who *were* those

133

clowns? And where were they now? Parker said, 'I don't know any other bunch.'

'It's a sad story,' Thorsen told him. 'Carmody had a girlfriend. He told her what was going down here.'

'Everybody talks to everybody,' Parker said.

'They do,' agreed Thorsen. 'The girlfriend talked to her brother, who's an asshole. He talked to two other assholes he knew, and they decided to come hit the hitters.'

'Did they,' Parker said.

'Before they left,' Thorsen went on, 'the other two assholes went to see what else the sister might know, and killed her. Not meaning to, I guess.'

Parker said, 'The sister?'

'They didn't mention that part to the brother,' Thorsen said. 'They just all came here.'

'To the motel, you mean. So they could follow the heisters.'

'That's right.'

'Liss told Carmody this was the motel, Carmody told the girlfriend, the girlfriend told the brother.'

'As you say,' Thorsen said, 'everybody talks to everybody.'

'The question is,' Parker said, 'who do I talk to?'

'The second bunch is in custody,' Thorsen told him. 'Calavecci was teasing the brother about the sister's death, not quite telling him, when I left.'

'Uh huh.'

'But I don't know that that bunch has much you want to know.'

'They're nothing to me,' Parker said. He was thinking, trying to find a way to turn this meeting into something useful. 'I might want Carmody,' he decided. 'He could

134

know associates of Liss, people Liss might go to if he has to go to ground.'

'Calavecci and his people squeezed him pretty good, I think,' Thorsen said.

'But they're thinking about the stadium, and the money. I'm thinking about Liss.'

'That's true.' Thorsen thought it over, and said, 'I could phone, say we want to drop by—'

'You and the insurance man.'

Thorsen grinned. 'That's right. Just get an okay, a phone call from Calavecci to the hospital saying we're cleared to go in. That way, Calavecci won't have to come with us.'

'He's a busy man anyway,' Parker suggested.

Thorsen got to his feet. 'I'll just make the call.'

Also rising, Parker said, 'Give me a minute in the john, and I'll be with you.'

As Thorsen went over to the telephone on the bedside table, Parker went into the bathroom, shut the door, and looked through Brenda's cosmetics until he found a round black compact. He opened it, and the inside of the top was mirrored. With eyebrow pencil, he wrote on the mirror *11 pm*. Then he closed the compact and put it down a different place from where he'd found it, then flushed the toilet before leaving the room.

The one place he was sure Brenda would look was in a mirror.

FOUR

Thorsen was still on the phone, saying, 'Yeah,' and, 'I see,' and, 'How about that.' He held a finger up toward Parker – one minute – and went on listening to the phone. Then he said, 'Well, we'll come over and hang around until you're done,' and hung up, and said, 'I could grow to dislike that slimeball.'

'The detective? Whatsisname?'

'Calavecci. He's waiting for the doctors to say he can go over and have a conversation with Carmody himself, probably by ten o'clock. When he's done, then we can go in.'

The clock radio in the room read 9:23. 'So we wait a while,' Parker said.

'The thing is,' Thorsen said, 'what he's waiting to do. He wants to bring Quindero over there, let him and Carmody have a conversation.'

'Quindero?' This was a new name to Parker.

'The brother,' Thorsen explained. 'This is just the sadistic son of a bitch wanting to turn the knife a little more. Let Quindero and Carmody reminisce together about good old Mary.'

'A nice guy, your detective.'

'Let's get out of here,' Thorsen said, looking around, disgusted. 'There's more, I'll tell you in the car.'

'Fine.'

Thorsen nodded at the connecting door. 'Nothing in there?'

'Same as here. They didn't leave any address books.'

'These are not people with address books,' Thorsen said. 'Come along— What do I call you? John, or Jack?'

'Jack.'

'And I'm Dwayne.'

'Fine.'

They went out, switching off the lights, and Thorsen said, 'I parked across the street.'

In the Professional Building parking lot, which was now half full. Thorsen's car was a rental, a blue Chevy Celebrity. He unlocked them into it, and on the console between the front seats was a black scanner, which he immediately switched on, saying, 'I've got this fixed to the local police band. I'm not official, so Calavecci won't tell me anything unless I ask, and then he has to play around a little.'

Thorsen had the volume low, so that the police dispatcher's voice was a raspy buzz that wouldn't interfere with conversation. Parker said, 'There's more?'

Thorsen started the car, and drove out of the parking lot, and as they headed across the city he told Parker about the mess at the gas station this morning, and the kid hospitalized with a bullet in his leg, and the description of the station wagon and the duffel bags and the two men and a woman.

'The thing is,' he finished, 'my security people in the money room where it happened, they say it was three men. The kid's sure it was two men and a woman. During the

137

robbery, the hitters had ski masks on, so maybe one of them was a woman all along.'

'Wouldn't be the first time,' Parker said.

'Then the other thing,' Thorsen said. 'Nobody knows if it's connected or not, but the locals have lost a cop. And his car.'

Knowing this was Liss's work, Parker said, 'Lost a cop? How do you mean?'

'The guy was on duty at an on-ramp someplace, by himself. When the relief showed up at six this morning, he and the car were gone. He doesn't respond to radio calls – you'll hear them, from time to time, they're still trying to raise him – and they don't know what it means.'

'If the heisters have a police car,' Parker said, 'they could probably just drive on out of town and nobody think twice.'

'Then why are they still in that gas station an hour later, with a station wagon? That's why nobody knows if it's connected.'

'They'll find him,' Parker said. 'Their cop. Sooner or later. One way or another.'

'What's driving them nuts is,' Thorsen said, 'if the hitters have that car, they've got the radio, just like this. They're listening to the pursuit.'

'They're probably not enjoying it much,' Parker said.

The hospital was well across town. Parker sat in the passenger seat as Thorsen drove from traffic light to traffic light, and the radio kept talking. From time to time, it called for an Officer Kendall, who never answered. Sometimes there was stuff about who would be on duty in and around the hospital, to guard Carmody. Then they found the station wagon.

Thorsen said, 'What? Turn it up.'

Parker turned it up, and they listened to the reports. A woman had reported her car stolen, a Toyota Tercel, from in front of her apartment building, discovering it when she went out to go to her morning class at the local college, and when the officers responded they found the battered station wagon in front of a fire hydrant directly across the street. So now the fugitives were presumed to be traveling in a dark green Toyota Tercel, license number S46 8TJ.

Except that Parker knew they weren't. He knew what Mackey would do now, because they'd both done it before, when they needed to buy time and they didn't dare travel in stolen wheels. Mackey and Brenda and the duffel bags, in the Toyota, would drive directly to a downtown parking garage, the kind where a machine gives you the ticket on the way in. There they'd park the Toyota, grab another car, wait in it twenty minutes or so, and pay on the way out with the ticket they'd got on the way in. This new car would take them to a motel, either the old one or more likely a new one. Once they had a room, Mackey would bring the new car back to where he'd got it, leave it there, and take a cab to the new hidey-hole.

Somewhere in this city. All Parker had to do was find them.

Up ahead, on the right, a patrolman strolled his beat, slow and relaxed, showing that not the entire local law was all caught up in the excitement. Parker saw him up ahead, from the back, saw how casual he was, then noticed how sloppy the uniform looked.

They drove by. Parker turned his head to look. It was Liss.

FIVE

Stop? Get out of the car? Go after Liss right now?

No. Too complicated to strip away Thorsen. At this point, Thorsen was Parker's only way to find out what the law knew and what they were doing and whether or not anybody was close to Mackey and Brenda. There was time to reach out for Liss, if the law didn't scoop him up first. Carmody might know just the one thing that would lead Parker to Liss after this was all over. In the meantime, if Liss was killing time and nothing else, strolling around in the sunlight with his cop imitation, that meant he was just as far away as Parker from the duffel bags full of money. Liss could wait.

There was excitement at the hospital. Television news vans, sprouting antennas like the whiskers on a witch's chin, lined both sides of the curved entrance road. Police vehicles took up the rest of the space in front, and cops were a heavy presence both inside and outside the main entrance. Thorsen left the Chevy in the very full visitors' parking lot, then talked himself and Parker into the main hospital building past any number of cops with questions, some of them local and some of them state. Everybody had to walkie-talkie to somebody else to get approval to let Thorsen through, but nobody questioned it when Thorsen vouched for Parker: Jack Orr, the insurance investigator.

In addition to Carmody, in a private room on four, there was also the kid from the gas station, Bill Trowbridge, in his own room on three. Trowbridge, having answered every question the cops could think of to ask, was now doing press and TV interviews and grinning like a goof at his mother, seated on an uncomfortable nearby chair, being firmly kept out of camera range. Among the reasons he gave for climbing the bins in the storage room and ripping his way through the roof, he did not mention his need to pee.

The hall leading from the elevator to Carmody was also full of cops. One of them, that Thorsen seemed to have met before, was a plainclothesman named Macready, who gave Parker a hello and a handshake at Thorsen's introduction, then said, 'Lew's on his way here with Quindero. He wants everybody else to wait.'

Thorsen said, 'Not here yet?'

'The Quindero family's lobbed a lawyer in,' Macready said. 'It's delaying things a— Oh, here they are.'

Out of an elevator and down the hall came a group of four, led by a big self-satisfied man who'd have to be Calavecci. Behind him came a skinny young scared guy with hands cuffed behind his back, and flanked by two serious-looking uniforms, each of them holding one of the cuffed guy's elbows. Parker looked at him past Calavecci and thought the young guy was probably one of the people from that car in the stadium parking lot.

But Calavecci was the point here. He said a smooth word to Thorsen, then was introduced to Jack Orr, insurance investigator. He shook hands too hard, grinned, and said, 'So you've been chasing our boys longer'n we have.'

'Just one,' Parker said. 'George Liss.'

'A real piece of work,' Calavecci said, with a pleased shake of the head. 'I'm looking forward to a discussion with him. What a rap sheet.'

'Yeah?'

'Got a record in the top ten,' Calavecci said. 'With a bullet. Why don't you and Dwayne wait in the dayroom over there, they got coffee and stuff for the nurses. We'll just have a little conversation, Ralph and me, with his pal Tom.'

Parker saw that Ralph Quindero was trying not to cry. When he got in front of Carmody, he'd quit trying. They'd have a nice little tearfest in there, with Calavecci lapping it up, like a cat.

The dayroom was too bright, with fluorescents. A few nurses, trying to be cool but sneaking looks at the strangers, were clustered over coffee at a table in the corner. Thorsen and Parker got coffee of their own, both passing up the powdered near-milk, and carried the cardboard cups to another of the green Formica tables. They sat there in silence, waiting, the taste and smell of the coffee both a little obnoxious, and then Thorsen said, 'This fella Liss.'

'Yeah?'

'Does he work with a regular bunch? Same people all the time?'

'No,' Parker said. 'He isn't in a crew. He's too untrustworthy. He's just as likely to turn on his partners.'

'Maybe he did this time,' Thorsen said. 'Maybe he's all any of us is looking for, at this point.'

'Anything is possible,' Parker agreed.

A few minutes later, Calavecci came in, got his own cup

of coffee, and joined them at the table. He seemed very content, as though he'd just had a good meal. 'They're forgiving each other in there now,' he said.

'That's nice,' Thorsen said. He remained very flat and still when talking to Calavecci.

'I believe they're about to start praying for Mary's immortal soul,' Calavecci went on, 'so I left them in there with the guards. I'll go back in a few minutes.' He gave Parker a measuring look. 'You root around in the garbage a lot,' he suggested.

'That's where the people are,' Parker told him.

'You been chasing Liss a long time?'

'Eight months. He was part of a bank thing in Iowa City, took a hostage, killed her.'

'What does the insurance company care?'

'They need Liss,' Parker said, improvising from what he knew of previous situations, from the other side, 'to prove the bank guards weren't incompetent. If they can prove the guards did what they were supposed to do, the company's liability goes way down.'

Smiling pleasantly, Calavecci said, 'And screw the survivors, right?'

Parker smiled back at him, just as pleasant and just as false. 'That's the job,' he said, and three shots sounded, flat and small but not far away. They could have been the sounds of somebody hitting a floor with a baseball bat, but they were not.

All three at the table knew it, and jumped to their feet. They were all moving toward the door before the first yells sounded outside. Calavecci went through the doorway, then Thorsen. Parker lagged, because he thought he knew what this was. He thought it wasn't a coincidence he'd seen George Liss walking toward the hospital.

Yes. The hall was full of armed men and women in blue, all facing the same way, frozen. Parker came through the doorway behind Thorsen and looked down the hall and Liss was backing away down there, waving the pistol he must have taken from the missing cop. He was still in the uniform, but what was protecting him now was Ralph Quindero. He backed away down the hall with Quindero in front of him, Liss's left arm tight around Quindero's waist, Quindero the shield, helplessly facing all those helpless armed people as he and Liss backed steadily away. There was a stairwell door back there, at the far end.

Liss, looking at everything, suddenly saw Parker, and laughed with surprise. 'Well, look at you!' he cried, and fired at Parker's head.

SIX

Thorsen's lunge drove both Parker and himself back through the doorway into the dayroom, bouncing off the floor while the bullet hit the doorframe behind them. As they untangled themselves, there were sudden shouts from the hall, and a quick flurry of gunfire, almost immediately stopped.

Parker got to his feet as the uniforms in the hall rushed forward in a body, meaning Liss had made it to the stairwell. But how much farther could he go?

Parker turned and held out his hand to help Thorsen back to his feet. He said, 'I owe you one.'

Thorsen looked slightly ruffled, but then he shook himself and became completely neat again. He said, 'That was Liss, wasn't it?'

'It was.'

'Looks like he knows you're behind him.'

'Looks that way.'

'And doesn't like it.'

'I didn't think he would,' Parker said, and started out of the room.

Thorsen, not moving, said, 'Let the police run him down. Shouldn't take more than five minutes.'

Over his shoulder, Parker said, 'Carmody,' and walked away down the now-deserted hall. Big eyes in shocked faces looked out from corners of cover at the nurse's station along the way.

Carmody's room was on the other side, just before the nurse's station. Parker went to that doorway and looked in, and it was a mess. Carmody had been shot in the head, and was lying back on the pillow, three eyes staring upward. The two cops who'd been in here with him, mostly to keep watch on Ralph Quindero, had been shot any which way, just to take them out of play, and were alive, but both lying like flung dolls on the floor, being worked over by nurses.

For Liss, Carmody was the only person except the rest of the crew who could positively say he'd been one of the heisters. It didn't matter if Carmody had given statements to the law, just so he wouldn't be around later to make the positive ID. Liss could afford a lawyer who'd fend off all that crap, dependent on there being no live Tom Carmody to stand up in court and point and say, 'That's him there.'

And what Liss was counting on right now, in the hospital, was too much confusion and nobody who'd ever seen him before. A guy in a police uniform, moving fast, shooting people, who came in and went out. There might be some potential IDs of Liss, but once again, not enough for a conviction. Not if he got away clean and hired his lawyer and established his alibi in some place like San Diego, or one of the Portlands.

'Gangway! Gangway!'

Parker stepped back, and white-coated people hurried by, pushing two gurneys into the room. Working delicately but hurriedly, moving fragile creatures who could break at any second, they put the two wounded cops on the gurneys.

146

Parker looked down the hall. Some of the cops had followed Liss into the stairwell, while others milled around down there, barking into walkie-talkies. Some had come the other way down the hall and were just now piling into an elevator. To go which way, up or down? Liss wouldn't be as easy to catch as these people thought.

Thorsen had also looked into Carmody's room, and now he came over to Parker to say, 'You can hold your questions.'

'There's nothing for me here,' Parker agreed. He was thinking, there was nothing for him around Thorsen any more, either. Get rid of him – maybe take him out of the action and borrow that little automatic of his – and then go find Mackey and Brenda. Liss was attracting too much attention right now, Parker didn't need to be around him.

Particularly since he was supposed to be the Liss expert, the insurance guy tracking him down. Calavecci had immediately gone running off to lead the search for Liss, but sooner or later he'd be back, and he'd be full of questions, and he'd probably even want to call Jack Orr's head office at Midwest Insurance, a company that so far as Parker knew didn't exist.

Down the hall, the plainclothesman called Macready came out of the stairwell and walked this way. Thorsen said, 'Get him?'

'Not yet,' Macready said.

Parker said, 'You lost him.'

'We know he's in the building,' Macready said. 'He isn't going anywhere.' Frowning at Parker, he said, 'He does seem to have a special interest in you, though, doesn't he?'

'We're interested in each other,' Parker said. 'He knows I don't mean him well.'

An elevator door opened and cops came out. They looked both purposeful and confused, and they milled with the gurneys coming out of Carmody's room. Macready went over to talk to these new cops, and Parker said, 'Time to get out of their way.'

'As a matter of fact,' Thorsen said, 'I was just thinking the same. Come to the hotel.'

Parker looked at him. 'What hotel?'

'Archibald and the Crusade,' Thorsen explained. 'We're all supposed to leave town today, go back to Memphis, but it looks like at least some of us will be staying on. You and I can go there, phone Broad Street from time to time, find out what's going on.'

A peaceful place. A good place to hole up until tonight; if nothing else happened, Parker could go back to that motel at eleven o'clock, see if Brenda'd been reading her compact lately. 'Good idea,' he said. 'Thanks for the invite.'

SEVEN

Macready rode down in the elevator with them. He had an air about him of gloomy satisfaction, as though taking pleasure in something he knew to be a sin. He said, 'We got a situation here, I don't know if you two realize this.'

Thorsen said, 'A situation? What kind of situation?'

'I mean,' Macready said, 'Lew Calavecci went out on a limb when he brought the Quindero kid over here, and now maybe the limb broke off.'

The elevator reached the ground floor. They stepped out to find a snag, a traffic jam of people being funneled slowly through one checkpoint at the main entrance. Everybody in and out was being closely studied.

Macready stood on line with them, and Thorsen asked him, 'Out on a limb? Why?'

'What have they got Quindero on?' Macready asked. 'Nothing, or next to nothing. His two pals killed the girl, his sister, but everybody acknowledges Quindero didn't know about it till long afterward, so he isn't a party to that crime at all. The three of them came here *intending* to commit a crime, but they didn't do it. The other two they're holding on murder one, to be shipped home, but all they have on Quindero, here or anywhere else, is obstruction of justice, because he knew the robbery at the stadium was going to take place and he didn't inform the police.

But that's Mickey Mouse, and everybody knows it, that's just to hold onto him a couple days. His lawyer's going to laugh at that one. In fact, he's already laughing at it. But now we got a different situation.'

Thorsen said, 'What?'

Macready seemed to consider whether or not to go on. The line inched forward, people irritable but obedient, one at a time leaving the building, one at a time entering it. Macready said, 'I don't know if you two got much of a sense of Lew Calavecci.'

'I think we do,' Thorsen said.

'Enough to go on,' Parker said.

'Well,' Macready told them, 'Lew let Quindero believe he was in a lot deeper shit than he actually is. You know, he put the screws to him a little. More for fun than to get anything out of him. And he didn't get clearance from anybody to bring Quindero here to confront Carmody because he knew damn well nobody would *give* him clearance.'

'Oh,' said Thorsen.

'And now,' Macready said, 'it looks like Quindero's teamed up with our shooter.'

Thorsen said, 'Teamed up? He was a hostage.'

'In the stairwell,' Macready said, 'the shooter took the time to shoot the lock on Quindero's cuffs, free him up. We found them there. Quindero must figure he's got nothing to lose, so he's thrown in with the shooter, and they're somewhere together. Two instead of one.'

Parker said, 'Calavecci needs Quindero back safe and sound, doesn't he? Not a scratch on him.'

'Good luck, say I,' said Macready. Looking at Parker, he

150

said, 'I hear the shooter was the guy you're looking for, is that right?'

'George Liss,' Parker agreed. 'Looked like him.'

They were nearly to the head of the line; Macready would usher them through. Waiting, he nodded and said, 'I can see where, following George Liss around, it wouldn't be dull work.'

EIGHT

It wasn't a manger. Carlton Tower, where William Archibald and his Christian Crusade were resting their heads while they saved local souls, was a many-tiered wedding cake, white and gleaming in the sun, with the flags of various Scottish clans dangling from horizontal poles stuck out from the facade just above the second level. (Most people had no idea what those colorful flags stood for, and the few who did know couldn't figure out what they stood for *here*.)

The lobby was broad and two stories high, with a figured carpet in which the dominant color was maroon. The bank of gold-doored elevators stood discreetly around a corner on the right. Thorsen led the way across from the revolving-doored entrance, through an atmosphere of hyper but hushed activity, and Parker looked at it all with approval. He liked this kind of place when he wasn't working. On the job, it was no good, of course, because the byword with a place like this was constant service of the guest, which meant constant observation of the guest. On the job, Parker preferred a place where, once you paid your money and they told you where the ice machine was, you were left alone.

Archibald and his people had taken all or most of the twelfth floor. Thorsen and Parker rode up in the elevator with blushing honeymooners, who continued on to greater heights. When Thorsen and Parker stepped out of the elevator, they found a very neat and muscular young man in dark gray suit and dark blue tie seated on the nice wing chair against the opposite wall, reading what looked like a missal. He glanced up, saw Thorsen, and said, 'Morning, sir.'

'Morning. Archibald in?'

'I believe everybody's in, sir,' the young man said, and gave Parker a flat look, merely recording him, to remember him. Parker already remembered the young man; he'd been one of the Crusade's guards in the money room at the stadium.

Thorsen led the way down the hall, saying, 'We'll drop in, have a word with Archibald, then go on to my office. He's an interesting fella to meet.'

'I suppose he must be,' Parker said.

They went to the end of the white-and-gold corridor, where the suites were, and Thorsen knocked on the door that instead of a number had the word *Macleod* on it. After a minute, this door was opened by another muscular youngster in a suit, a clone of the one at the elevator, though Parker didn't think this one had been in the money room.

Thorsen stepped in, murmuring a word to this guy, and Parker followed. They went through a small mirrored vestibule with two doors that probably led to closets, and then entered a large six-sided room with big windows in two walls showing cityscape. Paintings hung on the rest of the walls, cream-and-green broadloom was underfoot, and the furniture was large and dark, mostly imitation antique, and placed in separate groupings, the largest cluster being the two sofas and two chairs with several tables and lamps positioned in front of the now-idle fireplace. That detail surprised Parker; he'd thought Archibald would want a fire. Maybe too distracted by the loss of his money.

The remembered plummy voice from the night of the robbery oiled the room, coming from the man himself, seated at a small desk in front of the view, talking on the telephone. He gestured at Thorsen that he wouldn't be long, and went on with his conversation. Parker listened, and Archibald seemed to be on the line with his head office back in Memphis, arranging alterations in the television schedule created by the disruption that had happened here.

'Better coffee in this place,' Thorsen said, and went over to the bar – from the doorway, it was fireplace to the left, bar to the right, Archibald on the phone straight ahead – where he filled two hotel china mugs with coffee from a glass pot on a warmer there. Parker joined him, hiking one hip onto a stool in front of the bar while Thorsen stood behind it, leaning against the back counter. The coffee was in fact much better than the stuff at the hospital.

Parker looked around. 'Nice duty,' he said.

Thorsen offered a thin smile. 'Depends what you like.'

When Archibald got off the phone, everybody moved, Archibald rising and turning his smile toward the room as though it contained multitudes, Parker getting to his feet and standing there with the coffee mug in his left hand, Thorsen coming around the end of the bar to make the introductions. 'Reverend William Archibald,' he said, as the three moved toward one another, 'may I present Mr. John Orr, an undercover insurance investigator from Midwest Insurance.'

Archibald's handshake was firm but not aggressive. 'Mr.

Orr,' he said, in greeting. 'Here concerning our unfortunate loss?'

'Not exactly,' Parker said.

Thorsen said, 'Mr. Orr was on another case. He was already in pursuit of one of the fellas robbed us, for something else he did.'

Archibald smiled, with ruefulness in it. 'In that case, Mr. Orr,' he said, 'I can only regret that you didn't catch up with him last week.'

'I feel the same way,' Parker told him.

'But now you're here,' Archibald said, 'I presume you've taken our misfortune under your wing as well.'

'That would be a different insurance company,' Parker said.

Thorsen said, 'Mr. Orr's got a full plate, Will. This fella he's after is a very bad man. Just caused a ruckus down at Memorial Hospital.' His voice lowered, becoming as funereal as his boss, as he said, 'I'm afraid Tom Carmody's dead.'

That startled Archibald. 'Why, that's terrible!' Looking at Parker, he said, 'Tom was one of my failures, Mr. Orr. I'm not going to get over this.'

'Uh huh,' Parker said.

'But at least,' Archibald said, brightening, 'he expressed sorrow for his wayward ways. Toward the end, Dwayne, didn't he? You were there.'

'He was sorry, all right,' Thorsen said.

'We'll remember him in our prayers,' Archibald decided. A blonde woman came into the room, then, from somewhere deeper in the suite, and attracted everybody's attention; which is what she would do in any room she entered. Ripe to overflowing, she was almost a parody of the sexpot, but kept under strict control, her yellow hair in a tight bun, lush body completely covered in a sexless gray suit and high-necked white blouse, and dark horn-rim glasses worn to distract from the bee-stung mouth.

Archibald's smile when he turned to greet her contained the avarice of ownership; not much question who this woman was. 'Ah, Tina,' the Reverend said. 'Come meet Mr. Orr. He leads a very exciting life.'

When she came forward, Parker could see her rein herself in, deliberately hold herself within tight bounds. Her smile was small, almost prissy, and she didn't quite meet his eye as she murmured, 'Does he? How nice.'

'Mr. John Orr,' Archibald said, presenting his proudest possession, 'Ms. Christine Mackenzie, conductor of our Angel Choir.'

'How do you do?'

Her hand was soft, with toughness within. Holding Parker's a second too long, she said, 'What about your life makes it so exciting, Mr. Orr?'

'Not much,' Parker told her.

Archibald said, 'Mr. Orr's an undercover detective, working for an insurance company.'

'*Are* you?' The smile opened a bit more, showed a gleam of teeth. 'You must have some stories to tell.'

'Mostly, I keep them to myself,' Parker said.

He'd been aware of the transformation of Thorsen since Christine Mackenzie had come into the room. The man reacted with barely concealed rage and revulsion, covering panic; the sexuality of this woman was clearly far more than Thorsen could take. He wanted out of here, and now, gruffly, without looking at the woman, he said, 'Will, Mr.

Orr and I are going to my office, call Broad Street, find out if there's any developments.'

'Broad Street.' Archibald frowned slightly. 'That's what they call their police headquarters here?'

'They better not ever move it,' Christine Mackenzie said, and giggled, and showed Parker her tongue.

Thorsen turned away, his hands clenched into fists. 'Come on, Jack,' he said.

'Nice to meet you,' Parker told Archibald, and nodded to Mackenzie. 'Both of you.'

But Archibald said, 'Dwayne, you go ahead. Let me have a little word with Mr. Orr, if I might. I'll send him right along.'

'Fine,' Thorsen said. To Parker he said, 'I'm down on the right, 1237.'

'Got it.'

Thorsen left, and Archibald said, 'More coffee, Mr. Orr?'

'No, I'm fine.'

Archibald turned to Mackenzie, saying, 'Tina, go in the other room, please, and phone the concierge, and ask for somebody to come up and lay a fire, would you do that, please?'

She would rather stay, but that wasn't being given as a choice. 'All right,' she said, with a shrug that made her breasts call attention to themselves, even within all that nunnery. Approaching Parker, 'Glad to meet you,' she said, with another smile, and offered her hand once more. 'I hope we meet again.'

'That'd be nice,' Parker assured her.

Archibald was impatient for her to leave, and was

making it increasingly obvious. Now, he said, 'I'll be along after a while, Tina.'

Which meant don't come back, a message Tina understood. She rolled her eyes discreetly at Parker, and went away, and twitched just a little as she left.

Archibald said, 'Mr. Orr, sit down a minute, won't you?'

They sat on sofas at right angles to one another near the fireplace, toward which Archibald sent a fretful look, saying, 'I meant to call someone, have them lay a fire in there, but I just haven't had a minute to myself.' Smiling at Parker in amused self-pity, he said, 'I do think a fire cheers up a room, at any season. Don't you?'

'Sure.'

'What I wanted to talk about,' Archibald said, hunched forward slightly, becoming more confidential, 'is your job. You're a sort of undercover policeman, aren't you? But with the insurance company, not the regular police.'

'Something like that.'

'You have . . . contacts within the underworld, different from what the police might have.'

'I'm supposed to, anyway,' Parker said.

'People like you,' Archibald said, 'people in your position, they do moonlight, I believe, from time to time. Isn't that what it's called? To moonlight?'

'You mean collect from two bosses for the same work.'

'Well, slightly different work,' Archibald corrected him. 'Similar work. For instance, you're looking for this one man anyway, but my understanding is, there were at least three involved in the robbery at the stadium, and probably a fourth man to drive them away. When you catch the man you're looking for, and I have no doubt that you're very able at your job, that you will run this fellow to earth, but when you do, it's extremely unlikely he'll have all the money from that robbery on his person.'

'Very unlikely,' Parker agreed.

'If you could make it a part of your business,' Archibald said, looking Parker forthrightly in the eye, 'to retrieve the money stolen from me, whether it's in the possession of the man you're hunting or not, I'd be very appreciative.'

'Would you,' Parker said.

'I'd pay in cash, of course.'

'Uh huh.'

'And you ought to have— What do they call it in your business? A retainer?'

'That's one word,' Parker agreed.

'Let's say a thousand.' Getting to his feet, not waiting for an answer, Archibald turned toward the desk where he'd been on the phone before. Crossing to it, he said over his shoulder, 'Against, let us say, five percent of whatever you reclaim. That's a maximum of twenty-five thousand dollars, Mr. Orr, or just a little less.'

Parker got to his feet and watched. Archibald opened a drawer in the desk, took out a thick envelope that seemed to be full of cash, thumbed some bills out, and put the still-full envelope back in the drawer. Then he took up the bills he'd selected, slipped them into a hotel envelope, and came smiling back, envelope held out. 'An extra little blessing on your job,' he said. 'Shall we call it that?'

This was the first time Parker had ever been offered a bribe to help find the money he'd stolen. 'Let's call it that,' he said, and took the envelope and put it in his pocket.

NINE

Thorsen's office was converted from a normal hotel room. The wall-to-wall carpet showed indentations where the bed's wheels had been and the feet of the other furniture, all of which had been taken out and replaced by two desks, four office chairs and a number of telephones. The connecting door to the next room was slightly ajar; Parker guessed that was where Thorsen slept.

When he came in, Thorsen was at the desk nearer the window, just finishing a phone conversation. It didn't seem to be pleasing him. He said one or two brief things, and then he said, 'Thanks,' sounding sour, and hung up. 'Sit down,' he told Parker, gesturing toward the chair at the other desk. 'Your guy Liss got away.'

'Uh huh,' Parker said, and took the seat offered. Both desks were gray metal, basic models. The one he sat at had nothing on its surface, and probably nothing in its drawers.

Thorsen said, 'You don't sound surprised.'

'I'm not. How'd he do it? Is the other one still with him?'

'Quindero? Oh, yes. Calavecci is not a happy man.'

'Quindero,' Parker suggested, 'thinks he must be a desperate criminal, with nothing to lose.'

'And he isn't,' Thorsen said. 'But by the time this is over, he probably will be. Or dead.'

'How did Liss get out?'

'The hospital morgue is in the basement,' Thorsen told him. 'There's a special back way in, unobtrusive, from a side street, with a ramp, for the hearses from the different morticians. They don't like dead bodies and hearses around the front, gives the wrong image, looks like failure.'

Parker said, 'So the two of them went down there.'

'Where a body was being loaded. The hearse driver and a morgue attendant. I guess Liss didn't want to make too much noise, which was lucky for those two guys, because he just concussed them and tied them up. Then he and Quindero and the hearse – and the body, just to get even more people upset – went up the ramp and through a shit-poor roadblock there, and disappeared.'

'And now,' Parker said, 'Quindero has committed a felony.'

'He has, hasn't he? This mess is not getting neater,' Thorsen said. 'Did Archibald offer to pay you to find his cash?'

'A thousand now, one percent later.'

'Did you take it?'

'It was impolite not to,' Parker said.

'That's true. Excuse me,' Thorsen said, and turned away to one of his phones. He pressed four numbers, so it was a call inside the hotel. 'Okay,' he said, and hung up.

So it was going to be like that. Parker turned toward the slightly open connecting door, and in came four more of Thorsen's young troops, of the same standard issue: Dark suits, dark ties, dark shoes, white shirts, close-cropped hair, expressionless faces. They would do well at taking orders, and they would do well at giving orders, too. Parker smiled at them, then looked at Thorsen. 'And I thought we were getting along pretty good,' he said.

'Now, whoever you are,' Thorsen said, with no friendliness in it at all, 'let's hear your real story.'

TEN

What was it you didn't like about my story so far?'

'Everything,' Thorsen said. 'But to tell you the truth, and it's humiliating to say this, simple fuck that I am, I bought it for a while. Jack Orr, daredevil insurance spy.' He shook his head, discouraged with himself.

'Go on buying it,' Parker suggested. 'It's nice, and it's true, and it's the only story I've got.'

'We'll change your mind on that pretty quick,' Thorsen said.

The four young guys all shifted position and moved their shoulders around, like a herd that had just caught a whiff of something on the breeze. Parker looked at them, and then back at Thorsen, who said, 'Let me tell you when I finally got to singing in time with the chorus. It was when your friend Liss took a shot at you.'

'He knows who I am,' Parker pointed out. 'He knows I'm after him.'

'Everybody in that hall was after him,' Thorsen said. 'He didn't need to bust his own concentration to even some old scores. You said it yourself: He came there because Tom Carmody and the other robbers were the only people who could place him absolutely at the robbery, and he doesn't want anybody around who can do that. So he killed Tom, and the only other person he tried to kill was you.'

Parker grinned, as though Thorsen must either be kidding or crazy. 'Making me one of the heisters?'

'Heisters,' Thorsen echoed. 'That's a crook's word for it. We say robbers, or hitters.'

'Crooks are who I hang out with.'

'I'll tell you what happened,' Thorsen said, ignoring that. 'After the robbery, you all got split up somehow. One bunch spent the night in that gas station. Liss stole that police car and probably killed the poor cop. And you waited at the motel, until I showed up.'

'Wait a second,' Parker said. 'Am I a heister, am I a robber, or am I a guy waiting at the motel?'

'I figure the details have to come from you,' Thorsen told him.

Parker shook his head. 'It's your fairy tale,' he said, 'you'll have to fill it in yourself. George Liss takes one shot at the guy been chasing him eight months, and to you that means the guy's in on the heist.'

'That shot,' Thorsen said, 'made me start to think about something that had snagged me but I'd just let it go by. You know what that was?'

'You'll tell me,' Parker said.

'There's a lot of different words for the room that, when I was in the Marines, we called the head. There's the bathroom, the toilet, the lavatory, the washroom, the WC. The Irish call it the bog. I've been places they called it the cloakroom, don't ask me why. But one thing is constant and sure and solid and you could build your house on it: Nobody named John calls that room the john.'

Parker nodded. 'I think you're right about that.'

'So that isn't your name.'

164

'That's my joke,' Parker told him. 'My name is John Orr. Meaning, my name is John, or it isn't.'

'It isn't. You're one of the robbers. You and Liss had a falling-out.' Thorsen showed that thin smile again, thinner than ever. 'I think Liss makes a career out of having falling-outs with people. I think maybe he doesn't play well with others. What do you think?'

Parker said, 'Dwayne, I understand, the situation you're in, it can make you jumpy, paranoid. The story I told you is solid.'

'Then I'm gonna owe you an apology,' Thorsen said. 'But before I give you that apology, let's take a picture of you, and take your fingerprints, and ask the local law to check you out. And let's call your home office in— Where's Midwest Insurance located, by the way? I called our insurance guy in Memphis just now, and he never heard of it.'

'That's because he's in Memphis. He isn't in the midwest.'

Thorsen poised a hotel pen over a hotel notepad. 'Give me the phone number of your home office, and the name of your supervisor.' When Parker didn't say anything, he smiled again and said, 'And you might as well also give me the Reverend's thousand dollars, while you're at it.'

So this piece was played out. Parker glanced around at the four young guys standing there at parade rest, silent, watching, ready to do whatever they were told. He said, 'Are these guys armed?'

'You don't want to know,' Thorsen said.

'Oh, yes, I do. I've been without a gun for too long, I need one. I'm wondering, do I take that dinky thing of yours, or is one of these fellas better hipped?'

165

One of the youngsters spoke: 'We don't need to be armed,' he said, being tough.

Thorsen had put the pen down to stare at Parker. 'By God, you're sure of yourself,' he said.

'Why not,' Parker said, and rose from the desk. As he did so, he pulled the empty metal side drawer out of the desk and swung it around in a short quick arc into Thorsen's face.

ELEVEN

Always take out the brains first. Then you can deal with the hands and feet.

The four guys hadn't known it was going to play out like this. They'd thought their presence was supposed to keep trouble from happening. They were still working on their poses when Parker moved, so they were still reacting when Parker finished his first lunge, halfway across Thorsen's desk, Thorsen flying backward out of his chair, his face a red mess.

The return swing with the metal drawer caught the nearest young lion on the side of the head, and sent him reeling into number two, while Parker ran forward, the drawer held out in front of him like a battering ram, and caught number three as he was trying to duck away. One bottom corner of the drawer sliced his cheek as the other corner gouged his shoulder, and the whole drawer, Parker's momentum behind it, drove him straight back into the wall. He hit hard, crunched between the wall and Parker's weight on the drawer, and he dropped straight down when Parker let go of the drawer. The drawer and the man were both still falling when Parker spun around and kicked number four twice, first in the balls and then in the forehead as, in agony, he bent quickly down.

These four had trained in gyms, and knew a lot about

self-defense. They actually didn't have guns, and they'd never thought they would need such help. But they'd never been crowded into a small room before, getting in each other's way, with somebody who was trying to kill them and who didn't do any of the moves they'd learned about in gym.

Thorsen and numbers three and four were out of play. Number one, having been sideswiped with the drawer, was groggy but standing, and number two was moving in on Parker, hands splayed out, doing *all* the moves he'd learned.

Parker didn't have a lot of time. He didn't know how much noise he was making or who might be around to hear it. He didn't know when it would occur to one of these survivors to run the hell out of this room and go for help. He didn't know when it would be too late to get out of here, so he had to get out of here *now*, so he lunged in, ducked back, feinted for the balls, and sliced the edge of his left hand across number two's Adam's apple. Number two stopped, clutched his throat, made a strangled scream, and fell backward, trying desperately to breathe.

Number one, bleeding on the side of the head where the drawer had hit him, was getting less groggy by the second, but wasn't yet one hundred percent. He came in at Parker, arms in defensive position, looking to throw a punch, and Parker pointed at number two, on the floor, making terrible noises through his crushed throat: 'If I put you down, there won't be anybody around to get him breathing.'

Number one looked down and to his right, following the point of the finger and the sounds from his friend, and

Parker stepped in fast to clip the side of that jaw with his right elbow.

Forty seconds since he'd first reached for the drawer. They were all down. They were all out and silent except the one trying to breathe. Parker crossed to Thorsen, stripped off the coat, stripped off the very nice holster that was engineered to fit against the side without a strap across the body, and put it on himself, under his jacket. It would need some adjustment later, but it would do for now.

TWELVE

The hall was empty. Parker pulled the door to 1237 hard shut, to lock it, and walked at a steady pace toward the turn to the elevators. Behind him, way back at or near Archibald's suite, a door opened and closed, but he didn't look back.

The neat young guard was still in place on the wing chair facing the elevators. He nodded when Parker came around the corner, and put a finger in his missal to hold his place. Parker said, 'How you doin?'

'Fine, sir.'

Parker pushed the Down button and waited, but before it arrived someone else came walking around the corner. Christine Mackenzie. Dressed as before, but now with a simple gray hat and gray cloak as well, as though she were on her way to give alms to the poor. 'Well, hello,' she said, on seeing Parker, with a bigger smile than she'd permitted herself back in the suite. 'Fancy meeting you here,' as though she hadn't been watching Thorsen's office door, waiting for him to leave.

'How you doing?' Parker said.

'Well, I'm doing fine,' she told him. 'Since we have this unexpected stay here in this nice city, I believe I'm going to do some shopping.'

'Good idea.'

The elevator arrived. He gestured, and she boarded, and he boarded, and she pushed L. The young guard was back reading his missal again before the doors closed.

They were alone in the elevator. 'You should see the view on nine,' she said, and pushed that button.

Parker didn't have time for views, or anything else. A lot of people were going to be chasing after him in a few minutes. He said, 'Why's that better than the view on twelve?'

Here they were at nine already. 'They have a conference room here,' she said, holding the door open. 'Huge windows, all around. Come on and see, it's fabulous.'

It was easier to go along. 'Okay,' he said, following her out of the elevator. 'Show it to me.'

She giggled, a low contralto. 'I will,' she said.

He never thought about sex when he was working, but he was always hungry for it afterward. What situation was this he was in now? The heist was done, and yet it wasn't done. The job was finished, but it was still going on, with complications and trailing smoke. Was he going to have sex with this woman now, or not? He looked at her body, imperfectly hidden in somebody else's clothing, and it looked very good, but his mind kept filling with Liss, with Brenda and Mackey, with the duffel bags full of money; and now with Thorsen and Archibald and Calavecci and Quindero and who knew how many more. But still, it was a good body, walking along beside him here.

The conference room was at the opposite end on nine from Archibald's suite on twelve, so it was a view of a different quadrant of the city, but not that much different. Still, the room was large and airy and empty, with thick gray-green carpet and a large free-form conference table and some tan leatherette sofas along the inner wall.

'Come look,' she said, and when he went over to stand beside her she hooked her arm through his. 'I love the way the sunlight bounces off that roof,' she said, pointing with her free hand. 'See it?'

'Yes.'

She smiled at him, came close to laughing at him. 'You don't care much for views, do you?'

'Depends,' he said, and bit that swollen lower lip.

'Oo, careful,' she said. 'No marks.'

Beneath his hand, her breast was so firmly contained in place it might have been made of kapok. This wasn't going to work; she might as well be a sofa. 'Not a good idea,' he said, and backed away, disengaging her arm.

'You don't think so?' She stood by the window, facing him, letting the full light from outside make her argument.

Three floors up, they'd surely be making phone calls by now, and not all of them for a doctor. Parker said, 'Sometimes the time isn't the right time.'

'All times are the right time,' she corrected him, and slowly smiled. 'As the Bible says, Hope deferred maketh the heart sick.'

'That's the Bible?'

'I always do what the Bible tells me,' she said, and stretched, and smiled again. 'Come, let us take our fill of love, until the morning. It says that, too.'

She was a true pistol. He said, 'What about Archibald?'

She laughed at the idea that he cared about Archibald. 'Stolen waters are sweet,' she quoted, 'and bread eaten in secret is pleasant.'

172

'I'm sure it is,' Parker told her. 'And it'll be even better later. I'll take a rain check.'

The smile disappeared. The body snapped to attention. Behind the horn-rim glasses, the blue eyes flashed at him. 'Rain check? I'm not a *game*.'

That wasn't from the Bible.

PART FOUR

ONE

It was called Sherenden, and it was a house from the twenties, modern architecture of the time, designed by someone famous in his day and built at the edge of a ravine in what had then been the outskirts of town. On two steep acres of brush-covered rocky hill, at the end of a narrow winding road from the nearest city avenue, the house had been constructed of fieldstone and native woods and stainless steel, fitted into the broken shape of the landscape, with a large airy living room at the top, four windowed walls around a central black-stone fireplace. The rest of the house spread away beneath, for a total of four stories with an interior elevator, its shaft blasted into the rock.

The original owner was a lawyer, also famous in his day, and the bottom level of the house, enclosed by two jutting rock ledges of ravine, had been his study, with accompanying bath and small kitchen. From his desk in there he could look out through plate glass at the wildness of his ravine as though suspended from a balloon, and not see the slightest corner of the rest of the house.

When it was built, the place was considered daring and original and one of the templates that would describe the future. It was written up approvingly in newspapers and magazines of its day, and was still mentioned, with small black-and-white photos, in books on modern architecture.

Time had not been kind to the house. First there had been the divorce, as acrimonious as any divorce in the history of law, which had seen Sherenden fought over but unlived in for more than ten years. The winner, the ex-wife, had had no real use for the house but had wanted it out of spite, and had thereafter ignored it almost completely. Her heirs sold it as soon as they could.

Then there was the city, which had grown in ways and directions not expected by the town planners. This rocky area just within the city limits, full of inaccessible ravines, had seemed the least likely direction for the city to grow. But then, after World War Two, the interstate highway system was born, and an on-ramp was placed just outside the city line in this direction, and it suddenly made sense to knock down hills and fill ravines and put in working-class housing developments; a thousand homes from the same blueprint, girdling the two acres that contained Sherenden.

In the early sixties, one of the subsequent owners turned Sherenden into two apartments, by means of a lot of plywood and the removal of about half the original windows. (The elevator had ceased to function years before, and now became an additional closet on each level.) In the late seventies, another owner decided to restore the place to its former glory, despite the fact that the views from the living room were now of many small Monopoly-board houses stretching away toward infinity and the view from the bottom floor study was of the dump that had been made at the base of the ravine. However, he went bankrupt while the work was still under way, and so the plywood went back up, even more than before, sealing the house away.

The bank that took over at that point enclosed Sherenden with a tall wire fence, and waited. They were always on the verge of selling the two acres – nobody at the bank ever thought about the house itself, except as a problem – to someone who would demolish the 'existing structure' and level the land and put in eight houses, but the deals always fell through.

Kids and vagrants and drunks had made a sieve of the fence and a sty of the house. In the last decade, homeowners in Golden Heights and Oak Valley Ridge Estates, the neighboring development communities, had put forth a number of petitions against this eyesore in their midst, but the bank wouldn't tear the place down without a purchaser, and so the stalemate continued.

TWO

Parker took a cab to a shopping center, out away from the middle of town. He had lunch in a bar there – despite its fake Tiffany lamps, it was a bar – and watched the television up on its high shelf, full of excited local bulletins, one after another. A whole lot of stuff happening around here these days. The bartender thought it was probably the work of a private army, stocking up money and supplies for the revolution, and Parker said he thought the guy was right. The bartender had known after one look that Parker was a kindred spirit.

From the phone booth in the back of the bar, Parker called the Midway Motel and asked for Mr. or Mrs. Fawcett, and was told they'd checked out. No, the woman on the phone didn't know when they'd left, they were just gone. He asked to be connected to Mr. Grant's room, and let the phone ring in the black emptiness there for a good long time. The woman who'd switched him over never did come back to tell him his party wasn't answering and might be out and did he want to leave a message, so eventually he hung up.

Brenda had her compact, anyway. And Liss was probably not at the motel. Was he at the house, he and Quindero?

A city bus line ran past this shopping center and on out

to the developments by the interstate. Parker took it, at two-thirty that afternoon, a time when the passengers were a few schoolkids getting home early, some maids and cleaning women done with their day's work, and shoppers sitting slumped in the middle of their mounds of parcels.

Parker left the bus at the first corner in Oak Valley Ridge Estates and walked back down Oak Valley Ridge Avenue the way he'd come. In just over a hundred yards he got to the road leading in to the right. A pair of crumbling stone pillars, once graceful but now anemic, with bad rusted gouges at the top where the light fixtures had long ago been stolen, flanked a blacktop road that immediately curved down and away to the right, disappearing into a tangle of shrubs and trees. Wild rose vines knitted the underbrush together, interweaving their tough thorny stalks with the tamer junipers and maples, making it impossible for a human being to travel anywhere in there except on the road.

The road itself was receding back to nature. Frosts and rain had crumbled the blacktop, and weeds had grown through. Branches encroached from both sides, and closed completely over the top. Nothing here invited the passerby, and in fact the passerby was told to go away. PRIVATE PROPERTY NO ENTRY said the black letters on the yellow metal sign hung from the thick chain arced between the pillars. NO TRESPASSING said the black letters on the yellow plastic sign stapled to the pillar on the left, and DANGER KEEP OUT said the red and black letters on the white plastic sign stapled to the pillar on the right.

Parker slowed as he neared this welcome, waiting for two cars to finish going by. They did, and he stepped over the chain and walked briskly down the first curving slope.

He was now on the bank's two acres, an irregularly shaped parcel lying like a throw rug atop a lumpily unmade bed. The blacktop, almost disappearing in places, curved and climbed and dipped, covering nearly a quarter of a mile in what would have been much less distance in a straight flat line from entrance to house. Along the way, he saw nothing but shrubs and trees and vines, and at one point the faded blue trunk of a car that someone had years ago driven or pushed off the road into a deeper spot. The undergrowth grew up through the car, as though it weren't there.

In the old days, the first view of the house must have been something. You climbed a steep slope, came around a corner, and there in front of you was a wall of glass. Inside were the lights, and the graceful lines of the furniture, and the glow of the fireplace, and the confident movements of people. And beyond all that, seen through the house, was the view, already visible from here, of wild nature, tumbled scenery, and open sky.

Today there was the fence; that was the first thing. Eight feet high, chain link, it had one of its vertical metal support bars sunk into the middle of the road itself, to declare this no longer a road. Beyond the fence was the wall of plywood, darkened and discolored by time. It didn't look like a house any more. It didn't look like anything.

The fence had been snipped at the right edge of the roadway, as though for a prisoner-of-war escape, just enough to make it possible to push the flap of fence back out of the way and ease slowly through without ripping your clothes; though sometimes, to judge by the frayed threads on some of the sliced-off edges, clothes did get caught here.

Parker eased his way through, and moved to the right, over weedy ground that had once been lawn and had not yet been completely reclaimed by woods.

He'd been here before, with Mackey and Liss, when they'd been making ready for the job. It was Mackey who'd found the place, and researched it in architecture books in the library, and was as proud of it as if he'd designed it himself. 'Parker, it's a beauty. Nobody knows it's there, you got a million hiding places inside it, and it's right next to the entrance to the interstate!'

At first, Parker wasn't so sure. He had never liked places with only one entrance and exit. Given the situation with this house, once you were in it, the only way out was back that same road. On both sides of the house were woods that would eat you alive, and behind it was the ravine, too deep to get into and too steep to get out of, being very slowly filled as a town dump.

But Mackey was right about one thing: the house did have more than its share of hiding places for a few duffel bags. And they didn't intend to stay there at all, just drop the loot and go back to the motel. The idea was, if it so happened that any of them *was* made, or questioned, or shaken down by the cops, the swag would be nowhere near them.

So they'd gone through the house, Mackey leading the way, and it was Mackey who'd pointed out that there used to be an elevator in here where these closets were, and that its motor had been at the bottom of the shaft. The floors in all the closets that had been installed after the elevator car itself was removed and sold were plywood, and would pry up very easily. Mackey showed them how easy it would be to pry up the floor in the bottom-level closet, which revealed the old black motor, furred with dust on grease, leaving plenty of room for the duffel bags. It did mean lugging the bags down three flights of stairs and later back up again, but they would certainly be safe down in there for a few days.

If things had gone right.

Now Parker needed a place to lie low until tonight, when he could steal a car from the nearby development and go see if Brenda had caught up on her reading. At the moment, there were too many people looking for him, people who knew his face if nothing else about him. He had to give up the idea of settling with Liss until this whole operation was finished; unless Liss had also decided to hole up at the house.

Of course, the house still had its same disadvantage: one way in, one way out. But that could be an advantage, too. From inside the house, Parker could watch the road. If he saw anybody coming in, he might not be able to leave, but at least he'd know about them before they knew about him.

The loosened plywood, the new entry, was at the left corner of the house, near where the original front door had been. Parker looked over his shoulder, saw nothing, and eased inside.

THREE

The plywood sheathing made the interior dark, but cracks and spaces here and there provided some dim uneven light, in which Parker could see the truncated living room. A wall had been run across from front to back just beyond the fireplace, dividing the space in two, with the larger half out here. Later, the fireplace had been dismantled and covered over, leaving only a conical half dunce cap jutting for no apparent reason out of this new wall at chest height. The doors that had once been installed in the new wall were long gone. There was no furniture left in here, but rags and cans and bottles littered the floor.

The structure was still solid, having been built for a longer life than it was getting. When Parker crossed the living room, the floor neither squeaked nor sagged. He moved silently, a shadow in the shadows, to the nearer door in the new wall, which led to the kitchen that had been installed when this place became a duplex.

The kitchen equipment was now gone, leaving only holes in wall and floor with stubs of pipe where the plumbing had been. The elevator, on this level, had become a pantry, which now gaped open, doorless and empty. Near it was a spot where the outer sheathing of plywood didn't quite meet the original stainless steel corner post, leaving about an inch of unimpeded glass from top to bottom. Rain-streaked on the outside, the glass was still clear enough to see through, with the chain-link fence a silver grid in the afternoon sunlight out front, defining the location of the road.

Parker went over to that corner to lean close and look through, and saw nothing but the crowding woods and empty road. Then he stepped back, to study the glass itself, which was dusty and streaked all along here, its dirtiness hard to see because the plywood outside was flush against it. But the narrow band not covered by plywood was easier to look at, and just at eye level it had been roughly cleaned. The side of a hand, or maybe one of the rags from the floor here, had swept across the glass at just the right height for somebody to look out.

When was that done? Weeks ago, when Mackey first came to the place, before he brought Parker and Liss out? Earlier, or later, by somebody else completely, some vagrant or drunk just passing through? Or very recently?

Parker stood absolutely still for a long time, listening, alert, waiting. Facing the road as he was, he stood at the rear left side of the house, with the large living room making a C-shape to his right, around a central core. At his back was a wall separating this space from an interior coat-room and wet bar, its doorless doorway directly behind him. At the right end of that wall was the staircase, open to the living room up here, that went downward, flanked by interior walls, into the rear of the dining room one level below. To his left was the remnant of wall and the second smaller staircase that had been put in when the house was divided into two.

Not a sound in the house, nothing to be heard, not anywhere. Would he be able to hear people on the lower levels? Would they have heard him? The house was solid, even if very open, with these stairwells and open-plan rooms. What could be heard in here?

Very slowly his concentration shifted. There was still nothing to be heard, but he'd become aware of something else. Something very faintly in the air, something he could smell. Just a hint on the air, but it had to be very recent. A homely smell, almost a joke, but a warning.

Pizza.

FOUR

They're in here, Parker thought. Liss and Quindero. They would have seen me coming. Standing here, watching, eating the pizza they'd brought in. And now they're waiting. Liss didn't shoot, as I came in the door.

What are they waiting for? To see if Mackey is with me? No. To lead them to the money.

Parker stayed motionless. He seemed to be looking out at the fence and the road, but his attention was inward and behind him, and he was thinking. Liss had tried to kill him at the hospital, but was waiting now. Why? Because, at the hospital, for all Liss knew Parker had already been caught, and could be expected to trade Liss for lighter treatment for himself. But here and now, with Parker not in the hands of the law, and with the money not in Liss's hands, Liss wouldn't want to kill him. Not yet. Not until he had the duffel bags.

Where is he? Where's his new ball boy, the punk Quindero? Either he's hoping to stay out of sight and wait for me to leave, and then follow me to the money, meaning he's down a couple of flights right now, staying well out of the way, or he's close, in the room behind this one, wanting to make a move, waiting only to be sure I'm alone.

That was the way to play it. Liss hovering, just out of

sight, the way he did last night. Softly, not turning around, speaking in a conversational way as though the discussion had been going on for some time, Parker said, 'Well, George, here we are.'

Nothing. No response. Parker focused on the outside world, where nothing had changed. In the same easy tone, he said, 'Everybody makes mistakes. But then we move on.'

Still nothing. Maybe he really was alone in here, but he didn't believe it. 'George,' he said, 'we can go on making trouble for each other, but that way we both lose, and Ed Mackey takes home the whole jackpot. Or we can go back to the original idea, three guys, three splits.'

'What do I need you for?'

The voice was very faint, with that slur in it caused by the dead half of Liss's face. It came from well back, probably the doorway to the interior room. Parker didn't smile, but he relaxed, because he knew now everything would be all right. He'd kill Liss when the time came, and Brenda and Mackey would be waiting for him at eleven o'clock and all would be well. Still not turning, he said, 'George, you know what you need me for. Without me, you'll never see the money.'

'You know where it is?'

'Not now. I know where it's going to be.'

'When?'

'Twelve tonight.'

'Where?'

Parker shook his head, and smiled at the narrow view between the plywood and the stainless steel. 'George,' he said, 'why do you want me to lie to you?'

'We'll all go there together, is that the idea? At twelve?'

189

'All?'

'I've got a new partner.'

So Quindero was with him back there. Liss wouldn't call him a partner out of his hearing. Parker said, 'The kid from the hospital.'

'He's going to come over to you,' Liss said. 'He's going to frisk you. Don't turn around.'

Parker shrugged, with hands wide. Faint movement behind him was reflected in the glass in front, not clear enough to be of any use. He said, 'George, if you're holding a gun, put it away. I don't want to see it. We've got to get along if you're ever gonna see your share of the money.'

'Are you carrying?'

'Yes.'

'Here's my problem,' Liss's slurring voice said. 'Maybe I need you to get to the money. But if you know where it is, or where it's gonna be, why do you need me?'

That was the question. Parker had to finesse it and make it believable, or Liss would kill him here and now and try to figure out some other way to get to the money. The truth was, Parker needed Liss because Liss had a gun on him. Parker needed Liss only so long as Liss had the option to kill him. Parker needed Liss until they were back on an even footing. Then Parker would kill him.

Which was the thought he didn't want Liss to develop. He said, 'George, ever since you made that little mistake with the shotgun, we've both been looking over our shoulder. I need my concentration for other things, and so do you. We don't have to kill each other, and we don't have to lose out on the money. We team up again, we start new. Just until we get the money. Then you go your way and I go mine, and you know I won't work with you again.'

There was a long silence from behind him. Liss had to weigh it all, had to decide what was the likeliest thing to be the truth. But his judgment would be affected by the fact that he didn't know how to find the money and Parker did. That was why, at last, the slurring whispery voice said, 'I never heard you were a forgiving guy.'

'I'm not forgiving you, George. I know what a piece of shit you are. But I worked with a lot of guys over the years that I didn't want to see off the job. If I was only gonna work with gentlemen, I'd never work.'

Liss laughed. 'And isn't that the truth,' he said. 'All right, we'll try it your way for a while. But my partner's coming over there to take that gun off you. Or however many you have.'

'Not needed, George.'

'*I* need it, Parker,' Liss said, and for the first time the strain was in his voice. 'The other thing I could do, you know,' the strained voice said, 'I could gut-shoot you right now, and you'd still be able to lead me to the money later on but I wouldn't have to worry about you in between.'

'And if I went into shock?'

'I'd chance it.'

Liss might even do that, he was reckless enough. Parker didn't like giving up the gun he'd taken from Thorsen, but it was a risk he was going to have to accept. He said, 'One gun, George, on my left side, above the waist.'

'My partner's gonna pat you down.'

Parker shrugged.

Silence. Shuffling sounds. Panting in Parker's ear, and a hand that snaked around his chest, feeling for the gun.

Parker saw a scenario. He takes out this one with an elbow, spins around behind him, fires at the spot where Liss's voice had been coming from.

But Liss would know that scenario himself. By now, he would have moved to one of the two corners of the room back there. Parker would be firing at an empty doorway, and Liss would have an angle on him that the punk's body wouldn't shield.

The hand found Thorsen's gun, tugged it out. The panting breath receded. Hands patted his shins, his pockets, like being touched by a flock of passing bats. The hands missed anywhere he might have had a second gun, and then they left.

Parker said, 'George, when I turn around, I don't want to see your gun.'

A little pause. 'Fine,' slurred the voice.

Parker turned, and the Quindero kid was in the open doorway to the next room, his face full of exhausted panic, Thorsen's gun dangling from his right hand, barrel pointed downward. In the left corner of the room, just by the head of that open staircase downward, Liss stood, watchful, waiting. His hands were empty.

FIVE

One level down, there was more light because there was less plywood. This had originally been kitchen, dining room and maid's quarters, with bedrooms below that, and the owner's study at the bottom. With the conversion to the duplex, that fresh stairway had been cut in from the top floor to the maid's quarters, which then became the second bedroom of the upper apartment. The dining room down here became the living room of the lower apartment, with access via the original stairs, which were blocked off from the tenants up above.

The result was, this second level had been messed around with less. No new walls, no wholesale removal of windows. And, since below the top level access from without was very difficult on the ravine side, the windows down here had not been covered with plywood when the bank took over, and still showed the old view out over the ravine. From down here, in the original dining room, most of the development houses were invisible beyond the rim of the ravine, so you could look out and still see some of what had first attracted the site to the original owner and architect.

Squatters had lived in here from time to time. They'd pulled up the plywood that had been laid over the bathroom drains, so now you could use the space where the toilet had been as a toilet; but it was better to slide the plywood back over the hole when not in use. Some wooden boxes and old futons had been dragged down here by the onetime squatters as furniture. Nobody wanted to go near the futons, but the boxes made good chairs when placed against the wall.

Parker and Liss and the punk, Quindero, sat against three walls, Parker in the middle, facing the windows and the late afternoon view; sunlight on tumbled rocks and snarled woods, with the shadow of the building slowly creeping up the other side of the ravine. This place faced east, so the sunrise would look in on whoever was still here.

Liss sat to Parker's left, resting easy, legs out, back against the wall, hands in his lap with fingers curled upward. His eyes were hooded, and the active side of his face was almost as immobile as the frozen side. He was settled into a waiting mode, for as long as it took, patient, unmoving, a skill you learn on heists. Or in prison.

Ralph Quindero jittered to Parker's right. Nobody'd told him what to do with the little automatic, so it was on the floor between his feet, where his jittering made him bump into it with the sides of his shoes from time to time, each hit causing the automatic to scrape along the floor, each scrape sound making Quindero jump yet again. His hands twitched, moving from position to position, arms crossed, or hands resting on lap, or in pants pockets, or scratching his head and his arms and his knees. His eyes skittered back and forth, like a rodent, never looking at anything for long, bouncing every which way.

The stairway from above was just to Parker's left, a darker opening in this rear wall. The stairway down to the next level was along the right wall, between the windows and the jittering Quindero.

Did Liss count on this 'partner' of his? Did he think Ralph Quindero would be any damn use at all? If not, why keep him around?

They didn't have much to talk about, but after a while Liss roused himself and said, 'One thing.'

Parker looked at him.

The good half of Liss's face smiled a little. He turned his head enough to look at Parker, and said, 'What the hell were you doing in that hospital? You weren't after old Tom.'

'No. Not the way you were. You saw the guy gave me a shove.'

'Spoiled my aim.'

'That's him. He's Archibald's security man.'

Quindero, with his nervous whiny voice, unexpectedly joined the conversation: 'I remember him.'

They both ignored the interruption. Interested in what Parker had said, Liss raised the one eyebrow: 'Oh, yeah?'

Pointing, Parker said, 'That used to be his gun.'

'He gave it to you?'

'Not exactly. I went back to the motel, looking for Mackey—'

'They won't go back there,' Liss said, flat, with dismissive assurance.

'But they did,' Parker told him. 'Brenda and her cosmetics, remember?'

Liss didn't want to believe it. Gesturing at Quindero, he said, 'With these wild cards in the deck? The motel was spoiled, we all knew that.'

'Not later.' Parker shrugged. 'They went back, that's all,

and checked out. That's why I know where they'll be at midnight. George, you can call the motel yourself. Jack Grant's still registered, but the Fawcetts are gone.'

Liss thought that over, and decided he could believe Parker this time. 'Hell,' he said. 'I could have had them. I'd never have thought it.'

'While I was there,' Parker said, 'after Mackey and Brenda left and we made our arrangements, this guy Thorsen showed up, the security man. I told him I was an insurance investigator.'

Liss gave a little snort. 'You? Don't tell me he bought it.'

'For a while.'

'So the security guy's the one got you into the hospital. For the hell of it?'

'I wanted to talk to Carmody,' Parker said, 'only you got to him first.'

'What the hell you want to talk to old Tom about?'

'You.'

'What about me?'

'He was your parole guy. He might know people you knew, some way for me to track you down.'

Liss looked confused and irritable. 'Whadaya wanna track *me* down for? I didn't have the damn money.'

'I wanted to kill you,' Parker said.

Quindero jumped at that, the automatic scraping on the floor, but Liss laughed. Then he nodded a while, thinking that over, and when he looked again at Parker he said, 'You still want to kill me.'

'Not necessarily,' Parker told him. 'Not if we all get our money. Your new partner here gets his out of yours, you know.'

'Naturally,' Liss said.

Liss and Parker looked at one another with faint smiles, both knowing how unlikely it was that anybody would share with anybody, and how impossible that Quindero would come out of this with anything at all. Anything at all.

Liss thought some more, then said, 'You got any money on you?'

'A few bucks.'

'There's a deli about half a mile from here. We can send Ralph out for some more food. Another pizza. And sodas. Unless you want beer.'

Parker shook his head. As Liss knew, you didn't drink when you were working, and the both of them were working right now, very hard.

'Soda, then,' Liss said. 'You got a ten or a twenty?'

'You've got money, George.'

'I'll pay my share,' Liss assured him. 'And Ralph's, too, the poor bastard doesn't have a dime on him, the cops took it all. And his ID, and his shoelaces, and everything. Isn't that right, Ralph?'

'Uh huh,' Quindero said. He looked as though he suspected he was being made fun of, but knew better than to make an issue of it.

Parker took a twenty out of his wallet, and extended it toward Ralph, saying, 'You come over here to get it. Then you go over to George to get his. Leave that gun right where it is.'

Liss laughed. 'You gonna make a dash for it?'

'No,' Parker said.

Quindero looked at Liss, who told him, 'Do it that way, Ralph, it's fine.'

So Quindero got to his feet and came over to take

Parker's twenty, then crossed to Liss, who said, 'Lean down, Ralph, let me tell you especially what I want.'

Liss whispered to Quindero, while Parker watched the shadows inch up the opposite side of the ravine. Then Quindero started for the door, and Parker told him, 'George told you, call the motel, see did they really check out. Now, their name at the motel is Fawcett, be sure you get that right. And while you're at it, ask if Mr. Grant checked out, too.' Looking at Liss, he said, 'Because I didn't.'

Liss laughed. 'Shit, I was just hoping you'd lied to me. I mean, Parker, it's fine we're partners again and all that, but if it could turn out you don't know where that money is any more than I do, it would simplify my life, it really would.'

Parker said to Quindero, 'Be sure to make the call, and get the names right. George here is anxious to kill me, you know.'

Quindero threw frightened looks at both of them. He stood in the doorway, clutching the money in his right hand.

Liss said, 'Ralph. You know you'll come back.'

'Yes,' Quindero said.

'Because you got nowhere else to go,' Liss told him. 'I saved your ass, and I'll go on saving it. Just so long as you do what you're told.'

Parker said, 'Quindero. Have George describe his retirement plan some time.'

Liss laughed, but then he said, 'Parker, that isn't funny. Ralph is new at the game. Don't upset him.'

Parker looked out at the ravine again, and Liss made shooing motions at Quindero, who scurried away.

They were silent for almost five minutes, sitting against two walls at right angles to one another, resting, not seeming to look at one another. Then Parker said, 'What do you want him for, George? Besides to send for pizza.'

'To throw out of the sled,' Liss said.

SIX

It was unnatural to sit here like this. Parker needed Liss dead, and he knew Liss felt the same way about him, and they were both held back. Liss was held back because Parker was his only sure route to the duffel bags full of money, and Parker was held back because Liss had the gun.

After dark, Parker thought. A chance will come after dark.

The afternoon slowly descended outside, the sunny areas growing bright even as they narrowed, the shadows getting darker. The rock and the tangled underbrush out there would be full of creatures, wary, moving in sudden jumps, hidden away in the cat's cradle of vines and branches, living their lives with all senses alert. Darkness would be good for them, too.

Thorsen's gun was pale, standing out against the dark floor over next to the box where Quindero had been. Neither of them looked directly at it, but both knew it was there. Parker looked out the windows at the ravine and watched the light change. Liss didn't seem to look at anything.

Quindero was gone almost an hour, and when he came back he seemed more agitated than ever. He carried a brown paper shopping bag with handles, and when he came in he said, 'My picture's in the paper.'

They looked at him. Liss said, 'Is it a good picture, Ralph? Is it one you like?'

Parker said, 'Show me the paper.' And held his hand out.

Quindero dithered, not sure what to do, looking first at Parker, then at Liss.

Liss did his half-grin. 'You bought the paper, Ralph? Did you? For your scrapbook? Sure, go ahead, let Parker see it.'

Quindero put the bag on the floor, rooted in it, came out with a newspaper, handed it to Parker. Then he carried the bag over to Liss, to divvy up the food.

It was this city's one newspaper, full-size, not tabloid. It was heavy on the ads, heavy on the wire service reports, with just barely enough local staff to cover robbery, murder, arson and escapes all happening at once. Under the main headline:

WITNESS MURDERED IN
MEMORIAL HOSPITAL
Police Guard
Not Enough;
Killer Escapes

was an excited story about the events in the hospital, plus a recap of the robbery at the stadium, plus a lot of self-confident official pronouncements.

Three photos of equal size and importance ran horizontally under the main headline and next to the subhead and story. From left to right, they were the local police commissioner, Tom Carmody and Ralph Quindero. The newspaper couldn't have done a better job of taking attention away from Ralph Quindero's features if they'd decided not to run the picture at all.

The photo they'd used of Quindero was a black-and-white blowup of something from the family's collection, and it showed him in sunshine, full face, smiling and squinting, two things he wasn't likely to do for a while. When Parker looked at this picture and its placement, and then looked at Ralph Quindero, it seemed to him Quindero could probably walk through the newspaper's editorial department without anybody recognizing him.

Over next to Liss, Quindero squatted down and ripped up the paper bag into large irregular pieces to use as plates. On one of these, he brought Parker two slices of pizza, plus a can of some local bottler's cola. A bottle would have been more useful, but it didn't matter.

It was getting darker in here, hard to read, but once everybody was settled, with Quindero once again seated against the right wall, mouth full of pizza, Parker held the newspaper angled to catch the light from the windows and out loud read, 'Walter Malloy, the Quindero family attorney, issued a plea late this morning for fugitive Ralph Quindero to give himself up, saying, "There are no substantive charges against Ralph. At this point, the police merely want to talk to him as a witness. The longer he stays in hiding, the more he risks facing some sort of charge down the line." Police have announced a special telephone number for anyone with information on any aspect of the investigation.' Parker looked over at Quindero: 'You want the number?'

Quindero blinked a lot, staring back and forth between Parker and Liss. 'What does that— What do they *mean*?'

Parker said, 'Oley oley in free.'

Liss laughed, and looked at Quindero, and told him, 'It's a good thing we don't believe what we read in the newspapers, huh, Ralph?'

Quindero simply stared at him.

'Because, if you *did* believe that bullshit,' Liss went on, 'I'd have to kill you now. I can't have you go home and tell stories about me. But we don't believe it, so that's okay.'

Quindero said, 'We don't believe it?'

'Oh, come on, Ralph,' Liss said. 'That's the stuff they say every time. They'd say it to *me* if they could. Come on in, there's no problem, nobody's mad at you. Oh, okay, you say, I'm all right. And you go in, and the first thing, they slap the cuffs on you. You've had the cuffs on you, remember, Ralph?'

'I remember,' Quindero said.

'And that was *before* all this other stuff. Everything's okay and you should come in *now*? When back before old Tom got his, and you and I headed out of there, way back *then* they had the cuffs on you?'

'That's right,' Quindero said.

Liss looked at Parker, and shook his head. 'Parker, why do you want to upset my partner here? That's not a good thing to do.'

Parker looked at the top of the paper. 'It says there's a chance of rain tomorrow.'

'We don't care about that,' Liss said. 'We're long gone by then. One way or another.'

SEVEN

It's getting too dark in here,' Liss said.

They'd all been silent for a long while, Quindero brooding, Liss and Parker both waiting. But it was true; darkness had spread in this east-facing room, faster than outside, where the shadow across the way had not yet quite reached the rim of the ravine. Clear sunshine tinged with red made a kind of fire along the rim, a line of concentrated brightness, with the sky beyond it a deep blue turning gray. Inside, they could still see one another, but no one would be able to read the newspaper. Thorsen's gun no longer gleamed on the floor. And Liss wasn't happy.

Parker felt Liss's eyes on him, but didn't respond. He kept on watching the rim of the ravine out there. When the last of the sunshine left, there would be a sudden drop in reflected light into this room. Not a big change, not even very noticeable. But enough to make everything blur, everything out of focus, until their eyes could adjust. In that instant, Parker would go for Thorsen's gun.

But Liss was unhappy. 'Parker,' he said, 'I don't know about this.'

'What's the problem, George?'

'Same as always. You.'

Parker kept watching the rim. The sun moved very

slowly. 'Nothing's changed,' he said. 'We're all still like we were.'

'I don't want you loose when it's dark in here,' Liss said.

'Midnight doesn't come for a while, George.'

'Even if I had a flashlight, I couldn't use it,' Liss said. 'Not with all those windows. There's always some nosy son of a bitch with time on his hands to call the cops.'

'We've been doing fine up till now, George.' The light hung on the rim, golden red. The air was so clear you could see individual branches, fall shades of yellow and tan on the weeds and underbrush, turned Technicolor by the sun.

Liss abruptly stood. 'Ralph,' he said, 'put your foot on that gun.'

Parker didn't bother to watch Quindero obey. He also stood, watching Liss's hands, waiting for one of them to reach to a pocket or behind his back. 'George,' he said, 'don't fuck things up.'

'There's a closet,' Liss said. 'Ralph and me, we looked the place over when we first got here. Downstairs, next story down, there's a closet with a door on it and a lock on the outside.'

'George, you don't want me to—'

'It's that or I wound you,' Liss said. The strain was coming back into his voice. 'Maybe that'd be easier anyway. Don't have to gut-shoot you, I can take out both your knees, and Ralph can carry you when it's time to go.'

Quindero made a little startled sound, not quite a protest.

Parker said, 'Better have Ralph test that first. See how far he can carry me.'

Quindero stammered and said, 'I don't – I don't think I

could do that.' He was a reedy weedy thing, a poor specimen.

Liss had to know it, but he also had to protect himself. 'Goddamit, Parker,' he said. 'I want you out of the way, locked up, where I don't have to worry about you all the time. Eleven-thirty, we'll let you out, we'll all get out of here. Meantime, Ralph and me, we'll go get a car.'

'George—'

'We do it my way!'

Parker was silent, thinking. A closet till eleven-thirty? Half an hour after Brenda and Mackey would drive by the motel, and they surely wouldn't wait. But could a closet hold him that long? Liss and Quindero had to go get a car. He said, 'Make it eleven. It could take a while to get there.'

'Eleven,' Liss agreed. 'But I can't have you out here, Parker, you understand that. I'll have to shoot you, either to kill or wound. I can't have you around.'

'I'll wait, George,' Parker said. 'Where is this closet of yours?'

'Downstairs. Next flight down. You lead the way.'

The light hung on the rim of the ravine. Parker shrugged and turned toward the stairs. Behind him, Liss said, 'Ralph, bring along that fucking gun.'

EIGHT

It was darker down here, with all these interior walls separating off bedrooms and bathrooms, but Liss and Quindero were behind him, keeping their distance, and there was no advantage to be made of the darkness. Parker went down the stairs, and at the bottom, from behind him, Liss said, 'Around to the right,' which was the hall through the middle of the building.

Parker saw that the closet Liss was talking about was the one that used to be the elevator shaft. The lock was a hasp, with a wooden dowel stuck in it. Liss, still keeping well back, said, 'Take the dowel out. Hand it back to Ralph.'

Parker did that, and opened the door, and only a faint odor of dry wood came out. It was black inside there, impossible to see a thing.

Liss, sounding more and more nervous, said, 'What's the problem? Get in there.'

It wouldn't do to have Liss lose control; he was the one with the guns. Parker said, 'Take it easy, George. It's dark in here, I gotta feel my way.'

He took a step forward, reaching his arms out, and at first encountered nothing. The elevator, when it had been in place, had been deeper than wide, comfortable for two people, possible for three if they knew one another. Now that the space was a closet, the front half was empty, but when Parker stepped in deeper, his hands met the round horizontal wooden pole toward the back for hanging clothes on, and the wooden shelf above it. Both were empty, and so was the floor.

The pole and shelf were at head height, but there was plenty of room in front of them. Parker turned around to look out at Liss and Quindero, in the hall with the staircase behind them. 'All right, George,' he said. 'Go get your car.'

Liss said to Quindero, 'Shut it. Put the dowel in. Make sure it's goddam tight.'

Quindero came forward. His eyes met Parker's just before he shut the door, and they were full of panic. But he'd go on obeying Liss, because there wasn't one solitary other thing he could think of to do.

The door closed. In absolute darkness, he heard the dowel scrape into place. Then it sounded as though Quindero was pounding the dowel in tighter, probably with the butt of Thorsen's gun. Shoot his own elbow off, if he wasn't careful.

Late for Ralph Quindero to be careful.

Parker went down on the floor, pressing his cheek to the plywood floor and his head against the base of the door, his ear next to the space under the door. He heard Quindero back away, heard him say, 'It's good and tight.'

'Good.'

'Do we go get the car now?'

'No. When it's dark. Come on upstairs.'

The steps went away. Two pairs, receding down the hall, then mounting the stairs.

Parker sat up, rested his back against the plywood wall,

and crossed his forearms on his knees. His watch didn't glow in the dark, which was sometimes an advantage and sometimes not.

It didn't matter. He was better in here for now, not making Liss antsy. There was plenty of time to come out.

NINE

It was probably time. Parker had listened now and then at that space at the bottom of the door, but heard nothing, so Liss and Quindero weren't bothering to check on him in here. He'd seen the faint gray line of light under the door shadow and blur, until at last it disappeared into the general black. He'd gone on waiting, and now it was probably time to get out of here.

Did Liss understand what these closets were? Maybe not. They were afterthoughts, simple structures inserted to make use of the space. These closets were not structural, and therefore had none of the building's support beams going through their ceilings and floors. Simple stringers, two-by-six lengths of wood, had been toed into place to support plywood floors; that was it. And Ed Mackey had already showed them how to lift the floor in the bottom-level closet, to find the motor well for use as a hiding place for the duffel bags.

Parker went down on all fours and started in a front corner, patting the floor, looking for a seam. He found it where he expected it to be, about a foot and a half back from the doorway opening, the same place it had been downstairs. When they'd added these closets, they'd laid one sheet of plywood from the rear of the space to near the front, to give themselves leeway in fitting the piece in, and then they'd cut a second piece to fill the remaining space.

Next, he stood and felt his way to the back of the closet, where he patted the underpart of the shelf until he came to one of the two L-shaped brackets that the shelf rested on. It would have been easier if the shelf had just been placed there, but they'd screwed it to the brackets, so he stood under the shelf, bent down, kept out of the way of the wooden clothes pole, and punched upward with the heels of both hands, flanking one of the brackets, until the shelf broke loose.

When the shelf popped upward, with a quick ripping sound, one of the screws fell out and bounced on the floor. Parker paused, listening for a reaction. There'd been very little noise, but he couldn't be sure they hadn't heard it. If they were in the building.

After three or four minutes, when he still heard nothing, he went back to work, holding the shelf up out of the way with one hand while twisting the bracket back and forth with the other, until the screws holding it to the wall came loose. This part he managed to do with almost no noise at all.

Now he had the bracket for a tool. It was three inches along one side and four inches along the other, thin but strong metal. He put this to work on the floor, gouging along the seam line until he'd torn a slit wide enough to squeeze the bracket into. Kneeling on the larger section of floor, bearing down on the bracket, he pried the smaller section up one fraction at a time. Four screws had been drilled down into the corners of this piece, plus one each at front and back into the central stringer. It was the rear screw in the stringer that Parker pried out first, then the left corner, then the right. Then he could peel this piece up and back toward the door, until the other three screws gave way.

Now he had a space a foot and a half by five feet, with a two-by-six stringer across the middle and Sheetrock underneath. Using the bracket, Parker sliced through the Sheetrock a piece at a time, breaking the pieces off to bring them up into the closet and lay on the floor here, not wanting pieces of ceiling to fall and make a racket.

When he made the first hole in the Sheetrock, he saw gray light again, very dim, defining the jagged hole. There was no door on the ground floor closet, and whatever light was coming in the study windows reached back to here.

Parker removed chunks of ceiling, clearing the space, then slid down through the opening feet first. He had to wriggle his torso through the narrow opening, had to hold his arms over his head and at last just permit himself to drop.

He landed with knees bent, and let himself fall forward, hands hitting the floor, elbows flexing, allowing his body to drop to the left, until his shoulder hit the side wall of the closet. He stayed in that position, awkward, crouched on hands and knees, bent body leaning leftward, shoulder against wall, back to the open doorway. He listened, and waited, and heard nothing.

In silence, he shifted away from the wall. He put his left hand on the wall, and straightened. On his feet, he turned to look out across the stripped study at the angled row of windows, and they were bathed in blue-gray light. He moved toward them. There was stiffness to be worked out of his system, so as he crossed the study he moved his arms and shoulders, limbering up, feeling the sore points.

A half moon had risen above the ravine, and now looked down toward this side of the house. The newspaper had said it might rain by tomorrow, and there was just a hint of haze over the moon, but for right now it gave plenty of light. Maybe too much. Later it would climb above the house and give almost no light to the interior. And if the clouds came in, there'd be nothing but darkness inside here.

Parker moved slowly through the house, up through the levels, carrying the L bracket, his only weapon and tool. He searched the rooms as he went through, but they'd all been stripped, there was nothing left he could use.

And there was nobody here. The moonlight let him see his watch, and the time was nine-twenty. So Liss and Quindero must be out picking up a car. Parker needed them to come back soon, so he could finish this in time to meet Brenda and Mackey.

The dining room, where they'd waited out the afternoon, was very bright, being closer to the top of the ravine and with all those large windows facing right at the moon. Quindero had left his newspaper on the floor near the box where he'd been sitting, and the light was bright enough to read the headlines. If you held the paper close to a window and squinted, you could probably read everything in it, but there was nothing in there Parker needed to know.

He went on up to the top floor, and crossed to the spot in the rear corner where you could look out through the plywood sheathing at the road and the fence. The fence now gleamed silver, reflecting the moonlight, to make everything behind it a fuzzy blurry black.

Parker leaned against the wall and watched the road. He had come here to this house in the first place only because there were too many people in this town looking for him. He'd needed somewhere to lie low until it was time to go meet Brenda and Mackey, and this was the best place he knew. Finding Liss here had been an extra gift, a way to close the books on this job entirely, but if it wasn't going to work out it wasn't going to work out.

If Liss and Quindero didn't come back by ten, he'd have to leave, forget about them. Go meet with Brenda and Mackey, if they were there, and worry about dealing with Liss later.

Ten o'clock. Half an hour from now. Working the stiffness out of his shoulders and arms, Parker waited.

TEN

Nine-fifty. Light, moving through the woods.

Is he driving the car in here? Over *that* road?

But maybe it made sense. The road was almost nonexistent, but Liss might be more comfortable driving on it than having to walk back to the main road in total darkness. Particularly with Parker at his side.

Yes, here it came, very slowly. Some sort of four-door sedan. Liss drove with parking lights only, just enough amber illumination out front to give him a sense of where the road was. Now he swung the car to the left, just the other side of the fence, reversed, swung forward again, and backed up almost to the fence, facing out. Making it easier for himself for the return.

Liss hadn't removed the interior light. It flashed on as they got out of the car, and Parker saw that Liss had been driving and his new partner was still alive.

Parker moved into the shadows away from where they would enter the house. He could hear them talking as they neared it, and when they came through the break in the plywood he could make out the words. Liss was saying

'—trust him. He doesn't trust me, and he's right, and I don't trust him, and I'm right. If he can take us down, he will. Ralph, you listening?'

'Yes.' The voice was small, quavery, frightened, but determined.

'We gotta work together,' Liss said, 'or he'll kill us both. You hear what I'm saying?'

'Why don't we just leave him?' Quindero asked. 'Just walk away now and take the car and get away from here and just *leave* him down there.'

'I need the money,' Liss said. '*We* need the money, Ralph, you and me. Your half is two hundred grand, just keep thinking about that. You need that money, if you're gonna get to Canada, start over.'

So that's the fairy tale they're telling each other. Parker followed, well behind, as they went downstairs toward the dining room.

Liss said, 'We gotta keep him with us, and we gotta keep him alive, until we see if he really does know where the money is. Then we can deal with him. But before then, we gotta keep *him* from doing *us*. Jesus, it's bright in here.'

They were in the dining room now, Parker on the stairs behind them.

Quindero said, 'That's good, isn't it? If there's light, we can see him.'

'Here's what we're going to do,' Liss said. 'I'll wait here. You go down and— Wait. Where's that gun of his?'

'Here.'

'Give it to me,' Liss said. 'I don't want him taking it off you.'

'You want me to go down there without a gun? Where are *you* going to be?'

'Up here.'

'But—'

'Just listen,' Liss said, and Parker sat down on the stairs

216

to listen. Liss said, 'You go down there and take that piece of wood out of the lock. Do it quiet if you can. Then get back into some dark corner somewhere that he's not gonna see you, and then shout to him to come out. Then *I'll* shout from up here, and I'll tell him to come up. Then he'll come up and you'll come up behind him.'

'So he's in between us.'

'That's right,' Liss said.

Quindero said, 'But if I don't have a gun? What good is it if—'

'Does *he* know that? What if he sees you, and instead of coming upstairs he makes a jump for you? If you've got a gun, you're not gonna use it. So you show him your hands, you tell him you don't have any weapons on you, they're all up with me. He knows he has to come up past me before he can get out. And I'll call to him, I'll say, "Don't mess with my partner, I'm up here, come up." And he'll come up.'

Liss was explaining all this as though Quindero was a six-year-old, and he was probably right to play it that way. Another professional would already know most of what Liss was saying, but Ralph Quindero was not a professional.

And now Quindero said, 'Okay, he comes up here. And then what?'

'I'll move ahead of him,' Liss said. 'I'll go up those stairs over there, ahead of him, and we'll tell him to follow, and you come along behind. And we'll go out to the car that way, me always in front of him, you always behind him, so he can never get the both of us.'

'What if he jumps you?'

'I'll put one in his arm,' Liss said. 'It'll stop him, but it

217

won't kill him, and it won't put him into shock. Maybe I ought to do that anyway.'

Quindero said, 'Don't,' pleading.

Liss was amused. 'What, you don't like loud noises? Or is it blood you're afraid of?'

'We don't have to shoot him,' Quindero said. Now he sounded sullen.

Liss said, 'Haven't you been listening? Of *course* we have to shoot him, sooner or later. We have to shoot him dead. When we get there, wherever the money's supposed to be, we're gonna shoot him then.'

'Why? Why do we have to?'

'You want him behind you, the rest of your life?'

Quindero didn't say anything to that. They were shuffling around down there in the dining room, doing something Parker couldn't see, because he didn't want to descend the stairs far enough that he might be noticed, and then Liss said, 'Okay, go on down and let him out.'

Parker rose, silent, as he heard Quindero thump down the next flight of stairs. He eased downward, step by step, until he could see into the room, bluish gray in the moonlight, the boxes and trash throwing long black shadows across the gray floor. He looked left and right, and at first he didn't see Liss at all. Where was he?

Oh. Smart. Liss was seated on the floor directly under the windows, in the middle of that long wall. It was the one place in the room where he'd be hard to see, and he'd stay there until he was sure things were going right with Quindero.

But things wouldn't go right with Quindero. And where Liss had placed himself, Parker couldn't get at him. He'd never get across that large room without being seen, and shot.

'Hey! Mr. Parker! Come on out!'

Parker eased back up the stairs. He'd have to come at them in some other way.

It was too late now to get away from here. If he took the car, he wouldn't be able to drive it at better than a walking pace between here and the main road. Liss would have no trouble catching up. If he went on foot, Liss could get close enough to him with the car's headlights to bring him down.

He had to stay here, and finish it.

ELEVEN

When the house had been divided into two, the main staircase had been segregated from the top floor area by a new wall, but when the failed attempt had been made to restore the place to its original condition that extra wall had been removed, which meant Parker could now come up to the top floor, go to his left, and in the far corner find the additional set of stairs that had been added to give access to what had originally been the maid's quarters.

As he moved, he could hear them shouting back and forth:

'He's not coming out! He isn't coming out!'

'Ralph! Go over and open the door!'

'I don't want to!'

'Shit. Parker! Ralph doesn't have the gun, I do! Come on out of there!'

Construction materials were still scattered around, particularly up here where the duplex had been made and then unmade. Parker had earlier noticed a few scraps of plywood and other junk along the partition where the second staircase had been cut in, and now, while Liss and Quindero went on shouting at one another, he felt around in that rubbish, and came up with a stub of two-by-four about two feet long. He hefted it, and it wasn't very heavy, but it was the best he could find.

Carrying the two-by-four in his right hand and the L bracket in his left, he went quietly down the new stairs into the maid's quarters, and from there into the original kitchen. He was now one room away from Liss, who was yelling, 'Ralph! Dammit, open the door!'

Silence. Parker edged around the doorway between kitchen and dining room, and Liss hadn't moved, except to go up on one knee. But he was still in the same place, against the windows, unreachable.

'He isn't here! Jesus, I almost fell! There's a *hole* in the floor!'

'Parker!' Liss shouted, looking from doorway to doorway. 'Parker, dammit!'

'He's gone!'

'Ralph! Come up out of there!'

But still Liss wouldn't move away from that safe position against the outer wall. Parker could see his head framed against the window, now that he was up on one knee. He was turning left and right, watching everything. He was going to be hard to get at.

Watching him, Parker considered. What if he were to come out now, show himself to Liss, go back to the idea that they were all traveling together?

No. Not any more. Liss was too spooked by now. He *would* put a bullet into Parker, just to slow him down.

Quindero came clattering up the stairs. When he appeared, Liss at last got to his feet, still wary. Quindero hurried across to him, crying, 'He got away! He's gone!'

Quietly, Liss said, 'He's here.'

Quindero, bewildered, looked around at the moonlit room. 'What? But he escaped.'

'He's in the house,' Liss said, 'waiting his shot at us.'

'What are we going to do?'

'Pull those rags and shit into the middle of the room,' Liss told him. 'What we need is more light.'

'You mean a fire?'

'Then we go upstairs and wait. When he gets hot enough, he'll come up and visit.'

Parker watched them shift the trash to a low mound in the middle of the room. Liss used Quindero's newspaper to start the fire, then stood over it until a few rags and some scraps of wood also caught. Then, looking around, he called, 'Parker! Whatever you got in mind, it isn't gonna work. Come on out.'

Voice hushed, Quindero said, 'He must have heard us before, what we were talking. What we were gonna do.'

'Shut up, Ralph,' Liss said, almost absent-mindedly. 'We didn't say anything he didn't already know.' He now had his own pistol in his right hand, Thorsen's automatic in his left. 'Okay, it's burning,' he said. 'Time to go upstairs. You watch for him, in case he comes up over there. Let me get about halfway, and then follow me.'

'All right.'

Parker waited in the kitchen doorway, as Liss started up the stairs to the top floor, going almost immediately out of sight. Quindero stood staring at the stairs from below until Liss called down to him, 'Come on, Ralph.'

'I don't see him,' Quindero said.

'You will,' Liss said. 'Come on up.'

The instant Quindero turned toward the upper staircase, Parker came out from the kitchen. Moving fast, two-by-four cocked over his shoulder, he crossed the dining room, firelight throwing his shadows around the walls, and reached the staircase when Quindero was only up to the third step.

Liss yelled, 'Ralph! Down!'

But Quindero was too slow. He didn't drop, the way Liss wanted, but spun around, openmouthed, so the two-by-four, instead of hitting him in the back of the head, smacked into his left ear and cheek.

Liss fired anyway, and the slug punched into Quindero's right shoulder blade, spinning him farther around. Dazed, stunned, Quindero would have fallen, but Parker grabbed him with his left arm and held him as a shield, the way Liss had done in the hospital. The difference was, Liss didn't care about shields. He fired three more times, trying to hit Parker around Quindero or through him, he didn't care which.

Parker felt the impacts in Quindero's body, felt him go limp. His hand that held the L bracket pressed Quindero tight to him, and he backed hurriedly away from the stairs, dragging the body. In the middle of the room, he tossed Quindero across the small fire, hoping to smother it, or at least cut down on all that light.

Liss would come down, so Parker had to go up. Below here, there was only the one staircase, and he'd be trapped. On the top floor, where the glass was covered by plywood all around, there was almost no light. A two-by-four and an L bracket and darkness, that was what he had. Liss had two guns.

TWELVE

Parker eased off the stairs into the darkness of the top floor. He stopped, and listened, and heard nothing. Liss must be doing the same thing. But where? Had he gone down where the light is, to be safe? Or was he still up here?

He waited, hand against the partition wall, trying to see shapes in the dark. Ahead of him, where the main stairs would be, there was no light at all, but faint gray lines of light were visible at the periphery, where sheets of plywood didn't quite meet.

Very slowly, Parker moved to his right, along the partition wall. He meant to circle around until he was the other side of the main stairs. Then he could look down and see if Liss was framed against the light down there.

Two quick shots, in this room, echoing in the big open empty space. Then a third, from a different gun, that bit into the wall just to his left. In the flashes, Parker got an afterimage of Liss, at the head of the stairs, firing both guns. Then he realized what Liss was doing. He was firing his pistol just for the flashes of light, shooting it anywhere, not aiming at anything in particular, and then firing Thorsen's automatic at Parker when he had him fixed.

Parker crouched and hurried along the wall, and now there were two shots, one from each gun, and he heard one bullet whack into the wall above his head. Liss was closing with him. It was a good system, it was going to work, Liss firing one gun for the light, the other for the kill.

Parker stopped, stepped back the other way, and threw the two-by-four at the spot where the flashes had been. Then he ran forward, hearing Liss yell when the two-by-four hit, following that sound, seeing the flash very close when Liss fired again to use the light. The afterimage of Liss's staring face was with him as he launched himself low, under the second shot, and crashed into Liss's legs.

They went down in a tumble, Parker grabbing for anything he could find, Liss swinging with the gun in his right hand, Parker chopping with the L bracket. Liss screamed, and a gun went skittering away across the floor. Parker chopped and chopped with the L bracket, climbing up Liss as though he were a steep hill. Liss shrieked again, and kicked out, desperately, and rolled free.

Parker sat up and heard Liss tumble down the stairs. He went over onto hands and knees and scrambled to the head of the stairs, and saw the bulky shape of Liss crawl away across the dining room down there.

The fire on the floor was out, though from the smell it must have burned a little of Quindero before it died.

Parker sat still, trying to remember. He'd heard the rattle of one of the guns, spinning away across the floor. Which way? Not down the stairs. Left? Yes; over there, to the left.

He crawled in that direction, patting the floor. There was silence from below, but Liss wasn't done, not yet. Where was the gun? Where was it? Where was it?

Here. Parker touched it, picked it up. It was Thorsen's automatic. How many rounds were left in it? Three or four at most.

He'd hurt Liss, he knew that, but didn't know how

225

badly he was wounded. Was Liss still agile? Was he coming up the other stairs, or had he retreated to that position under the windows again? Or would he try to restart the fire?

Parker went on hands and knees back to the head of the stairs. He heard scuffling sounds from down below, but couldn't see Liss. He slid forward, and went slowly down the stairs head first, keeping his descent under control with his elbows on the steps. At the bottom, he looked over at the windows, but Liss wasn't there. He looked the other way, still saw nothing, and slid from the stairs down to the floor.

He had just started to rise, getting hands and knees under himself again, when Liss's head and arm and pistol appeared just above the stairs down to the next level. He'd been standing down there, just out of sight. He fired one shot, but Parker had dropped back to the floor when he heard the first sound of Liss's movement. The bullet hit the wall behind him, and lying there he twisted around to fire at Liss's retreating face, but missed.

He rolled away to his left, came upright, and Liss popped up again, aiming, firing.

They both heard the click.

Liss made a small strangled sound and dropped out of sight. Parker got to his feet and ran across the room and could just make out Liss's retreating shape at the foot of the stairs. He fired, but didn't hit anything, and Liss scurried away.

Parker went rapidly down the stairs. This level was the little maze of bedrooms and bathrooms, and the closet where they'd held him for a while. Standing at the foot of the stairs, Thorsen's automatic in his hand, he listened. Sooner or later, he'd have to hear Liss's breathing.

'Parker.'

Liss was off to the right, sounding as though he'd taken cover inside one of the rooms off this central hall. Parker turned in that direction, and waited.

'Parker, I'm hurt.'

Parker moved two quick quiet steps forward while Liss spoke, then stopped.

'I just want out of here. Parker? Take the car, do what you want. Call it quits. We can only mess each other up even more. Call it off.'

Parker moved when Liss spoke, stopped when he was silent. He'd reached the doorway now. Liss would be in the darkness just inside this room.

'Parker, why should we—? You son of a bitch, you're right *here*!'

There must have been some light behind Parker, that he'd now blocked with his body. Liss suddenly leaped at him, punching, kicking, trying to get past him. Parker pushed him off, to get a good shot, but Liss bounded away into the hall, and Parker fired after him, at all the noise he was making.

They both heard the click.

Silence. Parker reversed the automatic, gripping it by the barrel. What would Liss do now?

'Parker? Parker, listen, we're done, we're both done. Quit it. Neither of us has anything any more. Forget it, it's over.'

Parker had moved forward while Liss talked, and now he swung the butt of the automatic at the spot where the voice had come from. He hit something, something solid

that recoiled away. Liss yelled and retreated, and suddenly
he went thundering down the final flight of stairs, down to
the first owner's study.

Parker stood at the head of the stairs, listening to Liss
gasp and curse down there. Bottom of the house. No way
out.

Time to go down there and end it.

THIRTEEN

The moon was higher now, and only one narrow band of its light reached into the study, a stripe of silver-gray along the floor next to the windows. In that stripe Liss stood, panting, hunched, his right arm across his torso, protecting wounds.

Parker came down the stairs and stopped, still in darkness. Liss couldn't see him, but he looked across to where he knew Parker must be, and said, 'I'm all done, Parker. Leave me here.'

'I'm going to,' Parker said, and moved toward him.

Liss waved his left hand back and forth, as though to stop him. His breath was heavier and more ragged, his body hunched in tighter. 'Let it go!' he cried. 'You'll get the money, you'll get everything. Let it go.'

'If I leave you here,' Parker said, 'you'll rat me out, for a plea bargain.'

'Then take me along. Not to the money, just to get away from here.'

'I don't need you,' Parker said, and reached for him, and Liss came around hard with the knife he'd been concealing under his right hand and arm, pressed to his torso. A switchblade, with four inches of knife.

Parker jumped back, and the knife sliced shirt and skin just under his heart, scraping on bone. Parker kicked Liss's knee, but then had to retreat again as Liss swung the knife once more.

Parker still held the automatic by the barrel, but it wouldn't be any good as a club against that knife. He'd have to be in too close, and Liss could cut him up from farther out.

They moved in little jerks and pauses, back into the darkness, away from the band of light beneath the windows. The knife was a faint gleam, moving like a dowsing rod in Liss's hand, dowsing for blood.

Parker paused, and Liss lunged. Parker chopped the butt of the automatic at Liss's wrist, but only hit it a glancing blow, and then had to skip backward again.

They circled one another in the large room, slowly, with sudden dashes by Liss, trying to get that knife in among Parker's ribs. Parker dodged a dozen lunges, but Liss cut him twice more, and then again.

Parker's back was to the windows. There was nothing useful down here, no trash on the floor, nothing he could turn into a weapon. And Liss was crowding him closer, trying to get him into the corner of the room, the windows to his right, the solid wall to his left.

He couldn't let that happen, he couldn't let Liss corner him. He was still a few feet from the windows, there was still time. He feinted left, and then right, and then threw the automatic at Liss's head. He jumped in when Liss ducked, grabbed a double handful of shirtfront, and then rolled himself backward down onto the floor. His feet went up as he went down and back, his ankles catching Liss in the groin, lifting him up, the double grip on his shirtfront pulling him inexorably up and over, Liss swinging desperately back and forth with the knife, slicing

Parker's forearms as Parker heaved him up into the air and over in a midair somersault, and through the window behind him with a great shout of smashing glass.

Parker rolled quickly away from descending dishes of jagged glass. A scream rolled back into the window from the cool outer air, cut short.

Parker sat up. His chest and forearms stung where the knife had drawn its lines, and his body was sore all over, but he had no serious wounds. The dizziness he felt right now would soon pass.

Leaning forward, he put his watch into the moonlight, and forced his eyes to focus. Almost quarter past ten. Just time enough to make the meet with Brenda and Mackey.

Slowly he got to his feet, and looked around, at the ruined house and the gaping hole in the window. Then he went up the stairs.

CLICK

I'm getting bored,' Brenda said.

Ed kept on looking at the TV: CNN, multi-vehicle collision in fog on an interstate in California, blonde-haired woman solemn over her mike with ambulances in the background. He was waiting for the TV to tell him something new about events in this town right here, far from California and its fog. Outside this motel room, halfway around town from their first motel, the late afternoon sky was clear, visibility perfect. Inside, nobody on television, not local or network or cable, wanted to tell him what was happening *here*.

Brenda said, 'Ed? When are we getting out of here?'

'Late tonight,' Ed told her, pretending to be patient. 'You know why. You saw the TV.'

'California,' she said, and gave the television set a look of scorn.

'Come on, Brenda. Before.'

She knew, of course, he meant the business about Liss shooting up the local hospital, then taking off with some goon called Quindero that the cops wanted back unharmed for some reason. The law had been irritated already with just the robbery, but then you throw in Liss killing a guy the cops have under guard, right in front of them, and you could expect the locals were truly itching by now to get their hands on somebody. Anybody at all.

Which was the point Ed wanted to make. 'They're all over this town like a bad smell,' he said. 'We did enough running around here today. When it turns dark, I get us a nice little car, not flashy, nothing you look at twice, and *then* we clear out of here.'

They'd each been out of this room once since they'd checked in at this motel, Ed paying cash and using a driver's license for ID that had no history on it at all. First Ed had taken the most recent borrowed car back to the parking garage, to make their trail loop back on itself, and then he'd walked from there to a luggage store, where he'd bought three suitcases from a matched set and cabbed them back here, so they'd no longer be people with duffel bags. And then, a little after noon, Brenda had said, 'The hell with it, I want my stuff,' and over Ed's objections she'd cabbed back across town to their old motel.

She hadn't been completely careless, not at all. She'd left the cab two blocks from the motel, walked around the area, studied it, was very patient, and only when she was sure nobody had the place staked out did she go boldly back to their old room, where she packed up all her goods plus Ed's shaving kit and change of underwear. On her way out she noticed the woman in the office eyeballing her, so she went over there and checked out. 'The people in the room next to you,' the woman said, half-whispering, afraid the cockroaches might hear and pass it on, 'they had something to do with that big robbery.'

Brenda widened her eyes. 'They did?'

'Might have killed us all in our sleep,' the woman said.

'That's not much of a recommendation for your motel,' Brenda pointed out.

The woman lowered her eyebrows and hunched down over her counter. 'You can't be too careful,' she said.

'Words to live by,' Brenda agreed, and took another cab back to the new motel, where Ed hadn't moved, and CNN was showing distant explosions on a green mountainside. 'Piece of cake,' she said.

Ed kept his eyes on the screen. 'Everybody else,' he said, 'has a woman constantly nagging: "Be careful, be careful." I got a woman, *I'm* the one says be careful.'

'I was careful,' Brenda assured him. 'I didn't want you to see *me* on that TV.'

'Be nice to see something, though,' Ed said.

They saw something, at six o'clock, on the local news. They saw ambulances and stretchers and hundreds of official people, all in front of some big hotel downtown, behind an excited reporter yelling into his microphone about how one of the stadium robbers had posed as an insurance investigator until Reverend William Archibald's head of security unmasked him, when the robber damaged a whole lot of people and escaped. 'Huh,' Ed said. 'Parker's a woolly guy.'

'And all I did,' Brenda reminded him, 'was go back to the motel.'

'Well, Parker's far from here by now, anyway,' Ed suggested.

'And I wish I was,' Brenda told him.

'Patience. Later. Patience.'

The guy in the motel office had said there was a good Italian restaurant two blocks down to the left, so that's where they'd go, around eight o'clock, and pick up a car on the way back, and be on the road by ten. At quarter to eight, Brenda went into the bathroom to freshen up her makeup for the journey to the restaurant, and two minutes later she came out with a scrunched-up expression on her face and an open compact in her left palm. 'Ed,' she said. 'Take a look at this.'

He looked. 'It's dirty,' he said. 'The mirror's all streaked.'

'It's a message. Come here in the light.'

So he went back into the bathroom with her, where the light was brighter, and she said, 'Eleven P.M. See it?'

'Shit,' Ed said.

'He wants us to pick him up.'

Ed looked shifty. She could tell he didn't like this idea. 'He doesn't say where.'

'Come on, Ed. Back at the motel.'

'Not a chance,' Ed decided. 'You ready? Let's go eat.'

They fought about it through dinner, leaning toward one another over their plates, Brenda hissing while Ed muttered. The waiters thought it was a lovers' quarrel, and gave them space.

Ed had all the arguments, and all Brenda had was persistence. He said, 'We don't know who wrote that, even. It could have been George, and we walk right back into shit.'

'It's Parker, and you know it,' Brenda said. 'And he expects us.'

'If it was the other way around, he wouldn't come back for me, you can bet on it. And I wouldn't expect it.'

'It isn't the other way around,' Brenda said. 'You aren't him, you're you, and he knows we'll come back for him.'

'Then it's *you* he's counting on, not me.'

Brenda shrugged. 'Okay.'

'Brenda, he's got the whole fucking *state* looking for him, they've probably even got him by now. *And*, if they pick him up anywhere near that motel, they'll figure he was making a meet with us, and they'll wait, and we'll drive right into it.'

'He won't get caught,' Brenda said. 'He'll be there at eleven, and so will we.'

'He can't be sure we even got the message,' Ed insisted. 'That's a pretty weird delivery system.'

'I checked out of the room,' Brenda reminded him. 'He can find that out, and then he'll know I got my stuff.'

'We're not copping his goddam money, Brenda,' Ed told her. 'We'll call him in a week or two, make a meet, give him his half.'

'He wants to meet tonight,' Brenda said. 'So we'll be there.'

'*Why*, dammit? Why do a risk when we don't have to do a risk?'

'Because,' Brenda said, 'you'll meet him again. You'll work with him again. And he'll look at you, and what will he say? That's the stand-up guy came back for me? Or does he say, That's a guy I don't trust so much any more? What do you want him to say, Ed, next time you see each other?'

Ed leaned back, muttering to himself. After a minute, he shrugged, shook his head, and waved for the check.

The staff didn't think there was much hope for the relationship.

*

'I'll drive around the block twice,' Ed told her, as they neared the neighborhood, 'and if he doesn't show up, that's it.'

'He doesn't know the *car*, Ed.'

This was true. The car they had now was a black Honda from a side street near the restaurant where they'd had dinner. But Ed wasn't going to stop, and no argument. 'I'm not gonna be a sitting duck,' he said.

'There's a church, the next block, behind the motel,' Brenda told him. 'Drop me there, drive somewhere else, come back in five minutes.'

Ed clearly didn't like it, but Brenda wasn't going to change her mind, so he said, 'All right, five minutes. But if he isn't there, we go. We don't wait.'

'Naturally,' Brenda said. 'He put down eleven o'clock. He isn't there at eleven o'clock, we did our part, we go away.'

'Sense at last,' Ed said, and stopped in front of the church.

The quick way to the main road and the motel was through the small graveyard beside the church. Brenda went the long way around the block, and slowed as she approached the long brick motel building, with half a dozen cars parked at intervals in front of it. Traffic moved on the avenue, but she was the only pedestrian, and there were no cars parked along the curb. Come on, Parker, she thought, don't make me a dunce. I go back to Ed without you, he'll crow all the way to Baltimore.

She went past the motel office, walking slowly, just walking her dog, but without the dog, on this main traffic road where nobody walked. The office door opened and

237

closed behind her, and she thought, hell. Dammit, godda-mit, Ed, will you drive by now, please?

The voice behind her was smooth and non-threatening: 'Miss? Just a second. Miss?'

She turned, and the guy facing her was in plainclothes, but he was a cop, all right. Big and burly, with an open raincoat and that arrogant smile. She said, 'Yes?'

'Detective Lew Calavecci,' the burly man said, and flashed a badge from a leather folder. 'City police.'

Be polite, be a civilian, be not afraid. 'Yes?'

'Could I see some ID, Miss?'

Be a civilian, know your rights. Polite but firm, she said, 'Why?'

He grinned, suddenly changing, as though he'd just remembered a dirty joke. 'Come on now,' he said. 'I showed you mine, you show me yours.'

'Of course I could,' she said, wondering if a civilian would get indignant now, or scared, or what, 'but I don't see—'

'Yeah, you're it,' Detective Lew Calavecci said, and grinned all over his face.

Ed, where are you? Drive *by*, Ed. She said, 'It? What do you mean, it?'

'Three men and a woman,' Calavecci said. 'When we finally listened to those other clowns. And the woman came *back* here and checked out. Nobody expected that. You play a tough game.'

Indignant: 'I don't know what you—'

Calavecci brought handcuffs out of his raincoat pocket. 'Let's just see your wrists,' he said.

'But – I don't—'

'You could turn and run,' Calavecci told her, 'and I'd

238

wing you. I'd like that, relieve my feelings a little. Because I'm alone here, nobody could say it was excess force.'

'Detective, please, I don't—'

'I *need* you,' he said, with sudden passion. 'They relieved me, sent me home, but I can still make it all right. I've had a tough day, I lost some . . . But *this* makes up for it, I was right, I knew they'd come back. You'd come back. Put out your goddam *wrists*.'

'Lew!'

They both turned, and somebody was getting out of one of the cars parked nose-in along the front of the motel. 'Lew, let me talk to you,' he said, and straightened, and strode this way, and it was Parker.

Calavecci saw him, and his jaw dropped. 'You! By God, *you're* a dead man!'

Calavecci dropped the handcuffs to the ground in his hurry to get at the gun in his shoulder holster. Parker was still too far away, but coming fast. Brenda lifted a leg, pulled off her shoe, and did a roundhouse right with it, the heel digging into the side of Calavecci's neck, missing the main veins but almost giving him a tracheotomy.

Calavecci yelled, slapping her away, yanking the shoe out of his neck. He threw the bloody shoe at her, gasping loudly, blood pumping over his collar, and he reached for his gun again as Parker got to him and put him down with two quick movements.

Brenda hopped around on one leg, getting the shoe back on, while Parker went to one knee and took Calavecci's wallet, badge and gun. Straightening, he said, 'Where's Ed?'

Two cars had stopped out at the curb, wondering what

was going on with the guy on the ground. Brenda said, 'The church—'

Parker took her arm and hurried her away, back past the office, where the woman stood staring out, afraid to move. They went through the cemetery, dark and uneven but with just enough illumination from streetlights on both sides. Parker said, 'Church. He's praying?'

'Probably,' Brenda said.

As they came out to the next street, the Honda was just rolling down past the church. Brenda waved, and the Honda stopped, and they piled in, Brenda in front, Parker in back with the suitcases.

They drove down the street, and at the corner Ed turned right, away from the main road. 'We'll circle around,' he said. 'Then get out of here.' He glanced in the mirror at Parker in the back seat. 'You seen George?'

'Yes,' Parker said.

FLASHFIRE

ONE

1

When the dashboard clock read 2:40, Parker drove out of the drugstore parking lot and across the sunlit road to the convenience store/gas station. He stopped beside the pumps, the only car here, hit the button to pop the trunk lid, and got out of the car. A bright day in July, temperature in the low seventies, a moderate-sized town not two hundred miles from Omaha, a few shoppers driving past in both directions. A dozen blocks away, Melander and Carlson and Ross would be just entering the bank.

The car, a forgettable dark gray Honda Accord, took nine point seven two gallons of gasoline. The thin white surgical gloves he wore as he pumped the gas looked like pale skin.

When the tank was full, he screwed the gas cap back on and opened the trunk. Inside were some old rags and an empty glass one-point-seven-five-liter jug of Jim Beam bourbon. He filled the bottle with gasoline, then stuffed one of the rags into the top, lit the rag with a Zippo lighter, and heaved the bottle overhand through the plate-glass window of the convenience store. Then he got into the Honda and drove away, observing the speed limit.

2:47. Parker made the right turn onto Tulip Street. Back at the bank, Ross would be controlling the customers and employees, while Melander and Carlson loaded the black

3

plastic trash bags with cash. Farther downtown, the local fire company would be responding to the explosion and fire with two pumpers, big red beasts pushing out of their red brick firehouse like aggravated dinosaurs.

The white Bronco was against the curb where Parker had left it, in front of a house with a For Sale sign on the lawn and all the shades drawn. Parker pulled into the driveway there, left the Honda, and walked to the Bronco. At this point, Melander and Ross would have the bags of money by the door, the civilians all facedown on the floor behind the counter, while Carlson went for their car, their very special car, just around the corner.

When there's an important fire, the fire department responds with pumpers or hook and ladders, but also responds with the captain in his own vehicle, usually a station wagon or sports utility truck, painted the same cherry red as the fire engines, mounted with red flashing light and howling siren. Last night, Parker and the others had taken such a station wagon from a town a hundred miles from here, and now Carlson would be getting behind the wheel of it, waiting for the fire engines to race by.

Parker slid into the Bronco, peeled off the surgical gloves, and stuffed them into his pants pocket. Then he started the engine and drove two blocks closer to where he'd started, parking now in front of a weedy vacant lot. Near the bank, the fire engines would be screaming by, and Carlson would bring the station wagon out fast in their wake, stopping in front of the bank as Melander and Ross came running out with the full plastic bags.

Parker switched the scanner in the Bronco to the local police frequency and listened to all the official manpower in town ordered to the convenience store on the double. They'd all be coming now, fire engines, ambulances, police vehicles; and the fire captain's station wagon, its own siren screaming and red dome light spinning in hysterics.

2:53 by this new dashboard clock. It should be now. Parker looked in the rearview mirror, and the station wagon, as red as a firecracker in all this sunlight, came modestly around the corner back there, its lights and siren off.

Parker wasn't the driver; Carlson was. Leaving the Bronco engine on, he stepped out of it and went around to open the luggage door at the back, as the captain's car stopped beside him. A happy Melander in the back seat handed out four plastic bags bulging with paper, and Parker tossed them in the back. Then Carlson drove ahead to park in front of the Bronco while Parker shut the luggage door and got into the back seat, on the street side.

Ahead, the three were getting out of the captain's car, stripping off the black cowboy hats and long tan dusters and white surgical gloves they'd worn on the job, to make them all look alike for the eyewitnesses later. They tossed all that into the back seat of the station wagon, then came trotting this way. They were all grinning, like big kids. When the job goes right, everybody's up, everybody's young, everybody's a little giddy. When the job goes wrong, everybody's old and nobody's happy.

Carlson got behind the wheel, Melander beside him, Ross in back with Parker. Ross was a squirrelly short guy with skin like dry leather; when he grinned, like now, his face looked like a khaki road map. 'We havin' fun yet?' he asked, and Carlson put the Bronco in gear.

Parker said, as they drove deeper into town, 'I guess everything went okay in there.'

'You'd have thought,' Carlson told him, 'they'd rehearsed it.'

5

Melander, a brawny guy with a large head piled with wavy black hair, twisted around in his seat to grin back at Parker and say, 'Move away from the alarm; they move away from the alarm. Put your hands on your head; they put their hands on their heads.'

Carlson, with a quick glance at Parker in the rearview mirror, said, 'Facedown on the floor; guess what?'

Ross finished, 'We didn't even have to say, "Simon says."'

Carlson took the right onto Hyacinth. It looked like just another residential cross street, but where all the others stopped at or before the city line, this one went on to become a county route through farmland that eventually linked up with a state road that soon after that met an interstate. By the time the law back in town finished sorting out the fire from the robbery, trying to guess which way the bandits had gone, the Bronco would be doing seventy, headed east.

Like most drivers, Carlson was skinny. He was also a little edgy-looking, with jug ears. Grinning again at Parker in the mirror, he said, 'That was some campfire you lit.'

'It attracted attention,' Parker agreed.

Ross, his big smile aimed at the backs of the heads in front of him, said, 'Boyd? Hal? Are we happy?' Melander twisted around again. 'Sure,' he said, and Carlson said, 'Tell him.'

Parker said, 'Tell him? Tell me?' What was wrong here? His piece was inside his shirt, but this was a bad position to operate from. 'Tell me what?' he said, thinking, Carlson would have to be taken out first. The driver.

But Ross wasn't acting like he was a threat; none of them were. His smile still big, Ross said, 'We had to know if we were gonna get along with you. And we had to know if you were gonna get along with us. But now we all think it's okay, if you think it's okay. So what I'm gonna do is tell you about the job.'

Parker looked at him. 'We just did the job,' he said.

'Not that,' Ross said, dismissing the bank job with a wave of the hand. 'That wasn't the job. You know what that was? That was the *financing* for the job.'

'The *job*,' Melander added, 'the real job, is not nickel-dime. Not like this.'

'The real job,' Ross said, 'is worthy of our talents.' Parker looked from one to another. He didn't know these people. Was this something, or was it smoke and mirrors? Was this what Hurley had almost but not quite mentioned? 'I think,' he said, 'you ought to tell me about the job.'

2

It had started with a phone call, through a cutout. Parker returned the call from a pay phone and recognized Tom Hurley's voice when he said, 'You busy?'

'Not in particular,' Parker said. 'How's the wing?' Because the last time they'd been together, in a town called Tyler, Hurley had wound up shot in the arm and had been taken out of the action by a friend of his named Dalesia.

Hurley laughed, not as though he was amused but as though he was angry. 'Fucked me a little,' he said. 'I feel it in cold weather.'

'Stay where it's warm.'

'That's what I'm doing. In fact, that's why I'm calling.'

Parker waited. After a little dead air, Hurley did his laugh again and said, 'You never were much for small talk.'

Parker waited. After a shorter pause, Hurley cleared his throat and said, 'It's a thing with some people I don't think you know.'

'I know you.'

'Well, that's just it, I won't be there. If you want it, you're taking my place.'

'Why?'

'I got a better something come up, offshore. I'm fixing to be a beachcomber. A rich beachcomber.'

'Because of the arm,' Parker suggested.

'That, too,' Hurley agreed. 'These three are good boys.

8

They know how to count at the end of the day, you know what I mean.'

Parker knew what he meant; they wouldn't try to hog it all, at the end of the day. He said, 'Why don't I know them? They civilians?'

'No, they just work different places, different people, you know how it is. But then, it could pan out with them, and then you know them, and who knows.'

'Who knows what?'

'What happens next,' Hurley said.

Letting that go, Parker said, 'Where are they now?'

'They move around, like people do,' Hurley told him. 'Lately, they're based around the Northwest somewhere, or maybe Vancouver. Over there someplace.'

'Is that where this thing is?'

'No, they like to work away from home.' So did Parker. He said, 'Not around me.'

'No, in the Midwest, one of those flat states out there. I told them about you. If you're interested I'll give you a number.'

So one thing led to another, and here he was in the back of the Bronco with Melander and Carlson and Ross, and after all he was going to be told the who-knows that Hurley hadn't wanted to talk about.

3

'It's jewelry,' Ross said.

Parker wasn't impressed. 'That's a dime on the dollar, if you're lucky.'

'That's right,' Ross said, 'that's what we'll get.'

Melander said, 'We got three buyers, ready to go. That's what they all give us.'

Parker said, 'Three?'

'There's too much for one fence,' Ross explained.

Parker was beginning to get interested. 'What are we talking about here?'

Carlson steered them up onto the interstate ramp as Ross said, 'Four of us will walk home—'

'Ride home,' Melander corrected him. 'In a limo.'

'Right,' Ross agreed. 'Four of us will ride home with three hundred grand apiece.'

Parker looked from Ross to Melander and back.

They both seemed serious, if happy. Nobody in the car was taking any mood changers. He said, 'This is twelve million in jewelry?'

'That's the floor,' Ross said. 'That's the appraisal. It's a charity sale. If we let it alone, it'll go higher, but what we'll get is the floor.'

'A charity sale. Where?'

'Palm Beach,' Ross said.

Parker shook his head. 'Deal me out.'

Ross said, 'You don't want to listen to the job?'

'I just heard the job,' Parker told him. 'Twelve million in jewelry all in one place draws a lot of attention. Cops, private cops, guards, sentries, probably dogs, definitely helicopters, metal-detecting machines, all of that. Then you put it in Palm Beach, which has more police per square inch than anywhere else on earth. They're *all* rich in Palm Beach, and they all want to stay that way. And besides that, it's an island, with three narrow bridges, they can seal that place like it's shrink-wrap.'

'All of this is true,' Ross said. 'But we got a way in, and we got a way at, and we got a way out.'

'Then I still know the job,' Parker told him, 'and I still don't want it.'

Melander said, 'Just out of curiosity, why?'

'Because to even think about doing your job,' Parker told him, 'and to do it in Palm Beach, there's two things you got to have. One is the insider, who's the amateur, who's gonna bring you down. And the other is a boat, which is the only way off the island, and which is even worse than an island, because there's no way off a boat.'

Ross said, 'That's yes and no. We got the insider, that's true, but he's *before* the job. He's nowhere near Palm Beach on the day, and he's not exactly an amateur.'

Melander said, 'He's one of our buyers, we worked with him before.'

'What he is,' Ross said, 'he's an art appraiser, estate appraiser, he tells you what the paintings are worth, what the rugs are worth, what the jewelry is worth, for the taxes and the heirs.'

Keeping his eyes on the road, Carlson said, 'He has a little trouble with nose powder, so he needs extra money. But he doesn't let it make him a problem, at least not for us.'

11

'What his occupation is,' Melander said, 'he spends his life casing the joint.'

'Then he tips off you guys,' Parker said.

'Right.'

'And then you go in and take out the best stuff. And how long before somebody notices, when this guy does the appraisal, step two is a robbery?'

'We don't do it that way,' Ross told him. 'Our agreement is, we never touch a thing until at least two years after he's been and gone. And this time, the Palm Beach, he wasn't one of the appraisers.'

'He gets access to the appraisals,' Melander added, 'like anybody else in the business.'

'He's done other stuff in Palm Beach,' Ross said, 'so he knows the place, he knows the routine, he knows everything about it, but he isn't one of the people that looked at this particular bunch of jewels.'

Melander said, 'He's moved in that territory, but on different estates, different evaluations.'

'If they're looking for an insider,' Ross said, 'they won't look at him, because he wasn't inside.'

'Possibly,' Parker said. 'What about the boat?'

'No boat,' Melander assured him. 'I a hundred percent agree with you about boats.'

'Then how do you get off the island?'

'We don't,' Ross said.

'You stay there? Where? You know, you rent a condominium, the cops are gonna look at recent rentals.'

'Not a condominium,' Ross said.

'Then where?'

'At my place,' Melander said, and grinned like a bear.

Parker tried to see around corners, but couldn't, not quite. 'You've got a place there?'

'It's fifteen rooms,' Melander told him, 'on the beach. I think you'll like it.'

'You've got a fifteen-room mansion on the beach in Palm Beach,' Parker said. 'How does this happen?'

'Well, I looked at it a few weeks ago,' Melander said.

'But he's just buying it today,' Ross said. 'We got the down payment from that bank back there.'

4

The motel, and the car Parker would be using, was in Evansville. When they got there, while Melander and Ross counted the money on the bed, Carlson and Parker sat in the room's two chairs, across the round table from one another, and Carlson told him more. 'The mansion is cheap. I mean, for a mansion in Palm Beach.'

'Why?'

'It was sold maybe eight years ago to this movie star couple, you know, he's a star and she's a star, so when they make a picture, he gets twenty million, she gets ten million—'

From the bed, Melander said, 'Still not equal pay, you see that?'

Carlson and Parker both ignored him, Carlson saying, 'They bought the place, they thought they'd be stars in Palm Beach, but Palm Beach ignored them. They're stars, but they're trash, and in Palm Beach you can't be trash. Or, if you are trash, you hide it, and you spread your money around.'

'Charities,' Melander said.

'They love charities in Palm Beach,' Carlson agreed. 'But these stars didn't do it right. They thought they were already entitled. They threw big flashy parties, they brought in *rock bands*, for Christ's sake, and nobody came.'

'Well, a lot of people went to those parties,' Ross said.

14

Carlson said, 'Not the right people. Also, the parties were playing hell with the house, messing it up. Then the stars went away to be stars someplace else—'

'Where stars are looked up to,' Melander said.

'So the house was abandoned,' Carlson said, 'and the alarm systems would break down all the time, and bums would sneak in there from the beach, and they had a couple little fires, and the cops finally said, we can't keep a man on this house twenty-four hours a day, you got to put in your own security patrol, and the stars said fuck it, and put it on the market.'

Laughing, Melander said, 'A fixer-upper for sale in Palm Beach. A do-it-yourselfer.'

'These stars couldn't do anything right,' Carlson said. 'If *they* do the fix-up, they make a lot more money when they sell the place. But they're not interested, they're off somewheres else, and the house sits there until Boyd comes along.'

Melander got off the bed and took a stance, shoulders squared, big body relaxed, big smile, big wavy hair framing his head. He said, in a strong Texas accent, 'I do like this little town you got here, I'd like to contribute if I could, make it even better. I like that ocean you got, you know, it's bigger than the Gulf, I like the idea of that whole ocean out there and then Europe on the other side, not Mexico. Not that I have anything against Mexicans, hardworking little fellas, most of them.'

Melander sat down to the money again while a grinning Carlson said to Parker, 'Boyd can fit right in. And with all that oil money in his family, he'll fix up that mansion good as new. Better. And when he's got the house all done, he wants to host the big library benefit there.'

Parker nodded. 'All right, he can be plausible,' he said.

Carlson looked pleased. 'So you're in?'

'No,' Parker said.

All three were disappointed, gazing at him as though he'd let them down in some unexpected way. Carlson said, 'Could I ask why?'

'You've got a place to stay,' Parker said. 'If I ask, you'll tell me how the mansion won't trace back to any of you after it's all over.'

'Sure,' Carlson said.

'But that isn't the job,' Parker told him. 'That's nothing but the safe house. The job is still a whole lot of jewelry, twelve million dollars' worth of jewelry, completely surrounded by people with weapons who don't want you to get your hands on it. From this idea today – blow up something a little farther out of town as a distraction – I can see you guys like to be gaudy. That's fine, fires and explosions have their place, but I think you mean to be gaudy in Palm Beach, and it won't work out for you any better than it did for the movie stars.'

Carlson wanted to say something, but Parker held up his hand. 'Don't tell me,' he said. 'I'm not in this, so I don't want to know what the plan is, and you don't *want* me to know.'

The three of them looked at one another. Parker watched them, waiting to see what his move should be, but nobody seemed ready to offer any threat. At last, Carlson said, 'How's the count coming?'

'Done,' Ross said. 'Eighty-five and change.'

'That's short,' Carlson said.

Mclander said, 'Well, we knew it could be.' Carlson turned back to Parker. 'The down payment on the place is a hundred grand. It was higher, but Boyd haggled them down to that, but that's it, rock bottom. Two days from

16

now, this cash here is gonna be an electronic impulse out of a bank in Austin, but it isn't enough. As it is, we're gonna have to borrow black to top it up.'

Parker waited.

From the bed, Ross said, 'You see how it is. We gotta borrow fifteen, that means we gotta pay back thirty. Man, if we give you your' – he consulted a slip of paper on the bed in front of himself – 'twenty-one thousand three hundred nineteen bucks, we're gonna have to borrow almost forty, that's a payback eighty, that begins to cut in.'

'Also,' Carlson said, being very reasonable about it all, 'we still need a fourth man, the way we got it set up, so *somebody* has to get that fourth share. That's why we want it to be you.'

'No,' Parker said.

Again they looked at one another, and again Parker waited for them to make a move, but again it didn't happen. Melander simply said, 'He isn't gonna change his mind.'

'Well, that's a bitch,' Carlson said.

Melander said, 'We knew it could happen.'

'Still.'

Meanwhile, Ross was counting out a little stack of money onto the bed while Carlson got to his feet and crossed over to the closet. Opening the closet door, he pulled out two of the three suitcases in there, leaving Parker's. Ross got off the bed and came over to hand the little stack of cash to Parker, saying, 'Sorry it didn't work out. We'll catch up with you later.'

Parker looked at the money, and it wasn't enough, no-where near enough. He said, 'What's this?'

'Ten percent,' Ross told him. 'Just over two grand. When we're done in Palm, you'll get the full amount, so this is like interest on the loan.'

17

'I'm not loaning you anything,' Parker said.

Melander and Carlson were stuffing the rest of the cash into the two suitcases. Melander said, 'I'm afraid you got to, pal. You don't have a choice, and we don't have a choice.'

Ross showed Parker a pistol but didn't exactly point it at him. 'You shouldn't stand up,' he said, 'and you shouldn't move your hands off the table.'

Parker said, 'Tom Hurley told me you guys weren't hijackers.'

'We aren't hijackers,' Ross said with simple sincerity. 'You'll get your money. The job goes down two months from now, and then the money's yours. With interest.'

Melander said, 'Pal, I'm sorry we got to act this way, but what's our choice? We thought you'd come in with us, and then everything'd be fine. I'm sorry you feel the way you do, but there it is.'

Carlson said, 'You can count on us to pay you. I never stiffed another mechanic in my life.'

You're stiffing me now, Parker thought, but what was the point talking?

The three exchanged glances, as though they thought there might be something more to say, and then Melander turned to Parker and spread his hands: 'You know where we're going.'

'Palm Beach.'

'If we were hijackers, we'd kill you now.'

The only thing to do, Parker thought, and waited.

Carlson said, 'But that isn't our style.'

Then you're dead, Parker thought, and waited.

Melander said, 'It's just, we'd like you to stay at home the next couple months. We'll phone you sometimes, we'd like to know you're there.'

18

Parker shrugged. There was nothing to say to these people.

Apparently, they now themselves thought they'd said enough. They moved toward the door, Ross putting the pistol away, and left, not looking back at him.

Parker sat there, hands palm-down on the table, little stack of bills between his hands. His money was gone, about to become an electronic impulse in Texas. This wasn't what it was supposed to be, and it wasn't what it was going to be.

He got to his feet, and crossed to the phone, and called Claire, at the house up in New Jersey. When she answered, without identifying himself he said, 'You remember that hotel with the shark scare,' meaning a place they'd stayed once in Miami Beach.

'Yes.'

'Go there for a couple months, I'll call you.'

'Now?'

'You can wait a couple days, till the phone rings, but don't answer,' he said, and hung up.

5

He was starting from Evansville, and he had two months to get to Palm Beach. In that time, there would be preparations to make, and preparations cost money. So what he had to do, most of the time, for the next month and a half, was collect money.

Cash is harder to find than it used to be. There are no cash payrolls. Stadium box offices, travel agents, department stores, all deal mostly in credit cards. An armored car can't be taken down by one man working alone. A bank can be taken by a single-O, but all he gets is what's in one teller's cage, which isn't enough for the risk. So it's hard to find cash, in useful amounts. But it isn't impossible.

What he had, including the 'interest' his three former partners had given him, was a little over three thousand dollars in cash. The car he was driving, a tan Ford Taurus with Oklahoma plates, was clean enough for a traffic stop, not clean enough for an in-depth study of the paperwork. Clipped under the dash of the Taurus, to the right of the steering wheel column, was a .38 Special Colt Cobra, while under his shirt on the left side, in a narrow suede holster, was a Hi-Standard snub-nose Sentinel .22, useless unless the target is within arm's reach. He also had a few changes of clothing of utilitarian type, to make him look like somebody who works with his hands, and that was it.

What he needed first was better guns, then more money, then better clothing and luggage, then better wheels. He needed to change his appearance, too, not for the three guys he was going to kill but for the Palm Beach police; he needed to be somebody who wouldn't make the law look twice.

Melander had paid for this motel room with a credit card that would probably self-destruct by tomorrow, so the first thing to do was get out of here. Parker carried his bag, lighter than it should have been, out to the Taurus. Five minutes later he was on Interstate 164, headed south into Kentucky.

Throughout the South, there are more gun stores out along the state highways than there are in downtowns or shopping malls, and there's a number of reasons for that. The stores need good parking areas, they don't want to have to deal with antsy neighbors or troublesome landlords or the wrong kind of pedestrian traffic, and most of their customers are rural rather than urban.

So the stores are in the country, but they aren't countrified. They have first-rate security, with solid locks, burglar alarms wired to the nearest state police barracks, shatterproof glass in their display windows, iron bars, and some even have motion sensors.

Parker chose a place called 'A-Betta-Deala – GUNS,' mostly because it didn't have a dog. It was a broad onestory building beside a state road in central Kentucky, with its name in red letters on a huge white sign on the roof. Flanking the barred and gated double front doors were two wide display windows on either side, three of them featuring rifles and shotguns, the fourth showing handguns.

Two and a quarter miles to the south of the gun shop

21

was the garage and storage lot of the County Highway Department, and four miles beyond that was the nearest state police barracks. Parker left the Taurus at the side of A-Betta-Deala at quarter after three in the morning, where it wouldn't be readily noticed from the road. Then he walked the two and a quarter miles south along the hilly, curvy road through mostly scrub forest. The four times he saw headlights coming, he stepped off the road into the trees until the vehicle went past.

There was much less security at the Highway Department garage; just a bolted chain to keep closed the two sides of the chain-link gate. First putting on the surgical gloves, Parker climbed over the gate and found his way in the darkness to a yellow Caterpillar backhoe with a four-foot-wide bucket. Briefly using his pencil flash, he found the number painted on the side of the cab, then went over to the garage. The side door had a simple lock and no alarm system; he went through it, and used the pencil flash to find the locked plywood cabinet on the wall where the keys were kept. A nearby shovel made a good lever; he popped the cabinet door open and found the backhoe key. He also picked up a yellow hard hat to wear, to look legitimate, then went back outside.

The backhoe was loud but powerful. He had to back it out of its parking space, and it went *ping ping ping* until he shifted into Drive. Then he swung it around, extended the bucket, rotated it so the open part was facing rearward, and drove it through the locked gate.

The machine's top speed was around twenty miles an hour, and it didn't like to do that much on curves. It took eleven minutes to drive back north to A-Betta-Deala. In that time, one pickup passed, headed south, loud country music trailing from its open windows.

There were no headlights visible up or down the road when Parker reached the gun shop. Without pausing, he angled the bucket with the maw forward and down, then drove directly into the window displaying the handguns. He rotated the bucket, scooping up the window and everything in it, then backed away from the building while the backhoe pinged some more. Clear of the building, which was now screaming a high-pitched alarm wail, he rotated the bucket to spill everything onto the blacktop parking lot, then shut off the backhoe's motor, took off the hard hat, climbed down from the cab, and picked through the rubble, shining the pencil flash. He chose four pistols, went away to the Taurus, put the handguns under a motel blanket on the back seat, stripped off the gloves, and drove north, away from the gun shop, the Highway Department garage, and the state police.

6

Six days later, in Nashville, at eight-thirty in the morning, Parker sat in the Taurus on Orange Street, across the way and up the block from AAAAcme Check Cashing. The place wasn't open yet, so all that showed on the ground floor of the narrow three-story building, one of a row of similar structures along here, was the gray metal of the articulated grille that was drawn down over the facade at night. Once that was raised, the storefront was merely a small-windowed metal door in the middle of a brick wall, with a small wide window high on each side, both windows containing red neon signs that said 'Checks Cashed.'

This was Parker's fourth morning here, and he now was sure of AAAAcme's opening routine. The business hours of the place were nine A.M. to six P.M., Monday through Saturday. At about eight forty-five every morning, a red Jeep Cherokee would pull up to the store with two men in the front seat. The driver, a bulky guy in a windbreaker no matter how warm the weather, suggesting a bullet-proof vest underneath, would get out of the Cherokee, look carefully around, and cross to unlock and lift the metal grille. Then he'd unlock and open the front door, and stand holding it open, looking up and down the street. The other man, also bulky and in a windbreaker, would get out of the Jeep, open its rear door, take out two heavy metal boxes with metal handles on the tops, and trudge

24

them across the sidewalk and into the store. The first man would let the door close, then go back to the Jeep, shut the rear door his partner had left open, and drive half a block to a private parking lot reserved for the bailsmen, pawnshop owners, used musical instrument dealers, liquor store owners, dentists, and passport photographers who ran businesses in the neighborhood. After parking the Jeep in its labeled spot, he'd walk back to the store, knock, and be let in. Fifteen minutes later they'd open for business.

This was more of a late-night than an early-morning neighborhood. There was almost no traffic at this time of day, rarely a pedestrian until mid-morning. The three days Parker'd watched, AAAAcme hadn't had a customer before nine-thirty, so their opening time must be merely a long-standing habit.

This morning, the routine was the same as ever. Seeing the Cherokee approach in his rearview mirror, Parker got out of the Taurus, made a show of locking it, and walked down the street toward AAAAcme. The Cherokee passed him and stopped at the curb, and he walked by between Cherokee and storefront. He continued to walk, pacing himself to the normal speed of their movements behind him, and the Cherokee passed him again just before he got to the entrance of the parking lot.

Today he was dressed in a gray sweatshirt over black chinos. The Sentinel was in the right pants pocket, and a Colt.45 from Kentucky was tucked into the front of the chinos under the sweatshirt. Turning in at the entrance to the parking lot, he put his hand in his right pocket.

The driver was getting out of the Cherokee. He gave Parker an incurious look, turned to lock the Cherokee, and Parker stepped rapidly toward him, taking the Sentinel out of his pocket, holding it straight-armed in front of

25

himself, aiming as he moved. He fired once, and the .22 cartridge punched through the meat of the driver's left leg, halfway between knee and hip, then went on to crack into the door panel of the Cherokee, leaving a starred black dent.

The driver sagged, astonished, falling against the Cherokee, staring over his shoulder at Parker: 'What? What?'

Parker stepped very close, showing him the Sentinel.

'I shot you,' he said. 'The vest doesn't cover the leg. It doesn't cover the eye, either. You want one in the eye?'

'Who the fuck are *you*?' The driver was in shock, the blood drained from his face. He pawed at his left leg.

Parker held the Sentinel close to his face. 'Answer me.'

'What'd I do to you? I don't even know you!'

'I'm robbing you,' Parker told him.

'Jesus! You want my – oh, my God!' he cried, staring at his blood-red hand. 'For a fucking *wallet*?'

'The store,' Parker said. 'We'll go there, and we'll go in together.'

'My partner—'

'Will do what you tell him. You do right, in a few minutes you're on your way to the hospital. You do wrong, in a few minutes you're on your way to the morgue.'

The driver panted, trying to catch up, get his wits about him. 'They'll get you, you know,' he said.

'So don't sweat it,' Parker told him. 'It's only money, you're insured, and they'll get me. Let's go.'

'I can't walk.'

'Then you're no good to me,' Parker said, and brought the Sentinel up to his face again.

'I'll try!'

He could walk, with a limp. He kept looking at his red

26

hand, in disbelief. 'This is crazy,' he said. 'You don't just shoot people.'

'Yes, I do,' Parker said. 'What's your name?'

The driver blinked at him, bewildered again. 'What?'

'Your name.'

'Bancroft. Why, what's—'

'Your first name.'

'Jack. John – Jack, people call me Jack.'

'Okay, Jack. What's your partner's name?'

'First?'

'First.'

'Oliver.'

'Ollie?'

'No, he's no Ollie, he's Oliver.'

They were approaching the shopfront. Parker said, 'Tell him, "I'm shot, this man helped." Nothing else. Show him your hand.'

Jack nodded. He was panting pretty badly, limping more. His face was still ashen.

As they reached the shopfront, Parker put the Sentinel away and took out the Colt. Jack knocked on the glass in the door, and it was opened partway by Oliver, who stopped abruptly with the door less than a foot open when he saw Parker. He said, 'Jack?'

Jack held up his red hand. 'I was shot, Oliver, this man helped.' He gestured at his leg.

'What?' Oliver looked at Jack's trouser leg, now wet with blood. 'Jesus Christ!'

Oliver backed away, and Jack limped in, Parker following, shutting the door behind himself, pushing Jack to one side, showing Oliver the Colt. 'Oliver, don't move,' he said.

Oliver looked tough and angry, but he hadn't been shot. 'You son of a bitch, you—'

27

He was starting to make a move when Jack called, 'He knows about the vests!'

Oliver stopped, frowning at his partner.

'That's right,' Parker said. 'Your chest is safe from me. Oliver, help Jack to lie on the floor, facedown.' Oliver hesitated. Jack said, 'Oliver, I'm hurting. Get this over with, let the cops have it.'

Oliver nodded. He told Parker, 'They'll get you, you know.'

'Jack already told me. Move, Oliver.'

Oliver helped Jack to lie facedown on the linoleum floor in front of the counter. The counter was stained wood panel, chest-high, with bulletproof Lucite above and small openings where checks and cash could be passed through. A windowless gray metal door was at one end of the counter, to give access to the rear.

When both men were facedown on the floor, arms behind them, Parker put the Colt away and took from his back pocket a small roll of duct tape. He taped their wrists and ankles, Oliver first, then got Jack's keys from his pocket. He made sure he had the right key to get back into the shop, and left to walk up the block toward the Taurus.

There was still almost no morning traffic around here. Parker drove the Taurus down to AAAAcme, went back inside, and found Oliver and Jack where he'd left them. Jack was breathing like a whale. When he heard Parker move around, he said, 'Willya call 911, for chrissake?'

'Somebody will,' Parker told him, and went through the metal door to the rear part of the shop, where the two metal cases stood unopened on the floor. He lifted their lids and found the stacks of bills he'd expected.

Looking around, he saw an open safe, which Oliver

must have just unlocked for the start of the day. Inside were more stacks of bills, and on top of the safe was a lockable gray canvas money sack. Parker put the bills from the safe in the sack, then opened the cash drawers under this side of the counter, and found more bills. There was change, too, which he left.

The two boxes and the sack were now full. Parker carried everything through to the front door. Oliver kept twisting around to glare at him, but Jack merely lay there, eyes closed, cheek on the floor, mouth open, wheezing.

It took two trips to get everything from the store to the Taurus. Parker propped the store door slightly open, so the first customer would be able to get inside and find Oliver and Jack and make that 911 call, and then, at seven minutes to nine, he drove away, looking for the signs to Interstate 65.

In this part of Memphis, integration was complete. There were as many white junkies in this neighborhood as there were black. A number of old-fashioned drunks wandered around here, too, and that's what Parker was passing himself off as.

For nine days, while getting to know this territory, he'd been living in a small bare room in a moth-eaten residence hotel, blending in with the misfits and losers, paying cash, one day at a time. The Taurus, with most of AAAAcme's thirty-seven thousand dollars in the door panels, was stashed in the long-term-parking lot out at Memphis International. Parker kept a bottle of fortified wine sticking out of his hip pocket, and sat around on the sidewalks with the other boozers, though he wasn't the friendly type. He was the sort that kept to himself.

The problem with snooping in a neighborhood like this is not that people will think you're a heister, but that they'll think you're a cop. Whatever might be going on at higher levels, at the street level the cops around here were on the job, not on the take. The drug dealers had lookouts to warn them when legal trouble was near, and all at once the bazaars would disappear, into alleys and doorways and the back seats of rusted-out cars.

If these people were to decide that Parker was undercover, marking them, they would be determined not to let him live. But he needed to be curious, he needed to trail them, identify them, he needed to follow the money.

It was the scarcity of cash again. AAAAcme had been fine, very easy, but he couldn't keep doing that. If he cut a swath of check-cashing heists across the Southeast, the law would scoop him up before he had anywhere near the amount of money he needed. Every job had to be different, in order to lay no trails, leave no patterns. He didn't want anybody even to think there might be one man out there, doing his work, aiming at something.

So here he was, living on the street in Memphis, letting his beard grow, looking and acting like a stumblebum drunk. It was drug money he wanted now. The dealers are swimming in cash; they concentrate it on and around their persons. But they're constantly getting ripped off, sometimes killed, because that much cash attracts attention, and because everybody knows a robbed drug dealer isn't going to complain to the law. So they're not easy to get at.

On these streets, it seemed as though there were as many dealers as users, and while the dealers are mostly young and combined the cocky with the furtive, the users came in all kinds, from twitching hobos handing over wrinkled dollar bills they've just panhandled to men in suits driving into the neighborhood in Lotuses and Lexuses, pausing for a conversation out a window and an exchange of package for cash.

But it wasn't the street dealers Parker was interested in, not money at that level. What he wanted was higher.

The last nine days, he'd started to work out the delivery system. There were two cars he'd marked, one a black TransAm with fire streaks painted on the hood, the other a silver Blazer with Yosemite Sam brandishing his revolvers

31

on the spare wheel cover. Each would come around two or three times a night, starting and stopping, and the dealers would come out of their holes, and this time the exchange of package for cash would be in reverse: money into the car, package out.

There were at least three people in each of those cars, and Parker was sure there were others as well, scouts who moved ahead of the deliveryman and trailed along behind, looking for law, looking for trouble. Some of the scouts carried walkie-talkies, and all of them were suspicious of every single thing they saw, stumblebum drunks included.

It was the Blazer he started following, on the ninth night, moving away from the area where he'd been hanging out, shuffling six blocks to where he'd seen the Blazer turn onto a side street, then going one block down that side street.

This was a somewhat better neighborhood, but at eleven-thirty at night he didn't look totally out of place. He sat on the sidewalk, back against the front wall of a closed drugstore, and half an hour later the Blazer went by, not moving too fast. Parker watched it, and it ran at least a dozen blocks in a straight line before it went over a small ridge and disappeared.

Different neighborhood; different style from now on. Parker shuffled back to his fleabag, shaved everything but the mustache, which hardly existed yet, and dressed in somewhat better clothes; good enough to hail a cab. Then he packed everything into the small dirty canvas sports bag he'd bought at a pawnshop, left the hotel, walked half a mile, and caught a cab out to Memphis International. Collecting the Taurus, he checked into an airport hotel and paid cash for one night. After room-service dinner and a long shower, he felt more like himself.

The next afternoon, he checked into a motel closer to the city, paying cash for one night. At eleven, he drove into Memphis and parked where he'd last seen the Blazer.

It went by him at twenty after twelve, and kept the straight line for another eight blocks before turning left. When it was out of sight, he started after it, expecting it to be gone and ready to come back to the next post tomorrow night, but when he turned that corner the Blazer was parked at the curb, two and a half blocks away.

He drove slowly by. There was only the driver in the car, and he watched Parker, blank-faced. The Blazer had stopped at a storefront church, its windows blocked with white paper on which was printed outsize biblical quotations. A bright light was over the door, and benches on the sidewalk in front of the windows, and half a dozen hard men on the benches, watching everything; at the moment, watching Parker. He kept going and drove back to the motel.

He set the alarm for five, got up then moved out of that room, found an all-night diner for breakfast, then drove back to park in the block before the storefront church, which was now dark, the benches in front of it empty.

There was a service at seven-thirty, the congregation mostly old women who had trouble walking, then nothing happened until a little after eleven, when a dark blue Ford Econoline van stopped at the church. A big man got out on the passenger side, looking in every direction at once, and walked into the church.

A minute later he was back out, to open the sliding door of the van. A second man came out after him, carrying two pretty full black trash bags. They were heaved into the van, the second man went back into the church, and the first one slid the door shut. He got in on the passenger side, and the van drove off.

For the next three days, Parker leapfrogged the van, the way he'd done with the Blazer. Every night he checked into a different motel, paying cash for one night. Then, the fourth day, he watched the van drive into the basement garage under a downtown office building. It was a commercial garage, open to the public, so he drove in after it, collecting his ticket at the barrier, seeing the van stopped near the elevators. When he drove by, the passenger was on a cell phone. So these people didn't carry the cash up; someone up there would come down and get it. Probably in something more upscale than trash bags.

There were no parking places free on the first level. He spiraled down to the second, found a spot, left the Taurus, and went over to take the elevator up to the lobby. He stood there by the sidewalk, as though waiting for someone, and watched the display lights on the elevator bank. Three elevators were going up. None went to the first parking level for the next five minutes, so the exchange had already been made while he was parking the Taurus. He took the elevator down to the first level himself, and the van was gone. He walked on down to the Taurus.

The next day, he was there early, standing on the sidewalk in front of the building when the van drove in. He walked into the lobby, waited there, and in a minute saw an elevator descend to the first parking level. It held there for a minute while Parker crossed to the elevators and pushed UP.

The elevator arrived, and Parker boarded. Already in there were two white men in suits and a large black wheeled suitcase. The 9 button was lit; Parker pushed 11.

As they rode up, he watched the numbers light above the door. When 7 came on, he took out the Sentinel and

34

shot the nearer man in the arm, then pushed him into the other. 'It isn't your money,' he said, holding the gun high for them to see, and they stared at him, shocked, too startled to know what to do, both of them still in the process of realizing that one of them had been shot.

Parker waited for the door to slide open at 9. If they had a third guy up here, in the hall, he'd have no choice but to kill them, but he'd prefer not to. Death draws more police heat than wounding.

The ninth-floor hall was empty. Parker pushed DOOR CLOSE, and the unwounded man said, 'Do you know who owns this money?'

'Me,' Parker said.

The man said, 'They'll stuff your nuts in your mouth, and they'll make you watch your children die.'

'I can hardly wait,' Parker said, and the door opened at 11. 'Bring that,' he said, gesturing with the Sentinel at the wheeled suitcase.

They came out into the hall, the wounded one holding his arm and watching Parker with a wary look, the other one pulling the suitcase and watching for his chance to make a move.

The hall was empty. A sign said the stairs were to the left. Parker said, 'You know I don't want to kill you, or you'd be dead already, but you know I will if I have to. You both have pieces under your coats, and you'll leave them there. Let's walk to the stairs.'

They walked to the stairs. A sign on the door there said 'No Reentry.' In checking the building this morning, Parker had noticed that security arrangement. In case of fire, people could get to the staircase on every floor of the building, but only the door at the lobby level would open from the staircase side.

He'd also looked at the company names on the building directory in the lobby, and Vestro Financial Services on 9 was one of the three outfits that had seemed likely. 'You'll get back to Vestro in a little while,' he told them, 'with a story to tell. Leave the case in the doorway.'

They did, propping the door partly open, and the three of them stood close on the concrete landing. The stairwell was bright yellow and had an echoing quality.

Parker took a pair of shoelaces from his pocket, still in their paper band, and gave them to the unwounded one, saying, 'Use one to tie your pal's thumbs together. Behind him.'

The wounded one said, 'Man, don't do that. I can't move this thing.'

'He'll help you,' Parker said.

The other one hefted the shoelaces on his palm. 'You can still walk away from this,' he said.

'I'm in a hurry,' Parker told him. 'Do I have to do this the very fast way?'

The guy shrugged and said, 'Sorry about this, Artie.'

'Oh, shit,' Artie said, and hissed through his teeth when the other one moved his arm.

Parker watched, and the unwounded one tied the knot well enough. Then he turned to Parker and said, 'I suppose you want this one back.' He extended the shoelace, but it dropped through his fingers.

He'd been expecting Parker to be distracted by that, as his hand darted in under his jacket, but Parker was not; he stepped forward and shot him in the gut, just above the belt buckle.

The man grunted, folding in on himself, the revolver coming in slow motion out from inside the jacket. Parker plucked it from his hand and pushed his chest; as the man

36

toppled backward down the stairs, he turned to Artie and said, 'That makes it easier.'

'*I* didn't do anything! *I'm* no trouble!'

Parker put his new revolver on top of the suitcase, reached under Artie's jacket, and found its twin. He tucked both guns under his belt, beneath his shirt, and put the Sentinel back into its holster.

Artie watched him, fearful but not pleading. Parker turned away from him, wheeled the suitcase back out to the hall, and the No Reentry door snicked shut behind him.

8

When he rented the post office box in Pasadena, an industrial suburb southeast of Houston near NASA's manned space center at Clear Lake, Parker used the name Charles O. St. Ignatius. He paid for the first six months and pocketed the small flat key. Then he drove into Houston, where he bought the black suit and the clerical collar he wore when he went to the banks.

'We've started a fund drive at our church,' he told the first banker. 'We are in desperate need of a new roof.'

The banker didn't yet know if he was about to be hit up for the fund drive, so his expression was agreeable but noncommittal. 'That's too bad, Father,' he said.

'The Lord has seen fit to give us three near-misses the last several years,' Parker told him. 'Two hurricanes and a tornado, all just passed us by.'

'Lucky.'

'God's will. But the effect has been to loosen the roof and make it unstable.'

'Too bad.'

'Our fund drive is doing very well,' Parker told him, and the banker smiled, knowing he was off the hook. 'Well enough,' Parker went on, 'so we'll need to open a bank account, just temporarily, until we raise enough money for the repairs.'

'Of course.'

Parker pulled out the two white legal envelopes stuffed with cash. 'I believe this is four thousand two hundred dollars,' he said. 'Is cash all right? That's the way the donations come to us.'

'Of course,' the banker said. 'Cash is fine.' And under five thousand dollars meant that none of it would be reported to the Feds.

Parker handed over the envelopes, and the banker briskly counted the bills: 'Four thousand two hundred fifty dollars,' he said.

'Thank you,' Parker said.

There was a form to be filled out: 'In what name do you want the account?'

'Church of St. Ignatius. No, wait,' Parker said, 'that's too long. Signing the checks …'

The banker smiled in sympathy. 'Just St. Ignatius?'

'All right,' Parker said. 'No, make it C. O. Ignatius, that's the same as "Church of."'

'And the address?'

'We've opened a post office box for donations, so let's use that.'

'Fine.'

A little more paperwork, and Parker was given a temporary checkbook and deposit slips. 'My deposits will be in cash, of course,' he said.

'We recommend you don't mail cash.'

'No, I'll bring it in.'

'Fine,' the banker said, and they shook hands, and Parker went on to the next bank.

That day, he opened accounts in nine Houston banks, never going to more than one branch of the same firm. When he was finished, thirty-eight thousand dollars was now in the banking system, no longer cash, with nearly eighty thousand still in the side panels of the Taurus.

After the last bank, he drove on down to Galveston and spent the night in a motel with no view of the Gulf. In the morning, he rented a post office box under the name Charles Willis, for which he carried enough ID for any normal business scrutiny, then went to a bank not related to any of the ones he'd used in Houston. As Charles Willis, and using checks from two different St. Ignatius accounts, he opened a checking account with fifteen hundred dollars and a money market account with four thousand, giving the post office box in Galveston as his address. Then he took the free ferry over to Bolivar Peninsula and headed east.

9

The six theaters at the Parish-Plex out at St. Charles Avenue had a total seating capacity of nine hundred fifty, ranging from the largest, two hundred sixty-five, where the latest Hollywood blockbusters showed, to the smallest, seventy-five, where art films from Europe alternated with kung fu movies from Hong Kong. When Parker put down his eight dollars for the final screening of *Drums and Trumpets* on Sunday night, it was the fourth time he'd paid his way into this building this week; it would be the last.

Three runs per movie Friday night, five on Saturday, and five on Sunday. First thing Monday morning, the weekend's take would be delivered to the bank, but right now it was still in the safe in the manager's office. The entire multiplex had run at just under eighty percent capacity this weekend, which meant that, once Parker's eight dollars and the rest of the final intake were added, there would be just under seventy-eight thousand dollars in the safe, which was opened only when the cashier brought her money tray up from the box office.

The first time he'd come here, Parker had watched how the system worked for moving the money. When the box office closed, the cashier brought that low flat open tray full of cash upstairs to the manager's office. The manager then closed and locked the door, and about five minutes later she unlocked and opened it again; that would be the

41

time the safe in there stood open. Tomorrow, the cashier would bring starter cash for change back down to the box office in that metal tray.

His second visit, coming to an early show, Parker had waited until the manager left on one of her rounds, then tried the four keys he'd brought with him against the lock in the office door and found the one that worked. The third time, he'd watched the ticket-taker at the door, the only other employee in here except for the concession-stand girl. He was a college kid in a maroon and gray uniform; what did he do when the money was in motion?

Nothing, or nothing that mattered. Once the box office closed, the kid crossed the lobby, went through an Employees Only door and down a flight of stairs to change out of his uniform. So the cashier and the manager were all he had to think about.

Tonight, he stood looking at a poster for a coming attraction, mounted on the wall down the corridor from the manager's office. He read the names and looked at the colored drawing of an exploding train going over a cliff, as the cashier went by behind him, carrying the metal tray. Farther down the hall, the manager stood in the open doorway. She and the cashier had been doing this routine for years. Neither of them was wary, neither of them looked at the customer reading the poster. The cashier went into the office, the manager shut the door, and Parker heard the sound of the lock as it clicked shut.

He waited just over a minute, then slipped on the surgical gloves and moved quickly down the hall. The key was in his right hand, the Sentinel in his left. He opened the door with one quick movement, stepped into the office, and shut the door.

The manager was on one knee in front of the open black metal box of the safe in the corner behind her desk. The cashier had put the money tray on the manager's desk and was just starting to hand the cash to her. They both had stacks of bills in their hands. They looked over at Parker, and neither of them was yet alarmed, just startled that somebody had come through that door.

The manager's name was on a brass plate on her desk. Stepping forward, showing the Sentinel, Parker said, 'Gladys, keep that money in your hands. Turn toward me. Turn toward me!' He didn't want her thinking about hurriedly slamming shut the safe.

Gladys merely gaped, thinking about nothing at all yet, but the cashier, a short stocky round-faced woman, stared at the gun in open-mouthed shock, then sagged against the desk, the stacks of bills falling from her fingers. Her face paled, sweat beaded on her forehead, and her eyes glazed. Parker said, 'Gladys! Don't let her fall!'

Gladys finally got her wits about her. Scrambling to her feet, tossing onto the desk the money she'd been holding, she leaned toward the cashier, stretching out an arm while she snapped at Parker in a quick harsh voice, 'Put that gun away! Don't you know what you're *doing*?'

A short green vinyl sofa stood against the sidewall. Parker said, 'Come on, Gladys, help her to the sofa.' Gladys had to come around the desk to reach the cashier, but she still glared at Parker. 'She's from Guatemala,' she said, as though that explained everything. 'She saw ...'

The cashier was moaning now, sliding down the desk, the strength giving out in her legs. Parker said, 'Get her to the sofa, Gladys, and she won't have to look at the gun.'

'Maria,' Gladys murmured, helping the other woman, moving her with difficulty away from the desk and over toward the sofa. 'Come on, Maria, he won't do anything, it's all right.'

That's right, Parker wouldn't be doing anything, at least with the Sentinel, not this time. He wanted not to use it unless he absolutely had to, because that, too, could become a pattern, a series of robberies that always began with the wounding of one of the victims.

The two women sat on the sofa, Maria collapsed into herself like a car-crash dummy, Gladys hovering next to her, murmuring, then turning to glare again at Parker and say, 'Are you *robbing* us? Is that actually what this is? Are you actually *robbing* us?'

'Yes,' Parker said, and moved around the desk toward the safe.

'For *money*?' Gladys demanded. 'The *trauma* you're giving this poor woman for *money*?'

'Keep her calm,' Parker said, 'and nobody's going to get hurt.'

He had brought with him a collapsible black vinyl bag with a zipper, inside his shirt at the back. Now he took it out, put the Sentinel handy on the desk, and stuffed cash into the bag. When it was full, he zipped it shut and put the rest of the money in his pockets.

There was one line in here for both phone and fax. He unplugged the line at the wall and at the phone, rolled it up, and pocketed it, then carried the vinyl bag and the Sentinel over to the two women on the sofa. 'Gladys,' he said.

She looked up at him. She was calmer now, and Maria was getting over her faint. Gladys was ready to stop being angry and start being worried. 'You wouldn't dare shoot that,' she said. 'Not with all the people around.'

'Gladys,' Parker said, 'there's gunshots going off in the

44

movies all around us. I could empty this into you, and nobody'd even look away from the screen.'

Gladys blinked, then stared at the gun. She could be seen braving herself to stare at it. Maria moaned again and closed her eyes, but wasn't unconscious.

Parker said, 'I'll wait out in the hall for a few minutes. If you come out too soon, I'll shoot you. You know I will, don't you?'

She looked from the Sentinel to his face. 'Yes,' she whispered.

'You decide when to come out, Gladys,' he told her. 'But take your time. Think what a trauma it would be for Maria, to see you lying in a lot of blood.'

Gladys swallowed. 'I'll take my time,' she said.

10

From a pay phone in Houston, Parker called a guy he knew named Mackey and got his girlfriend Brenda.

'Ed around?'

'Somewhere,' she said. 'I don't think he's looking for work.'

'I don't have any. What I want is a name.'

'Yours or somebody else's?'

'Both,' Parker said. 'Maybe he could call me at – wait a minute – two o'clock your time.'

'You're in a different time?'

'Yes,' he said, and gave her the number of another pay phone, backward.

'I'll tell him,' she promised. 'How've you been keeping yourself?'

'Busy,' he said, and hung up, and went away in his dog collar to make today's cash deposits into his nine bank accounts, and then shift more of that money into the accounts in Galveston.

At three, changed out of the religious clothes, he went to that second pay phone, mounted on a stick to one side of a gas station, by the air hose. He stopped the Taurus in front of the air hose, got out, stepped toward the phone, and it rang.

Ed Mackey sounded chipper, like always. 'Brenda says you're looking for a name.'

'There was somebody you knew, in Texas or somewhere, could give me a name.'

'I know who you mean,' Mackey said. 'I think he specializes in Spanish names, though, you know? People that wanna bring their money north.'

'That doesn't matter,' Parker said.

'Okay. He's in Corpus Christi, he's in the phone book there, he calls himself Julius Norte.' He pronounced the last name as two syllables: Nor-tay.

'Julius Norte,' Parker echoed.

Mackey laughed. 'I think maybe his first customer was himself.'

'Could you give him a call? Tell him Edward Lynch is coming by.'

'Sure. When?'

'Tomorrow sometime,' Parker said, and the next day, when he'd finished his bank transactions, he drove south the two hundred miles to Corpus Christi, the southern-most Texan port on the Gulf, nearest to Mexico and South America.

Corpus Christi International Airport is just west of town, down Corn Products Road from Interstate 37, and near there he found tonight's motel. A Southern Bell phone book for the area was in the bottom drawer of the bed-side table, and Julius Norte was listed. Parker dialed the number and got an answering machine: 'You've reached Poco Repro, nobody in the office right now. Please leave your name and number and we'll get back to you.' Then it repeated the same thing in Spanish.

'Edward Lynch,' Parker said, and reeled off the phone and room numbers here. Then he went back to the phone book and a local map for restaurants, but hadn't made his decision yet when the phone rang. So Julius Norte was home after all, and screening his calls.

'Yes.'

'Mr Lynch?'

'Yes.'

'A friend of yours said you might call.'

'Ed Mackey.'

'That's the fellow. Where are you?'

'Near the airport.'

'You want to come down now?'

'Yes.'

'Know where Padre Island Drive is?'

'I can find it.'

'Okay,' he said, and gave quick precise instructions, and Parker followed them and found himself in a neighborhood that could have been anywhere in the south or west of the United States, from Mobile to Los Angeles: small one-story pastel stucco houses without garages or porches, a little shabby, on small weedy plots of land, with not a tree or a tall bush within miles.

The address Parker wanted was on a corner, with a carport added on the side away from the intersection, and the first surprise was the car in the carport: a gleaming black Infiniti with the vanity plate 1NORTE1. This car cost more than all the other vehicles up and down the block, all combined together.

Parker left the Taurus at the curb and walked up the cracked concrete walk to the small stoop at the front door. Beside the door was a bell button, and above the button on a small hook hung a sign that read 'Ring And Walk In.'

So now Parker knew a number of things. This was not where Norte lived. He wasn't worried about who might walk through his door. And he was richer than this neighborhood.

48

He rang the bell, as instructed, and pushed open the door, and stepped directly into what had once been the living room but was now an office, with two desks. The desk to the left rear, facing this way with its side against the wall under the carport window, was a simple gray metal rectangle, and seated at it, just putting down a *fotonovela* to give Parker the double-O, was a guy who looked like a headliner in TV wrestling: long greasy wavy black hair, a neck wider than his forehead, and a black T-shirt form-fitting over a body pumped up with weights. His nose was mashed in, mouth heavy, eyes small and dark under forward-thrusting eyebrows. The look he gave Parker was flat but expectant, like a guard dog's.

The other desk, nearer the door and off to the right, was a much bigger affair, more elaborate, a warm mahogany that took the light just so. A green felt blotting pad, brass desk lamp and gleaming desk set, family photos in leather frames; it had everything.

And the guy seated at the desk had everything, too. He wore a white guayabera shirt that showed off his tan, and his head was topped by a good rug, tannish brown, medium long, nicely waved. Below, his bland nice face had the smooth non-committal look of much plastic surgery, and when he rose to smile at his visitor it was as though he were holding the smile for somebody else. 'Mr Lynch,' he said.

'Mr Norte,' Parker said, and shut the door behind himself.

Norte came around the desk to offer a strong working-man's hand that had not had plastic surgery and so was more truthful about where he came from. Parker shook it, and Norte gestured with it at the brown leather armchair facing the desk. 'Sit down, Mr Lynch,' he offered. 'Tell me about it. Our friend Ed is well?'

'He didn't say,' Parker said.

Norte gave him a quick smile as they both sat, on opposite sides of the desk. The guard dog had gone back to his *fotonovela*. 'Down to business, eh?'

'Might as well,' Parker said, but took a second to look around. Gray industrial carpeting, a few beige filing cabinets, a closed interior door opposite the entrance. A paper company calendar and a few diplomas on the wall. 'You call this place Poco Repro,' he said. 'What's that?'

'Printing,' Norte explained. 'Mostly yearbooks, annual reports, banquet programs. More Hispanic than Anglo. But that's not what you want.'

'No,' Parker agreed. 'What I want is ID.'

'How good?'

'Real. Good enough to buy a car, take out a loan. I don't need it forever.'

Norte nodded. A fat gold pen lay on the green blotter in front of him. He rolled it in his fingers and said, 'You must know, real is the most expensive.'

'Yes, I know.'

'It doesn't matter how long you want it for, you can't sell it back, or even give it back. Once you've got it, it's yours.'

Parker shrugged. 'Fine.'

'Do you care about the backstory?'

'Just so there's no paper out on the name.'

'No, of course.' Norte considered, looking past Parker at the front window. 'The Social Security won't be real,' he said. 'I can't get a legitimate number that works in their system.'

'That should be okay,' Parker said.

'I'm thinking of some friends of mine,' Norte said, 'naturalized citizens. Is that okay?'

'I gotta have a name that looks like me.'

'Oh, yes, sure, I know that. You could be Irish, no?'

'I could be.'

'Many Irish went to South America,' Norte told him, 'in the nineteenth century, did well, the names survive. In Bolivia, other countries, you've got your Jose Harrigan, your Juan O'Reilly.'

'I can't use "Juan,"' Parker said.

'There are names that cross over,' Norte said. 'Oscar. Gabriel. Leon. Victor.'

'Fine.'

'And when would you like this?' Norte asked, but laughed before Parker could say anything and said, 'Never mind, that was not a smart question. You want it as soon as you can get it, no?'

'Yes.'

'Texas resident?'

'That would be best,' Parker said.

'And easiest for me. So you want a driver's license and a birth certificate. Do you need a passport?'

'No.'

'Now you surprise me,' Norte admitted. 'Most people, that's the first thing they want.'

'My troubles are domestic,' Parker told him.

Norte laughed. 'All right, Mr Lynch,' he said, 'you can stop being Mr Lynch, I think, in three days' time. Is that all right?'

'That's fine,' Parker said.

Norte said, 'But then again, you haven't been Mr Lynch all that long, have you? Never mind, that wasn't a question. You didn't bring a photo, did you?'

'No.'

'We can do that here,' Norte assured him. 'The other thing is money.'

'I know.'

'Driver's license, birth certificate, both with legitimate sources. Ten thousand. Cash, of course.'

'I like cash,' Parker said.

'There's so little of it around these days,' Norte said. 'That would be in advance. Sorry, but it's best that way.'

Parker said, 'Will you be here in half an hour?'

'If you intend to be,' Norte told him.

Parker got to his feet. 'Nice to meet you, Mr Norte,' he said.

'And you, Mr Lynch.'

11

When Parker went back to Norte's office half an hour later, he'd made two stops, the first at a drugstore where he'd bought reading glasses of the lowest possible magnification, 1.25, and a dark brown eyebrow pencil. The glasses were squarish and blackframed, and the eyebrow pencil would work to emphasize his new mustache. And the second stop he'd made, in the far corner of a supermarket parking lot, had been to open a door panel and remove from inside it ten thousand in cash.

Again he rang the bell and walked in, and again the guard dog looked up from his *fotonovela* to watch Parker cross the room. Norte was on the phone, but he said something quiet in Spanish, hung up, and got smiling to his feet. 'Right on time,' he said.

He wanted to shake hands again, so Parker shook his hand, then took out the money and placed it on the desk. Norte smiled at it. 'You don't mind if I count.'

'Go ahead.'

Norte did, then said, 'Bobby will take your picture.'

'Bobby?'

Norte indicated the guard dog. 'Roberto,' he said. 'Not a name you could use.'

'No.'

Norte spoke to Bobby in Spanish, and the guard dog

put down his *fotonovela* and stood. Norte said to Parker, 'You go with Bobby.'

Parker went with Bobby, through the door at the back of the room into what still was a kitchen, though not many meals would be made here. Bedrooms and a bathroom were off the kitchen to the right and rear.

A camera was set up on a tall tripod at head height, facing a blank wall. Bobby, moving toward the camera, made a shooing gesture for Parker to stand by the wall. When Parker went over there, he saw a pair of white footprints painted on the floor and stood on them.

Bobby was efficient, if silent. He moved his head to show Parker how to pose, then quickly took three shots. Still saying nothing, he led Parker back to the other room.

The money was gone from the desk, and Norte was standing beside it, smiling farewell. 'Phone me Friday afternoon,' he said. 'It should be ready by then.'

'Good,' Parker said, and left, and drove back to the motel. Later, after dinner, he put on black clothing, took his b&e tools out from under the trunk bed in the Taurus, and drove south again, one hundred fifty miles almost to the border, turning east at Harlingen toward South Padre Island, where the rich boaters keep their country villas and retirement homes.

Bay View, Laguna Vista, Port Isabel; this is where the Gulf Intracoastal Waterway begins, where the rich sea-loving Texans are based, alternating between agreeable 'cottages' and even more agreeable yachts, moored just at the end of the lawn. In the evenings, they visit one another, play bridge, drink, gossip, plan excursions across the Gulf to the islands of the Caribbean. Half the houses are full of light, warmth, good cheer; the other half are empty.

A little after nine in the evening, Parker left the Taurus

in the parking lot of a chain drugstore that wouldn't close till midnight. He left the parking lot over a chain-link fence at the back, and kept to the rear of houses, moving as far as possible from the lit-up noisy ones, crossing only side streets and only at their darkest points. This area was patrolled almost as heavily as Palm Beach, but he was keeping himself dark and silent.

All of the houses along the Waterway are equipped with alarm systems; enter through any door or window, and if the alarm is not switched off at the control pad within forty-five seconds it will signal both the town police and the security service. But where is the control pad to be found? In every house, it is just inside, next to the door nearest to where the car is parked. It was never hard to figure out which door that was.

In the next hour and a half, Parker went into nine houses, and the method was always the same. Interior pockets in the back of his coat carried his tools, which included a telephone handset with alligator clips, a special one used by telephone company repairmen to check lines. With this, he could attach to the house's phone line outdoors, where it came in from the pole, and call that line. He could always hear it ring, inside the house. If the answering machine picked up, or there was no answer after ten rings, and no dog barked, it was his. He'd go to the door nearest where the car would normally be parked and use his small pry bar to pop it.

Inside, on the wall, its red light lit, would be the alarm control pad. He never needed the full forty-five seconds to short-circuit and disarm it. Then he'd move through the house, looking only for cash. He had to leave behind hundreds of thousands of dollars' worth of jewelry, bonds, paintings, cameras, watches, and all the other toys of the leisured rich, but it didn't matter: there was always cash. There was often a wall safe, which he would find by lifting pictures along the way and get into with hammer and chisel, and the wall safes always produced bundles of cash, often still in the paper band from the bank.

Nine houses, a little over a hundred twenty thousand dollars. Finished, he skirted the areas he'd already been through, made his way back to the drugstore fifteen minutes before it would close, and drove back north to Corpus Christi.

Tomorrow, he'd have more money for the banks in Houston.

12

On Friday, from a different motel in Corpus Christi, Parker phoned Norte, got the Poco Repro machine, left a message, and Norte phoned right back: 'We're ready, Mr Lynch,' he said.

'I'll come right down,' Parker told him, and drove down to Norte's place, but when he turned the corner a black Chevy Blazer was parked in front of the house, with white exhaust visible at the tailpipe. Parker decided not to stop, but drove on by, and saw the driver alone in the Blazer, a chunky man in a white dress shirt, with the thick black hair of the Mayan Indian. He sat facing front, hands on the steering wheel, waiting, patient.

Another customer was with Norte. Parker drove on down to the next corner and went around it. He didn't want Norte's other customers to meet him, and they probably didn't want him to meet them.

He spent ten minutes driving around the neighborhood before going back to Norte's house again to see the Blazer still there. But this time its engine was off and the driver was gone.

Parker slowed, peering at the house. The 'Ring Bell And Walk In' sign, which had been there ten minutes ago, was gone now from its hook above the bell button.

Something wrong. Parker drove three-quarters of the way around the block, parked, and walked on to the house.

Blazer still there, sign still gone. No one visible in the windows. He walked up to the house and around it to the left to the carport. The Infiniti was there, as before. There was just enough room between the car and the house to slide down there and look through the high window over Bobby's desk.

Norte was at his own elegant desk, on the phone. Bobby stood in the middle of the room, an automatic loose in his hand. Three men lay facedown on the floor, wrists and ankles and mouths swathed in duct tape. One of them was the Mayan driver.

The thing to do was go away somewhere and phone. Parker moved back from the window, sidled past the Infiniti, and when he got to the front corner of the house Bobby was there, the automatic pointed at Parker's chest. With his other hand he gestured: *Come with me*.

Parker shrugged. He walked past Bobby and around to the front door and in, Bobby trailing after him.

Norte was off the phone now, standing behind his desk, looking aggravated. 'Bad timing, Mr Lynch,' he said.

'Hand me the papers and I'll go,' Parker told him. Two of the men, not the driver, had twisted around to stare up at Parker, not as though he might help but as though he might be more trouble. Norte, with a sad smile and a harried look, shook his head. 'I'm sorry,' he said. 'You see the situation here, no?'

'Dissatisfied customers,' Parker suggested.

But Norte shook that away. 'No, I don't have dissatisfied customers. What I got, I got a customer doesn't want anybody alive that knows who he is now and what he looks like now. That fuckhead sent these fuckheads to kill Bobby and me.'

'He sent the wrong fuckheads,' Parker said.

'So now I gotta take *them* down,' Norte said with a disgusted gesture at the men on the floor, 'and I gotta take their boss down, because I don't need this shit.'

'It's not my fight,' Parker said. 'Just give me the papers and I'll go.'

'I wish I could,' Norte said, and he sounded as though he meant it. 'But you're a witness here, no?'

'I don't witness things,' Parker told him.

Norte didn't like it. He chewed the inside of his cheek, and then he said, 'I tell you what. When I get this shit straightened out here, I'll call Ed Mackey, tell him the situation, see what he thinks I should do.'

Parker watched him.

Norte tried a smile while still chewing his check. He said, 'That'll work, no? Ed Mackey knows you.'

'He knows me.'

'In the meantime,' Norte said, 'just lie down on the floor here.'

'Sure,' Parker said, and as he bent forward he reached inside his shirt. He pivoted the holster down, lifted his left arm, and fired through his shirt.

The bullet hit Bobby somewhere, it didn't matter where. It wouldn't stop him, only confuse him for a second; long enough, maybe, for Parker to drop to his knees, turning, pulling the Sentinel out, hearing the big boom of the automatic bounce in this enclosed room, knowing the bullet had gone over his head. He thrust his arm out as Bobby adjusted his aim, and shot the guard dog in the face.

That still didn't finish him, but it made him drop the automatic as he whipped both hands up to his ruined face. He tottered there as Parker dropped the Sentinel, grabbed the automatic, and lunged to his feet.

Norte was pulling a blunt revolver out of a desk drawer, ducking down low behind his desk, calling, 'Drop that!'

'Fuck you,' Parker said, and pulled Bobby in front of himself to take Norte's first three shots. Now he held the dead Bobby up in front of himself and moved forward toward the desk as Norte, still hidden behind it, called, 'All right! I'm done!'

'Put the gun on the desk,' Parker told him.

Norte stayed out of sight behind the desk. 'We don't have to kill each other,' he said.

'We're not gonna kill each other.'

'I was worried, I was upset, I was too hasty. Ed Mackey said you were okay, I should've remembered that.'

'Put the gun on the desk.'

Still he remained out of sight. 'People need me,' he said. 'They won't like it if you take me down. Ed Mackey won't like it.'

Parker waited.

'I was wrong,' Norte said. 'I was too hasty.'

Parker waited.

'There's no reason to do anything anymore.'

Parker waited.

Norte's hand appeared, with the revolver. He put it on the green blotter and pushed it a little forward.

Parker let Bobby fall, on top of the men on the floor. He went forward and walked around the side of the desk to where Norte crouched there, looking up. Norte, voice shaking a little, said, 'You don't need to do a thing. I got your documents, middle drawer. You'll see, they're beautiful.'

'Let's see them.'

Norte hesitantly rose, then looked at his revolver still on the desk. 'Aren't you gonna take that?'

'You intend to reach for it?'

'No!'

'Let's see this ID.'

Norte opened the middle drawer, took out a manila envelope, shook two official papers out onto the green blotter. He was careful to keep as far as possible from the revolver. He stepped back to the wall, holding the manila envelope, and gestured for Parker to look them over.

His name was Daniel Parmitt. He'd been born in Quito, Ecuador, of American parents, and the birth certificate was in Spanish. His Texas driver's license showed he lived at an address in San Antonio. The photo on the driver's license, with the glasses and the mustache, made him look less hard.

He pocketed both documents, looked around the room. What had he touched? The carpet, Bobby; nothing that would leave prints. 'Come here,' he said.

Norte didn't move. His hands fidgeted with the manila envelope the documents had been in as he said, 'It's a mis-understanding, it's all over. Bobby and me, we were gonna take these shits away, not mess up the office, then all of a sudden we got you here – it was too much goin' on, I got too hasty.'

'Come here,' Parker said.

It finally occurred to Norte that he was still alive and that he needn't be. With small steps, he came forward to the desk and Parker took the manila envelope out of his hands. 'Pick up the gun,' he said.

'No!'

Parker held the automatic leveled at Norte's forehead. 'You aren't gonna point it at me,' he said. 'You're gonna finish those three.'

'Here? We didn't want to—'

'Bobby's messing your rug already. The other way is, I do you and I do them and I go.'

'But what—'

'Ed says you're useful. I say you're too jumpy to be reliable, but you do good work. If you make it possible, I'll help you stay alive. Pick up the gun.'

'And, and kill them?'

'That's what it's for,' Parker said.

Norte stared down at the three men. The driver was still stoic, but the other two were now staring up at Norte, hoping something different was going to happen now.

No. Abruptly, as though to get it over before he had to think about it, Norte grabbed up the revolver, bent over them, and shot each one in the head. The carpet would have to be replaced for sure.

'Keep shooting,' Parker said.

Norte grimaced at him. 'They're dead. Believe me, they're dead.'

'Keep shooting.'

Norte looked down at the bodies and fired at random into their backs. One, two, *click*; the revolver was empty.

Parker held out the manila envelope. 'Put it in here.'

Norte frowned, studying Parker's face. 'You want a hold over me.'

'You make all this go away, what hold? All I need is, *I* was never here.'

Norte managed a twisted smile. 'Oh, if only that could be true, no?'

'We can make it true. Put the gun in here.'

Norte shrugged and reached forward to slide the revolver into the envelope.

Parker said, 'Stand back over there by the wall.'

Obediently, Norte moved back to where he'd stood

62

before. He kept his arms at his sides, palms forward, to show he wasn't going to try anything, but Parker already knew that.

Parker put the envelope, bulging and heavy with the revolver, on the green blotter. He went around the desk, found his Sentinel near Bobby's feet, and put it back in its holster. Then he picked up the envelope. Automatic in his right hand, envelope in his left, he backed to the door, as Norte looked around at the mess he had to clean up. His face had gone through too much surgery to permit it to show his emotions, but they were there in his eyes.

With a little trouble, Parker turned the doorknob with the hand holding the envelope. He stepped outside, let the door snick shut, and put the automatic under his shirt, keeping his hand on it in there, like Napoleon. But, as he walked away, Norte did not come outside. He had enough to think about.

13

Daniel Parmitt's address in San Antonio, according to his driver's license, was an office building downtown; nobody lived there.

Parker stayed in three motels off Interstate 10 for three nights while setting himself up in town. A real estate agent showed him rental houses, and the second day he found what he needed in Alamo Heights, between McNay Art Museum and Fort Sam Houston National Cemetery. It was a three-bedroom two-story fake-Gothic yellow clapboard house with a turret, set back from a winding, hilly street among modestly upscale houses. Parker knew it was right, but didn't tell the real estate agent; they looked at another four places before he suggested they try again tomorrow.

It was then two-thirty in the afternoon, time enough to get to a bank and open a checking account for Daniel Parmitt, using the address of the house he hadn't rented yet, starting the account with a thirty-eight-hundred-dollar check from Charles O. St. Ignatius in Houston and a forty-two-hundred-dollar wire transfer from Charles Willis's money market account in Galveston, so the money would be available at once. From there he went to the post office and the Department of Motor Vehicles, putting in a change of address from the office building to the new house at both.

Next day, he said to the real estate agent, 'Let's look at that yellow house again.'

'I thought you'd like it,' she said, and this time he did.

Daniel Parmitt signed a two-year lease and left a check for two months' rent plus one month deposit. Parker bought a sleeping bag, the only furnishing he'd need in the house, and settled down to wait.

What he mostly had to do now was move money through his bank accounts, gradually cleaning out all the St. Ignatius accounts in Houston, emptying the two accounts Charles Willis had in Galveston, and concentrating the money into Parmitt's checking and money market accounts in San Antonio.

While doing that, he also went shopping. Daniel Parmitt was a rich Texan with a background in the oil business, a man who may have worked at some time in his life but happily doesn't have to anymore, and Parker should dress the way Daniel Parmitt should look. He bought casual slacks and blazers, gaudily colored dress shirts with white collars, shoes with tassels or little gold figures attached to the vamp, yachting caps and white golf caps. He also bought obviously expensive luggage to put it all in.

During this time, he waited to see what the Department of Motor Vehicles would do. If Parmitt's license was real, as Norte had promised, the change of address would go through without a hitch, and he'd be safe to show that license anywhere. If Norte had lied, or made a mistake, the request would bounce back to him.

But it didn't. Two weeks into his stay at the turreted yellow house in San Antonio, Daniel Parmitt got his first piece of mail at his new address: his revised driver's license.

His local Jaguar dealer was happy to talk about leases.

There was a little frown of doubt when, on the credit application form, he put down that he'd been at his present address for one month, and gave his previous address as Quito, Ecuador, but then he said, 'I was in the oil business down there,' and it was all right. Texans understand the oil business.

Six weeks and two days after Melander and Carlson and Ross had made their mistake in Evansville, Daniel Parmitt got behind the wheel of his yellow Jaguar convertible, top down, rear full of luggage, left his yellow home in San Antonio, and drove eastward on Interstate 10. Three days later he'd covered the thousand miles to Jacksonville, Florida, taking his time, not pushing it, and there he turned southward onto Interstate 95. A day and a half later he turned off at Miami.

14

Claire was not in her room. He found her out by the pool in a two-piece red bathing suit, on one of the white chaises there, ignoring the interest she aroused and reading a biography of Aphra Behn.

It had been a while since he had seen her at a different angle like this, coming upon her as though she were a stranger, and it reminded him of the first time they'd met, when he'd opened a hotel room door expecting some flunky driver and had seen this cool and beautiful woman instead. When he told her then he hadn't expected a woman in the job because it was unprofessional she'd said, 'It doesn't sound like a very rewarding profession,' and already he'd been snagged. Closed off before then, indifferent to the world except as it had to be tamed and manipulated, he hadn't known he could be snagged, but here she was. And here again. Still here.

In his dark blue yachting cap, sunglasses, mustache, pale green blazer, candy-striped dress shirt, white slacks, and tan shoes with tassels, he walked through the sun and the people and the coconut smells of sunblock to sit on the chaise next to her, sideways, to face her. Without looking away from her book, she said, 'That's taken.'

'By me,' he said.

She, too, was in sunglasses, dark green lenses and white plastic frames. She turned her head to give him her cool look through those lenses, then frowned, removed the sunglasses, looked him up and down in astonished distaste, and said, 'Good God!'

He grinned. She was the only thing that made him grin. He said, 'It works, I guess.'

She studied him, detail by detail, then gave him a small quirk of a smile as she said, 'This person. Can he be any good in bed?'

'Let's find out,' he said.

'Now I remember you,' she told him, smiling, and ran her finger along the purplish furrow on his left side, just above the waist, where a bullet once had passed him by, fired by a man named Auguste Menlo, now dead. 'My human target.'

'I haven't been shot for a long time,' he said, and stretched beside her on the bed.

'Not since you met me. I'm good luck for you.'

'That must be the reason I'm here,' he said, and reached for her again.

He'd been shot eight times, over the years, with puckered reminders still visible on his body, but the only one that showed when he was dressed was the little nick in the lobe of his right ear, as though he'd been docked for branding. A man named Little Bob Negli, who hadn't yet figured out that his Beretta .25 automatic was shooting high and to the right, had made that nick, firing at him from behind. Negli, too, was dead, but Parker was alive, and in the cool dimness in Claire's hotel room he felt that life quicken.

In the morning, she said, 'The mustache is wrong.'

'Tell me.'

'It's a policeman's mustache, too bushy. What you want is a lounge lizard's mustache, smaller, daintier. Think of David Niven or Errol Flynn.'

'You do it.'

'All right.'

They stood in the shower together, she very intent with her nail scissors, and he watched her eyes, how the light took them.

Later he put on his strange clothes, and she watched him, amused. 'Is that what you'll wear when you come back?'

'No.'

'Don't get shot any more,' she said, and kissed him, which covered the fact he didn't have an answer for her. But she hadn't asked him any questions, and she still didn't.

At two-thirty that afternoon, in bright sunlight, temperature 76, humidity not too bad, he drove in the yellow Jaguar over the Flagler Memorial Bridge onto Royal Poinciana Way, in Palm Beach.

TWO

1

'Welcome to the Breakers sir.'

'I have a reservation. The name is Parmitt.'

'Yes, sir, here it is. You'll be staying with us three weeks?'

'That's right.'

'And what method of pay – oh, I see. We will be billing your bank in San Antonio, is that right?'

'They keep all my money. I'm not permitted to walk around with it myself.'

The clerk offered an indulgent smile; he was used to the incompetent rich. 'It must take a worry off your mind,' he said.

Parker touched the tips of two fingers to his lounge lizard mustache; it felt like half a Velcro strip. 'Does it?' he asked, as though the idea of having a worry *on* his mind had never occurred to him. 'Yes, I suppose it does,' he decided. 'In any case, I'm not worried.'

'No, sir. If you'd sign here.'

Daniel Parmitt.

'Will that be smoking or non, sir?'

'Non.'

'And will you be garaging a vehicle with us during your stay, sir?'

'Yes, I left it with the fellow out there. He gave me a – wait, here it is.'

73

'Yes, very good, thank you, sir. You keep this, you'll show it to the doorman whenever you want your car.' Parker held the ticket, frowning at it, then sighed and nodded and put it away in his trouser pocket. 'I can do that,' he decided.

'And will you be needing assistance with your luggage, sir?'

'The fellow put it on a cart, over there somewhere.'

'Very good. Front! Do enjoy your stay with us, Mr Parmitt.'

'I'm sure I will,' Parker said, and turned to find a bell-boy at his elbow, who wanted to know what room he was in. Parker didn't know until the bellboy helpfully read it aloud for him off the little folder containing his keycard.

'I'll meet you up there, sir, with your luggage.'

'Fine. Thank you.'

He stood where he was until the clerk said, 'The elevators are just over there, sir.'

'Thank you.'

He rode the elevator up, alone in the car and strode down the quiet hall to his room. Entering, he faced a wide window, thinly curtained, with the ocean and the bright day visible outside. When he looked at the king-size bed, he thought of Claire, whom he would see again ... when? In three weeks? Sooner? Never?

A rapping at the door meant the bellboy with the luggage. Parker went through the usual playlet with him, being shown the amenities, the luggage placed just so, lights switched on and off, then the bellboy accepting the rich tip Parker gave him and smiling himself back out the door.

About to start unpacking, Parker caught sight of himself in one of the several mirrors and stopped. He studied himself and knew that what he was doing was the thing to do, the way to be here without being seen, without causing questions to be asked, but still, it felt strange and it looked strange. This person, in these clothes, in this room, on this island.

Well. Whatever tactics he decided on in the next couple of weeks, he knew one thing for certain: he wouldn't be intimidating anybody.

2

'This is my first time in Palm Beach,' Parker told the real estate woman, 'and I find I'm taking to it quite a bit.'

The real estate woman was pleased. A round-faced blonde of about forty, an ex-cheerleader with padding, she wore a beige suit, matching shoes, paler plain blouse, a gold pin of a leaping dolphin on her right breast, and a simple strand of pearls at her throat. She was one of an interchangeable half dozen of such women in this spacious cool office on Worth Avenue, where the only difference was in the color each woman had chosen for today's suit (skirt, not pants); there was peach, there was avocado, there was coconut, there was canary yellow, and there was royal blue. It was a garden of padded real estate women, and how did they decide each morning which one would be Kim, which Susan, which Joyce? The one talking with Parker had chosen to be Lesley today.

'Palm Beach isn't for everyone,' she said, though still with her welcoming smile. 'Those who will find it *the* place in their lives tend to know that right away.'

'I don't know as how it could be *the* place for me,' Parker told her, leaning into the characterization, knowing he would never be as seamlessly plausible as Melander, talking about the little Mexicans, but thinking he could do it well enough to pass. 'I have other places I like,' he explained. 'South Padre Island. Vail. But Palm Beach has something that appeals to me.'

'Of course,' she said with that smile. Her teeth were large and white and even.

'To have a place here, oh, for a month a year, January or February, that might not be bad.'

She made a note, on the form on which she'd already filled in his particulars: name, home address, bank, staying at the Breakers. She said, 'Would you be entertaining?'

'You mean, how big a place would I need. Yes, of course, I'd have guests, I'd want room to spread out.'

'Not a condo, then,' she said.

He already knew that much about Palm Beach. 'Lesley,' he said, 'the condos aren't Palm Beach. They're south on the island, their own thing, little places for retired accountants. I'd want something – well, you tell me. What's the neighborhood I want?'

She opened a desk drawer, pulled out a map, and laid it in front of him. With a gold pen, she made marks on the upside-down map as she described the territory. 'The most sought-after section, of course,' she told him, 'is what we call between-the-clubs, because *real* Palm Beachers want to belong to both of the important clubs, so to have a place between them is very convenient.'

'Sounds good.'

'The Everglades Club, at the north, is here on Golf Road. Then the area of County Road and Ocean Boulevard here is the section I'm talking about, down to the Bath and Tennis Club, here where Ocean Boulevard turns inland at the Southern Boulevard Bridge.'

'These are all oceanfront?'

'Well, they're both,' she said. 'Lake Worth runs along here, on the mainland side of the island. Here, just below

77

Bath and Tennis, where Ocean Boulevard curves in away from the sea, we have estates with ocean frontage, but some of them have tunnels under Ocean Boulevard to the beach on Lake Worth, so the property actually extends through from ocean to lake.'

'And the lake is more protected than the ocean.'

'Exactly.' Then she smiled and said, 'One of our ladies, some years ago, to keep from being served papers in a divorce, ran through the tunnel to escape. Unfortunately, they were waiting on the other side.'

He saw that that was gossip that was supposed to make them more comfortable with one another, and that he was supposed to laugh now, so he laughed and said, 'Too many people know about the tunnels, I guess.'

'Not that they aren't *secure*,' she assured him. 'No one you don't want could get in.'

'But if you go out,' he said, 'they'll be waiting for you.'

She smiled, a bit doubtfully. 'Yes,' she said.

'But this area,' he said, running his finger along it on the map, 'isn't between the clubs, it's south of them.'

'But very close,' she said. 'It would be in the same range.'

'And what is that range? What are we talking about along there?'

'*When* something's available, and nothing is at the moment, you could expect to pay fourteen or fifteen.' Parker shook his head, looking solemn. 'My bank wouldn't let me do that,' he said. 'For a month a year? No. I wouldn't even raise the issue.'

'Then you're not going to be between the clubs,' she said. She was very sympathetic about it.

'I understand that,' he assured her. 'But there's got to be something that's not all the way up to these places but not

78

all the way down to the condos.'

'But with ocean frontage, you mean.'

'Naturally.' He shrugged. 'You don't come to Palm Beach *not* for the water.'

'Well, you can go south of Bath and Tennis,' she said. 'For quite a ways along there, you'll find some *very* nice estates, mostly neo-Regency, on the sea, or some facing it across the road. Of course, the farther south you go, the closer you are to the condos.' As though to say, the closer you are to the Minotaur.

'I tell you what,' he said. 'Take half an hour, show me these neighborhoods, give me some idea what's out there.'

'That's a good idea,' she agreed, and pulled her purse out of the bottom drawer of her desk. 'We'll take my car.'

'Fine.'

It took more than half an hour; they spent almost two hours driving up and down the long narrow island in bright sunshine. Her car was a pale blue Lexus, heavily air-conditioned, its back seat full of loose-leaf ledgers and stacks of house-description sheets, many with color photos.

She drove well, but didn't give it much attention; mostly, she talked. She talked about the neighborhoods they were going through, about the history of Palm Beach, the famous people connected with the place, who mostly weren't famous to Parker, and the 'style' of the 'community.' *Style* and *community* were apparently big words around here, but both words, when they were distilled, came down to money.

But not just any money, not for those who wanted to 'belong' – another big word that also meant money.

Inherited money was best, which almost went without saying, though Lesley did say it, indirectly, more than once. Married money was okay, second best, which was why people here didn't inquire too much into new spouses' pasts. Earned money was barely acceptable, and then only if it acknowledged its inferiority, and absolutely only if it wasn't being earned anymore. 'Donald Trump never fit in here,' Lesley said, having pointed out Mar-a-Lago, which for many years had belonged to Mrs Merriweather Post, who definitively *did* fit in here, and which after her death had been for years a white elephant on the market – nobody's inherited money, no matter how much of it there was, could afford the upkeep of the huge sprawling place – until Trump had grabbed it up, expecting it to be his entrée to Palm Beach, misunderstanding the place, believing Palm Beach was about real estate, like New York, never getting it that Palm Beach was about money you hadn't earned.

'I should be pleased Mr Trump took over Mar-a-Lago,' Lesley said, 'I think we should all be pleased, because we certainly didn't want it to turn into Miss Havisham's wedding cake out there, but to be honest with you, I think a place must be just a *little* déclassé if Donald Trump has even heard of it.'

Parker let all this wash over him, responding from time to time with his Daniel Parmitt imitation, looking out the windshield at the bright sunny day, looking at the big blocky mansions of the unemployed rich. Neo-Regency style in architecture, when it was pointed out to him, seemed mostly inspired by the Tomb of the Unknown Soldier: molded plaster wreaths on the outside walls, marching balustrades, outsize Grecian urns dotted around like game pieces.

But although Daniel Parmitt was supposedly looking at all this with the eye of someone who just might want to buy into it, into the whole thing, the property, the *community*, the *style*, in which case Lesley would be the real estate agent, the mentor, and the guide, what Parker was looking for was something else. What he wanted was the house Melander had bought, partly with Parker's money.

And there it was.

They'd traveled south, out of the commercial part of town, through between-the-clubs, where the big houses were mostly hidden behind tall hedges of ficus and, less successfully, sea grape. They'd driven on south beyond the Bath and Tennis Club, driving over the tunnels that let the ocean-facing residents swim in the lake, then past Mar-a-Lago, and past one of the very few public beaches on the island, Phipps Ocean Park, and then more big houses, and in the driveway of one of them, just barely visible past towering sea grape and a closed wrought-iron gate, squatted a Dumpster.

'Work being done there,' he said.

'Oh, there's always renovation, here and there,' she told him. 'There's a more than adequate workforce over in West Palm, and people add things to their houses constantly. Lately, people have been putting lots of lights outside, to light up the ocean, so they can have their view all night long.'

'And no burglars,' Parker said.

Lesley laughed, dismissing that. 'Oh, no, there aren't any burglars,' she said. 'Not here.'

'The paper says there's burglars.'

She was still dismissive. 'Oh, every once in a while, some idiots come up from Miami, but they never last long, and they always get caught. And the city keeps wanting to put some sort of control on the bridges, to get identification on everybody who comes to the island. There's some sort of civil rights problem with the idea, but I really believe they'll figure out how to do it someday. And you know, just here in Palm Beach, we have a sixty-seven-man police force.'

Parker had been seeing patrol cars in motion every minute or two since they'd started to drive. 'A lot of cops,' he said.

'*More* than enough,' she assured him. 'Crime is not the problem here.' Then she giggled and said, 'Liver transplants are more the problem than crime in Palm Beach.'

'I suppose so,' Parker said. 'But that place back there got me to thinking. The bank might like it if I found a fixer-upper.'

Surprised, she said, 'Really?'

'Well, they always talk about value-added, you know,' he explained. 'God knows I don't want to *work*, I wouldn't even oversee the job, but my man at the bank does like it if I put my money somewhere that it grows itself.'

'Oh, I see what you mean. You'd put money into that kind of house, but then when you were finished it would be worth more than you put in.'

'That's what they like,' Parker said.

'Well, we don't get that sort of thing very much, not around here,' she said. 'People tend to take care of their places in Palm Beach.'

'Oh. That one back there just looked – I suppose they were just renovating.'

'No, you have a very good eye,' she told him. 'That place *was* a wreck. A very sad history. They'd had a fire, and I don't know, it had just been left alone too long.'

'But somebody got there before me.'

'I believe,' she said, remembering, pleased by the memory, 'I believe he's also a Texan, like yourself.'

Melander and his little Mexicans. 'Lucky him,' Parker said.

'There's nothing else like that around right now.'

'Just a thought,' he said.

'You know,' she said, 'I might still have the sheet on that. I didn't sell it, but – let me pull in at Monegasque.'

That was a restaurant, not far ahead, a rare spot on this road where it was possible to pull off to the side. Lesley stopped in front of the place, ignored the valet parkers watching her, and grabbed the stack of house-description sheets from the back seat. She riffled through them and pulled one. 'Here it is. You can see the trouble you missed. I don't think fixer-uppers are worth the trouble, frankly.'

Here it was. Color photo, taken from an angle to minimize the neglect. Floor plan. Entrances. Description of alarms.

'I'll keep this, if it's okay with you,' Parker said.

'Go ahead,' she said. 'I don't need it. That house is sold.'

3

A mile or so south of Melander's house, the private estates began to give way to the hotels: Four Seasons, Hilton, Howard Johnson, all tending down toward the condos. Parker left the Jaguar, top up, in a parking area of the Four Seasons a little after midnight, made his way out to the beach, and walked north. Far ahead, he could see lights along the shore, probably for the night-time views of the sea Lesley had talked about, but along here the land and sea were both dark, the estates as private and closed away on this side as on the roadside.

There was no moon, but starshine bounding from the sea outlined everything in shadowed silver. Walls and gates marked the properties, with more of those big urns looming at the corners. Almost all the houses tucked far back in there showed interior lights, but they were far away, screened, indirect; only twice did he see doors open to terrace or lawn, lights and sound spilling seaward, small parties in progress. Both times, he kept his head down so his pale face wouldn't show, and moved closer to the shush of the waves, out of reach of the lights.

He wasn't carrying tonight and was dressed in dark but casual clothing and carried Parmitt's identification. If he were to have a confrontation at all tonight, it would be with cops or private security, and with either one a gun would be more of a problem than a help.

He had tried to count the number of estates down from Melander's, driving here, and now he tried again to count, walking north, but wasn't sure he'd seen them all in either direction. When he came to the one he thought was probably Melander's, it showed toward the sea a seven-foot-high pale concrete wall. In the middle of the wall was a fairly narrow opening, in which a wrought-iron gate stood shut and locked, with concrete steps behind it leading upward, flanked by walls of more concrete.

At the northern edge of the wall, it met the next property's barrier, which was sea grape entwined with chain-link fence, stretching even higher than the neighboring wall. It looked to Parker as though the people who'd built the Melander place, if this was the Melander place, had put up this wall along the beach, and sidewalls back, then filled in behind it to make a high terrace at the same level as the road out front. Instead of that, the people next door had left the slope of the land as it was, down toward the sea, and merely fenced it.

Chain-link fence is a ladder, even when encumbered with sea grape. Seeing only a few lights in the house behind the fence, Parker climbed it at the corner, moving slowly, not wanting to make a lot of noise and also not wanting to leave a trail for Melander and the others to notice tomorrow.

When he was a few feet off the ground, he could see over the top of the wall, and it was lawn at that upper level, stretching back to the house. A few lights glowed inside the house, but there was no sound, no movement. An ornamental wrought-iron fence was fixed along the top of the wall, waist-high, and was most likely there to keep guests from falling off the lawn onto the sand seven feet below.

Parker stepped over the fence onto the ground above and behind the wall, and crouched there, waiting for a response. He knew the kind of security this sort of place could have, but he doubted Melander and Carlson and Ross were keeping it up; they weren't the type. Still, it would be better to be cautious, especially if he'd counted wrong and this wasn't their place after all.

What he waited for now was a motion sensor. That would be the first line of defense for these estates, and it should react to his presence as soon as he was on the property. If this house had such a thing, it would not only sound alarms, it would most likely also switch on floodlights around the exterior of the house, because the residents would be less interested in capturing anybody than in repelling them. If anything happened now, Parker would go over the wrought-iron fence, jump to the sand below, and move south, back toward the car.

But nothing happened. He stood there, waiting, listening, and looked around. The ground where he stood had once been lawn, but hadn't been cared for in a long time; ocean air had killed it, leaving hard crumbly earth. So this was probably the right house.

It loomed ahead of him, pale in the starlight, centered on its property, with broad open swaths that had been lawn on both sides. Screens of tall ficus along both sides blocked any sight of the neighbors, but the ficus wasn't being cared for; instead of the smooth wall-like appearance the professional gardeners would give them, the lines of trees had a messy, shaggy, unshaven look.

After a long minute, Parker moved forward toward the house. It looked as though only two lights were burning in there, one upstairs and one down; almost a guarantee that nobody was home. The lights were dim, amber, deep in the house, but they showed the rectangles of windows and glass doors.

Lawn gave way to stone patio closer to the house. There was no furniture, and sand scraped underfoot. Ahead, a line of glass doors like a theater entrance showed a large dim room. Parker stepped close to the glass to look in.

The light in there came through a broad doorway at the far end. This had once been the main public room of the house, but now there was nothing in it but a piano, pushed at an angle into a far corner, with no bench or stool in front of it.

The doors were locked; naturally. Would the alarm system be functioning, and would it connect with the local police station? Parker didn't think Melander and the others would want police coming around, not for any reason, but there was no need to be hasty or careless.

He stepped back to the outer edge of the patio to look at the second floor. There was a setback up there, and a terrace. And where the house was not glass it was large rectangular blocks of pale stone; not much harder to climb than a chain-link fence.

Parker went to the right rear corner of the building and climbed the stones to the second-floor terrace. Here there were signs of occupancy: three cheap chrome and strap chaises, an upside-down liquor carton used as a table, an empty beer bottle standing on the floor near one of the chaises.

Glass doors led to three rooms up here. The center one had been a library and television room, but was now stripped, the shelves bare. Beyond its interior open door he could see the second-floor light source: a chandelier at the head of a flight of stairs.

The two side doors led to what had been and still were

bedrooms, though now very simply furnished with nothing but mattresses. These doors were also locked, but the locks were a joke. Parker opened the one to the bedroom on the right, then stepped back to the outer edge of the terrace to wait for a response.

Nothing. No lights came on, no alarm sounded. Two minutes, three minutes, and no sound of police sirens headed this way. The door he'd opened hung ajar.

Parker crossed the terrace and entered the house. He closed the door behind himself.

It didn't take long to search the place. There were fifteen or sixteen rooms, but Melander and Carlson and Ross were only using five: three bedrooms upstairs, the kitchen and dining room downstairs. They were getting along with a minimal amount of furniture.

And they weren't here. The refrigerator was switched on, but it contained only half a dozen beer bottles, nothing perishable. There was almost no clothing in the bedrooms. There were no towels hanging in any of the bathrooms, though a stack of folded towels was on the floor at the head of the central staircase, as though they'd just come back from a laundry.

So they'd moved in here, they'd established the place, and then they'd gone away. They wouldn't come back until it was time for the heist. Parker could make his own presence here, be waiting for them.

He found two alarm systems, the main one with its control pad by the door from the attached garage, and a supplemental one with a control box in a closet near the front door. Both were switched off. Parker rewired them so that, if they were armed, they would seem to be working but were not.

He went out the front door, leaving it open. He studied

the grounds, then went over to look into the Dumpster, which was the largest size, big as a longhaul truck. It was a third full of trash: broken chairs, mirrors, wadded mounds of curtains, things the previous owners had not wanted to take with them. There was no construction debris, though, from the road, this big container would make it look as though construction or reconstruction had to be going on.

Back in the house, he shut the front door and went to the garage, big enough to hold three cars but now standing empty, except for a metal footlocker in a rear corner. The footlocker seemed strange, and was padlocked. Parker crossed to it and studied the padlock, which was new and serious. He lifted one end of the footlocker, and it was very heavy; something metal slid inside there.

So this must be their stash of guns. Parker switched on the garage light long enough to study the footlocker and its padlock, then he switched the light off again, left the garage, left the house, climbed down the neighbors' chain-link fence, and walked back to the Four Seasons. He walked toward the Jaguar, stashed among a dotting of other cars in the dim-lit parking area, then veered off, away from the Jag, moving around into another section of the lot.

There was someone in the Jag. A dark mound, in the passenger seat.

Parker, empty-handed, came slowly at the Jag from the rear, trying to keep out of any mirrors the passenger might see. At the end, he crouched against the rear bumper and moved his head slowly to the left until he could see the rearview mirror, see the reflection of the person, move farther left, see the person better ...

Lesley.

4

When he straightened and moved around to her side of the car, she saw him coming and reacted by opening the door. The interior light came on and she squinted, smiling up at him. 'Have a nice walk?' she said.

He said, 'Who knows you're here?'

'Oh, don't be silly,' she said, still smiling, pretending to be unconcerned, but clutching tight to the handle of the open door to hide her nervousness. 'I'm no threat to you,' she said, 'so you don't have any reason to be a threat to me.'

He said, 'Who knows you're here?'

She was still in uniform, the beige suit and the dolphin pin. She shifted her legs to get out of the car, saying, 'Buy me a drink at the bar over there.'

He reached out and cupped his palm over the top of her head feeling the tight blond curls. He didn't exert pressure, just held her there, so she couldn't go on getting out of the car. 'Lesley,' he said, 'when I ask a question, you answer it.'

She tried to move her head, to twist out from under his hand so she could look up at him, but he wouldn't let her move. 'You're hurting my neck,' she said.

He knew he wasn't, but it didn't matter. 'Who knows you're here, Lesley?'

'No one! All right? No one.'

He released her and stepped back a pace so she could get out of the car. She did so, tottering a bit as she got to her feet, leaving the door open so she could lean on it and there'd be some light. Sounding resentful and flustered, she said, 'You want to know who I told your *business*, is that right?'

That was half of it. The other half was, how complicated would it be if he had to kill her. He said, 'What *is* my business, Lesley?'

'That's what I'm trying to figure out,' she said.

'You smelled something.'

'I certainly did.' She was getting her self-confidence back, feeling they would deal in words now and words were her territory. She said, 'Everything you did in the car today was almost right, al-most, but I didn't buy it. Is Daniel Parmitt your real name?'

'Why wouldn't it be?'

'Because you're less than two months old,' she said. 'When we finished driving around today, I thought, That man doesn't really want a house here, but he wants *something*, and the only thing he showed any interest in at all was the house Mr Roderick bought.'

'Roderick.'

'Also a Texan, or so he says,' she reminded him. 'And I looked into him, too, and he's only six months old. The two of you, there isn't a paper, not a line of credit, a history of any kind that goes back even a year.'

'I've been out of the country,' Parker said.

'You've been off the planet,' she told him. 'Listen, do we have to stand here in the parking lot? If you won't buy me a drink, I'll buy you one.'

He said, 'Where do you live?'

'Me?' She seemed surprised at the question. 'With my

mother and sister,' she said, 'over in West Palm.'

He didn't want a drink with her in a hotel bar, because it was seeming as though she might have to die tonight, and he didn't want to have been seen with her just before. But visiting the mother and the sister in West Palm was also no good, and taking her to his room at the Breakers would be worst of all.

On the other hand, *had* she talked to people about this strange new man? Had she left a note somewhere? He said, 'Let's go to your office.'

That surprised her. 'What for?'

'You have keys, you can get in. We'll have the talk you want to have, and we won't be interrupted.'

'I really do want a drink, you know.'

'Later.'

She frowned at him, trying to work him out.

'Lesley,' he said, 'where's your car?'

'Over there,' she said, and pointed generally toward the hotel.

'I'll meet you at your office,' he said, and walked around to the driver's side of the Jag.

She hadn't moved. She went on standing there, in the V of the open door, her beige suit bouncing the light, her face in semi-darkness as she frowned at him over the top of the car.

'Shut the door, Lesley,' he said. 'I'll meet you at your office.'

He got into the Jag, and she leaned down to look in at him 'Daniel Parmitt is not your real name,' she said, and straightened, and shut the door at last, and walked away across the parking lot.

He left the Jag in the other long block of Worth Avenue,

among the very few cars parked there, and walked to the office, where she was waiting for him on the sidewalk. 'You could have parked here,' she said.

'I like to walk.'

She shook her head, turned away, and unlocked the office door. 'We'll use Linda's office in the back,' she said. 'It's more comfortable, and we won't have to leave a lot of lights on in front.'

'Fine.'

An illuminated clock on the sidewalk, gift of an insurance company, served as the office night-light. In its glow, he followed her through the desks to a doorway at the back. She stepped through, hit a switch, and overhead fluorescents came stuttering on.

He said, 'Aren't there better lights?'

'Hold on.'

The office was wider than deep, with a large desk on the right, filing cabinets across the back, and shelves and cabinets on the left. A dark brown vinyl sofa, with a coffee table, stood out from the cabinets, facing the desk across the way.

While he stood in the doorway, she turned on a brass desk lamp, a tulip-globed floor lamp in the corner behind the desk like something in a funeral parlor, and a group of muted strip lights under the shelves. 'You can turn the overheads off right there,' she told him, pointing to the switch beside the door.

Now the room was comfortable, illuminated in pools of amber. Crossing to sit on the right side of the sofa, he said, 'Tell me what you think you've got so far.'

'You're a wooden nickel, that's all I know right now,' she said. 'Linda usually keeps white wine in the refrigerator here. Want some?'

She herself did, of course: keeping the tension held down below the surface was hard work. He said, 'If you do.'

She smiled. 'At last, a human response.'

The refrigerator, a low one, was in a cabinet behind the sofa. Real estate magazines and old news magazines were on the black Formica coffee table. She brought a bottle of California chardonnay and two water glasses and shoved magazines out of the way to put them down. The bottle was already open, cork stuck back in, not much gone. She pulled the cork and poured for them both. 'To truth,' she said, toasting him.

He shrugged, and they both drank, and she sat at the other end of the sofa, knees together, holding the glass in her left hand, body angled toward him. 'You're new at your bank,' she said, 'you're new at your house. One thing you get good at in this business is credit checks, and your credit doesn't exist. You never owned or leased a car before the one you have now, never had a credit card, never had a mortgage, never had a bank account until the one you just started in San Antonio.'

'I'm an American citizen,' he told her, 'but I was born in Ecuador. I don't know if you saw my birth certificate.'

'That isn't one of the things I can get at.'

'Well, you'll see I was born in Quito of American parents. I've still got family down there, I've lived most of my life down there. The family's in oil.'

'Banana oil,' she said. 'Who is Roderick to you?'

'Nobody.'

'That's why you were looking for his house? That's why you walked to his house in the middle of the night?'

'Who says I walked to his house?'

'I do.'

He glanced at her shoes, which were medium-heel

pumps, not much use on sand. 'I just went for a walk,' he said.

'Coincidence, you headed straight for Roderick's house.'

'Coincidence,' he agreed. 'You say you've got problems with this Roderick, too.'

'Well, I didn't have, until I started thinking about you and looking into who you really are. That led me to run the same thing on Roderick and he's another guy out of a science-fiction movie, suddenly dropped onto the planet from the mother ship five or six months ago.'

'Why don't you ask him about himself?'

'I don't know the man, I didn't handle the sale. We carried the house, but it was a different broker made the deal.' She sipped wine, put her glass down, leaned toward him. 'Let me tell you what I know about Mr Roderick,' she said.

'Go ahead.'

'He wanted a presence here on the cheap. There was a house nobody wanted because it should be a teardown, but he wanted it, and now he's got it, and he isn't doing anything with it.'

'No?'

'No. There's a general contractor Mr Roderick was going to hire, to do the renovation work. I called him this afternoon, and Mr Roderick hasn't got around to starting the work yet. Says he's still dealing with his architect.'

'Maybe he is.'

'What architect? There's nobody there. The place is empty. Nothing's happening at all.'

'Architects are slow sometimes,' he said.

'Particularly when they don't exist.' She finished the wine in her glass, looked at his, poured herself a second. Before drinking, she said, 'Now you show up, and you want to know about Roderick, but you don't want Roderick to know about you.'

'You watch too much television,' he told her.

'Yes, I do,' she said. 'And I drink too much. And I worry too much. And I live with my mother and my sister. I'm divorced, and I don't want that son of a bitch back, and I don't need any other son of a bitch to take his place, in case you were wondering, but I want more than *this*.'

'Uh-huh.'

'I want more than driving obnoxious fat cats around to show them empty houses, fending off gropes from ninety-year-olds wearing white ascots – oh, yes, white ascots, and they're all wonderful *dancers* – sitting at my goddam desk out there every day, waiting for my life when my life is *over*.'

'Now you're watching too much daytime television,' he told her.

'I would if I didn't have to work.' Her glass was empty again; she refilled it and said, 'I look at you, and I say, what does this man want? He playacts to be somebody that belongs here, but he doesn't belong here. And Roderick doesn't belong here. So who are these people and what do they want?'

'You tell me,' Parker said.

'Palm Beach has only got one thing,' she told him. 'Money.'

'Sun and sand,' he said. 'Parties. Charity balls. Shopping on Worth Avenue.'

She laughed. 'I'd like to see you shopping on Worth Avenue,' she said. 'I really would. You could buy a white ascot.'

'I might.'

'Daniel – I'm going to call you Daniel, because I have to call you something, so, Daniel, what *I* need, to get out of here, to get a running jump on a new life, is *money*. And what you are here for, and what Roderick is here for, is money.'

'You want me to give you some money,' he suggested.

'Oh, Daniel,' she said, and shook her head. 'Dan? No, Daniel. Daniel, I don't want you to *give* me money. Do you really think I'm stupid? Do you really think I don't know why you parked a block away and didn't want to be seen with me in a public place?'

'Why's that, Lesley?'

'Because if I'm a problem,' she said, and sat tip straight, and looked evenly at him, 'you intend to kill me.'

'Lesley,' he said, 'while you're watching all this television I think you've also been smoking some weed.'

She brushed that aside. 'I'm being serious,' she said. 'I want to *earn* the money. Do I go to you, or do I go to Roderick? I've met you—'

'And Roderick isn't here,' he pointed out. 'At least you tell me he isn't here.'

'So here's what I'm telling you now,' she said. 'Whatever you have in mind, robbery, I suppose, or maybe a kidnapping, kidnap one of these dowagers here, whatever it is, you need somebody who knows the territory.'

'You.'

'Why not me? I sell real estate, I've been in probably a third of the important houses around here, and I know the rest. I know the town, I can answer questions, and I can tell you what questions you're forgetting to ask. Roderick doesn't have anybody local, and I think you and Roderick are competitors, so if you have me you have an advantage over him.'

He watched her, thinking about what she was saying, who she was, what she wanted.

She gave him another level look; she didn't show any nervousness at all now. 'To even find Roderick,' she reminded him, 'you had to come play that roundabout game with me. And all it did was make me suspicious. How many people do you want wondering about you?'

'None,' he said.

'It's too late for none, but I can help you limit it to one.'

He picked up his glass and sipped from it. She watched him, and then said, 'One thing. I'm not talking about sex.'

He looked at her. 'I didn't think you were.'

She said, 'I find it a strain just to talk with you. I certainly don't ever want to take my clothes off in front of you.'

'But you're going to have to,' he said.

She shook her head. 'No, I—'

'I mean, you're going to have to now,' he said.

She stared at him, panic leaching through. 'I can't – I thought you—'

'Lesley,' he said, 'I have to know if you're wearing a wire.'

She gaped, trying to make sense of the words. 'What?'

'A wire. I have to know. One way or another, Lesley, I have to know.'

'You mean—' She was blinking a lot, catching up with the situation. 'You mean you think I could be taping you?'

'Come on, Lesley.'

'But – I wouldn't, I don't – honestly, no.'

'Now, Lesley. You stand up over there, and I'll sit here,

and you'll show me whether or not you're wearing a wire.'

'I'm not,' she said, her voice fainter.

'Good. Show.'

'And then what?'

'If you're not wired, I leave here and walk back to my car, while you turn the lights off and lock the place. Tomorrow, you bring Linda another bottle of wine, and I'll be in touch. Now Lesley.'

She wasn't wearing a wire.

5

Her last name was Mackenzie. The phone book gave her a listing on Utica Street in West Palm Beach. The reverse phone book also gave a listing for Laurel Simons at the same address.

Parker left the phone company building and drove the Jag across Flagler Bridge out of Palm Beach and through West Palm to the airport, where he left it in long-term parking and walked around the lot until he found a red Subaru Outback station wagon, a much less noticeable car than a yellow Jaguar convertible, in any neighborhood except Palm Beach. It had almost no dust on it, so it hadn't been here long. Breaking into it, he hot-wired the ignition and drove to the exit, where he turned in the ticket he'd just picked up.

The tollbooth clerk, a Hispanic who looked or tried to look like Pancho Villa, frowned at the ticket: 'You don't stay long.'

'I forgot my passport,' Parker told him. 'I've gotta go back and get it, screwed up my whole day.'

'Tough,' the clerk said, gave Parker his change, and Parker drove to Utica Street.

It was a neat but inexpensive neighborhood of single-family homes on small plots, most with an attached garage. Basketball hoops over the garage doors, neatly maintained lawns, tricycles and toys around some front doors. A lot of aluminium siding in shades of off-white or pastels.

Number 417 was ranch-style, two stories on the left with the garage below and most likely bedrooms above, one story on the right. The garage door was closed, with a green Honda Accord parked at the edge of the black-top driveway, out of the way of access to the garage. So Lesley's Lexus, being more important to their livelihood, got the garage, and the mother's car got the weather.

Parker circled the block once, then stopped in front of a house half a block short of 417. There was a Florida map in the driver's door pouch; he opened it on the steering wheel.

This was a working-class neighborhood, and everybody was away working. Very few cars drove down Utica Street, and no pedestrians appeared at all. It was now eleven-thirty in the morning; Parker was ready to wait until school children started to return this afternoon.

But he didn't have to. At twenty to one, the front door at 417 opened and two women came out. One was an older, bulkier version of Lesley, with a harsher blond in her short hair and an angry thrust to her head and a similar conservative taste in clothing. The other was gross; she wore a many-colored muumuu and she waddled. Her black hair was fixed in a bad home permanent, a thousand tight ringlets like fiddlehead ferns, as though in a lunatic attempt to distract from the body. She tripped on the driveway, over nothing at all, and her mother snapped at her. The daughter cringed and lumbered on.

The two women got into the car, the mother at the wheel, and drove away. After lunch, they go out and shop for dinner. Parker drove the Subaru closer, stopping in front of the house next door, then got out of the car,

101

walked around to the back of the house, and forced the kitchen door.

There wasn't much he needed to know – Lesley was hardly a mystery woman – and he found it all in fifteen minutes. Her former husband was named Gerald Mackenzie, he lived in Miami, and there was cold, correct, formal communication between them if something like old taxes caused them to make contact with one another.

Lesley kept small debts going in several credit card and department store accounts. She didn't seem to have a man in her life, and maybe hadn't since the no-fault divorce from Gerald eight years earlier. She had occasional correspondence with a woman friend in New Jersey.

She had not written anything anywhere about her discoveries concerning Daniel Parmitt. She didn't seem to own a gun, unless it was in the glove compartment of the Lexus.

She was the alpha member of the family. Her room, facing the backyard from above the garage, was larger than the other two bedrooms up here, and had its own bath. She'd made an office out of a corner of the room, with a small desk and a low filing cabinet and a computer hooked to the Internet. She had done her best to make herself comfortable and at home here, and her mother and sister had done what they could to help, but it hadn't worked. Her room was impersonal, and she was willing to take a leap into the unknown rather than stay in this life.

What she had said last night, about him needing somebody local to smooth the way, made sense. The question was, did *she* make sense? The move she'd made was a strange one; did it mean more strange moves ahead?

Most people in Lesley's position wouldn't have been bothered by his Daniel Parmitt imitation, wouldn't have noticed anything wrong with it. Of the few people who might have picked up his errors, or seen a glimpse of his actual self under his performance, what were the likely reactions? First, most common, to do nothing, to chalk it up to eccentricity. Second, if really snagged by some false note somewhere, to mention it to a friend, somebody in the office, or a member of the family at home, and maybe even follow up with a conversation with a local cop; more likely if the person already knew a local cop. But the least probable reaction, Parker thought, was what Lesley had done: follow the ringer, try to figure him out, try to use him for her own purposes, which was to get out of this dead-end life and start over somewhere else.

So she was quick, and she didn't let her fear hold her back. And she didn't intend to get cute and try to use sex as a weapon, as she'd demonstrated last night by her awkwardness and discomfort when she'd had, very briefly, to strip.

So did all that mean she was reliable, or did it mean she was a loose cannon? There was nothing in her house to tell him for sure. For the moment, then, make use of her, but keep watch.

Before he left the house, he phoned her at the real estate office. 'Lesley, it's Daniel Parmitt.'

'Oh, Mr Parmitt,' she said. 'I was wondering if I'd hear from you again.'

'Today,' he said, 'I'm interested in looking at some condos.'

'Very different.'

'Very. Around four o'clock? You have a nice one to show me?'

'Does it need to be furnished?'

'Doesn't matter.'

103

'Good,' she said, sounding relieved. 'There's a lovely two-bedroom in the Bromwich, ocean view. I could meet you in the lobby.'

'Fine,' he said, and hung up, and drove the Subaru back to the airport. He left it in its old spot in long-term parking, picked up the Jaguar, and drove to the exit.

This clerk was a Hispanic woman, chunky and bored, who said, 'You come in today? This the long-term.'

'I forgot my passport, gotta go back for it, screws up the whole day.'

'Tough,' she said, and gave him his change.

6

The condos along the narrow strip of island south of the main part of Palm Beach yearn toward a better life: something English, somewhere among the landed gentry. The craving is there in the names of the buildings: the Windsor, the Sheffield, the Cambridge. But whatever they call themselves, they're still a line of pale concrete honeycombs on a sandbar in the sun.

Parker arrived at the Bromwich at five after four. Two Hispanic gardeners worked on the long bed of fuchsia and impatiens along the low ornamental wall in front with the place's name on it in block gold letters. Signs at the entrance indicated residents' parking to the right, visitors' to the left. The visitors' area was farther from the building.

Parker drove to the gleaming blacktop expanse of the visitors' parking lot and left the Jag next to Lesley's blue Lexus. He walked through the sun to the boxy cream-colored building, seeing none of the residents, though the other lot was full of their cars, mostly big old-fashioned boats, traditional Detroit iron.

The lobby was amber faux marble with a uniformed black security guard at a long chest-high kidney shaped faux-marble desk. The lobby seating was several round puffs of magenta sofa; Lesley rose from one of them. Today her suit was peach, her pin a gold rose. 'Mr Parmitt,' she said with her working-hours smile, and came forward to shake his hand. 'Right on time.'

'Afternoon, Ms Mackenzie,' he said. Her hand was soft and dry and without pressure.

She turned to the guard to say, 'We're looking at 11-C, Jimmy.'

'Yes, ma'am.' He gave Parker a uninterested look, then looked downward again. He had the *Globe* newspaper open on his desk, among the phone systems and security screens.

The elevators were around behind the desk. As they rode up together, she said, 'You don't want a condo, you want a place to talk.'

He shrugged. 'What else?'

'So I'm hired,' she said with a bland smile, as though it hardly mattered.

He said, 'It doesn't work exactly that way.'

'You'll explain it,' she said, and the elevator slowed to a stop.

He waited for her to lead the way, but instead of leaving the elevator she held down the button that would keep the door open and said, 'If you have to check me for a wire again today we'll leave now.'

He shook his head. 'Once was enough.'

'It certainly was,' she said, and led the way out of the elevator and down to unlock them into 11-C.

It was completely empty, as bright and bare as the beach down below. Their shoes made echoing sounds on the blond wood floor, bouncing off the hard white walls and, in the living-room, the uncurtained wall of glass doors that opened to the balcony. The place had been repainted, to make it ready for sale, and the smell of the paint was a faint tang in the air.

Parker crossed to open the sliding balcony door. It was hot out here, but with a breeze. The afternoon shadow of the building lay on the beach down below, where no one sat or swam.

Pink plastic-sheet walls on both sides shielded the view of the balconies to right and left, and openwork iron benches were built into both of those walls. Pointing to one of them, 'We'll sit here,' he said.

'You have to know,' she told him, 'that wall isn't sound-proof.'

The outer edge of the balcony was a waist-high pink plastic-sheet wall, with a black iron railing along the top. Parker held to it, leaned forward, and looked around the outer edge of the privacy wall at the balcony next door. Potted plants filled the bench he could see over there, and the rest of the space was occupied by a white plastic table, four chairs to match, a gas grill, and a StairMaster. That apartment's glass wall was completely shielded inside with white drapes. There was no one on the balcony.

He leaned back to turn and say, 'There's nobody there.'

She was wide-eyed, both hands pressed to her chest. 'Don't do that,' she said.

'Sit down, Lesley.'

They sat side by side on the iron bench against the pink wall, he facing inward, she facing the view. He said, 'I'm going to tell you what's going on.'

'All right,' she said. Now she looked solemn, as though she were being inducted into somebody's secret rites, like the Masons or Cosa Nostra.

He said, 'Don't ask me any questions, because I'm only going to tell you what I want to tell you.'

'I understand.'

107

'All right. The guy you know as Roderick owes me some money.'

She looked disappointed. 'It's some kind of debt?'

'Some kind. He's with two other guys. Have you seen them?'

'I've never even seen Roderick.'

'Well, the three came here with just enough cash to put the down payment on that house. Some of the cash they used was mine.'

She said, 'Do they intend to roll it over? Don't tell me they have a buyer.'

'Lesley, listen,' he said. 'What they are is thieves. I don't mean from me, I mean that's what they do, who they are.'

'You, too,' she said.

He said, 'They want the house because there's a job going down and they know they can't get off the island afterwards.'

'If anything big happens,' she said, 'they raise all the drawbridges. And they patrol the Waterway very seriously.'

'That's why they don't want to have to leave. They want to be established here, already known and not suspect. If I rented this condo here right now, and two weeks from now it happens, the cops would be at the door, they'd want to know all about me.'

'And you two months old,' she said.

'So that's why Melander – he's Roderick – that's why he wanted to be already in place, nobody wondering about him.'

'They're going to do a big robbery,' she said, 'and then go back to that house and wait for the excitement to die down.'

'That's right.'

'But they used your money to buy the house.'

'A quarter of it.'

'For the down payment,' she said. 'So when they do this robbery, you're going to be there to get your part of the money back.'

'To get it all, Lesley,' he said. 'They shouldn't have taken my money.'

She studied him. 'You mean that.'

'Of course I mean it.'

She nodded, thinking about this. 'So it's a lot of money.'

'Yes.'

'And some of it will come to me, because I'm not cheating you, I'm helping you.'

'Yes.'

'If they hadn't cheated you, you would take a quarter.'

'Yes.'

She looked past him, out at the ocean. 'This is a little scarier than I thought,' she said. He waited, and she looked at him again. She said, 'You're here to find out if you can trust me, and I'm here to find out if I can trust you, and if either of us guesses wrong, we're in trouble.'

'That's right.'

'But I think,' she said, 'if I guess wrong, I can be in a lot worse trouble than you.'

'Trouble is trouble,' he said.

'Maybe so. What is this robbery?'

'That's the first thing you can do for me,' he said. 'You can tell me what the robbery is.'

'You don't know?'

'I know some things about it. I know it's a charity thing.'

'There are charity events all season,' she told him. 'There are balls here that are five thousand dollars a ticket. But that isn't cash.'

'Neither is this,' he said. 'It's a charity auction of jewelry. It's sometime probably in the next two weeks, and they told me the market value of the jewelry was twelve million dollars. Can you tell me what it is?'

She looked surprised, and then she laughed. As though disbelieving, she said, 'Mrs Clendon's jewels?'

'Is that it?'

'That's it, oh, absolutely, that's it.' She seemed to find the whole thing very funny. 'Oh, Daniel,' she said, 'and I had such hopes.'

'What do you mean?'

'There's nothing there to help anybody, Daniel,' she said. 'There's nothing for me, and there's nothing for you, and there's nothing for your friend Roderick.'

'They're gonna do it.'

'Then they're going to jail,' she said. 'And if you're there, you'll go to jail.' She rose, stood facing him. 'But I won't be there,' she said. 'Don't worry, Daniel, I'm going to forget this entire conversation.' She turned away, toward the living room.

He said, 'Lesley.' When she looked back at him, he said, 'Unless you want to go off the balcony, Lesley, you'll sit down.'

She gave a frightened look at the air beyond the balcony railing. 'They'd know you're in the building,' she said.

'Let me worry about that.'

They looked at each other. He was deciding to stand when she came over and sat beside him. 'If I tell you about it,' she said, 'and if you see it can't work, will you let me go?'

110

'Yes,' he said.

'Daniel,' she said, 'I really wish it was something that could work. I could taste it, Daniel.'

'Freedom.'

'The new me.'

Parker said, 'Tell me about Mrs Clendon, Lesley.'

7

The first thing you ought to know, Lesley told him, is that there are no basements in Palm Beach, the water table is too high. And the rich people are seasonal, they're *never* here between May and November, so they need somewhere to store all their valuables while they're gone, and for the last fifty years that place has been the First National Bank.

The First National Bank doesn't just have safe deposit boxes like other banks, they have entire vaults down under the bank. They store about three thousand fur coats down there every summer, and everything else people don't want to leave in their empty houses: rare wines, gun collections, paintings, silverware and goldware, even furniture, antique chairs and things like that.

You don't want to break in there, believe me you don't; the bank is very serious about its responsibilities. The closest anybody ever came to robbing that bank was back in 1979, when a college student got into a crate and had himself shipped into the bank as antiques. His idea was to come out of the crate at night, fill it up with valuable things, and then wait to slip out of the bank during regular business hours. Then he'd come back later to get the crate. Except the bank is guarded at night, and he was found before he could get out.

Even now, during the season, the bank is full of valuables. The rich women keep all their most expensive jewelry in the bank, and the bank opens up late every night that there's one of the important charity balls. They open so the women can come get their stuff, and then they open again later that night so they can bring it all back. Somebody told me the mirror down there by the vaults isn't regular glass; it's tinted gray because that makes people look better when they're trying on their jewels. So the bank takes very good care of its customers.

One of the most important customers the bank ever had was Miriam Hope Clendon. On the Hope side, her family was important in transatlantic shipping up till the Second World War, when they sold everything and became the idle rich. The same thing on the Clendon side, except they were railroads out west.

By the time you got to Miriam Hope Clendon, the money was so old it didn't have any bad suggestions of trade on it anymore; it was as though Miriam Hope Clendon had money only because God wanted her to. So naturally she was very important in Palm Beach, and important to the bank. And also she lived longer than anybody – she was something like ninety-seven when she finally died, in Maine, last August.

Her family didn't live as long as she did, and most of her children didn't have children, or if they did the children died in accidents or suicide, so when she passed away she was the last of her line except for some very distant cousins, none of whom had ever even met her or had ever been to Palm Beach. Still, they'll get most of what she left.

But not all of it. One of the assistant managers in the bank had become a kind of pal of hers in her last years, when she didn't have anybody else except employees, and he was very interested in raising money for the library here.

It's only the last few years there even *is* a library in Palm Beach. He talked to Miriam about the library sometimes, and she contributed some money every once in a while, but it wasn't much of a big deal.

But then she died, and in her will she left all the jewelry she'd kept in the bank to this manager, not for himself, but to do a charity auction and raise money for the library. They'd known each other in the first place because of her jewels, so that's what made her think about doing it that way.

The auction and the ball – there has to be a ball, of course – were set up by a couple of the women who do all that sort of thing here, with the man from the bank to consult. *Everybody* wants some of the Miriam Hope Clendon jewelry, because she used to knock their socks off at the charity balls, glittering like a chandelier. And the ball is going to be a week from this Thursday, with the auction the next night.

So right now, all that jewelry is still in the vault in the bank, and you aren't going to get at it in there, and neither is Roderick, or whatever his name is. On the Wednesday before the ball, the jewelry is all going to be transported by armored car to the Breakers, because the Breakers has the biggest ballroom on the island, and that's where it's going to be displayed, under heavy guard, during the ball on Thursday, so people can see it all, under glass and behind electrified fencing.

Then on Friday, the display will be taken down and it will all be moved over to the Fritz estate, because now Mrs Helena Stockworth Fritz is the most important person in Palm Beach society, now that Miriam Hope Clendon is dead, and Mrs Fritz insisted the auction be held at her house. *Hundreds* of people are invited to the ball on

114

Thursday, but to go to the auction on Friday you have to make a contribution to the library fund and you have to make a sealed bid on at least one piece in the collection. So no freeloaders.

I'm not sure exactly when the jewelry's all going back to the bank, either late Friday night or early Saturday morning, but that's what's going to happen. The successful bidders won't get to take the jewelry home with them from the auction; they'll have to go to the bank the next Monday morning and show their bidding slip and collect their jewelry then.

So what's going to happen is, this huge collection of very important and very valuable jewelry is going to leave the bank on Wednesday, under extremely heavy guard. It's going to the Breakers to be set up along the sides of the ballroom. Then after the dance it's going to be moved to Mrs Fritz's house, still with the same armored car and guards, and it'll be guarded all the time it's there, and after the auction it's going back, all together, to the bank. I don't know what your friends have in mind, but if they're going to try to break into the bank, they'll be caught. If they try to steal it all from the Breakers or from Mrs Fritz's house, they'll never get out. If they try to attack the armored car on any one of its three trips, they'll probably be shot. The people here know what Mrs Clendon's jewels are worth – they're not going just to leave them lying around.

I'm sorry to have to tell you this, Lesley finished, because I'd like them to get their money, so you can get your money, so I can get my money. But it isn't going to happen. Forget it.

8

The shadow of the building was a little longer, reaching out across the sand toward the sea. Out near the horizon two boats, widely separated, both slid south. Parker stood and paced, and she watched him. After a minute, he stopped and put his hand on the railing and looked out at the sea. He said, 'This Mrs Fritz's house. I'm thinking it's on the ocean but it doesn't have a beach.'

'No, it doesn't,' she said, sounding a little surprised. 'It's a seawall along there. It's not far from where that drifting cargo ship ran onto somebody's terrace a few years ago.'

'I know these guys,' Parker said. 'They're gaudy. They're going to like Mrs Fritz's house because it isn't a commercial space, it's a private space, so control can never be one hundred percent. They're going to like it because they can come in from the sea, go back out to the sea, and duck right back in again down at their own place, while everybody's searching the Atlantic Ocean for them.'

'It isn't that easy,' she insisted.

'They don't expect it to be easy,' he told her. 'They expect it to be tough, and that's why they'll be gaudy. I don't know what they have in mind, but it'll shake people up.'

'If you mean scare them,' Lesley said, 'it would take a lot to scare people in Palm Beach. Not so long ago, you had a militia of these octogenarians on the beach, still in their white pants, with their big-game hunting rifles, marching back and forth on the sand, drilling, ready to repel Castro.'

'Good thing for them Castro didn't show up,' Parker said. 'But the point is, Lesley, I'm not going to steal the package, Melander and the others are. I don't have to have a plan, just have to know what theirs is. But I know them, I know what business they're in, I know they're sure enough of themselves to sink all their cash into this thing, and I know how their minds work. They won't mess with bank vaults, and they won't try to get into the middle of a huge hotel on its own acres of grounds. An armored car on this island is hopeless – where would you take it? So that leaves Mrs Fritz, in a private house on the ocean with a seawall. That's where they're going to do it, so the question is when.'

'After everybody's gone home,' she suggested, 'and before the jewels are loaded back into the armored car.'

'No. I told you, these guys are gaudy, they won't want to sneak in and out. A lot of rich people all dressed up in one confined place, wearing their *own* big-dollar jewels. That's the time to come in, when you can make the maximum trouble, the maximum panic. What are guards gonna do if there's a thousand important people running back and forth screaming?'

'I don't know,' she said.

'They won't do a lot of shooting,' he said.

'No, I suppose not.'

He said, 'Show me Mrs Fritz's house.'

'I can't take you *in* there,' she said, surprised. 'It isn't on the market.'

'Drive me by it.'

'You won't see much, but all right. We'll take my car.

We'd better find a place where you can put yours in some shade.'

'Good.'

She stood and looked out at the ocean. 'Are they really going to do that, do you think? Come in from the sea?'

'That's their style.'

'Like James Bond,' she said.

He shook his head. 'More like *Jaws*,' he told her.

9

Mrs Fritz's mansion was invisible from anywhere, except, probably, the ocean. Parker and Lesley drove past it twice, first northbound and then southward again, and both times she drove as slowly as she could when they went by, but there was nothing to be seen.

An eight-foot-high stucco-covered wall in a kind of beige color, dappled with climbing ivies, faced the road and ran back both sides of the property. In the dead middle of the road-facing wall a broad opening was filled by massive wood-beam doors, vertical planks held together with thick black bands of iron. These must be electrically operated, and would only be opened when Mrs Fritz or some other acceptable person was going in or out.

'You see what I mean,' Lesley said, the second time they drove by it.

'Those doors will be open the night of the auction,' Parker said.

'With security standing there and a Palm Beach police car in the driveway. You don't crash Mrs Fritz's parties.'

'Melander will.'

She dropped him back at the Jaguar, in the corner of a real estate office parking lot where tall sea grape offered some shade. 'What now?' she said.

'We wait for party time,' he said, and got out of the car.

To get where he was going next, he had to drive past Mrs Fritz's estate one more time, and the thing was just impossible. There was no parking along here, no useful shoulder, nowhere even to stop. You couldn't find anywhere to sit and watch the place.

Well, that wasn't Parker's problem. That was somebody else's problem.

He drove over to West Palm, parked the Jag a little after five-thirty, and found a hardware store open, where he bought a cordless drill and an inch-wide metal-routing bit and a small hacksaw and a glass cutter and a pair of pliers and a roll of clear tape and two rubber suction cups with handles. Then he drove back to the Breakers and, in one of the shops off the lobby, bought a bright blue canvas shoulder bag with a flap. Everything from the hardware store went into it.

That night, with the shoulder bag, he left the Jag in the Four Seasons parking lot and walked to Melander's house. This time he was armed, carrying the Sentinel in his hand so he could toss it into the sea if he had to.

But he didn't have to, so when he got to the house he put the Sentinel in the shoulder bag with the rest of the tools. He went in through the same second floor bedroom as the last time and then down to the kitchen, where the refrigerator was exactly as it had been before, nothing added or subtracted. So they hadn't yet come back.

He switched lights on as he moved through the house to the garage, where he tipped the footlocker onto its face and drilled an inch-wide round hole through the metal as close as possible to the bottom right corner.

The rear of the footlocker was stiffened with bands of metal that divided it into six sections. Parker hacksawed three sides of the lower right section, then peeled it open and looked inside at the six guns lying in a jumbled heap: three shotguns and three Colt .45 automatics.

One by one he snaked the guns out of the footlocker, then carried them all away to the kitchen. He put them on the table there, sat in front of them, and misaligned the firing pins on the automatics and drained the shot from the shotgun shells. Then he carried them all back to the garage and dropped them into the footlocker. He bent the opened flap down flush again and used the clear tape to put the round plug he'd cut out back into position. If anybody were to open the footlocker and study the interior, the cut would be obvious, but the three wouldn't be looking at the footlocker, they'd be looking at the guns.

Back in the house, he went to the dining room, the only other downstairs room beside the kitchen that they'd furnished, with a simple black Formica Parsons table and three mismatched armless kitchen chairs, all probably bought used over in West Palm. Two floor lamps in the corners gave light, the original chandelier having been messily removed.

If he were in here with them, it would be because they were in control and they wanted a conversation. Would they sit and have him stand? No, they'd rather be the ones on their feet. On which side of the table?

There were three doorways in three walls in here, two broad ones opposite each other opening onto living rooms at the front and rear, and a narrower one with a swing door leading to the kitchen. They would want him with his back to the fourth wall because, without thinking about it, they wouldn't want to be looking at escape routes behind him.

The good thing about a Parsons table is that it has a strip of wood all around, just under the top, that creates a recess. Parker taped the Sentinel to the underside of the tabletop, on the side where there was no door. Then he went looking for a window.

The exterior doors, upstairs and down, were all large expanses of plate glass, too big to be of use. But on the road side of the house, flanking the front door, were pairs of double-hung windows with panes, four over four. Going outside, he chose the corner window farthest from the door and the garage. First he fixed the suction cups onto the top right pane of the lower half of the window, then used the glass cutter to slice the glass through just inside the wooden sash bars, scoring it four times all the way around before he got completely through. Tugging on the suction cups, he removed the rectangle of glass, then made sure he could reach the lock inside. Then he put the pane back in place, fixing it there with small pieces of the clear tape. The suction cups he buried under the shrubbery along the footing.

Walking back along the beach toward the Four Seasons, one by one he threw into the sea the drill, the routing bit, the hacksaw, the glass cutter, the pliers, and the roll of tape. The shoulder bag he left on the ground in the parking lot; some tourist would take it home.

10

The question was Lesley. She'd been useful, but she was an amateur, and an amateur is never entirely reliable. Could she be useful again? Or could she be a problem?

So far, she was doing everything right. She came up with the answers he needed, and she didn't ask a lot of her own unnecessary questions. She didn't try to push herself closer to the job. She showed patience. All of these were rare qualities in an amateur and were keeping her alive.

So the real question was, how tight a leash should he keep on her until the day? He finally decided the answer was to keep no leash at all. If she kept herself to herself, as she'd been doing, fine. If she started phoning, or coming around, he'd deal with it.

It was ten days till the job. There was nothing to do now but wait, and make sure that when Melander and the others came back they didn't notice Parker in the neighborhood. So why not go back to Miami for a few days, spend some time with Claire?

He left in late morning, took Interstate 95 south, and got off the highway at Fort Lauderdale to find a diner lunch. After, he came out of the diner to the bright sunlit parking lot, and the Jaguar was gone.

Stupid; to let that get ripped off. He looked around the parking lot for another car to take, and a guy came out of the diner behind him, working at his mouth with a tooth-pick. He said, 'Hot day.'

'Yes,' Parker said. He waited for the guy to go away.

But the guy pointed across the parking lot with his toothpick and said, 'You see that white Toyota Land Cruiser over there?'

Parker didn't look at the white Toyota Land Cruiser, he looked at the guy with the toothpick. He was bulked up, tanned, about forty, grinning like a man with a secret. He nodded, not looking at Parker, and said, 'There's a guy in there with a thirty ought six – you do anything he doesn't like, any single thing at all, he'll blow your head off.'

'Maybe he'll hit you,' Parker said.

'Funny thing about Herby,' the guy said. 'He never misses what he aims at. Never been known to happen. Why don't we go over there, he can tell you about it himself.'

Now Parker looked at the Land Cruiser, a Land Rover clone, then back at the guy. These people weren't from Melander and Carlson and Ross; that trio would handle their own problems. He didn't see how they could be connected with Lesley. So who were they and what was their interest?

The guy said, 'I'm walking over there now myself. If you don't walk with me, they'll be hosing down the pavement here later.'

Parker said, 'We'll walk together. I'm trying to remember where I know you from.'

The guy chuckled, not as though he thought Parker had said something funny, but as though it was a skill he'd learned one time, chuckling, and he liked to practice from time to time. As they walked across the parking lot to the Land Cruiser, that was the only answer he gave.

Herby, a sharp-nosed skinny man in a wrinkled white

dress shirt and black pants and mirror-lensed aviator sunglasses, sat in the back seat, the big hunting rifle on his lap, right hand loose near the trigger, left hand loose under the barrel. There was no way to tell if he was looking at Parker or not, but it really didn't make any difference.

The first guy, still cheerful, said, 'You can ride up front with me.'

They were willing to kill him in public, if they had to, but they'd rather do it in private. So there was still a little time. Parker went around to the right side of the Land Cruiser and opened the door, and saw a small square photo on the passenger seat. He picked it up, slid onto the seat, shut the door, and looked at the photo. It was himself, one of the pictures Bobby had taken for his driver's license.

He looked from the picture to the guy, now behind the wheel, grinning at him around the toothpick. 'So Norte's dead,' Parker said, and dropped the photo out the window.

The guy stuck the key in the ignition. 'Hell, pal,' he said as the engine started, 'everybody's dead. Some people just don't know it yet.'

11

They were going to kill him in the Everglades. A good place for it, obviously; the idea had been thought of before.

The white Land Cruiser headed out westward along Alligator Alley, the Everglades Parkway, a two-lane black binding tape laid on the uncertain green land, straight as a rifle shot across the flat landscape. Big trucks groaned along, and the smaller cars zipped around them and sped on. The guy with the toothpick in the rear corner of his mouth moved the Land Cruiser along at a steady unhurried speed. There was time enough to get the job done.

Parker thought about the Sentinel, now taped to the underside of the Parsons table in Melander's dining room. There were two guns stashed in the Jaguar, but he had nothing on his body. Here there was Herby in the back seat with his rifle and maybe some other things. The driver wasn't obviously armed but he could have a pistol in a pants pocket or in a spring-loaded holster under the dash on the far side of the steering column.

They couldn't do anything on this road, with this traffic. There were always at least half a dozen vehicles in sight. They'd have to turn off, and that was the point where he'd have to make his move. They were pros, and they would know that was when he'd have to move, but he had to anyway. And they knew that, too.

Although it didn't matter now, he couldn't help but

wonder if it would have made a difference if he'd decided not to let Julius Norte live. He'd thought the man could handle himself against the fellow who'd sent those killers after him, but maybe without Bobby, Norte hadn't been so invulnerable anymore.

It seemed to Parker that this guy, whoever he was, who'd hired these two in the Land Cruiser, would have been on Daniel Parmitt's trail whether he'd left Norte dead or alive. There would have been papers in Norte's office, evidence, things Parker wouldn't have had the time or knowledge to find and destroy, to tell who the other customer had been that day, who'd dealt himself a hand. It was revenge that guy wanted now, as well as his grim determination to leave nobody alive who could possibly lead back to him. Nothing to do with Parker, but he was stuck in it anyway.

They drove for over an hour, passing the occasional tourist place, offering cold drinks or airboat rides into the swamp or views of caged alligators, and no one in the car spoke. The air-conditioning kept everything cool and dry. They passed small side roads from time to time, bumping away on rough bridges over the canals, and Parker waited.

Over an hour. The driver lowered his visor because the afternoon sun was rolling down the sky, dead ahead, and Parker did the same. There were warnings on notices attached to this side of the visor, but he didn't read them.

The driver tapped the brake. Parker squinted, and maybe that was a road out there, still some distance off, leading to the right. He became very still, and the driver tapped the brake again, and the rifle barrel came to rest against the base of Parker's skull, just below and behind his left ear, a cold hard smoothness of metal.

Parker sensed, but didn't turn his head to see, the driver grin. Still facing front, feeling the steel against his skull, he said, 'Try not to jounce on the turn.'

The driver practiced his chuckle again, and slowed some more, flipping on his directional.

It was a dirt road, heading north over the scrub near the highway, then going on into the ripe green of the swamp shrubbery. Parker watched it coming and knew he couldn't do the move, not now. He'd have to wait until they thought he wasn't going to do anything. Eventually, they'd believe he'd given up the idea of doing anything, because eventually everybody gives up, and they'd know that. Eventually, he, too, might give up.

The driver made the turn, smooth and slow, but then they bumped a little when they crossed the wooden bridge over the nearby canal, and the rifle barrel jounced hard against his skull, but the gun didn't go off. And a minute later, with the car up to a good speed again and the mangroves and palmettos getting closer, the rifle barrel went away.

Parker adjusted the air-conditioner vent so it wouldn't blow directly on him. He looked at the driver, who concentrated now more completely on his driving on this imperfect road, then twisted around to look back at Herby, who was seated sideways in the left corner back there, so he could hold the rifle with its trigger handy to his right hand and its barrel aimed at the back of Parker's seat. The aviator glasses reflected Parker, darkly. He faced front again.

Once in the swamp, the road veered left and right to keep on the dry ground. Water glinted among the trunks on both sides. The road was one lane wide, but here and there were wider spots where one car could pass another.

128

A straight stretch, and down at the end a sharp curve to the left. The driver accelerated, and Parker watched his foot on the pedal. At the end of this stretch, he'd have to brake.

There. The foot started to lift, and Parker moved everything at once. His left foot mashed down on the driver's foot and the accelerator, jolting them forward, maybe spoiling Herby's aim for just a second. His right hand shoved the door open against that acceleration as his left hand swung up backhanded to mash that toothpick into the driver's mouth. And his right foot shoved down and leftward, propelling him backward out of the Land Cruiser, as the crack of the rifle shot banged around inside the car.

He landed hard on his back, the Land Cruiser spraying dirt back at him as the driver tried to brake, to steer, to keep the Land Cruiser from running off into the swamp. Herby was rolling out of the car on the other side, not waiting for it to stop, rolling with the rifle cupped against his chest under his crossed arms.

Parker rolled away from the road, hoping for water, but a low berm had been built along here to keep the swamp away from the road, and it stopped him. He had to rise, not wanting to, if he would get over the berm, and as he came up on his knees he heard the crack behind him, much smaller in the outer air, just a firecracker. Except that a punch in the back threw him forward across the top of the berm, and when he lifted himself, suddenly very heavy, there was blood spreading across the front of his shirt. The bullet had gone through him.

He *shoved* with his arms, but they were heavy as trees and he only dropped forward, rolling onto his back. There was no sky, only the darkness of the leaves.

He felt their feet when they rolled him down into the water, but when he hit the water he wasn't feeling anything anymore.

THREE

1

He wasn't there. The house at Colliver Pond was empty, and that was bad news. Melander and Carlson and Ross wandered the empty rooms, looked out the windows at the frozen lake, and they were not happy.

Dissension had started among them not twenty minutes after they'd left Parker at the motel in Evansville, with a handful of earnest money instead of his share of the bank job. Carlson had started it; being the driver, he was the brooder, the one with extra thinking time on his hands. 'I don't like it,' he'd said.

The other two had known immediately what he was talking about, and Melander had said, 'Hal, we didn't have a choice. We thought he'd come in. Tom Hurley would've come in.'

'But Hurley left. And he sent us this guy Parker, and I can't help thinking we made a mistake.'

'No choice,' Melander said again.

'We had choices,' Carlson told him, keeping his eye on the road, Interstate 64, headed east, going to switch to 75 southbound at Lexington, aimed for Palm Beach.

Ross, seated beside Carlson up front, with Melander in back, said, 'What choices, Hal? The Clendon jewels is the only thing we got, and this is the only way to get it.'

'If we were going to rob him—'

'Hey!' Surprised, a little angry, Melander said, 'Rob him! Who, Parker?'

'Who else?'

'We didn't rob him, we borrowed the money, he'll get the whole thing, we explained it to him.'

'If you did it to me,' Carlson said, 'I'd say you robbed me.'

They all thought about that for a minute, trying to imagine the situation reversed, and then Ross shrugged and said, 'Okay, he thinks we robbed him. So what?'

'So maybe,' Carlson said, 'we shouldn't have left him alive.'

Ross stared at him. 'Meaning what?'

'Come on, Jerry, you know what I'm saying. If we're going to rob him, maybe we should go ahead and kill him.'

Melander, firm about it, said, 'Hal, we don't do that. We don't kill the people we work with. How could we *do* that?'

'Then there he is,' Carlson said, 'behind us, thinking how we robbed him. He didn't strike me as a let-it-ride kind of guy.'

They thought about that awhile, going over their brief knowledge of Parker, and then Melander said, 'We can keep in touch with him. We'll call him, time to time, let him know we're still gonna pay him, let him know it's gonna be all right.'

'And make sure he's in place,' Carlson said.

'That, too,' Melander agreed.

When Tom Hurley had bowed out of the bank job and suggested Parker to take his place, he'd given them a way to make contact, if they had to. There was a phone number, and they should ask for Mr Willis. But they shouldn't start off with that call, they should wait for him to make the first move, to let them know he was interested. As it happened, he'd done everything with that first move, so they hadn't had to use the Mr Willis number, but now they could.

Except, four days later, with their freshly installed telephone at the estate in Palm Beach, when they tried that number there was no answer. They had a go at it on and off for three days, and then Carlson said, 'He's following us.'

Melander didn't like that. He walked around the empty living room, with the out-of-tune piano shoved into a corner, and he glared out at the terrace and the ocean and all the beautiful weather he was supposed to be enjoying instead of that icy northern shit, and he didn't like it at all. 'We left the son of a bitch alive,' he complained.

'Like I been saying,' Carlson pointed out.

'We left the son of a bitch alive,' Melander insisted, 'so he'd know we were good for it, he can count on us, we'll come through. Not so he could follow us around and make trouble. We're busy here, we got a lot on our minds, we don't need this shit.'

'Like I been saying,' Carlson said.

'Jesus, Hal,' Melander said, 'what made you so fucking bloodthirsty all of a sudden? You never wanted to go around popping people before.'

'I don't want to this time,' Carlson said. 'It just seems to me before we did what we did, we should have thought it through a little more.'

'Well, we didn't,' Melander said, 'and I don't see what more fucking *thought* was gonna do about it. We did what we had to do, what we agreed we had to do, and we did it and it's done and I swear to God, Hal, I want you out of my fucking face on this topic.'

'I'm just saying,' Carlson said.

'I *hear* you saying, and I'm tired of hearing you fucking saying, you follow me?'

Ross, speaking quietly as though in a room with some possibly dangerous dogs, said, 'Maybe what we should do is go there.'

They stopped glaring at each other to frown at Ross. Melander said, 'Go where?'

'Where that phone number is,' Ross said. 'With a phone number, you can always get an address.'

Melander, feeling belligerent toward everybody, said, 'Go there and do what? What's the purpose?'

'Maybe there's something there tells us where he is,' Ross said, still being very mild. 'Or how to get in touch with him. And he's supposed to have a woman there, too, maybe she knows where he is. Or maybe she should come stay with us awhile to make sure Parker doesn't get to be too much.'

'The woman,' Melander said, nodding, losing his belligerence. 'That's a good idea.'

'I don't know about that,' Carlson said. 'Maybe that just makes it worse. First we rob him, then we kidnap his lady friend, maybe he's gonna—'

Exasperated, Melander said, 'Why do you keep worrying about how *he's* gonna take it? Whose side are you *on*?'

'Mine,' Carlson said.

Ross said, 'Let's go take a look at the house.'

So they did, driving up the east coast to the still-icy North, and the house was in northwest New Jersey, seventy miles from New York, on a lake where most of the houses were seasonal, still shut up for the winter. The house the Mr Willis phone number led to, behind a rural mailbox that said 'Willis' on the side, was small, part gray stone and part brown shingles, with an attached two-car garage. It was surrounded by trees and brush, and it was empty.

People lived here. There was much evidence of the woman, less evidence of the man, who had to be Parker. They found three guns stashed in the house, one clipped under the living room sofa, one clipped under the bed, and one in a sliding wood panel in the garage, next to the kitchen door, just above the button to operate the overhead garage door. That last was the one that got to Carlson. He could see it: the guy makes an innocent turn to push that button, open or close the overhead door, and turns back with an S&W Chiefs Special .38 in his hand.

They could see that the woman had packed, and probably for an extended stay. But there was nothing to show where she'd gone, no travel agent's itinerary, no notes about airline connections, nothing. There was nothing at all about Parker; his footprint was not deep in this house.

They stayed four days in the house, finding a couple of diners and a supermarket not too many miles away, waiting to see if anybody showed up or if there was a phone call. If Parker phoned, looking for his woman, they'd talk to him, see if they could cool him out, discuss it with him.

But nothing happened, no calls, no visits, and after four days Melander couldn't stand it anymore. 'And it's fucking cold,' he said. 'This isn't where I was gonna be right now.'

Carlson said, 'We aren't doing anything here except act like jerk-offs.'

Melander, who'd been thinking the same thing, didn't like the thought when he heard it expressed. 'Jerk-offs? What are you talking about?'

137

'We're sitting around here,' Carlson told him; 'waiting for people who aren't here and aren't gonna be here and in fact are probably themselves in Palm Beach.'

'Getting warm,' Ross said.

'Fuck it,' Melander said. 'Nobody's coming here, let's go back.'

'Like I said,' Carlson said.

They didn't want Parker to know they'd been there, in case he did happen to drop by before the Clendon job went down, so they put everything back the way they'd found it, including restashing the guns. There was a late snowstorm, which delayed them another day and got Melander's back up even more, and then they drove south, grousing at one another most of the way. They usually got along together, but the wait this time was getting to them, and the complication of Parker just made everything worse.

They got back to the estate in Palm Beach at almost midnight and went through switching on lights, echoing through the empty rooms, all of them looking for signs of Parker's presence, but none of them saying so. They met again in the kitchen and Ross said, 'No change.'

'Exactly like we left it,' Carlson said.

Melander opened the refrigerator and got out three beers. 'Well, wherever he is,' he said, 'at least he hasn't been here.'

2

The funny thing is, she showed that condo two days later, the place where Daniel Parmitt – as if that was his name – told her about the three men who'd cheated him and who were going to steal Mrs Miriam Hope Clendon's jewels. And the funnier thing is, Mr and Mrs Hochstein from Trenton, New Jersey, loved the condo, didn't want to haggle at all, didn't want to look at a thousand other places, loved the Bromwich, wanted to close right this second. The first place she showed them, and they were hooked, they were hers, which has never happened in the entire history of real estate. It was a sign.

Lord knows she needed a sign. Lesley hadn't heard from Parmitt since their discussion at the condo, and she would dearly love to know what was going on, but knew better than to call him and ask. He was a very private person, Mr Daniel Parmitt. He would let you know how close you could get, and woe betide you if you crossed the line. She thought she understood Parmitt now, and how to deal with him. In a nutshell, he was everything that Gerry Mackenzie, her brain-dead ex, was supposed to have been but, it turned out, was not.

Gerry Mackenzie had been young Lesley Simons's first attempt to break out of the third-rate life she'd been dealt, growing up poor in West Palm, right next door to the ultra-rich, but never being quite poor enough just to throw in the towel. No; all the time she was growing up, her mother's favorite word had been 'appearances.' They had to keep up appearances, God knows why. They had to spend money for show, not for necessities. With a divorced mom who worked as a supermarket cashier and a slightly retarded older sister who was never going to be useful for anything and was never going to marry and become somebody else's burden, this meant for the young Lesley Simons an endless life of dreary pretense.

Gerry Mackenzie, a wholesale salesman for a big computer company, a glad-handing upbeat guy full of talk about the latest advances in the 'industry,' full of expertise and inside dirt, as though he himself were just on the verge of becoming the next software billionaire, had seemed just precisely the right prince to rescue Lesley Simons from the dungeon of her life. Only after she'd married him had she discovered that her mother had been an *amateur* when it came to keeping up appearances; Gerry was the pro. It was all sparkle and flash with him, all salesman's hype, all toothy grins and pay-you-back-next-week. It all came clear to her, one day in the second year of the marriage, when she'd heard two of Gerry's fellow salesmen talking about him, and one said, 'He comes on so great, but you know? He just can't close.'

She understood there were salesmen like that, failed salesmen. (Not her, though; in real estate, she was a shark for closing.) As a talker, Gerry Mackenzie was a winner; as an earner, he was a flop. She got her real estate agent's license during the marriage because somebody had to put food on the table, and after a while she realized all she was getting out of this deal was the opportunity to listen to Gerry gasbag all the time. Home wasn't that great an alternative, but, until something else came along, it was better than Gerry. At least, she got to keep more of her earnings.

Was Daniel Parmitt the something else? Not to marry, God knows, or even to sleep with, but to make it possible for her to get *out* of here. On her own, this time. Far away from Palm Beach, far away from Florida entirely. Maybe the U.S. Virgin Islands, where she could kick back in her own little place and let the world go screw itself. On her own, strictly on her own.

Which had been the other thing she'd learned from marriage to Gerry Mackenzie: she didn't much like sex. She never had, in the few times she'd tried it with other people before Gerry, but then she'd always assumed it was because she and the guy didn't know each other well enough or weren't compatible or whatever. With Gerry, they got to know each other very well, and Gerry certainly knew how to turn his salesman's charm to the question of sex, so that was one area in which she couldn't find him at fault.

No, it was her. She didn't think she was a lesbian, she'd never had any interest in that direction, either. She thought it was just that she didn't particularly need sex, so why go through with it? Messy, disorganized, and frequently embarrassing; the hell with it.

That was one of the good things about Daniel Parmitt; he didn't mistake her interest for a sexual one, and he was too focused on his own plans to have time for irrelevancies like sex with his local girl guide. There were moments when she thought it might be interesting to go to bed with him just once, just to see what it was like, but then she'd remember how cold his eyes had been the time he'd made her strip so he could be sure she wasn't tape-recording their conversation, and she knew that wasn't the look

141

of somebody interested in her body. Even today, Gerry Mackenzie would give her a better time than that, if that's what she wanted.

It still surprised her that she'd been bold enough to go after Parmitt, before she'd known enough about him to know it was the right thing to do. Desperation, maybe, an antenna out frantically in search of a sign. Whatever it was, some instinct had grabbed her, that's all, and said, This guy will get you out of here. He'll get you out of here, and then he'll get out of your life. Grab him.

Would he? Would the people he was mad at really steal Mrs Clendon's jewels and get away with it? Would Daniel Parmitt really take the jewels away from *them*? And would he really share some of the profit with her?

Maybe. Maybe. Maybe.

Did she have anything else going? Nothing. The commission on the Bromwich condo sale was very nice, but not what she needed. She'd known for a long time, you don't change your life on commissions. You need a score. Somewhere, somehow, a score.

Keep healthy, Daniel Parmitt, she thought. I've bet the farm on you.

3

Elvis Clagg saw the whole thing, from the beginning, right there in front of him. It was incredible. It was like a movie.

At twenty-three, Elvis Clagg wasn't the youngest member of the Christian Renewal Defense Force (CRDF), but he was the most recent recruit, having joined up only four months ago, bringing the CRDF's strength up to twenty-nine, its highest enlistment in more than fifteen years. Still, not one of those guys had ever themselves seen anything as amazing, and they were the first to admit it. Even Captain Bob, in his years in Nam, had never seen the like, and Captain Bob was over fifty years of age.

Captain Bob Hardawl himself had founded the CRDF not long after he'd come back to Florida from Nam and had seen that the blacks and Jews were about to take over everywhere from the forces of God, and that the forces of God could use some help from a fella equipped with infantryman training.

Armageddon hadn't struck yet, thank God, but you just knew that sooner or later it would. You could read all about it on the Internet, you could hear it in the songs of Aryan rock, you could see it in the news all around you, you could read it in all the books and magazines that Captain Bob insisted every member of the CRDF subscribe to and *read*.

That was an odd thing, too. Reading had always been tough for Elvis Clagg. It had been one of the reasons he'd dropped out of school at the very first opportunity and got that job at the sugar mill that paid shit and immediately gave him a bad cough like an old car. But now that he had stuff he *wanted* to read, stuff he *liked* to read, why, turned out, he was a natural at it.

They oughta figure that out in the schools. Quit giving the kids all that *Moby Dick* shit and give them *The Protocols of Zion*, and you're gonna have you some heavy-duty readers.

But the point is, with all the reading everybody'd done, and all the sights that everybody'd seen – and three of the CRDF troopers had done time up at Raiford, so you know they're not exactly pansies – still and all, nobody had ever seen anything like this.

The entire troop of twenty-nine, Captain Bob Hardawl commanding, was deep in the Everglades on maneuvers, keeping up their tracking skills, learning jungle infiltration, when they heard the car. There was a road over there, of course, they'd just marched out on it, but you never heard a *car* on that road, it didn't go anywhere. Just to some fallen-down shacks used to belong to alligator hunters or maybe even older, egret hunters, from when the fancy ladies up north liked to wear egret feathers in their hats. So why was a car coming this way?

Billy Joe, one of the more excitable members of the group, called, 'Captain Bob, interlopers! Suppose they're Feds?'

Feds! The deadly battle with government lawmen, always a possibility, always the threat out there waiting. Was it here now? Elvis searched the sky, clutching his Uzi to his chest, but he saw no black helicopters.

'Easy, boys,' Captain Bob called to his line of men, and held his Colt .45 automatic up in the air to signal they should stand where they were. The rest of them all carried Uzis adapted to fire only one shot at a time, to make them legal, which of course would be unadapted in a flat second once Armageddon started, but Captain Bob, as the leader, was the only one with a side arm.

'I see it!' Jack Ray called, and then they all saw it. A white utility vehicle, it was, looked foreign, moving along the road toward the curve where they themselves had turned off into the glades not five minutes ago.

Captain Bob gestured downward with the .45, and they all crouched, twenty-nine men in camouflage uniforms with greasepaint and Off! on their faces. In a minute, the car would go around that curve and on out of sight.

And then it happened, astonishingly. Instead of slowing, the car abruptly *speeded up*, and its right front door opened, on the side away from the CRDF, and a man fell or jumped out of it.

The car yawed this way and that, brakes on hard, tires slipping on the muddy road, and the *near* side rear door opened and *another* man came rolling out, and this one was clutching a rifle in vertical position against his chest, exactly the way Captain Bob had taught the CRDF to do, if they ever had to bail out of something big, moving fast.

The car slewed around, the first man started to his feet as though to run off into the glades, and damn if the second man didn't come up on one knee, aim, and shoot the first man in the back. *Whang*! Down he went; son of a bitch!

And tried to get up. They could see him struggle as the man with the rifle got up and walked toward him and the white car finally came to a stop, and the driver stuck his head out to yell something to the shooter.

Captain Bob started yelling then, too: 'Hey! Hold on there! You men stop there!'

But they couldn't hear him, or they were concentrating too much to pay attention, so the whole CRDF watched the rifleman kick the man he'd shot to roll him down into the water, and then take aim to shoot him again up close.

That was when Captain Bob fired his side arm into the air to attract their attention.

Which it did. The driver of the car and the rifleman both turned to stare at the crouching CRDF, and then, quick as a wink the rifleman whipped up his rifle and fired at *them*!

A fella named Hoby that had bad teeth and was three guys to Elvis's left flopped backward like a cut line of wash. Just back and down.

The truth is, if it wasn't for the CRDF, Elvis personally would have panicked at that point and gone running like a greyhound into the glades. But there *was* the CRDF, and he was part of it, and he stuck.

'Two lines!' called Captain Bob while the rifleman fired again and a fella named Floyd did the back-flop thing, and the remaining twenty-six troopers, with Captain Bob tall at their right end, quickly formed into two broad lines facing the foe. The front rank dropped to one knee.

'Front rank!' yelled Captain Bob as the rifleman suddenly took off running toward the car. 'The vehicle!'

Which meant the rear rank, which included Elvis, was to take out the rifleman. Okay. Not much leading at this distance. Hands steady as a rock.

'Fire!'

Thirteen bullets went into the driver and thirteen bullets went into the rifleman.

The CRDF's first military engagement. They'd taken two

casualties out of a force of twenty-nine, and the opposing force was completely wiped out. As far as Elvis Clagg was concerned, the CRDF had just kicked ass.

4

'Dear,' said Alice Prester Young, 'do we know a Daniel Parmitt?'

Jack Young looked up from his *Wall Street Journal* to smile across the breakfast table at his bride. 'Who, dear?'

'Parmitt, Daniel Parmitt. It says here he's staying at the Breakers.'

'It says where?'

'In the *Herald*.'

Jack Young's smile was the soul of patience. 'Dear,' he said, 'why is Mr Parmitt in the *Herald*?'

'Because he was shot. Not expected to live.'

'Shot!' Jack's surprise was genuine. 'Why would we know anybody that was shot?'

'Well, it says he's staying at the Breakers, so I'm wondering if he's here for the ball.'

'Well, if he's been shot,' Jack said, 'he isn't likely to come to the ball.'

'No, dear, but I was just wondering.'

'If we knew him,' Jack said.

'Yes, dear,' she said, although by now she had realized that wasn't the actual question at all. It wasn't did *they* know this Daniel Parmitt, it was did *she* know him. Jack wouldn't be likely to know anybody from *her* past, would he?

This was her first season at the beach as Alice Prester

Young, after having been Alice Prester Habib forever. Eleven years; hard to believe. Before that, somebody else, before that, somebody else, who even remembers anymore?

It was very nice to bring an attractive new husband to the beach for the season, introduce him around, let the biddies turn green with envy. And it was especially nice to know that one could still look *all right* on the arm of such a husband. One didn't look exactly like a girl anymore, but one certainly did look *all right*.

Particularly the body. Between the doctors and the dietitians and the personal trainers, it was possible, though not easy, to keep a hard youthful body forever, to offer an attentive young husband something interesting and responsive in bed. The face could be kept smooth and attractive, but never quite exactly girlish. The softnesses and roundnesses of youth can never be recaptured on the face, so the best you can hope for in that department is angular, slightly hollow, good looks, more striking than beautiful. But who could complain? At sixty-seven, to have a striking face above the body of a twenty-year-old wasn't bad. And a twenty-six-year-old brand-new husband.

Why had she stayed so long with Habib?

Jack broke into her thoughts by saying, 'Somebody shot this fellow at the Breakers?'

'No, dear, he's *staying* at the Breakers. They kidnapped him—'

'What!'

'—and took him into the Everglades and shot him there.'

'Who? Why?'

'Apparently it was a case of mistaken identity. They

149

were professional killers, and whoever they were supposed to kill they took this man Parmitt by mistake.'

'Now, that's what I call bad luck,' Jack said, and laughed. 'And besides that, he doesn't get to go to the ball.'

'Oh, that reminds me, the auction,' she said. 'Dear, would you be a dear?'

'Of course,' he said. He'd been just as attentive when he'd been an insurance company claims adjuster and they'd met after that silly automobile accident in Short Hills. Now, his bright blue eyes eager, he said, 'What do you need, dear?'

'My albums,' she said. 'Not last year's, but the two years before that.'

'Coming up,' he said. He rose, smiled, folded his *Journal*, put it on the chair, and went off to her study, leaving her in the cool and quiet breakfast room, all pink and gold, with its view over the sea grape at the limitless ocean.

In a minute he was back with the two albums she'd asked for, both big thick volumes with padded pastel covers and glassine sheets within, inside which, every year, Alice inserted all photos and social-page stories involving her. Which meant, naturally, that most of the other important Beachers would also be seen in the various photos.

'What I'm looking for ...' Alice said, pushing her coffee cup aside and riffling through the first album, 'what I want ... is ... yes! There, see it?'

She had found a newspaper photo showing the three co-chairs of a charity ball from two years ago, the last year Miriam Hope Clendon had still been active in society. The three over-dressed women were lined up in a row to face the camera, Miriam in the center, of course, being the grande dame, with Helena Stockworth Fritz on her right

150

and Alice on her left. But this time it wasn't at herself Alice wanted to look, nor even at the rather portly and snout-faced Miriam, but at the necklace around Miriam's neck, on which she tapped a mauve false fingernail.

Jack leaned attentively over her shoulder, smiling vaguely at the photo. 'What am I looking at, dear?'

'The necklace, Miriam's necklace. *That's* what I'm going to bid on. I've had my eye on that necklace ever since I first met Miriam, oh, some years ago.'

'It's beautiful,' Jack said, and in his eye was the glint, though Alice didn't see it, of a man looking at a necklace he expects to inherit someday.

'We have to do a sealed bid on *something* to get into the auction,' she said with satisfaction, 'and that's what I'm after, and I believe I'll get it.'

'Won't other people bid for it?'

'Not for long,' she said. 'It's extremely valuable, you know.'

'Yes, it looks it.'

'*Most* people, *I* believe,' Alice said, 'will just go for the baubles, because they won't want to spend an awful lot of money this late in the season. Just so they take home some little thing. But *I* will bid on this necklace, and I'll bid low, and because it's so valuable it won't come on the block until very late, when everybody else will already have their little something, and I wouldn't be surprised if I get it for my opening bid.'

'How clever you are, Alice,' Jack said, and patted her shoulder before he went back around to his seat and his *Wall Street Journal*.

She continued to smile at the necklace in the photo. 'What a coup,' she said. 'To get that necklace cheap, and to wear it on *every* occasion.' Like all very wealthy women, Alice had strange cold pockets of miserliness. Her eyes shone as she looked across the table at Jack. 'It will be an absolute *steal*,' she said.

5

Trooper Sergeant Jake Farley of the Snake River County sheriff's department had never seen anything like *this* before. Four dead, one dying, all questions, no answers. Nothing but frustration, all the way around.

Starting with blowhard 'Captain' Robert Hardawl and his collection of retards and misfits that he called the Christian Renewal Defense Force. Hardawl and his scruffy gang had been a thorn in Sergeant Farley's side for years, always threatening violence, never quite going far enough to get themselves busted up and put away where they couldn't be an offense to decent law enforcement people anymore.

Two, three times a year, Farley would sit down with Agent Mobley from the Miami office of the FBI to discuss the various hate groups and paramilitary loonies wandering around these swamps, and Hardawl and his crowd were always prominent in that discussion. And now they've gone ahead at last and killed two men, and there wasn't one blessed thing Farley could do about it, because, goddammit, it was self-defense, and Hardawl had his own two dead bodies to prove it, shot with the same firearm that shot Daniel Parmitt.

Who was another frustration. Who the hell was he? Some rich fella from Texas, that's all, spending part of the winter in Palm Beach, grabbed up by two professional killers from Baltimore either because somebody wanted Daniel Parmitt dead – to inherit his money, maybe? – or because they got the wrong man.

Being unable to ask Gowan and Vavrina who hired them because they'd been all shot to shit by Hardawl's people, and being unable to ask Parmitt who might want him dead because he damn near *was* dead, unconscious and slowly slipping away, meant Farley had nobody to ask anything except Hardawl and his pack of losers, who didn't know anything. It was enough to make a man bite his badge.

Four days. The Baltimore police and the Maryland state police had shared all the information they had on Gowan and Vavrina, which was a lot, but didn't include the name of their most recent employer. The San Antonio police had passed on to Farley what they could find out about Parmitt, which wasn't much: never been in trouble with the law, owned a house in a nice part of town, was loved by his bankers. The Breakers had sent along Parmitt's possessions from the hotel, which consisted mainly of resort wear. He traveled with his birth certificate, which was about the only oddity Farley had seen in it all.

Snake River County didn't get much of what Jake Farley thought of as big-city crime, meaning gangland killings, professional armed robbery, that sort of thing, but what they did get was all his; he was the one man in the sheriff's department who'd been through the FBI courses and the state CID courses and had even been sent off with the help of federal funding for a couple of courses at John Jay College of Criminal Justice up in New York City; *that* had been an experience.

But even that hadn't prepared him for this situation. He had the victim, he had the perps – far too many perps, in fact – he had the weapons, he had every damn thing, and yet he couldn't have known less about what was going on if he was a brand-new baby boy. So here he was on the fourth day of the so-called investigation, seated at his corner desk in the bullpen at the sheriff's department, trying to think of somebody to call, when his phone rang. He gave it a jaundiced look before he answered: 'Farley.'

'Meany here, Sarge.'

Meany was the deputy on duty at the hospital, to report any change in Parmitt's condition, so this was the one phone call Farley had definitely not wanted: 'So he's dead, huh?'

'Well, no, sir. The reason I'm calling, he woke up.'

Farley's back lost its slump: 'What?'

'And there's a woman here to see him.'

'A woman? For Parmitt?'

'Yes, sir. Read about it in the *Miami Herald*, she said, said she had to talk to him.'

'Not before me,' Farley said. 'Hold her there, keep him awake, I'll be right over.'

The woman was a good-looking blonde of about forty with some heft to her; the kind of woman Farley was attracted to, in his off-duty hours. In fact, the kind of woman he was married to, which meant his off-duty hours were few and far between.

And this wasn't one of them. He entered the waiting room, saw Meany standing there, saw the woman rise from one of the green vinyl sofas, and crossed to her to say, 'Trooper Sergeant Farley, sheriff's department.' He did not offer to shake hands.

She said, 'I'm Lesley Mackenzie.'

'And you're a friend of Daniel Parmitt's.'

'Yes. I'd really like to talk with him.'

'So would I,' Farley told her. 'Rank gets its privileges here. I go first, then we'll see if the doctor says it's all right for you.'

'I'll wait,' she said, 'however long it takes.'

So she was *that* kind of friend, a little more than a friend but not quite family. Farley said, 'You can probably tell me more about him. We'll talk in a while.'

'All right,' she said.

Farley turned away, giving Meany a quick frown and head-shake that meant don't-let-her-leave, then went out and down the hall toward Parmitt's room.

This was only the second time he'd visited Parmitt, the first being shortly after the man was brought in, when visiting him was nothing but a waste of time. Parmitt was a real wreck then, shot, nearly drowned, and some of his ribs caved in.

What had happened was, he'd been shot in the back, the bullet passing through his body, hitting nothing vital, missing the spine by an inch, nicking a rib on the way out. Then the killer rolled him into the water, unconscious, and by the time the war with Hardawl's crew was over, the fella was drowned.

One thing you had to give Hardawl credit for – and Farley hated to have to admit it – he did give his people good training, including drowning rescues and CPR. They knew enough to lay the man on his stomach, head to the side, somebody's finger in his mouth to keep him from swallowing his tongue, while somebody else did some heavy bearing-down on his back, in slow rhythmic movements, to get the water out and start the process of breathing again. This can crack ribs, the way it did this time, and this time was even worse, because that was rough treatment for a torso that had just had a bullet pass through it, but Hardawl had realized there was no choice. If you don't get the water out, the man's dead anyway.

Well, he was a tough son of a bitch, Parmitt, and he survived the drowning rescue just the way he survived the shot and the drowning, but when they brought him in and Farley got that one gander at him, he sure did look like a candidate for the last rites. So what would he look like now?

Not that much better. They had the upper half of the bed cranked partway up, to make it easier for him to breathe, and his entire torso was swathed in bandages. His eyes were deep-set and ringed with dark shadow, his cheeks were sunken, and that snaky little mustache looked like somebody's idea of a bad joke, painted on him as though he were a face in an advertising poster. His arms, held away from his body because of the thicknesses of wrapping around his chest, were above the blanket, lying limp, the big hands half-curled in his lap. He was breathing slowly through his mouth, and when he saw Farley the look in his eyes was dull and without curiosity.

A white-coated intern was in the room, looking at the patient, just standing there, and he turned to say, 'Sheriff.'

Farley never bothered to correct people's use of titles; he was in the tan uniform of the sheriff's department, so if they wanted to call him Sheriff or Deputy or Officer or Trooper or anything else, he knew it didn't mean much more than *hello*, so why fret it. He said, 'How's our patient?'

'Conscious, but barely. I understand you want to question him.'

'More than you can imagine.'

'Try to make it short, and if he starts to get upset, you'll have to stop.'

157

'I understand,' Farley said. 'I've been at bedsides before.'

There were two chrome and vinyl chairs in the room. Farley brought one over to the side of the bed and sat on it, so he and Parmitt were now at the same height. 'Mr Parmitt,' he said.

The eyes slowly moved to focus on him, but Parmitt didn't turn his head. Maybe he couldn't. But it was a strange gesture; here the man was the victim, nearly dead, weak as a kitten, but in that eye movement he suddenly looked to Farley extremely dangerous.

Which was foolish, of course. Farley said, 'How do you feel, Mr Parmitt?'

'Where am I?' It was just a whisper, no strength in it at all. The intern, at the foot of the bed, probably couldn't make out the words.

So Parmitt gets to ask the questions first. Okay, Farley could go along with that. He said, 'You're in the Elmer Neuman Memorial Hospital, Snake River, Florida.'

'Florida.' He whispered it like a word he didn't know, and then his brow wrinkled and he said, 'Why am I in Florida?'

'On vacation, like everybody else,' Farley told him. 'Don't you remember? You're staying at the Breakers, up in Palm Beach.'

'I live in San Antonio,' Parmitt whispered. 'I was ... I was driving to my club. Was I in an accident?'

And this was something Farley had seen before, too. In bad accidents, or after bad scenes of violence, often the victims don't remember any of the events leading up to the trauma. Later on it would come back to them, maybe, but not right away.

Unfortunate. Farley could see there was no point

questioning the man now, he didn't remember enough, and if he were told somebody out there was trying to kill him it just might put him into shock. So he said, 'Yeah, you were in a kind of accident. You're still getting over it, Mr Parmitt. We'll talk again when you feel better.'

'Was I driving?'

Farley had to lean close to understand the man. 'What? No, sir, you weren't driving.'

'I have … an excellent safety record.'

'I'm sure you do, Mr Parmitt,' Farley said, and got to his feet, and said, 'We'll talk later.'

Lesley Mackenzie was again seated on the vinyl sofa. She started to rise when Farley entered, but he patted the air, saying, 'Stay there, Ms Mackenzie, we'll sit and talk.'

He sat at the other end of the sofa, half-turned to face her, and said, 'You're a friend of Mr Parmitt's. Known him long?'

'Only a few weeks,' she said, and opened her purse on her lap. 'I'm a real estate agent in Palm Beach,' she explained, and produced her business card. 'My card.'

He accepted it, looked at it, tucked it away in his shirt pocket, looked at her.

She said, 'Mr Parmitt was thinking of buying in Palm Beach, and I showed him some places, and we started to date. In fact, we had an appointment – to look at a house, not a date – and when he didn't show up, I didn't know what to think. Then I read about the – what is it? attempted murder – in the *Herald*, and I came here as soon as I could get away.'

Farley saw no reason to disbelieve the woman. She was who she claimed to be, and her relationship with Parmitt sounded about right. In fact, her hurrying down here all the way from Palm Beach suggested to Farley she'd had some idea of her friendship with Parmitt blossoming into something more. She wouldn't be the first real estate woman in the world to wind up marrying a rich client. They walk into all those bedrooms together, and finally something clicks.

Well, more power to her. Farley said, 'I have to tell you, Ms Mackenzie, at the moment he doesn't remember much. Doesn't remember the shooting at all, doesn't remember coming to Florida. Right now, he might not remember you.'

The slow smile she gave him was startlingly powerful. 'Trooper,' she said, 'or Sergeant. What do I call you?'

'Sergeant,' he said, pleased and grateful that she made the effort to get it right.

'Sergeant,' she said, 'if Daniel Parmitt doesn't remember *me*, I'm not half the woman I think I am.'

Farley always found himself growing awkward and foolish when a woman talked dirty in front of him. He blinked, and tried a half smile, and said, 'Well, you can go and have a word with him if you like. The only thing, the doctor said, try not to get him excited.'

She laughed. After she left, he could feel the blush still hot on his face.

6

Lesley was shocked by the look of him. She hadn't known what exactly to expect, but not this. He was like some powerful motor that had been switched off, inert, no longer anything at all. The look in his eyes was dull, the hands curled on his lap seemed dead.

Would he remember her? It had seemed to her that the best way to handle that sheriff sergeant was to give him the idea she and Daniel had something sexual going, because if that wasn't the reason for her being here, what *was* the reason? Also, she could see that he was one of those men made uneasy by talk about sex from a woman, and it would probably be a good idea to keep him off balance a bit.

But in fact, if Daniel was as harmed as he looked, maybe he really wouldn't remember her, maybe her imprint wasn't that deep with him.

There was a white-coated intern in the room, seated in a corner on a chrome and vinyl chair, writing on a form on a clipboard. He nodded at Lesley and said, 'You can talk with him, but not for long. You'll have to get close, though, he can't speak above a whisper.'

'Thank you.'

A second chair stood over beside the bed. Reluctant, wishing now she hadn't come, that she'd merely tele-phoned to find out what his situation was – though then

161

she wouldn't have found out what she needed to know about the three men – she went over to that chair and sat down and said, 'Daniel.'

His eyes had followed her as she crossed the room, and now he whispered, 'What day is it?' The whisper was hoarse, rusty, and barely carried across the space between them.

She leaned closer. 'Monday,' she said.

'Four days,' he whispered.

'Four days? What do you mean?'

'Auction.'

'What? You aren't still thinking about *that*.'

He ignored her, following his own lines of thought, saying, 'How do you know I'm here?'

'It was in the *Herald*. You were shot and the people who shot you were killed by—'

'*Herald*? Newspaper?'

'Yes. On Saturday. I couldn't get here till now.'

'Lesley,' he whispered, 'you've got to get me out of here.'

Now she was whispering, too, almost as inaudible as him, because of the intern, who was paying them no attention. She leaned closer yet to whisper, 'You can't leave! You can't even move!'

'I can do better than they think. If I'm in the paper, somebody else could come to finish me.'

This was the subject she really wanted to talk about, and the main reason for her trip here. The three robbers. She whispered, 'It's the people you want to steal from, isn't it? Do they know about me?'

'Different. Not them.'

That was a surprise. She'd taken it for granted it was the three men planning the robbery who'd discovered Daniel

162

and had him shot, and quite naturally she'd wondered if they also knew about *her*. She whispered, 'There's somebody *else*? Who?'

'Don't know. Don't care. Just so I get out of here. Lesley.'

'What?'

'The longer I'm here, the more the cops are gonna wonder about me. My background, my name. And I can't have them take my prints.'

'Oh.'

She sat back, considering him. He was really in a terrible situation, wasn't he? Battered, weak, being pursued by killers he didn't seem even to know, trapped in this hospital with police all around, and now it turns out his fingerprints would lead the police to something dangerous in his background. And the only person in the whole entire world who could help him was her.

This time, she wasn't surprised by him, she was surprised by herself. She felt suddenly very strong. Her emotion toward Daniel Parmitt wasn't love or sex, but it *was* tender. It was almost, oddly, maternal. Now, she was the strong one, she was the one who could help. And she *wanted* to help; she wanted him to know that when he asked the question, she would be there with the answer.

She leaned even closer to him, one forearm on the bed as she gazed into his eyes, seeing they weren't really as dull as he pretended. She whispered, 'How bad off are you, really? Can you walk?'

'I don't know. I can try.'

'In the paper, it said you weren't expected to live. Won't that make these other people wait?'

'Awhile.'

'All right,' she said. 'I don't know how I'll do it, but

I'll do it. I'll see what I can arrange, and I'll come back tomorrow.'

He watched her leave. The intern sat in the corner, writing.

7

Mrs Helena Stockworth Fritz was an extremely busy woman, never more so than since the death of dear Miriam Hope Clendon. There were the foundation boards to sit on, the press interviews, the arrangements for the charity balls, the lunches, the shopping, the phone calls with friends far and near, the yoga, the aura therapist, the constant planning for this or that event; and now the auction of dear Miriam's jewelry, right here at Seascape.

And not merely on the grounds, but inside the house as well. Most times, charity occasions at Seascape were held out on the side lawn and the terrace above the seawall overlooking the Atlantic, but this time it was necessary to have the jewelry on display, and to have the auctioneer where all the attendees could see and hear him, and so it was necessary to open the ballroom at Seascape with its broad line of tall French doors leading out to the terrace and the famous view. So in the middle of all this frenzy of activity, the last thing Mrs Fritz needed was the delivery, three days early, of the musicians' amplifiers.

Jeddings came with the news, to the parlor where Mrs Fritz was deep in concentration on her flower arranging. Jeddings looked worried, as she always did, and clutched her inevitable clipboard to her narrow chest as she said, 'Mrs Fritz, deliverymen at the gate.'

'Delivery? Delivering what?'

'They say the amplifiers for the musicians.'

'Musicians? We aren't having musicians tonight.'

'No, Mrs Fritz, for the auction.'

The auction. Yes, there would be music that night, of course, dancing and the drinking of champagne before the auction began, to loosen up the attendees. But that wasn't till Friday, the day after the ball at the Breakers when the jewelry would first be publicly displayed, and today was only Tuesday. 'What on earth are they delivering amplifiers *now* for?'

'I don't know, Mrs Fritz, they say this is the only time they can do it.'

'Let me see these people.'

Mrs Fritz accompanied Jeddings to the vestibule, which was what they called the very well-equipped office at the front of the house, near the main door. Jeddings and two clerks operated from here, helping to keep all of Mrs Fritz's many charities and social events and other activities on track, and the video intercom to the front entrance was here.

Mrs Fritz stopped in front of the monitor to frown at the TV image there. Once again, as always, that stray thought came and went: Why can't these things be in color like everything else? But that, of course, wasn't the point. The point was that, stopped just outside the gate, half blocking traffic, was a small nondescript dark van, containing two men. The driver was hard to see, but the passenger, a burly man with a thick shock of wavy black hair, was half-leaned out his open window, where he'd been speaking on the intercom and was now awaiting a reply.

'Tell him,' Mrs Fritz said, 'this is a very inconvenient time.'

'Yes, Mrs Fritz.'

Jeddings sat at the desk, picked up the phone, and said, 'Mrs Fritz says this is a very inconvenient time.' Then she depressed the loudspeaker button so Mrs Fritz could hear the reply.

Which was polite and amiable, but not helpful. Mrs Fritz watched the burly man smile as he said, 'I'm sorry about that. I don't like no dissatisfied customers, but they give us this stuff and said deliver it today, and we got no place to keep it. We got no insurance for this stuff. These amplifiers, I dunno how much they cost, I don't wanna be responsible for these things.'

Jeddings covered the phone's mouthpiece with a hand and turned her worried face toward Mrs Fritz. 'We could store them in a corner of the ballroom, Mrs Fritz. They wouldn't be in the way.'

Mrs Fritz didn't like it, but she could see it was simply going to be one of those inconveniences one had to put up with, so grumpily she said, 'Very well. But I don't want to be tripping over them.'

'Oh, no, Mrs Fritz,' Jeddings promised, and spoke into the phone: 'Very well. Come in.' And she pushed the button to open the outer doors.

Mrs Fritz could see that the burly man said something else, but this time Jeddings had not pressed the loudspeaker button. 'That's fine,' Jeddings said, and hung up, and the big wooden doors out there began to roll open.

Mrs Fritz said, 'What did he say?'

'He said thank you, Mrs Fritz.'

'Polite, in any event. *That's* a rarity.'

'Yes, Mrs Fritz.'

'I'll come along, see where you intend to place these things.'

'Yes, Mrs Fritz.'

They went out to the front hallway, with the double curving staircase and the pink marble floor, cool in the hottest weather, and Jeddings opened the front door as the van came crunching across the gravel around the curving drive to roll past the entrance and then back up. 'Shore Fire Delivery' was not very professionally printed in white on the doors.

The two men got out and came around to the rear of the van, the burly man smiling up at Mrs Fritz and saying, 'Afternoon, ma'am. Sorry about the inconvenience.'

'That's all right,' she said, to be gracious, though everyone present was well aware it was not all right.

The driver was a smaller man, skinny, sharp-featured, with very large ears. The two were dressed in normal workman's clothes, dark shapeless pants and T-shirts, the burly man's advertising beer, the driver's advertising the Miami Dolphins.

Why did the underclass so enjoy turning itself into billboards?

When the van doors were opened, two very large black boxes became visible inside, along with a hand truck, which the burly man brought out first. Then the two of them wrestled one of the boxes out of the van and onto the hand truck, and Mrs Fritz and Jeddings backed out of the doorway as the two men thumped the thing up the broad stairs and into the house. It had the usual dials and switches across the top, and black cloth across the front, and the brand name Magno in chrome letters attached to the front near the bottom.

Jeddings led the way through the house, the burly man wheeling the hand truck ahead of himself, the driver walking beside him with one hand on the amplifier to keep it from falling over, and Mrs Fritz brought up the rear, looking to be sure their wheels didn't hurt the parquet.

Fortunately, the placement of the display tables for the jewelry and the auctioneer's dais had already been determined, and tables and dais were now all in place. Mrs Fritz had not wanted to worry about details like *that* on the day. So they'd be able to place the amplifiers where they would not be underfoot while the rest of the preparations were being made, and would not be in a spot where it turned out something else had to be put.

It was the burly man, in fact, who suggested where to put the amplifiers. Pointing to the corner farthest from the display tables, he said, 'Ma'am, if we put them over there, I don't think they'd bother you.'

'Good,' she said, 'do that, then.'

They did, and repeated the operation with the second amplifier, placing it beside the first. Then they wheeled their hand truck back to the front door, the burly man smiled his way through another set of apologies – Mrs Fritz was gracious again – and then she went into the vestibule to watch on the monitor as the van drove away and the big doors were shut once more.

Jeddings said, 'Mrs Fritz, I'll have staff put a tablecloth over them – you won't even notice them.'

'Good. You do that.'

Jeddings did do that, and the amplifiers disappeared under a snowy damask tablecloth, and nobody gave them another thought.

8

'I don't want to,' Loretta whined.

Loretta always whined, but her whines were different, sometimes merely expressing her general attitude toward life, other times standing for specific emotions, like anger or fear or petulance or weariness. This one right now was her bullheaded stubborn whine, with that extra twang in it, and rumbles of mutiny.

Time to put a stop to that. Lesley turned to her mother, across the table. 'Mom,' she said, 'I don't ask much.'

Her mother, Laurel, put down her fork and frowned deeply, her leathery beige face creasing like a supermarket paper bag, because she never liked to have to mediate disputes between her daughters, between Lesley the quick one and Loretta the slow one, slightly retarded, badly overweight, never quite grasping what was going on.

The three were seated together at the dinner table on Wednesday evening, and Lesley knew she had to force the issue now because tomorrow would be the last day to try to get Daniel Parmitt out of the hospital. She'd thought and she'd thought, and this was the only idea she'd come up with for a way to slip him out of there, and it just simply required Loretta's cooperation. No other choice.

But her mother was making trouble, as well. 'Lesley,' she said, 'if only you'd tell us *why* you want to do this.'

Which, naturally, she could not. But why should she

have to? *She* was the provider in the family, she was the one who held it all together, how dare they question her?

'Mom,' she said, forcing herself to be calm and reasonable, 'this man is a friend. Not a lover, it's not like that, a friend. He's in trouble, and he asked me to help, and I'm going to help, and I need Loretta.'

'I don't want to get in trouble,' Loretta whined.

'You won't get in trouble,' Lesley told her, not for the first time. 'You just do what I say, and it'll be *easy*.'

'Mom,' Loretta whined.

Lesley looked at her mother. 'Or,' she said, slow and deliberate, to let her mother know she was serious about this, 'I could move out.' She didn't mention, nor at this moment did she more than barely think about it, that if this all happened the way it was supposed to, she'd be moving out anyway.

Loretta looked stricken. She had only the vaguest idea what life would be like without Lesley in the house, but she understood it would be in some way horrible. Worse than now.

Their mother looked from one to the other. She sighed. She said, 'Loretta, I think you have to do it.'

Loretta lowered her head to aim her put-upon look at the food on her plate. Her mother turned to Lesley: 'What time will you want to leave?'

'At four,' Lesley said. 'And it really will be easy, Mom. Nothing to it.'

9

Alice Prester Young knew she was a herd animal, and enjoyed the knowledge, because the herd she moved with was the very *best* herd in all the world. For instance, here she was, at five-thirty on this Thursday afternoon, in her chauffeured Daimler, on her way to the bank with her new husband, the delicious Jack, to pick up just the *perfect* jewelry for tonight's pre-auction ball, and she knew when she arrived at the bank she would be surrounded by her own kind, chauffeured and cosseted women with attractive escorts, all coming to the bank (the only bank one could use, really) because this particular bank stayed open late whenever there was an important ball in town, just so the herd could come get its jewelry out of the safe-deposit boxes. And the bank would open again, later tonight, when the same herd left the ball and returned to redeposit their jewelry all over again.

The ritual of the bank was almost as enjoyable as the ritual of the ball itself, though shorter. The staff was quiet, methodical, servile without being obsequious. The herd cooed greetings to one another and exclaimed with pleasure over each other's choice of which pieces to wear to this special occasion. The mirrors that the bank had installed in the rooms outside the safe-deposit vault were very special mirrors, not clear like common mirrors but tinted the most delicate gray, so that when the ladies of

172

the herd looked at themselves as they put on their jewelry, they did not see as many wrinkles or age spots or other flaws as a common mirror might unfeelingly display. The bank cared about the feelings of the herd, and Alice Prester Young liked that, too.

How was it phrased, in that little map and pamphlet the tourists could pick up? The people of Palm Beach were 'those who feel they have earned the right to live well.' Yes. Precisely. That's exactly how Alice felt. She had – somehow – earned the right to move with this plump and comfortable herd, to ride in the Daimler with her brand-new husband, to the beach, to the ball, to the bank.

Another glorious night!

Five-thirty. Trooper Sergeant Jake Farley sat in a side booth at Cindy's Luncheonette and drank coffee with FBI Agent Chris Mobley, a big spread-out Kentuckian with an easy grin and cold eyes. They were discussing, yet again, the wounded man from Texas, Daniel Parmitt.

'I just don't know where else to get at this thing from,' Farley said. 'The shooters are a blind alley, but every time I try to talk to Parmitt he gets all vague on me, can't remember a damn thing. I asked him would he mind if I bring in a hypnotist, and he said yeah he did, so here I am, still stuck.'

Mobley said, 'Why'd he nix the hypnotist?'

'Said he didn't like 'em, thought they were phony.'

'If they're phony,' Mobley said, 'they can't do nothing to him.'

'You can't reason with a man in a hospital bed,' Farley said. 'I've learned that a good long time ago. Man in a hospital bed feels sorry for himself and sore at the world. You can't reason with him.'

Mobley sipped coffee and squinted toward the front of Cindy's and the street outside. 'You think he's a wrong one somehow?'

Farley frowned at him. 'How'd you mean?'

'Somebody shot him,' Mobley pointed out. 'Man gets shot, usually it means somebody had a reason. How come he don't know what the reason is?'

'He doesn't remember the last week at all,' Farley said.

'Well, how about two weeks ago?' Mobley asked. 'Wouldn't the people with a reason have a reason back that far?'

Farley frowned deeper at that. 'You think he's fakin'? Lyin'? Stallin'?'

'You've seen him, I haven't,' Mobley said. 'But the man oughta know who's mad at him, oughta know at least that much.'

'Mmm,' Farley said, and frowned at his coffee.

'I tell you what,' Mobley said. 'Tomorrow, you run off a set of his prints, fax 'em to me in Miami, we'll check 'em up at SOG.'

Farley thought that over and slowly nodded. 'Couldn't hurt, I suppose,' he said.

Six o'clock. Lesley drove south on Interstate 95, Loretta an unhappy lump on the passenger seat beside her. Loretta was already dressed in the long tan raincoat and the wide-brimmed straw hat with the pink ribbon, and she was staring mulishly out the windshield. She wouldn't look at Lesley and certainly wouldn't talk to her. Loretta would go along with the plan, because she had no choice and she knew it, but she was definitely in a grade-A snit.

Well, it didn't matter, just so she did her part. Everything

174

was falling into place, starting with this car. Another rep at Lesley's firm, Gloria, was what is called a soccer mom, which meant she spent all her non-working time transporting masses of small children and all their necessary gear to sub-teen sporting events. For this purpose, her second car was this Plymouth Voyager, with the middle line of seats removed and a ramp installed that could be angled out from the wide side door to accommodate wheeled trunks full of basketballs or hockey sticks or whatever was needed. Lesley had arranged to borrow this vehicle from Gloria for this afternoon and evening, explaining she had to take her sister to a complicated medical procedure that would leave her unable to walk for a few days, and now they were on their way.

She looked out ahead, far down the straight wide road, and said with surprise, 'Well, *there's* something you don't see every day.'

Loretta almost looked at Lesley, or asked what it was you don't see every day, but she caught herself in time and went on being a lump.

Lesley watched the fire engine down there, rolling north, moving very fast in the left lane, overtaking everything on the road. 'It's a fire engine, Loretta,' she said. 'A great big red fire engine. See it? I wonder where it's going.'

Loretta finally did focus on the fire engine, having to turn her head to keep watching it as they passed one another. She actually started to smile, but then became aware of Lesley observing her, and quickly frowned instead.

'I like fire engines,' Lesley said, expecting no response and getting none.

'I like fire engines,' Hal Carlson said as they highballed north.

Seated beside him, Jerry Ross grinned. 'What I like,' he said, 'is fire.'

Seven-thirty. Mrs Helena Stockworth Fritz was not part of the herd. She was, in fact, above the herd, as the whole world acknowledged, and that's why she did not, before each ball, pay a visit at the bank.

The late Mr Fritz (munitions, oil, cargo ships, warehouses, all inherited) had, many years ago, during a spate of politically inspired financier kidnappings, installed a safe room in the middle of Seascape, which Mrs Fritz still used for her most valuable valuables. The safe room was a concrete box, twelve feet square and eight feet high, built *under* the building, into the water table but sealed and dry. A dedicated phone line in a stainless-steel pipe ran underground from the safe room to the phone company's lines out at the road, though in fact that telephone had never once been used.

If, however, some phalanx of Che Guevaras actually had launched an attack on Seascape back in those parlous times, Mr and Mrs Fritz would simply have locked themselves into the safe room, which included plumbing facilities and stored food, very like a fallout shelter from two decades before, and would have phoned the Palm Beach police to come repel the invaders.

That had never happened, but the room was far from useless. It was impregnable and temperature-controlled, and in it Mrs Fritz kept her furs, her jewelry, and, in the off-season, much of her best silver. Which meant she never had to join the hoi polloi crowding around the gray mirrors at the bank.

The mirror in the safe room, before which Mrs Fritz now stood, studying the effect she would make in *this*

176

gown, with *this* necklace, *these* bracelets, *this* brooch, *these* rings, and *this* tiara, was not tinted a discreet gray, like the mirror at the bank. Mrs Fritz was a realist and didn't need to squint when she gazed upon herself. (Nor would she ever stoop to buy a thirty-year-old husband.) She had lived a long time, and done much, and enjoyed herself thoroughly along the way, and if that life showed its traces on her face and body, what of it? It was an honest life, lived well. She had nothing to hide.

Satisfied with tonight's appearance, Mrs Fritz left and locked the safe room, then rode the stairlift up to the ground floor, where her walker awaited. Charles LeGrand was her frequent walker, a cultured homosexual probably even older than she was, neat and tidy in his blazer and ascot, smiling from within his very small goatee. Offering his elbow for her hand, 'You look *charmante* tonight, Helena,' he said.

'Thank you, Charles.'

They walked through the ballroom on their way to the car. Mrs Fritz noted with approval the ranks of rented padded chairs for the bidders, now in rows facing the auctioneer's lectern, each with its numbered paddle waiting on the seat. The platform for the musicians was in place, the side tables were covered in damask but not yet bearing their loads of plates and glasses and cutlery, the portable bar-on-wheels stood ready for tomorrow night's bartender, and all was as it was supposed to be.

The amplifiers under their white tablecloths she didn't even notice.

177

10

The Voyager's dashboard clock read *7:21* when Lesley steered into the visitors' parking area outside the Elmer Neuman Memorial Hospital in Snake River. Perfect timing.

In her three previous visits to Daniel here, Lesley had learned what she needed to know about the hospital routine. Was this what criminals called 'casing the joint'? She knew, for instance, that visiting hours ended at eight P.M., to accommodate visitors who had day jobs. She also knew that down the hall from Daniel lay an old woman named Emily Studworth, who seemed to be permanently unconscious and never to receive visitors. And she further knew that the clerical staff at the hospital changed shift at six P.M.

Lesley shut off the Voyager's engine and looked in the rearview mirror at Loretta. 'Okay, Loretta,' she said. 'We just go and do it and come right back out.'

Loretta was already in the wheelchair that Lesley had rented from a place in Riviera Beach called Benson's Sick Room and Party Supplies. Her mulish pouting expression fit the wheelchair very well; she was great in the part.

Lesley got out of the Voyager, slid open its side door, pulled out the ramp, and carefully backed Loretta and the wheelchair down to the blacktop. Then she shut and locked the car, and pushed the wheelchair across the parking lot and up the handicap-access ramp to the hospital's front door.

Since this was the first time she was arriving at the hospital after six P.M., the receptionist who checked the visitors in had never seen her before, and had no way to know that before this she'd always visited a patient named Daniel Parmitt. 'Emily Studworth,' Lesley told her.

The receptionist nodded and wrote that on her sheet. 'You're relatives?'

'We're her grandnieces. Loretta really wanted to see her auntie Emily just once more.'

'You don't have much time,' the receptionist warned her. 'Visiting hours end at eight.'

'That's all right, we just want to be with her for a few minutes.'

Lesley wheeled Loretta down the hall to the elevators and up to the third floor. The people at the nurses' station gave them a brief incurious look as they came out of the elevator. Lesley smiled at them and pushed the wheelchair down the hall to Daniel's room, which was in semi-darkness, only one small light gleaming yellow on the wall over the bed. They entered, and she pushed the door mostly closed behind her.

He was asleep, but as she entered the room he was suddenly awake, his eyes glinting in the yellow light. She pushed the wheelchair over beside the bed and whispered, 'Are you ready?'

'Yes.'

'Help me, Loretta.'

Obediently, Loretta stood up from the wheelchair and removed the long coat and big-brimmed straw hat. She put them on the bed along with her purse, which had been

179

concealed in the wheelchair. Then she and Lesley helped Daniel get out of bed.

He was stronger each day, but still very weak. The muscles in the sides of his jaw bunched and moved with his determination. He got his legs over the side of the bed, and then, with one of them on either side of him, he made it to his feet.

Lesley said, 'Can you stand alone?'

'Yes.' It was whispered through gritted teeth.

He stood unmoving, like a tree. They helped him put on the long coat, over the hospital gown that was all he wore, then helped him ease down into the wheelchair. He folded his hands in his lap, not to be noticeable, and Lesley fixed the straw hat on his head.

Meantime, Loretta had sat on the bed to remove her fake-fur shin-high brown boots. She had soft pumps in her purse that she now slipped on instead.

The boots had been too big for Loretta; they were the right size for Daniel. The hat, the long coat, and the boots covered him completely. As long as he kept his head down and his hands in his lap, he would look exactly like the person Lesley had wheeled in here.

Loretta stood up from the bed, wearing the blue pumps. She had on a shapeless blue-and-white-print dress. 'Do I go out now?' she asked.

Lesley considered her. 'Don't forget your glasses.'

'Oh!' Loretta took her black-framed glasses from her purse and put them on, becoming again the owlish, gawky person Lesley knew.

Lesley said, 'You just walk out. We'll be along in a minute.'

'All right.' Now that they were doing it, and nothing bad was happening, Loretta's mood had improved considerably. She very nearly smiled at Lesley, and when she looked at Daniel in the wheelchair her expression became concerned. 'He should stay here,' she said.

'He has his reasons,' Lesley assured her. 'We'll be along.'

Loretta left, and Lesley looked in the closet, expecting to find his clothes, surprised to see nothing in there at all. 'Where's your things?'

'Cops kept.'

'Oh. Well, let's get you out of here.'

The return journey was simple, and outside, there was Loretta, waiting for them, standing over there beside the Voyager. As she pushed him across the parking lot, Lesley said, 'I don't know what you expect to do tomorrow night.'

'Kill some people,' he whispered.

11

Jack Young really did care for his new (old) wife, Alice, felt affection for her, enjoyed more about her than her money, though of course the money had come first. In fact, it had been just a joke at the beginning, when he'd met Alice Prester Habib up in New Jersey, where he'd worked for Utica Mutual as a claims examiner, and where, when he first became aware that this particular insured had the hots for him, it was nothing more than the subject of gags around the office.

It was Maureen, an older woman with the firm, computer processor, who'd put the bee in his bonnet. 'You could do worse,' she'd said, and when Jack thought about it, he *could* do worse, couldn't he? He'd almost *done* worse, two or three times.

It had been almost a year, at that time, since he'd broken up with his last serious girlfriend, or, more accurately, since she'd broken up with him. His life was a little boring, a little same-old same-old, and the idea of shaking it up in this really different and outrageous way came to appeal to him more and more. And don't forget the money.

But the fact is, Alice was okay. God knows she was older than his mother, almost older than his grandmother, but she kept herself in shape like an NFL quarterback, and she was of an age where she had no timidity left in bed at all. So that part wasn't so bad, and for the rest

– the knowledge that people laughed at him behind his back, the term 'boy toy,' which seemed to hover in the air around him like midges – fuck 'em if they couldn't take a joke.

Because you can take the boy out of the actuarial business but you can't take the actuarial business out of the boy, and Jack was fully aware that he was (a) Alice's only heir, attested to in the prenuptial agreement, and (b) likely to outlive her by forty to fifty years. Forty to fifty *rich* years.

So all he had to do was pay attention, in and out of bed, and otherwise be discreet. For instance, when he and Alice walked into the big ballroom at the Breakers Thursday evening for the pre-auction ball, with the tall gleaming mirrors reflecting the posh crowd, and the radiant chandeliers, and the band's swing oldies echoing in the high-ceilinged space, and the swirl of revelers in their sprays of bright colors and gleaming gold and winking silver and sparkling jewels, the very *first* person he saw was Kim Metcalf, and he barely gave her a smile of recognition. She, too, with her shrewd blue eyes under the cloud of fluffy yellow hair, returned only the briefest of impersonal nods, including Alice as much as himself, before she moved on, holding to the arm of her husband, Howard, a retired tax lawyer she'd met as a stew on a first-class flight New York to Chicago. (She was still so much a stew in her heart that to this day she preferred the label 'flight attendant.')

As the Metcalfs moved on, Jack turned his eyes firmly away from Kim's twitching creased behind within the shimmering pale blue satin, but his mind said: *Saturday*. The apartment Alice would never know about, down among the condos, where he and Kim managed to meet once or twice every week, came surging into his memory.

Kim's body was softer than Alice's, which was also nice, but by now, for the both of them, the main point was to be able to have a conversation with somebody whose memory bank had not become full before you were born.

Turning to Alice and away from all temptation, Jack said, 'Do you want to dance, darling, or meet people first?'

'We'll dance, darling,' she decided. 'We can always meet people.'

True enough.

The new red paint on the fire engine doors was dry, and the doors no longer read

CRYSTAL CITY F.D.
ENG #1

It's a good thing Crystal City, a sparsely populated area down near Homestead, had an Eng #2 as well, or the good folks there would be shit out of luck if a fire were to start up anywhere around town in the next couple of days. It was a volunteer fire department, like so many in the sticks, so there was never anybody around the small brick fire house except for fires and meetings, so it had been very easy, at five this morning, to bypass the alarm system and ease into the fire house and come roaring out with old Eng #1. By the time anybody started looking for it, Melander and Carlson and Ross would have finished with it.

At nine P.M., with the pre-auction ball in full swing up at the Breakers, Ross stood beside the driver's door of Eng #1, an open quart of gold enamel paint in his left hand and an M. Grumbacher fine-line brush #5 in his right, with Melander just behind him to hold the flashlight. The fire engine now stood on the lawn at the right side of the house, out of sight from anywhere off the property. Ross, who had learned to be a passable sign painter during the first of his two stretches inside, leaned close to the door and drew the first vertical, then the U-shape to the right:

P

Farley's wife had learned to sleep through the late-night phone calls, and Farley had trained himself to wake right up at the beginning of the first ring, his hand snaking out from under the covers toward the phone before his eyes had completely focused on the bedside clock: *1:14.* There'd been worse.

'Farley.'

'Higgins here, Sarge,' being one of the deputies on night shift at the office. 'We got a report of a missing man out to the hospital.'

'Parmitt,' Farley said.

'That's right, Daniel Parmitt. The night administrator just called. They did their usual late-night check on the patients, and that one's gone.'

How? He didn't walk out, Parmitt, he wasn't up to it. Somebody helped him. The real estate woman? Farley said, 'You sent somebody over there?'

'Jackson and Reese.'

'Call them, tell them I'm on my way.' There wouldn't be anything there; still, he'd have a look.

Damn; should've taken those prints yesterday.

He drove into Snake River at two in the morning in the rented Buick Regal. He'd be done here in an hour, then drive back to Miami International, have breakfast, take the morning flight west, be swimming in his own pool by mid-afternoon.

The woman who gave him his assignments, once or twice a year, was a lawyer in Chicago. They spoke guardedly on the phone, almost never met face-to-face, and unless he was on assignment he lived a quiet life indeed, writing occasional album reviews for music magazines. On assignment, he had a different name, different identification, different credit card, different everything. Different personality. He didn't even listen to music, driving south and west from Miami.

The lawyer in Chicago had told him this wasn't a rush job, but what was the point in dragging it out? Fly in, do it, fly away. 'Just so it's certain,' the lawyer had said, and he had said, 'It's certain,' because when you hired him, you hired the best. It had been certain every single time for the last twelve years.

Apparently, the client, whoever he was, had gone bargain basement the first time, brought in people who'd messed the job up, left the target alive but hospitalized. And the client really and positively wanted this target worse than sick; he wanted this target a fading memory.

He had never before had a target stationary in a hospital. And no guards on him round the clock, no steady police presence. It was almost too easy, as though he shouldn't take his full fee for the job. Though he would. Still, it hardly seemed like work for a grown man, and he had to talk to himself as he parked the Regal on a side street three blocks from the hospital to walk the rest of the way. He had to remind himself that *all* assignments are serious, even if this one seemed like shooting ducks in a rain barrel. He had to remind himself that every mistake was serious and that overconfidence is the cause of more mistakes than anything else. He had to remind himself to treat this assignment just as though there might be some danger in it.

He approached the hospital catty-corner, through the parking lots. He was a tall lean man dressed all in black. One Beretta was in a holster in the small of his back, just above the belt, and the other was in his left boot. The right boot contained the throwing knife. Other than that, and his knowledge of several martial arts, he was unarmed; he never carried more weaponry than needed when on assignment.

The hospital's main entrance and the emergency entrance around on the left side were both well lit, but the service entrance on the right was dark except for one small illuminated globe mounted on the wall above the door. He found the door unlocked – he'd have picked it if necessary – went in, and climbed one flight of concrete stairs before stepping through into a hallway. What he needed first was an operating room.

He avoided the lit-up nurses' stations, moved through the halls, and soon found what he was looking for. And in the scrub-up room next door were several clean sets of green O.R. coats and pants. He took the largest set and put them on over his clothing; then he'd be able to move more freely along the halls, though still keeping out of other people's way.

There had been no way to find out ahead of time what room the target was in, so all he could do was walk the halls and look at the patient names stuck into the labels outside the doors. How long could it take? Half an hour?

Less. Fifteen minutes after he entered the hospital, he came to the third-floor door labeled 'Parmitt,' and without breaking stride or looking around he walked right in. Never pause and look indecisive, it attracts attention.

The target should be asleep; the knife would probably do. He crossed the dim room to the bed, starting to reach down toward his right boot, then realized the bed was empty.

Bathroom? Not away to therapy or anything like that, not at this hour. He looked around, saw the closed bathroom door, and walked around the bed.

He was almost to the bathroom when someone entered the room behind him, saying, 'Doctor, we'd rather nobody touched anything in – what the hell, we can turn the light on.'

He spun around as the overhead fluorescents flickered on, and saw the rangy man in tan sheriff's uniform in the doorway, and thought, I can be a doctor. Thirty seconds and I'm out of here.

'Whatever you say, Sheriff,' he said with an easy smile, and started toward the door.

But the sheriff was suddenly frowning. 'What's that under your scrubs?'

He wasn't prepared for in-close observation. 'Just my shirt, Sheriff,' he said, already stooping toward the boot with the Beretta in it, as he casually talked on, saying, 'I get chilly at night.'

'Stop,' the sheriff said, and all at once had his side arm out and aimed, in the classic two-handed bent-kneed stance. 'Straighten up with your hands empty,' he said.

He didn't dare bend any more, but he didn't straighten either. 'Sheriff? What the heck are you doing?'

'I always hit what I aim at,' the sheriff told him. 'And with you, what I'll aim at is your knee.' Then he raised his voice, shouting toward the doorway behind him: 'Reese! Jackson!'

He heard the rumble of running footsteps as he said, 'Sheriff? I don't know what your problem—'

Two uniformed deputies appeared in the doorway, trying not to look excited, one of them black, the other one white. The black, staring, said, 'Sarge? Who's *this*?'

'Exhibit one,' the sheriff said. His hands holding that automatic were as solid as a rock. 'You two search him, see what armament he's got on him.'

He thought: Can I go through the window? Thick plate glass, I'd either bounce off or get cut to pieces on the way out. Third floor. Three of them; what to do?

The deputies approached him, keeping out of their sergeant's line of fire. The sergeant said, 'If it happens you do have to shoot the son of a bitch, take out his legs. *This* one we're gonna keep alive.'

12

After lunch, Lesley went shopping for Daniel, using the list he'd given her of his sizes. He had nothing, so she bought two sets of everything from the skin out, plus one pair of black loafers, and a small canvas bag to put it all in. It stretched her credit card, but he had given her a bank to call in San Antonio and a PIN, and the man there had confirmed that ten thousand dollars would be shifted to the real estate agency's escrow account by noon tomorrow, where she'd be able to withdraw it without trouble.

Be nice to have a banker in San Antonio who'd wire you ten thousand dollars whenever you felt like it. Be nice to understand Daniel Parmitt, too, but she doubted she ever would.

Done shopping and with the canvas bag in the trunk of her car, she next showed seven condos to a couple from Branson, Missouri, who didn't like any of them, and when she got back to the office Sergeant Farley was there, the sheriff from Snake River.

She'd been expecting this, she having been Daniel's only visitor in the hospital, but it still frightened her when she saw the man standing beside her desk in his crisp tan uniform. It made her tense up, suddenly unsure of her ability to deceive him.

'Why, Sergeant,' she said, smiling, coming boldly forward, 'what brings you here?' Then, affecting sudden concern to hide her nervousness, she said, 'Has something happened? Is Daniel all right?'

'Something happened, okay,' he said, and gestured at the client chair beside her desk. 'Okay if we sit for a minute?'

'Of course. Do.'

She was aware of the other reps throwing little surreptitious glances in this direction, but they were the least of her worries. She'd intended to bring Daniel his new clothes after writing up this afternoon's wasted work, but did she dare, with Sergeant Farley around?

They sat turned toward one another, and he said, 'To come right out with it, Parmitt's gone.'

She acted as though she didn't understand. 'Gone? You don't mean – no. I don't know what you mean.'

'He left the hospital last night,' Farley said.

'But how could he? He's so weak.'

'We figure,' Farley said, 'somebody gave him some help. I was wondering, would that be you?'

'Me?' Don't overplay this, she told herself. 'He never *asked* me,' she said, then frowned at the papers on her desk as she said, 'I don't even think I would. He shouldn't be out of the hospital, he's too sick.' Then she looked at Farley again, saw him coolly watching her, and said, 'He shouldn't *be* anywhere else. Are you looking for him?'

'Checked all the motels round about,' he told her. 'Talked to the cabbies, checked the bus terminal. Got no cars stolen. You're right, Parmitt didn't go out of there on his own, he had help.'

'Well, it wasn't me,' she said. 'Last night, was it?'

'Sometime before one. Between eight and one, we figure.'

'I was home,' she said, 'with my mother and my sister,

191

watching TV. I don't know if your own family is considered a good alibi, but that's where I was.'

'Okay,' he said, then seemed to think things over for a minute. 'The point is,' he said, 'anybody around Parmitt is likely to be in trouble.'

'For helping him, you mean.'

'No, a different kind of trouble. We caught a fella in the hospital last night, came there to kill our Mr Parmitt.'

That did astonish her. 'My God! No!'

'Yes. Might of slipped in and out, nobody the wiser, except we were already on the scene, account of Parmitt being gone. So now we got this fella, and pretty soon he'll tell us who hired him, and then we'll learn a lot more about Daniel Parmitt than we know right now.'

'Good,' she said.

'But the thing is,' Farley told her, 'this is the second try at him we know about, the first being the gunshot put him in the hospital. Before we catch up with the fella that's paying for all this, some other goon might catch up with Parmitt. And probably anybody standing too close to him.'

'Thank you, Sergeant,' she said. 'I understand what you're saying. Just in case I *am* involved with Daniel, I should know to watch out. But I'm not.' The laugh she offered was almost completely real. 'Speeding tickets is as big a criminal as I've ever been.'

'Good, keep it that way,' he said, and got to his feet, at last. She also rose, as he said, 'If you hear from him, I'd appreciate a call.'

'Absolutely,' she said. 'And if *you* find out anything about him, would you let me know?'

'Will do.' He extended a hand. 'Nice to meet you, Ms Mackenzie.'

He's got a thing for me, she thought, as they shook hands, but he'd never show it in a million years. She said, 'I guess I can cross Daniel Parmitt off my list of eligible bachelors.'

His grin was just a little sour. 'Good idea,' he said.

She had Daniel stashed in the condo where he'd first told her about the three men who planned to rob tonight's jewelry auction. That condo had now been sold, by her, but the closing hadn't happened yet, so nobody would have any reason to go in there for a couple of weeks. She'd brought him in last night, with the help of Loretta, who was suddenly happy and perky and full of good cheer now that the scary part was over, and they'd left him with milk and candy bars and two blankets.

Now, once she was sure Farley wasn't still around and following her, she drove back down to the condo, carried the canvas bag in with her, and found Parker seated on the bench on the terrace, where they'd talked the first time. He had one of the blankets wrapped around himself.

'I have clothes for you,' she said, and showed him the canvas bag.

He got up stiffly, but he could move better today than last night. He took the bag from her and went off to another room, and when he came back, dressed, he looked almost his normal self, but more gaunt, and still moving slowly. 'I could use a razor,' he said as he sat on the terrace bench again. His voice at last was above a whisper, was now a hoarse burr, like a palm brushing corduroy.

She sat beside him, saying, 'Okay. Anything else?'

'Can you pick me up at seven-thirty?'

'Daniel, you still want to go after those people? Tonight?'

'Tonight's when they're doing it.'

'But you're – I don't suppose I could argue you out of it.'

'If you argue me out of it,' he said, 'you don't get anything.'

'If they kill you I don't get anything either.'

'Maybe it won't happen.'

'Maybe,' she said, giving up. 'Sergeant Farley came to see me this afternoon.'

He watched her. 'Did he worry you?'

'A little,' she admitted. 'But he had more news.'

'What?'

She told him about the hired killer Farley had captured. He grunted at that and said, 'That's the end of it, then.'

'But who is he? Who's after you like this?'

'The stupid thing is,' he said, 'I don't know. The guy's making trouble, and he doesn't have to.'

'I don't understand.'

'I got some identification from a guy,' he said.

'Daniel Parmitt's identification?'

He shrugged. 'He's a guy who does that kind of thing. He did it for somebody else, South American or Central American I think, maybe a drug guy or a general, whoever. Turns out that guy wants to erase anybody knows about his changeover. He sent people to kill the guy did the work for him. I was there, he thinks I know his story, too, he's tracking me down. Only now the law's gonna follow the string back from the guy they just nabbed, and they're gonna find him, and his cover's blown. He must be wanted badly somewhere, and it'll come out. You'll read about it in the papers, a month or two from now, some guy everybody's after, he suddenly pops up.'

'But you're not concerned about him,' she said. 'He

tries to kill you, and it doesn't matter to you. These other people, you feel they cheated you, that's all, but you won't give up.'

'The other guy's gonna self-destruct,' he told her. 'He has to, he's too stupid to last. He's somebody used to power, not brains. But these three are mechanics, we had an understanding, they broke it. They don't do that.' He shrugged. 'It makes sense, or it doesn't.'

Did anything about Daniel Parmitt make sense? Getting to her feet, she said, 'I'll see you at seven-thirty. With the razor.'

13

At seven, the big doors were opened onto the driveway to Mrs Fritz's house, and the police car drove in to park just off the gravel, facing out. The private security people set up their lectern on the left side of the entrance and stood around waiting, but no one was going to be unfashionably on time, and the first guests didn't arrive till seven-twelve.

Each car stopped at the lectern, where the driver handed over to the guard the invitation the guest had received last night after making his sealed bid on one of the items up for auction. The guard checked the invitation against the list on his lectern, then politely nodded the guest through. At the main entrance, staff opened the car doors, the party-goers emerged, the driver was given a claim check, and the car was driven by a valet around to the parking area at the side.

Just over half a mile to the south, Melander and Carlson and Ross had started to dress. Stacked on the dining room table and on the floor were their fire boots, their rubberized gloves, red fire helmets, and black turnout coats with the reflective horizontal yellow stripes and, in block yellow letters on the back, PBFD. Leaning against a wall were their three black air canisters, also with PBFD on them in block white letters. When completely dressed, their visored eyeguards and the mouthpieces from their air canisters would cover their faces entirely.

'I love a costume party,' Ross said.

A few miles farther south, Lesley stood in the bathroom doorway and watched Daniel shave off that ridiculous little mustache. It changed him. Without the mustache, he was a hard man, very cold. She realized with surprise that, if she'd seen him this way at first, she wouldn't have dared approach him.

He was still battered, though, and she didn't see how he could hope to beat those three men. He'd stripped to the waist to shave, and his torso was still swathed in bandages, partly because of the bullet holes front and back but mostly because of the broken ribs. Why wouldn't they just ride right over him?

And what happens to me? she wondered.

Mrs Fritz's ballroom quickly filled. All the men wore essentially what they'd worn at the Breakers last night, and all the women wore something strikingly different. Staff moved among them with canapes and champagne, and special lights gleamed on the display tables where the jewelry was arrayed. Maroon velvet ropes kept the guests from getting within reaching distance of the jewelry. Everybody was here now except the musicians, who would arrive later, and play for dancing after the auction was complete. To one side, Mrs Fritz and the auctioneer, a professional man who'd worked any number of charity balls around here over the years, consulted together about timing.

'I think it's time,' Melander said, and the three of them, encumbered in their full firefighter gear, tromped out of the house and around to the fire engine parked at the side. Carlson climbed up behind the wheel while Melander and Ross took up standing positions on the outside of the fire engine, just to increase the visual plausibility of the thing.

Carlson said, 'Ready?' and the other two agreed they were ready. Carlson picked up the two small radio transmitters from the seat beside him and pressed down on the buttons.

In the ballroom, the incendiary rockets came thundering out of the amplifiers still in the corner. Some of the rockets flew straight up, to embed themselves in the ceiling and spray sparks and flame onto the people below. Some shot directly back into the wall, gouting flame and smoke, and the rest drilled down into the floor. None were aimed at the guests or the display tables of jewelry.

Shocking heat and noise and smoke abruptly filled the room. No one knew what had happened, where this sudden disaster had come from. A lot of people thought rockets were being fired from outside the house. Everybody milled around in sudden fear, trying to find a way out. The display tables and the auctioneer's stand blocked the terrace doors, so the only way out was through the broad interior doorway into the rest of the house. People jammed together, making a bottleneck in the doorway, clawing to get through.

Outside, the police and the security guards stared in amazement at the sudden fire burning on the roof, listened unbelievingly to the screams from inside the house, gaped at each other in bewilderment, not knowing what they were supposed to do. Then, almost immediately it seemed, they felt the great relief of hearing that approaching siren.

The fire engine came rushing up from the south, red lights flashing, siren yowling. Police and guards cleared everybody out of the entranceway, and the fire engine went tearing around the curve, Melander and Ross clinging to the handholds, the fire engine rushing full tilt at the house, where the first of the fleeing guests were just now beginning to stagger out into the clear night air.

Carlson didn't hit the brake until the very last second, the big fire engine spewing gravel as it shuddered to a stop. He switched off the motor and took the key with him, to cause a little extra trouble down the line, but left the siren on, screaming away, so communication among the other people present would be just that much more difficult.

Lesley helped Daniel into his shirt, and the two of them gathered up everything that had been brought into the condo. She said, 'Are you sure, Daniel?'

'Time to go,' he said.

The three firemen ran heavy-footed through the house, pushing the panicked guests out of their way, finally helping the last of the guests and staff out of the ballroom. They slammed the double doors and slid a massive sideboard over the polished floor and up against the doors to block them.

Alice Prester Young staggered out of the house alone, into the glare and scream of the big fire engine, with more fire engines coming now from far away, racing south. She'd lost Jack somewhere, she'd been terrified, she had to struggle through the awful crowd completely on her own.

Where was Jack? Was he hurt, crushed by the people back there? Where was Jack?

199

She stared around at the people collapsing on the lawn, and all at once she saw Jack, and he was carrying somebody, in his arms, like a groom carrying a bride. He was reeling like a drunken man, but he was carrying a woman, and as he at last put her on her feet on the lawn Alice saw she was young Kim Metcalf, Howard Metcalf's sexpot stewardess wife. And as she saw them, Jack saw her and stopped dead.

The stupid thing is, she hadn't thought anything until Jack stopped like that, like … like a caught burglar. And Kim's look of shock and guilt when she met Alice's eyes across the reeling, weeping, stunned crowd, there was that, too.

Movement to her left. Alice turned her suddenly heavy head, and Howard Metcalf stood there, near her on the steps, gazing out and down at his wife. With great difficulty, Alice turned her heavy head again and looked at Jack, and now he seemed to have no expression on his face at all, like a bad drawing, or a minor figure in the background of a comic strip.

In all that racket, there was a great silence, enclosing the four of them.

In the ballroom, Melander and Carlson and Ross quickly shimmied out of their gloves, helmets, air tanks, fire boots, and turnout coats. Beneath, they each wore a black wet suit and a large zippered bag on a belt around the waist. The bags now held nothing but divers' face masks and headlamps, which they removed so they could load the bags with all of Miriam Hope Clendon's jewelry.

Lesley and Daniel drove northward in her Lexus, neither saying anything, he resting his head back, eyes closed.

Conserving himself. Then he opened his eyes and looked out ahead and said, 'Slow down.'

She did, but said, 'Why?'

Instead of answering, he opened his window. She had the air-conditioning on, of course, and now the humid air billowed in, and with it a faint distant sound of sirens. She said, 'Police?'

He laughed, a sound like a bark. 'Fire engine,' he said. 'I told you they were gaudy. They aren't going in from the sea after all, they're going in from the land, in a fire engine.'

'But there isn't any fire,' she said.

'With them? There's a fire. It's along here now.'

He meant Mr Roderick's house, or whoever Mr Roderick really was. As he closed his window, she said, 'Do you want me to come in with you?'

'No. You go home. I'll call you tomorrow.'

'What if you don't?'

'Then I don't,' he said. 'Stop here.'

She rolled to a stop near the Roderick house, and he paused, his hand on the door handle. 'The question is, how do they get back out? Tuxes under the fire coats?'

She said, 'To mingle with the guests, you mean? Could they do that?'

'They think they can do anything,' he said, and opened the door. 'I'll call you tomorrow.'

At the Fritz house, more fire engines had arrived, blocked by the milling crowd and the still-screaming first fire engine that none of the later firefighters recognized. 'Whose is this? Is this from West Palm? What the hell's it doing here?'

In the ballroom, Melander and Carlson and Ross finished loading the jewelry into their waist bags. They put the air

201

canisters back on, put on the divers' face masks and the mouthpieces and the headlamps. From hooks inside their turnout coats they brought out pairs of black flippers.

Lesley found a place to park, locked the Lexus, and walked back down the road toward Mr Roderick's house.

Firemen hurried through the mansion and found the ball-room doors wedged shut. They had their axes and used them, splintering the doors.

Melander and Carlson and Ross heard the thuds of the axes. Melander shoved a display case out of the way and they went through the terrace doors and ran across the terrace, invisible in their black wet suits, holding their flip-pers in their hands. A little apart from one another, so they wouldn't collide underwater, they dove into the sea.

Firemen smashed their way into the ballroom. Police followed. As the rockets fizzled out and the fires began to fade, they looked around at the emptiness.

All gone.

FOUR

1

If he didn't exert himself, the pains in his chest were just a small irritation, a low grumbling, like far-off thunder. But when he had to move, even to do simple things like pull on pants, the pain punched him all over again, like brand-new, like the bullet thudding into him right now instead of a week ago. Still, he didn't mind the pain as much as the weakness, especially in his legs. He wasn't used to being dialed down like this; he kept expecting the strength, and it wasn't there.

The worst part of getting into the house was the climb over the windowsill. He found the suction-cup handles where he'd left them, attached them to the pane of glass he'd scored, removed the glass, and reached in to unlock and open the window. Then he put the glass pane through the opening and stretched to rest it on the floor inside, leaning against the wall.

That was the first punch. His breathing was constricted anyway, because of the bandages around his ribs, and the punch constricted it even more, so that he inhaled with hoarse sounds that he'd have to control later, in the house.

He hoisted himself over the windowsill, gritting his teeth, not blacking out, but lying on his back on the floor until the pain receded and his breath was closer to normal. Then he stood, shut the window, dropped the suction-cup handles through the open pane into the shrubbery outside, and fitted the piece of glass back into place.

He had time to search the house, but not long. There were two changes in the garage: the white Bronco was there, the same one they'd used after the bank robbery, and the trunk where he'd found their weapons was open and empty. Did they have the guns with them, on the job?

No. All six were on the dining room table, the three automatics and the three shotguns. The Sentinel was still under the table. He left it there; what he needed to do would be done differently.

In the living room, the alarm system had been switched on. Its warning light gleamed red, though Parker had seen to it that it would not respond to break-ins. And in the kitchen, the refrigerator was now full of food, as were the shelves. So they planned to spend a few days here, until things calmed down, which was smart.

Parker made his way through the house, slowly, noting the changes, pausing to lean against a wall when the weakness got to be too much. He came last to the big empty room with the piano in the corner and the glass wall facing the sea, and out there lights now moved back and forth, police boats with searchlights, roving this way and that, like dogs who've lost a scent. So the trio had gone to the robbery by land, in a fire engine or some other official vehicle, but they'd left by sea.

Soon they'd be back here. In a boat? Or were they diving? Probably diving.

He didn't have much time to find a hiding place. He had to be secure, but somewhere that would make it possible to move around. He went up to the second floor, tried all the shut doors up there, and found a staircase leading up to the attic. It was covered with black industrial carpet and didn't make a sound.

The attic area at the top of the stairs had been converted into a screening room, probably by the movie star couple, and then later all the projection equipment had been taken out again, leaving two dozen plush swivel chairs facing a screen attached to the wall. The screening room had been meant to look like a thirties movie house, with art deco lighting sconces and dark red fabric on the walls. There was no reason for the three to come up here, so this was where Parker would wait until he could get at them.

He went back down to the second floor and out one of the bedrooms to the upstairs terrace. Lights still moved back and forth in the thick darkness, but Parker knew the police boats were searching too far out, probably expecting to find a boat. But the three would stick close to shore as they made their way back, without a boat.

He sat on one of the chaises, feet up, and watched the lights roam out there. So long as they stayed out there, restlessly moving, Melander and Carlson and Ross had not been caught. So they had a good operation, and they were now on their way to Parker with twelve million dollars in jewelry.

It was good to sit here for a minute, after the exertion of moving through the house, but he didn't want to get too comfortable and fall asleep. He could sleep later.

The dim flashlight had been moving on the beach for a minute or two before his mind told him what his eyes were looking at. A small light, fainter and more diffuse than the searchlights out over the ocean, was headed this way up the beach from the water. The three, coming back?

One of them. And it wasn't a flashlight, it was a head-lamp. The figure beneath it was black, almost impossible to see as he came forward across the sand. Parker lost sight of the lamp and the hurrying man as he neared the retaining wall at the edge of the property, then he heard the loud rusty squeal as the gate at the foot of the narrow concrete stairs was opened.

Here came the headlamp, up the stairs to the terrace. And beyond him, two more lights were now coming from the sea.

All three of them. Parker got to his feet and stood back by the door, ready to go inside.

The first one down below stopped on the terrace and was taking something bulky off his back. A scuba tank. And now the other two came up, also removing scuba tanks, and the first one spoke, and it was Melander: 'Did you see the dolphin?'

'No. What dolphin?' That was Carlson, the driver.

'He crossed right in front of us.'

'You were out ahead, you were making some sort of race out of it.'

'I wanted to get back.'

Ross, the third one, said, 'In the morning, early, we gotta sweep the sand down there.'

Carlson said, 'Why?'

'You see those lights? They'll stay out there till daylight, and when they're sure we didn't get picked up in a boat they'll come back in and search the island, and one thing they'll look for is footprints coming in from the sea.'

Melander said, 'Jerry, you're right. I never would have thought of that, and tomorrow morning they'd be all over my ass.'

Carlson said, 'First light, the cops'll be out, too, maybe they see us sweeping. We should do it now.'

Melander said, 'Let me get out of this wet suit, and then I'll do anything you want.'

They started to move toward the house, carrying their scuba tanks. They were almost out of sight from Parker's vantage point, and he was about to step inside, when everybody heard the sudden squeak of the gate down below, abruptly stopped.

Melander was fast. He didn't bother with the stairs, just ran forward, vaulted over the railing, and dropped the seven feet to the sand below.

Parker heard the woman cry out in sudden fear, and knew immediately it was Lesley. Wanting to be sure she got hers, wanting to hang around and observe from just out of sight, and immediately got herself caught.

Ross and Carlson ran down the stairs to take a hand. Would they kill her? That would be the simplest, for Parker and for them both, kill her and throw the body in the ocean and forget about it.

No. They were bringing her up the stairs. They were curious, they wanted to ask her some questions, complicate things a little more.

Parker watched the three dark men come up, headlamps bobbing, the paler figure of Lesley struggling in their midst. She was protesting, stupid half-sentences, pretending to be just an innocent bystander, nothing to do with anything, which they would not buy for a minute. They've just come back from the biggest heist in Palm Beach history, and here's a woman trying to sneak into their house. Not a coincidence.

But Parker didn't expect the conclusion that Melander leaped to, as easily as he'd leaped over the wall. While Lesley continued to struggle and to argue, Melander shook her with the one hand holding her arm and said, 'Don't make me punch you, okay? You gotta shut up now so we can talk.'

She did shut up then, shrinking into herself as she looked at the three of them, looming over her, encased in black, with the headlamps shining in her eyes. Parker saw her face unnaturally white against the darkness all around as she forced herself to be silent.

And Melander had a touch of gloating humor in his voice when he said, 'Claire Willis, am I right? We visited your house, up north, sorry you weren't there.'

She blinked at them, baffled. 'What?'

Melander said, 'So that means our friend Parker's around someplace, too. He'd probably like us to take good care of you, right? Let's go inside. You could be valuable to us.'

Damn. Almost as irritated with Lesley as with the other three, Parker faded into the house and up the attic stairs. Lesley didn't have a purse with her, and probably didn't have ID, and wouldn't be able to prove who she was. So let them thrash it out together all they wanted. Sooner or later, they'd go to sleep.

2

But he went to sleep first, not intending to, and woke when the wall sconce lights came on, then heard them coming up the stairs. Why? To have a place to keep their prisoner.

When he'd first come up, in the darkness, he'd sat on one of the swivel chairs with his feet on another, but the curved position was bad for his ribs, bad all around, and he gave up and lay on his back on the black-carpeted floor. He didn't think he'd sleep, it wasn't that late. Melander and Carlson and Ross had done the robbery a little after eight, just barely night, then full night by the time they got back to this house, after eight-thirty. They'd be keyed up, and now they'd have Lesley to distract them, so they wouldn't go to sleep until late. Parker figured he shouldn't go downstairs until at least three in the morning, so he had six hours up here to rest.

But he hadn't expected to sleep. Normally, he could hold sleep off until the work at hand was done, but this was some other part of the weakness. He'd been awake, lying on his back in the darkness among all the swivel chairs, planning how he would take them out, and now he was awake again, the red-tinged lights clicking on, the swivel chairs like flying saucers above him.

He heard them coming up the stairs, Melander saying, 'This a nice quiet place for you till the morning, keep you out of trouble.'

Parker rolled against the wall farthest from the stairs, black clothing against black carpet, turned away so the paleness of his face and hands wouldn't show.

'What is this?' That was Lesley, still trying to catch up.

Melander, the grin in his voice, said, 'The previous owners used to watch their own movies in here. Think how much fun people used to have in this room. Maybe if you're real quiet, you can hear the singing and the dancing and the laughing.'

'And if you're not real quiet,' Carlson said, 'you'll hear from us.'

'Oh, come on, Hal,' Melander said. 'Claire's gonna cooperate, aren't you, Claire?'

'I've told you I'm not—'

Slap. Melander's voice, no longer humorous: 'And *I've* told *you*, quit insulting my intelligence. I'm losing my good disposition, Claire, you follow me?'

Silence from Lesley. Ross said, 'She'll be all right now, Boyd. Won't you?'

'Please …'

'See?' Now Ross was being the good cop, saying, 'Here's the light switch here, you can turn it on or off, whatever you want. The door's gonna be locked down there, but we'll let you out in the morning, we'll have a good breakfast, talk it over.'

'That's right,' Melander said, in a good mood again. 'No more excitement for tonight. You go on over there and sit down. Go on, now, just go right over by those chairs and—'

Her *shriek* at that second was not because they'd hit her again or anything like that. Parker knew exactly what it was. Coming deeper into the room, she'd piped him, and immediately tipped him to the others, like a bird dog.

She'd been better than the normal amateur, until it mattered.

Yes. Here came the footsteps and Melander's humorous surprise, saying, 'And what have we here?' Parker rolled over onto his back to look up at them. Carlson and Ross carried the automatics he'd ruined. He said, 'You boys pulled a nice one today,' hating the reediness of his voice.

Carlson said, 'And you thought you'd wait till we were asleep and take it away from us.'

'Just keeping an eye on my share,' Parker said.

Melander said, 'On your feet.'

'He's been *shot*!' Lesley blurted. 'He isn't even supposed to be out of the hospital!'

They frowned at her, and then down at Parker. Melander said, 'Is that right?'

'Shot in the chest,' Parker said. 'Some broken ribs. I'll live.'

'Maybe,' Carlson said.

Melander backed away a pace. 'Okay, Parker,' he said. 'You can stay up here with—'

Lesley said, '*That's* Parker?'

Before Melander could smack her again, Parker said, 'Give it up, Claire, we folded that hand.'

She blinked at him, but at last she was beginning to get her wits about her, and she didn't argue the point.

Ross came forward, saying, 'You bandaged and stuff?'

'Around the chest.'

'Where you carrying? I'll just ease it out without making trouble for you.'

Parker shook his head. 'Not carrying. I don't want you to think I'm still sore.'

They didn't believe him. Melander, laughing, said, 'We come in peace? Check him out, Jerry.'

213

Ross handed his automatic to Carlson and went to one knee beside Parker. 'Sorry about this,' he said.

'Go ahead.'

Ross patted him down without unnecessary pain, then shrugged and looked up at the other two. 'He's clean.'

'Will wonders never cease,' Melander said. 'Okay, Parker, we'll talk in the morning. Your investment came through, right?'

'Right,' Parker said.

Ross took his dead automatic back from Carlson, and the three of them went downstairs, murmuring together, a little confused. Parker was here, but hurt, and unarmed. What did it mean?

The lock clicked on the door downstairs. Lesley said, 'I'm sorry, Daniel. It's all my fault.'

'Yes,' he said.

3

He sat on the floor, back against the wall. The hard surfaces were best, when he was awake. She sat in one of the swivel chairs. She said, 'You were going to hide up here until they were asleep and then go down and kill them, weren't you?'

'Yes.'

'How?'

'Pillow for Carlson and Ross. Melander last, the big one, with a bullet. They're in separate rooms.'

'Are you strong enough to do that? With the pillow?'

'I'm not going to find out,' he said.

'Because of me.'

'Yes.'

'If you weren't strong enough, you'd use a knife?'

'No. You can't do a real job with a knife and stay clean. There's tools in the kitchen. Hammers.'

'Oh.' She blinked, and licked her lips, and moved on away from that, saying, 'If it wasn't for me, they wouldn't have had any reason to come up here, and they wouldn't have found you.'

'That's right.'

'But why tell them I'm Claire? Is Claire your girl-friend?'

'If they think you're Claire,' Parker said, 'they'll think I want to keep you alive, so you're a bargaining chip in their favor. Keeps them calm.'

'But you don't care if I live or die,' she said, 'do you?'

'I'd rather you were dead,' he said.

She thought about that. 'Are you going to kill me?'

'No.'

'Because of the bargaining chip.'

'Yes.'

'You're a little more truthful than I'm ready for,' she said.

He shrugged.

She said, 'Is there a bathroom up here?'

He pointed at the door in the rear wall, to the left of the stairs. 'No window, it's vented.'

'I wasn't planning to call for help or anything,' she said, and got to her feet and went away to the bathroom.

While she was gone, he thought it over. Should he wait until later, then try to get down through that door at the foot of the stairs? No; they knew he was here, and they didn't trust him, and they'd have the door covered with all kinds of traps, things to make noise, alarms going off. On the other hand, every hour that he kept still his body improved a little more. In the morning, he'd be better able to deal with them.

But the original plan was dead. And Lesley, who'd been a help before this, was now no help at all. Now she was trouble.

She came back out of the bathroom and came over to sit in a chair near him. She looked very solemn, as though she'd made an oath of some kind in the bathroom. She said, 'I've never been around anything like this before.'

'I know that.'

'The idea of killing somebody, that doesn't bother you.'

He waited.

'It does bother me,' she said, 'but that's all right. I got

216

us into a hard place, and I know I did. I don't think they'll just let me go.'

'No.'

'I think tomorrow,' she said, 'they'll decide to kill us both, once they've talked it over together.'

'Probably.'

'If it was just me, I wouldn't have a chance. If it was just you, without me, I think you would stand a chance.'

'Maybe.'

'I don't want to get in the way anymore,' she said. 'Whatever you say to do, I'll do. If it's just sit down and shut up, I'll sit down and shut up. If I can do anything to help, I'll do it.'

He said, 'That way, through that other door there, is the unfinished part of the attic. I didn't get a chance to look it over. I want to know about windows, and I want something soft between me and the floor, so I can sleep without getting too stiff.'

'I'll be right back,' she said, and was gone almost ten minutes, and came back dragging a large gray canvas painters' tarpaulin. 'Small windows, with bars,' she said. 'Decorative bars, but bars. There's this, and there's part of a roll of pink insulation. I thought we could put the insulation on the floor and part of the tarp on top of it, and put the rest of the tarp over us.'

'Good,' he said.

While she was gone this time, he went on all fours to the nearest chair and climbed it to his feet. The few hours of sleep had stiffened him, more than he liked to think about. He didn't have time for the body to heal; it had to come along no matter what.

She came in with the roll of insulation, pulling it along, and they worked together to put down four strips of it, pink side down, shiny paper side up. Then they stretched the middle section of the tarp over it, with extra material on both sides to pull over them. She said, 'Do you want the light on or off?'

'I'm going to sleep,' he said.

The laugh she gave had hysteria in it. 'Are you kidding? In the spot we're in, and in the condition you're in, who's going to do anything *except* sleep? I'll turn off the light.'

4

She said, 'What's Claire like?'

'No, Lesley.'

But she was following her own line of thought, answering her own question. 'I think she's very beautiful and very self-sufficient. Neither of you leans on the other, you both stand up straight.'

'Sure,' he said.

She considered him. 'I need somebody … a little different,' she decided.

He shook his head. 'You don't need anybody, Lesley.'

She surprised him by blushing. She turned away, then turned back and smiled sheepishly and said, 'I'd like to need somebody. I keep thinking, if I find the right guy, I'll need him.'

'Could be.'

'That's how it is with you and Claire, I suppose.'

He knew this talk was simply so she could distract herself from the people downstairs. Her watch had told them it was almost eight-thirty in the morning, so whatever was going to happen would happen soon. But he didn't feel like playing the game anymore, so he walked around instead, in and among the swivel chairs, rolling his shoulders, judging how his body felt this morning.

A little better, maybe, just a little better. His voice seemed stronger to him, and the night on the fairly hard flat surface – the insulation hadn't done much – seemed to have been good for his ribs.

She sat in a swivel chair, swiveling slowly back and forth, watching him move. They were both silent for a few minutes, and then she said, 'I'm hungry.'

'So am I.'

'Should we knock on the door or something?'

'Let them have their own pace.'

'Okay.' Then, in a rush: 'Are they going to kill us?'

'I don't know,' he said, and stood still, hand on the back of one of the chairs. Now that she was ready, they could talk. He said, 'Melander's the main guy, the big one with all the hair, and as far as he's concerned they were all reasonable back when. He just borrowed money from me, and he meant to pay me back, and he might even pay me back someday. He thinks he's straight in our world, that he doesn't heist a heister, and what happened with me was just business or something.'

She said, 'Could you let it *be* just business or something?'

'We'll see how it plays out,' he said, to keep her calm. 'There's Carlson, I think he'd prefer we were dead. He doesn't like it that I didn't wait at home like a good boy, that I'm here.'

'And the other one?'

'Ross follows. He'll follow whoever's on top.'

She thought about all that, slowly shaking her head. Her right shoe was half off, and she waggled it up and down with her toes. Then she said, 'What do you think is going to happen?'

'Nobody can leave this house for a few days,' Parker told her, 'that's the problem. If we could all just split now, go our separate ways, they'd lock us up here and take off, and that would be it. But you know this island's shut down, they're checking every car on every bridge, every boat in the water, they'll keep it up for three or four days.'

'I know,' she said.

'I'm going to make Melander itchy after a while,' Parker said. 'Just by being here.'

'And you can't leave, not now,' she said. 'Or could you? Could we leave together? We wouldn't tell anybody.'

He was already shaking his head. 'They don't want us loose. They want us under control. And for now, that means here. Later on, it could mean dead.'

'But not this morning, you think.'

'Parker!' Ross's voice called up the stairwell. 'You two up?'

'Yes,' Parker called. Lesley stooped to pull her shoe back on.

'Come on downstairs.'

Low, Parker said, 'Now we'll find out.'

5

Ross led them to the dining room, where Melander sat at the table with his back to the sea. The guns were gone from the table, and in their place were a box of doughnuts, a coffeepot, pound box of sugar, quart of half-and-half, white china cups, metal spoons, paper plates, and paper napkins. The shotguns leaned against the wall in a corner. The automatics were out of sight, probably being worn by the three. On a side table were three black mesh pouches attached to belts; Parker caught a glint of gold through the mesh. Carlson wasn't in sight.

Ross had gone into the room first, followed by Lesley, then Parker, so he was too late to stop it when Melander gestured to the chair on his left and said, 'Have a seat, Claire. You don't mind if we're informal here, do you?'

She was moving with small steps, arms against her sides; holding it in. 'No, that's all right,' she said, and went over to sit where Parker had salted the Sentinel.

'Take a seat,' Ross told Parker, while Melander said to Lesley, 'I'm glad. We can all be pals. I'm Boyd, and that's Jerry. Hal's in the kitchen, trying to figure out the stove. Maybe you could help him later.'

Parker, sitting to Melander's right, opposite Lesley, said, 'Claire's not too much for stoves.'

'No?' Melander grinned and shrugged. 'Okay, fine.

Either Hal figures it out, or he blows us all up.' He gestured at the things on the table. 'This is it for breakfast. Help yourselves.'

Lesley looked uncertainly at Parker, who pushed the doughnut box toward her, saying, 'Go ahead.' The coffee-pot was near Parker. Melander said, 'Parker, why don't you pour for her?'

'Claire likes to do that for herself,' he said, and pushed the coffeepot toward her, too, because they might think it strange that he didn't know if his Claire took milk or sugar in her coffee.

She took it black, as did Parker, and they both took doughnuts, as Melander continued the conversation, saying, 'Now, Parker, what are we gonna do about you?'

'Hold me until you leave,' Parker said, and sensed movement behind him. That would be Carlson, coming in from the kitchen. Parker faced Melander but kept aware of Lesley; her reaction would let him know if Carlson had anything in mind. He said, 'Then you'll get your money from the fences, and you'll send me what you owe me, and that's the end of it.'

Behind him, Carlson said, 'Forgive and forget, is that it?'

'No,' Parker said, still talking to Melander. 'I don't forgive, and I don't forget, but I don't waste time on the past, either. I won't work with you people again, but if you pay me my money I won't think about you anymore, either.'

'That would be nice,' Melander said. 'We were talking about that last night, Hal and Jerry and me, how we didn't like the idea of you thinking about us.'

'Showing up here,' Carlson said. He was still behind Parker, not coming into view.

Parker kept looking at Melander. 'This is where my money is,' he said.

Melander laughed. He was buying Parker's story, though maybe Carlson wasn't. He said, 'This is where your money is.'

'That's right.'

'What happens if we would have screwed up on the job? If we went up there and something went wrong?'

'I'd try to come in, get what I can.'

Carlson, back there, said, 'And help us out?'

'Not a chance,' Parker said.

'I just wish,' Melander said, 'you were a more easygoing guy,' and door chimes sounded.

Everybody in the room tensed. Carlson stepped forward to Parker's right, looking at him, saying, 'You got friends?'

'Only you people.'

Melander said, 'Jerry, take a look.'

Ross hurried from the room while Carlson crossed to pick up two of the shotguns, bringing one to Melander, neither shotgun pointed exactly at anybody.

Stupid with fear, mouth open, Lesley stared at Parker, and Ross ducked back into the room: 'It's cops!'

'For Christ's sake, why?' Carlson complained, glaring at Parker.

Parker said, 'They're searching the island. Hello, Mr Householder, you see anybody looked suspicious?'

Melander laughed and got to his feet, handing his shotgun back to Carlson as he said, 'Everybody I see looks suspicious. I'm the householder.' He left the room, smoothing his hair back.

Carlson and Ross went to stand to both sides of the parlor doorway, where they'd be able to hear. Parker waved a hand to get Lesley's attention, then pointed to

224

her side of the table. She stared at him, not getting it. He tapped his temple: Think. Carlson and Ross wouldn't be distracted forever.

'Hello, Officers, what can I do for you?'

'Mr George Roderick?'

'Yes, sir, that's me.'

Parker put both hands under the table, gesturing that his hands were touching the underside, then again pointed at her side of the table.

'May we come in?'

'Sure. Could I ask—'

'Are you moving in or out, sir?'

At last she reached under her table, and her eyes widened.

'Moving in. Slowly, slowly.'

'I suppose that would explain it.'

Parker patted the air with palms down: *Don't move it yet.*

'Explain what?'

'You are aware of the robbery last night.'

'Robbery? No, what robbery?'

'Mr Roderick, a massive jewel theft and fire took place last night just up the road from here, and you don't *know* about it?'

'No, I'm sorry, I don't have a TV here, I don't even have a radio. I stayed home and read last night. I didn't—'

'You don't have a phone, either.'

'No, I don't – it isn't in yet.'

'We're phoning residents, asking if anyone saw anything, but you don't have a phone.'

'No, not yet.'

'You haven't applied for a phone.'

'No, I haven't got a—'

'There's a Dumpster out here, but you have no contractor. No one's doing work on the property.'

'Officer, I live mostly in Texas. There've been business problems there recently. I've been delayed in—'

'How many of you are staying here, Mr Roderick?'

'At the moment, just me. My family's still—'

A different cop voice said, 'Someone else came into the living room, went back out again. I saw it through the window.'

'That was me,' Melander said, still sounding affable, while Carlson and Ross were getting more and more edgy, hands flexing on the shotguns. 'I had my coffee cup in my hand, went back to—'

'It wasn't you,' the second cop voice said. 'It was somebody shorter.'

The first cop, sounding tougher, less polite, said, 'Mr Roderick, how many of you are in the house right now?'

'Just me, I'm telling—'

'Mr Roderick, I'm afraid I'm going to have to search the house.'

'I don't see why. I'm just a guy from Texas trying to fix up this—'

'And we'll have to begin with a search of your person, sir.'

'Me? Search *me*?'

'Sir, if you'll lean against the wall, arms spread ...'

It was now. Parker snapped his fingers to get Lesley's attention, and gestured she should toss him the gun. Carlson heard the snap, saw the gesture, saw the Sentinel come up from under the table in Lesley's two hands, a piece of clear tape still curling away from it, and he swung the shotgun around to shoot at Lesley, trigger going click as he squeezed.

226

Lesley flinched and *screamed* and fired the Sentinel, the flat *crack* of it bouncing in the room, the bullet missing Carlson, beelining somewhere into the living room, where the cops and Melander were.

Parker was on his feet, turning in a quick circle to his left, away from the doorway, reaching for the chairback behind him with his left hand. The pains in his torso drove knives into him, shot arcs of lightning across his vision, popped the sweat beads onto his forehead, but he kept turning, picking up the chair at the end of his left arm, swinging it in a loop that intersected with Ross, who had already fired his shotgun uselessly twice at Parker's head. The chair knocked him off balance to his right, into the doorway.

There was already shooting out there. Melander had probably drawn his automatic when he saw the situation going to hell, and had gone down pulling a trigger that just wouldn't deliver.

Ross reeled into the doorway space to the living room, clutching the shotgun, and was brought up short by a sudden squadron of bullets that knocked him backward, knocked the shotgun from his hands, knocked him to the ground.

Lesley had emptied the Sentinel, two-handed, into Carlson, who sprawled in a seated position on the floor against the wall, gaping at her, stupefied.

Parker clapped once, to get her attention. When she stared at him, glassy-eyed, he pointed to himself, fast, urgent, then violently shook his head. *I'm not here, I don't exist, I'm not part of it.* She managed an openmouthed nod, and he turned, grabbed the three pouches full of jewelry, and ran.

But he couldn't run. His body wasn't up to it; he was

reeling from what he'd already done. He was one room ahead of them and couldn't go much farther.

He made it to the terrace. The morning sun glared dead ahead, breathing its humidity on him, sapping the rest of his strength.

They weren't pursuing anybody; they didn't know there was anybody else to pursue. They were staying with the mess they already had. But he couldn't just wander the beach, physically battered, carrying the loot from the robbery.

To the left was the chain-link fence he'd climbed the first time he'd come here, with the neighbor's sea grape crowding against it on the inside. Parker went to the corner of the terrace, looped the three pouch belts through his own belt, and went down the neighbor's side of the fence.

It was slow going, for many reasons. He didn't want to break a lot of branches, leave a trail straight to himself. He was bulky and cumbersome and the jewelry pouches kept snagging on branches and leaves. And his body kept trying to pass out.

At the bottom, the tangled stringy trunks were a failed Boy Scout knot. Years of dead leaves had made a mush of the ground. The air was cooler, but just as wet. A foot from the fence, you couldn't see the fence or the ocean beyond it.

Parker, feeling darkness iris in around his eyes, sank slowly into crotches and curves of branch until he'd given over his entire weight to the tree, as though he'd been hanging there forever and it had grown around him. He'd done what he could do. Arms around a trunk, cheek against a branch, he let the iris close.

6

Darkness and cramping, forcing him to be conscious. He tried to move, to ease the cramps, but he was all tangled in branches and leaves. Too dark to see where he was or what he could do.

He stopped the useless moving about. He ignored the cramps, in his ribs, in his legs, and took a slow deep breath while he oriented himself. Where he was. What had happened.

He'd slept the day away, laced into a sea grape. They hadn't found him, so they hadn't looked for him or they *would* have found him, so Lesley's story – whatever it had been – had not included him.

Could he get up out of here? The first thing was to try to stand, untie himself from this tree. Reaching this way and that for handholds, his knuckles brushed the chain-link fence, and he grabbed onto it, used it to pull himself forward and then upward until he was vertical and could try to do something about the cramps.

For the torso, just slow breathing, slow and regular breathing, holding it in. For the legs, flexing them and flexing them and flexing them, waiting it out. Until finally only the familiar pains in his chest were left, a little worse than before, but not crippling.

He could see nothing, but he could feel the three jewelry pouches, still looped onto his belt in front and on the left side. He still had hold of the fence, and now he began to climb it, slowly, with long pauses. The legs threatened to bind up on him again, and the breathing was very thick and soupy, but he kept moving upward, a bit at a time, and finally came out onto the terrace behind the late Mr Roderick's house. He sprawled there, on his back.

Light. A quarter-moon and many stars. The hushing sound of the ocean, rising and falling. No other sound and no other light.

Finally, when he felt he had the strength for it, he gathered his arms and legs under himself, and levered himself upward, and used the protective wrought-iron fence for support, and then he was on his feet.

The house was dark, its many glass doors dully reflecting the bright night sky. Something ribbonlike fluttered over there, horizontal, at waist height, and when he moved slowly closer to the building it was a yellow police crime-scene tape. They'd sealed the house.

How sealed was it? He needed this house. In slow stages, with many pauses, he worked his way around to the front, where the Dumpster still loomed in the moonlight and more crime-scene tape semaphored in the night breeze. But there were no vehicles, no guards. The crime at the crime scene, as far as the law was concerned, was over.

It took longer this time to find the suction-cup handles, but eventually he did, and got into the house the same way as before, but feeling the damage to his body even worse. He did pass out, for a while, lying on the floor inside the house, the window open beside him, but then he came out of it and stood and finished the job, tossing the suction-cup handles outside again, hoping never to need those anymore. He reinserted the loose pane of glass, and then he was inside.

230

The alarm pad by the front door gleamed its red warning, but had the police checked to be certain the alarm hadn't been tampered with? No, they hadn't. If the alarm was doing its job, his opening the window would have set it off.

And if he were his usual self, he'd have been much more cautious about coming in here. He could see that the physical toll was beginning to make him careless, sloppy in his thinking. He couldn't let that happen.

It wasn't really possible to search the place in this darkness, even if he had the strength. But the air had the flat silence of an empty house, and he was sure he was alone.

The same furniture was still in the dining room, though disarranged; nobody had bothered to pick up the chair Parker had knocked over. In the kitchen, the refrigerator was still full of food. There was cold fried chicken in there, and there was beer. He ate and drank, and then curled up on the floor and slept.

On Monday they came to clean out the house, where he'd been trying to recuperate since Saturday night. They didn't expect to find anybody inside the place, so Parker had no trouble keeping out of their way. They were two plainclothes detectives, one bored uniform, and a crew of movers. The detectives would check each room, okay it, and the movers would label everything and take it all out.

Having expected something like this, Parker had already made a stash of provisions, hidden in the unfinished part of the attic. In there were a razor and shaving cream and comb and some clothing, all things the dead heisters had left behind, plus an unopened box of cereal, a plastic bag of rolls, two cans of tuna, and half a dozen bottles of beer. But if they were going to shut this house down completely he wouldn't be able to stay much longer.

After they left, he came down to see what they'd taken, which was all the furniture, all the personal possessions, all the leftover food. The refrigerator was there, but had been switched off and the door propped open. There was still water and still electricity, so he started the refrigerator and put the beer and rolls in it.

What he was waiting for was Lesley. She'd come back, he knew she would. She'd figure some way to get back to this house, if only out of curiosity. Or, more likely, to try to find his trail. One way or another, she would show up here, and that's what he had to count on, because he needed her assistance just one more time. He knew he couldn't just walk out of here and down the road, looking the way he did. He wouldn't get half a mile before some cop would stop to ask questions. Any question at all.

Wednesday afternoon. He was spending most of his waking time seated on the floor on the secondfloor terrace, out of sight of anybody on the beach, but in the open air, giving his body a chance to relax, to heal itself. He had all the interior doors open in the house, and the door to the terrace open, so he'd hear if anybody came in.

Midafternoon, the terrace now in the building's shadow. He felt hungry, but otherwise not bad. The breathing was better, the ribs less painful. The bandages were now almost a week old, but he didn't want to remove them or fuss with them because he didn't have any replacements.

He heard the front door shut, and rose, grunting a little. In the doorway, he could look straight down the staircase to the front hall, where he saw Lesley just disappearing to the right. Going to switch off the useless alarm.

He stepped through the doorway, leaned on the railing at the head of the stairs, waited. She came into view again down there, looking around, as though deciding what to do first. Softly, he called, 'You alone?'

She lifted her startled face, saw him up there. 'My God! I thought you were a thousand miles from here!'

'Not yet. Wait there, I'll come down.'

He went down, and they sat together on the staircase, and he noted the clump of keys in her hand. 'It's okay you being here?'

She grinned, pleased with herself. 'I've got the exclusive,' she said.

'I don't follow.'

'The house reverted to its former owner,' she explained, 'so it's on the market again. I'm a heroine, so I've got the exclusive listing.' She grinned at him, as though bringing him a present. 'No one is going to come into this house unless they're with me.'

'That's good,' he said. 'But I can't stay here. Are they still doing traffic stops?'

'No,' she said. 'They think the fourth man escaped with the jewelry somewhere else.'

'Fourth man?'

'They searched the house all day Saturday and didn't find the jewelry, so there must be a fourth man.'

'All right.'

'They think the three who came here gave this fourth man the jewelry somewhere along the way, and I'm pretty sure they *think* he's somebody locally prominent, but nobody's saying so.'

Parker stretched his lips in a grin. 'Now it's an inside job,' he said.

'Exactly,' she said, grinning back, but then her expression clouded, and she said, 'Except for that sheriff. Farley.'

'He's still around?'

'He's decided,' she told him, 'that the fourth man was Daniel Parmitt, and the other three got him out of the hospital because they needed him in their plan. Nobody else cares about Daniel Parmitt or thinks he had anything to do with the robbery, only Farley. He thinks Parmitt had a boat or something. He keeps trying to find somebody to tell that story to, but the police here think he's just a small-town jerk from the Everglades.'

'He's a small-town jerk, but he's sharp,' Parker said. 'What story did *you* tell?'

'I said I thought this house had been abandoned, because there was never anybody around, and I wanted the opportunity to sell it if it was on the market, and I even thought *you* might be a prospect.'

'Parmitt.'

'Right. And I came here, and it was unlocked, and there was nobody home. And I was still looking around when these three terrifying men in wet suits came in and kidnapped me. And I didn't see them carrying any jewels, then or ever.'

'Good.'

'They held me overnight, and then they gave me breakfast in the morning, and I found that little gun taped under the table, I have no idea where it came from. There was still tape on the gun when I gave it to the police, and they found the rest under the table.'

'Good.'

'I told them I was afraid to touch it at first, but then the police arrived, and I thought they were going to go away again and not rescue me, so that's why I pulled the gun out to shoot it to attract their attention.'

'That's good,' Parker said. 'And you're a local, solid reputation, the story's good enough, so it might be true.'

'They believe me,' she insisted.

He shrugged. 'Why not? What do they think about the guns being rigged?'

She looked confused. 'Rigged?'

'Their guns didn't shoot,' Parker pointed out.

'That's right,' she said in wonder, 'I forgot about that. I thought I was *dead* when that man pointed that rifle at me, but then it didn't shoot.'

'None of them did,' Parker said. 'What do the police say?'

'Nothing. There hasn't been a word about that.'

Parker thought it over. 'Did nobody notice? Everything going by so fast. Or somebody noticed and they decided, why should we tell everybody we killed three guys that couldn't shoot back? Okay, just so they're not making a big deal out of it.'

'They're not.'

He said, 'You know that bank account of mine in San Antonio.'

She shook her head. 'I tried,' she said, 'on Monday.'

'Oh, yeah?'

'I went through a lot of trouble,' she told him. 'I wanted some money.'

'Sure.'

'The man was very nice,' she said, 'but he told me there was a temporary hold on that account, and he couldn't ship me any more money.'

So Parmitt was gone for good. 'All right. You've got some of the ten grand left.'

'Some,' she admitted.

'You've still got my clothing sizes. I need some Daniel Parmitt clothes, clothes I don't look like an ex-con in.'

'I bet you are an ex-con,' she said.

'Polo shirt. Khakis. Tassel loafers. Sunglasses. White yachting cap.'

'I love your disguises,' she said.

'Wait here,' he told her, and stood, and went into the kitchen, where the circuit breaker box stood on the wall beside the window over the sink. He opened the metal cover and snaked out the painted wooden one-by-four running underneath it that he'd loosened the other day. Under there, inside the wall, the three jewelry pouches hung from the Romex wire cables leading out of the box.

He removed them, put everything back, and carried them to the front hall, where Lesley abruptly got to her feet at the sight of them, as though she'd seen the Queen walk by.

'Is that it?'

'All of it. Will it fit in your bag?'

Like most career women, Lesley's brown leather bag was outsize, more utilitarian than fashionable. She said, 'Let me just get a couple of these maps and things out of here. You're *giving* it all to me?'

'You're holding it,' he told her. 'You take it home, you hide it someplace where your mother and your sister won't find it, and someday soon, a few weeks or a month from now, a guy's gonna come around and say he's from Daniel Parmitt. Only first I'll phone you, and I'll tell you what name he's using and what he looks like.'

She was very solemn, nodding at each thing he said. 'All right.'

'He'll take the stuff away,' Parker said. 'He and I'll work out a price. Then he'll come back and give you one-third. Okay?'

'One-third.' She was still awed. 'How much would that be?'

'We're guessing four hundred thousand for you, might be less.'

'Not much less.'

'No.'

She hefted the bag, her maps and Filofax in the other hand. 'You're trusting me with this?'

'It isn't trust, Lesley,' he said. 'What are you gonna do with it? Go to a pawnshop?'

'I think there's a reward.'

'Not four hundred thousand. And then you'd have to

explain where you got it. No, you'll hold on to it, and you'll take the four.'

'I certainly will,' she said. The awe was being replaced by a broad grin. 'This sure worked out, didn't it?'

'For some of us. Can you come back tonight around eight? With my new clothes.'

'Sure.'

'And drive me down to Miami.'

'Okay. Is that where Claire is?'

He said, 'You don't want to know about Claire, Lesley.'

'Of course I do,' she said.

He looked at her, and decided to finish that part once and for all. 'Claire is the only house I ever want to be in,' he said. 'All her doors and windows are open, but only for me.'

A blush climbed Lesley's cheeks, and she stepped back, looking confused, as though a door had just slammed in her face. 'You're probably anxious to see her again,' she said, mumbling, going through the motions. 'I'll see you at eight.'

8

Except, no. Not ten minutes after Lesley left, with Parker once more seated on the upstairs terrace floor, back against the wall of the house, he heard the sound of the front door, and when he stood up to look, it was Farley. The Snake River sheriff, in uniform, right hand on his holstered firearm, creeping cautiously into the house, looking every which way at once.

Followed Lesley. Thought she'd lead him to Parmitt, or to somebody else connected with the jewelry robbery. But giving Parker an opportunity to deal with some of the problems he still had.

It wasn't possible to go through the house, Farley was too alert for that. Parker went down the corner of the wall from the terrace, the way he'd come up from the lower terrace the first time he'd entered this house, and moved as fast as he could around to the front, where he saw Farley's official sheriff's car parked by the front door.

It wasn't locked, and the driver's window was open so it wouldn't get too hot and stuffy while Farley was away. Parker got into the passenger seat in front, read the owner's manual for a while, and twenty minutes later Farley came out of the house, grimacing in frustration. When he saw Parker seated in his car he at first looked enraged, then triumphant, as though he'd been proved right about something.

He came around and got behind the wheel and said, 'You were in there.'

'In where? In that house? No, I've been out here. I followed you. I wanted to talk to you.'

Farley's glare meant no-nonsense-pal. He said, 'You were in there, and the Mackenzie woman came to see you there.'

'Who? Oh, Lesley. No, I haven't seen Lesley since she came to visit me at the hospital.' Parker made a crooked-face grin and said, 'I think I scared her that time.'

'She helped you *escape* from the hospital.'

'What, that *woman*? Don't be stupid.'

Farley didn't like being called stupid, but he knew he wasn't on secure ground here, so he said, 'Have it your own way,' and turned to start the engine.

Mild, Parker said, 'Where we going?'

'Snake River, of course,' Farley said as he thumbed his window shut. 'I'm arresting you.'

'For what?'

'For running away from the hospital.'

'That's no crime,' Parker told him. 'Ask the hospital if there's any charges they want to press against me.'

The engine was running, the air conditioner blowing its cold breeze into the car, but Farley hadn't put it in gear. He glowered at Parker, thinking it over, and then said, 'You're mixed up in that big jewel robbery.'

'Wrong again.'

'Don't tell me. I *know*.'

'In the first place,' Parker said, 'that isn't your case, and in the second place, nobody who is working on that case thinks I had anything to do with it, and you know it.'

'They're wrong,' Farley said.

'Everybody's wrong but you.'

'It happens,' Farley said.

240

Parker nodded, looking at him. 'Happen often?'

'Oh, fuck you, Parmitt,' Farley snapped, and pointed an angry finger at him. 'And that's another thing. You aren't any Daniel Parmitt.'

'Everybody knows that,' Parker said. As Farley gaped at him, he gestured at the house. 'Why don't we go sit in there and get comfortable? There's nobody home, is there?'

'It's empty, it's got no furniture in it, as you damn well know.'

'Oh, really?' Parker looked at the house, shrugged and said, 'Then we might as well stay here. For a cop, you're goddam incurious.'

'About what?' Farley demanded. He was ready at this point to take offense at just about anything.

'At why I'm sitting in your car,' Parker told him. That took Farley aback. He thought about it and said, 'You didn't want me following you.'

'You weren't following me, I was following you.'

'Oh, goddammit, Parmitt, John Doe, whoever the hell you are, all *right*. Why are you in my car, if not to get arrested for a dozen different things I can think of?'

'Don't embarrass yourself, Farley,' Parker advised him. 'If you had any case at all, I'd be in cuffs right now.'

Farley sat back against his door to look Parker up and down. 'You've been getting me riled up on purpose,' he decided.

'You started it on your own.'

'I did. So you did it like a firebreak, I guess, to calm me down. Okay, I'm calm. Why are you in my car?'

'Because I want to know how you're doing with the guy who's hiring people to kill me.'

Farley nodded. 'All right,' he said. 'It's a good reason.'

'I know it is. How are you doing?'

241

'Well, the Chicago police—' At Parker's look, he made a sour face and said, 'Yeah, Chicago's taken over now. Bernson, the guy we caught in the hospital—'

'That his name? I only heard you got somebody.'

'Edward Bernson. A professional killer, according to the Chicago people. One of the guns on him tied him to two other murders over the last couple years. When he saw we had him cold, he flipped.'

'And gave you the name of the guy that hired him.'

'No, the go-between. It's a lawyer in Chicago named Gilma Yard, and now the Chicago police are looking into it. They think she's like a clearinghouse or an agency for killers, for hit men. They're not even sure that's her name, but her files are full of stuff that's gonna clear up a lot of murders around the country.'

Parker said, 'This Gilma Yard, she isn't the principal? She's just the one that runs the string of killers?'

'That's how it looks.'

'And they haven't flipped her.'

'Not yet. She's stonewalling, and she's a lawyer, and she seems to think she can skate out of it. I don't know if she can, but right now they've got her in protective custody in case there's any customers out there that wouldn't like to be mentioned.'

'So it's still that nobody knows who's hiring these people that are trying to gun me down.'

'Well, *you* must know,' Farley told him.

'I don't.'

Farley shook his head. 'That isn't possible. You must have *some* idea why you—'

'No. We'll get to that,' Parker promised, 'but what's happening with this lawyer and her files? Don't they at least have somebody who *could* be the guy?'

Reluctantly, Farley said, 'Yes.'

'In Chicago?'

'No, in Tulsa, Oklahoma.'

'We do get around,' Parker said. 'Who is this guy?'

Farley gave him an exasperated look. 'Just given the wild chance that you *don't* know who's gunning for you,' he said, 'why should I give you a name? So you can go out to Oklahoma and deal with him yourself? Level with me and let the law deal with him.'

'I want the law to deal with him.'

'Well, the law can't,' Farley said, 'not so far, because there's no connection between the man in Tulsa and Daniel Parmitt. But why should there be, when you *aren't* Daniel Parmitt and we don't know who you are? If we knew who you really were, we'd know the link.'

'Sheriff Farley,' Parker said, 'I'm going to make you an offer.'

Farley thought about that. He squinted at his white car hood, baking in the sun. He adjusted the air conditioner down a notch. He said, 'I can at least listen to it.'

'I will tell you the link between this man and me,' Parker said. 'It's a stupid link, but it's the only one there is. You will tell me the name of the guy in Tulsa, and then I'll give every law enforcement agency in the country a year to bring him down. You won't need a month, I think, given the guy. But if you all fuck up, in a year and a day I kill him.'

Farley said, 'Why do you want to do it that way?'

'Because he's already been too much of a distraction. Because I don't want to have to think about him anymore.'

'The man had you *shot*. You don't feel any desire to go deal with him yourself?'

'Why? You people are better equipped than me to be

sure he's the right guy. And I want him *out* of my life, not *in* my life. And the other thing, Sheriff, just between you and me, I don't want you on my backtrail anymore, either. You go live your life in Snake River, and I'll go live my life somewhere else.'

'If I see you again—'

'You won't.'

Farley thought it over. He said, 'If I took you in, took your prints, asked you questions a few days, showed you to my friends at the FBI, I bet we'd come up with a lot of answers we'd like.'

'Sheriff,' Parker said, 'if you make a single move in that direction, the two of us in the car here together, you're a much more stupid man than I think you are.'

Farley considered that. 'I'm armed,' he pointed out.

Parker held his hands up between them, fingers half-curled. 'So am I.'

'Jesus, you've got gall!'

Parker lowered his hands. 'Do we have a deal?'

'You'll tell me the link between you and the man in Tulsa, and you'll keep away from him for a year, and we should have enough to get the goods on him.'

'And,' Parker said, 'you'll tell me his name.'

'Zulf Masters,' Farley said.

'Zulf Masters.'

'All anybody knows is, he's rich, everybody thinks from oil. He's in real estate, office buildings and shopping centers, all through Oklahoma and Kansas and Missouri.'

'That's laundered money,' Parker said. 'It didn't come from oil. Zulf Masters,' he repeated, in case he'd have to remember it later.

'Nobody's sure if that's *his* real name, either,' Farley said.

244

'It isn't,' Parker said.

'These are very dubious people, Parmitt,' Farley said. 'Bad as you.'

'Take notes, Sheriff.'

Farley had pen and notepad as part of the console between the front seats. He obediently picked them up and said, 'Go ahead.'

'In Galveston, Texas,' Parker told him, 'there was a man named Julius Norte.'

'Was.'

Parker spelled the name. 'Sometime in the last month he was murdered. I think by the same two that shot me.'

'Oh ho,' Farley said.

'Norte created ID for people.'

'Like Daniel Parmitt.'

'That's right. He did very good stuff, you could do background checks, whatever. Only the credit history wouldn't be there.'

'You traveled with your birth certificate,' Farley said. 'That snagged at me, but I didn't think it through.'

Parker said, 'If the Chicago cops are right about this guy in Tulsa, he got his name from Norte. And whoever he really is, some South American warlord or drug dealer or whoever, he doesn't want anybody who can link the new guy to the old guy. So he must have had plastic surgery, and he probably killed the surgeon. He killed Norte. And because I was there, I happened to be there at the time, he's trying to kill me. It was whoever was gonna be Norte's customer that day was gonna have this guy breathing down his back.'

Farley looked up from his notepad. 'That's it? That's all of it? You were with Norte at the wrong minute, and this fellow wants you dead?'

245

'I think he's somebody comes from a former life where making people dead was the solution to most problems.'

Farley said, 'If we can prove the Zulf Masters identity is a fake, we can get through to the real guy.'

'The one thing Norte couldn't do,' Parker told him, 'was the Social Security number. He said he didn't have the access to the legit files.'

'That'll bring him down,' Farley said. 'You're right, we won't need a year.'

'He's going to be some stinking piece of work when you find out who he really is.'

Farley laughed. 'Worse than you and me?'

'Worse than you,' Parker said. 'You going back to Snake River now?'

'Naturally. So I can call Chicago.'

'Drop me off in Miami Beach.'

'That's out of my way.'

'Not that far. And you can give me a quarter for a phone call.'

Farley shook his head. 'You don't lack for nerve, Parmitt, I'll give you that.'

Forty minutes south of Palm Beach on Interstate 95, Farley said, 'It isn't Mackenzie.'

Parker looked at him. 'What isn't Mackenzie?'

'Who you're meeting in Miami Beach.'

'Farley,' Parker said, 'you've got that woman on your mind. You've got the itch for her, haven't you?'

'Don't be stupid,' Farley said, glaring at the traffic on 95. 'I'm a happily married man.'

'They all are,' Parker said, and Farley didn't talk about Lesley anymore.

*

Driving down Collins Avenue in Miami Beach, Farley said, 'Where do you want to get off?'

'Anywhere at all,' Parker said.

'No, I know you're still hurting, you don't want to walk a lot, I'll let you off wherever you say.'

'Anywhere along Collins is fine by me,' Parker said.

Farley laughed. 'You don't want to give me one clue.'

Parker looked at the hard-bodied girls on roller skates, weaving in and out among the retirees. Everything that was extreme was here.

Farley found a fire hydrant and stopped next to it. 'I give up,' he said. 'Hold on, here's your quarter.' It came from a cup on the dashboard.

'Thanks.'

'You know, Parmitt,' Farley said as Parker opened the door, 'it's kind of an anticlimax for me, you just walking off like this.'

'Yeah?'

'I'll always wonder,' Farley said, 'if I could have taken you.'

'Look on the bright side,' Parker told him. 'This way, you have an always.'